Beyond Indigo

Beyond Indigo

PREETHI NAIR

LARGE PRINT

Oxford

First published in Great Britain 2004
by
HarperCollins*Publishers*

Published in Large Print 2005 by ISIS Publishing Ltd,
7 Centremead, Osney Mead, Oxford OX2 0ES
by arrangement with
HarperCollins*Publishers*

British Library Cataloguing in Publication Data
Nair, Preethi 1971–
    Beyond indigo.– Large print ed.
    1. Deception – Fiction
    2. Women artists – Fiction
    3. Arranged marriage – Fiction
    4. Large type books
    I. Title
    823.9'2 [F]

ISBN 0–7531–7351–4 (hb)
ISBN 0–7531–7352–2 (pb)

Printed and bound by Antony Rowe, Chippenham

Thank you to whoever is responsible for making flowers pop up when I most needed them. To my family and friends, especially to Avni, Esperenza and Tricia whose constant support, encouragement and enthusiasm cannot help but inspire me. To my friend and agent Diana Holmes for believing in me and finally a big "thank you" to all the team at HarperCollins.

To my Dad and Amma.

"There are always flowers for those who want to see them."

HENRI MATISSE

2nd December 1999

I know now that hurling a saffron-stained coconut over London Bridge at six-thirty in the morning should have set some alarm bells off. The tramp peered up at me from his cardboard box as if to say that I would be joining him very soon. But the Guru had said that it would remove the stagnation from my life, me being represented by a hairy coconut and the water representing flow. The Thames did not glisten at me. Well, it couldn't really as it was pitch black and probably frozen, but I believed it was glistening, shimmering even, and leading me to better things.

Looking back, the only bit the Guru got right was the symbolism. Brown woman thrown further into murky waters.

I had met this Guru the previous day. I'd like to say that I met him at the foothills of the Himalayas or somewhere exotic but I bumped into him outside Pound Savers on Croydon High Street. It was one of those really cold December days when everything comes at you from all directions; the wind, the rain, puddle-slush, the odd hailstone, and anything else nature can find to throw at you.

It had been a really hard day at work and almost unbearable to get through: my best friend, Kirelli, had died exactly a year earlier. Sorting out the contract of some egotistical artist and checking the provenance of a painting for a client seemed irrelevant, so I told my boss that I had a headache and was leaving early.

"Two aspirins will clear it," he said.

"Right, I'll get some on my way home," I replied, with absolutely no intention of stopping off at the chemist's. I was good at pretending; it had become second nature to me because of the distinct worlds I lived in.

Having said that, there were certain parallels between the art world and the Indian subcontinent ensconced within our semi: both worlds were seemingly very secure with an undercurrent of unspoken rules and codes of conduct that were made and manipulated by a dominant few. One set fixed the price of art and the other fixed up marriages. The main difference was that the ones in the art world didn't have centre-parted hair and weren't dressed in saris, grey woolly socks and sandals.

The only way I was able to make the cultural crossover from the Hindi songs wailing from the semi to the classical music played subtly at the reception area in the law firm where I worked as an artist's representative was by pretending. Pretending to be someone I wasn't.

2

"Nina, Boo Williams is coming in tomorrow," my boss reiterated before I left. This was his coded way of saying, "Make sure you pull yourself together by the morning."

Boo Williams was one of the artists we represented at the firm. Her sculpture of Venus de Milo made from dried fruit and vegetables had failed to win the Turner Prize so she would be needing much consolation and bullshit from me in the morning. Forget the sickie, forget grief; Boo and her heap of fruit and vegetables needed me more.

"Right, see you tomorrow then," I muttered, grabbing my coat.

On the way back home there were no commuters hurling themselves onto the tube. The carriages were almost empty and I was relieved, because if I had had a group of wet strangers pushing against me, vying for space, that would have just about done it. I sat opposite an old lady with wispy white hair. She had the kind of eyes that made me want to tell her that my best friend had died in my arms at exactly this time — two-thirty, a year ago — and that since then I had been lost, truly lost. The old lady smiled at me and a lump began to form in my throat. I got up, moved seats and sat down beside a soggy copy of the *Guardian*. The page it was turned to showed the Turner Prize winner, Maximus Karlhein, trying desperately to pose seriously. He was standing next to one of his pieces exhibited at the Tate — an old wardrobe stuffed with his worldly possessions.

I pushed the paper away feeling exhausted. It was all nonsense; people posing in front of wardrobes, passing it off as art and making headlines. Where was the feeling? The passion? And that crap — that the relationship with his wardrobe was imbued on his soul and that he had no option but to express it — which PR person had thought of that line? Art was supposed to be passionate and full of emotion, not contrived, not like an Emperor's-new-clothes scenario where a group of influential people said that the work was good and therefore people believed it was. What had happened to art? Paintings done by artists who didn't even care if they weren't known, not some hyped artist giving a convoluted explanation behind a pile of dried fruit or a heap of junk. A year on, and despite promising that I would be true to myself after Ki's death, I still participated in the circus.

Tomorrow, no doubt I would have to console Boo. What kind of name was that anyway? Knock, knock, who's there? Boo. Boo who? Don't worry, love, your apricots didn't win the Turner Prize this year but you can sell them for at least five grand. That's what I would want to say, but what I would probably say was, "Ms Williams, Boo, it's an injustice, I just can't see how you didn't win. Your concept, the use of colour is simply . . . simply inspirational."

Was that what happened to you in life? You started off with such high hopes and ideals and then got sucked into all the bullshit and you pretended that that was reality. No, I didn't think that was the case with me — I knew deep down that life was too short to be doing anything other than what I really wanted to do; Ki had shown me that. But that wasn't the problem — there were the occupants living in the semi to consider. I had a duty to make sure that they were happy, and keeping my job as a lawyer was fundamental to their all-important list system.

Mum and Dad's short list was devoid of any kind of love or passion. Thinking about it, the Turner Prize short list and my parents' own were not that dissimilar: although the criteria was seemingly clear and transparent, the subject produced was, at times, truly baffling. In their case, the subject was a man and the objective of the list was to find me a husband. Like the art world, much went on behind the scenes that nobody really knew about. Favours were exchanged, backs were scratched and tactics employed so that the prospective candidate was over-hyped to an influential few in order to persuade them that he was the right man for the job.

The long list was drawn up by a group of well-connected elderly women in the community, whose demure presence betrayed what they were really capable of. The criteria that had been set to filter the candidates were that they had to come from a good family background, be well educated and have lots of money. One of my mum's roles was to whittle down the long list, but her primary task was to set the PR machinery in motion; to cover up any negatives, then to promote and hype the candidates and make sure they were shown to me in a favourable light. This week she had managed to get the list down to three potentials whose vital statistics were presented in the form of

5

handwritten CVs. There was a doctor, another lawyer and an accountant left on the dining-room table for me to look at. The hot favourite (who had been put to the top of the pile) was the accountant, because he had his own property: "Beta, this candidate was imbued on my soul." She wouldn't use those words exactly, she would just draw my attention to his flat. So, although it was seemingly my decision to choose one, go on a few dates with him and agree to marriage, the system was clearly rigged.

However, the panel had overlooked one very important thing: an outsider was trying to infiltrate the system. A man of whom they had no knowledge had just asked me to marry him. The judges were going to have a problem. At best there would be an uproar: my dad would pretend to go into heart failure and my mum would do her wailing and beating on the chest routine. At worst I would suffer the same fate as my sister, who had run off with her boyfriend and who they had not spoken to since.

I didn't know what to say to Jean Michel when he asked me to marry him. It wasn't a question of not loving him enough; it was a question of making a decision and then facing all of the consequences, and I was too tired for all of that. So for a while I hadn't been making any decisions; not even daring to venture slightly outside my routine. There was a certain sense of safety in catching the tube to work, dealing with clients, going back home to Mum and Dad and seeing the CVs on the table.

I hadn't been thinking about anything too deeply except on days like that when I had been forced to. I mean, I knew Ki was dead, I had watched her disintegrate before me and then be scattered into the wind, but for me she was still there in some kind of shape or form. She had to be. Pretending that she was still there, looking out for me, was the only thing that had helped me hold it together, because otherwise . . . otherwise, everything was pointless.

Her death was senseless. Good people weren't supposed to die young. I had bargained hard with God and promised to do all sorts of things if He let her live, and although He didn't listen I held steadfast in my belief. It was the only thing that I could really cling to. I don't know how best to describe what this *belief* was, but it's the feeling that someone out there is listening and responding; that there's a universal conversation going on where forces of nature conspire to look after you and give you strength. Occasionally you'd get a glimpse of the workings behind the scenes and these were termed by others as coincidences or luck. And then there were signs. Signs were things like accidentally finding a twenty-pound note when you most needed it; a song on the radio that comes from nowhere and that speaks to you directly; words or people that find their way to you at just the right time. Ki promised she would send me a sign. A year had passed and she hadn't. Or maybe she had and I'd missed it. I had become far too busy to see any signs.

I got off the underground and waited for the train that would take me home.

★ ★ ★

The High Street looked tired and depressed, like it too had had enough of being battered by the rain. Among all the greyness, the windswept umbrellas and the shoppers scurrying home, I suddenly spotted colour, a vibrant bright orange. I walked in its direction to take a closer look. It was a Guru, standing calmly in the rain amid a flurry of activity. I stopped momentarily, thinking that the scene would have made a good painting, and stared at the strangeness of his presence. He was wearing a long, orange robe over some blue flarey trousers and over his robe he had a blue body-warmer. As they walked past, school children were pointing and laughing at the enormous red stain across his forehead. The red stain did not strike me as much as the open-toed sandals on his feet. It was freezing, and as I was thinking that he must be in desperate need of some socks, someone called out to me.

"Nina, Nina," shouted the man as he came out of Pound Savers, clutching his bag. He knew my dad, I had met him a couple of times but I couldn't remember his name.

"Hello Uncle," I said, thankful that calling obscure friends of your parents "Uncle" is an Indian thing. Any random person that you've only met once in your life has to be bestowed with this title. "How are you?" I asked politely.

"Just buying the socks for his Holiness," he said, looking at the Guru, "he's finding the weather here a little colder than Mumbai. Guru Anuraj, this is Nina Savani. Nina, this is his Holiness, Guru Anuraj."

The Guru put his hands together in a prayer pose. If I was a well-mannered Indian girl, such an introduction and the use of the word "Holiness" would be my cue to bow down in the middle of Croydon High Street and touch his "Holiness's" icy feet, but instead I just smiled and nodded.

The Guru held out his hand. I thought he was angling for a handshake so I gave him mine. He took it, turned it palm up and muttered, "Been through much heartache. Don't worry, it's nearly over."

"He's very good, you know. For years Auntie was becoming unable to have baby and now we are expecting our child," acquaintance man interrupted eagerly. "Guru Anuraj was responsible for sending child," he beamed.

The Guru's warm smile spun out like a safety net as he told me my life would improve greatly in two weeks. Although his smile was warm I chose to ignore the fact that it was full of chipped and blackened teeth. If I had paid attention to his dental hygiene it could have given me some indication towards his character and all that was to follow without having to take his palm — "cleanliness being next to godliness" and all that — but as he made promises of being able to remove the stagnant energy which was the cause of much maligned obstacles, I chose not to see the warning signs. I wanted him to tell me more but the Guru had his socks to put on. He'd also spotted the grocer roasting chestnuts, and indicated to acquaintance man that he might like some.

9

Before he left, he delved inside his robe and handed me a leaflet. "Call me," he said, staring intently into my eyes.

"You must call him, his Holiness only gives out his number to the very special people," added acquaintance man. I took the leaflet and said goodbye to them both.

When I got home, Hindi music was blasting from the television set and both my parents were doing their normal activities. My mum was in the kitchen making rotis and my dad was in the sitting room, with a glass of whisky in one hand, newspaper in the other, looking like an Indian version of Father Christmas with his red shirt, white beard and big belly. He was the only person who was not engulfed by the enormous Land of Leather sofa.

"Good day, Nina?" he asked, turning back to his newspaper.

"It was really crap. Crap day, crap client, just awful."

"Good, good," he replied. My dad had very selective hearing and only chose to hear the words he liked or words that were of some threat to him. "Home early, no?"

"We were all made redundant."

He put his glass down, threw his newspaper to the floor and looked at me. Redundancy was his worst nightmare. I had to be a lawyer; years of both time and money were invested in this and it was pivotal to the list system (the spin on candidates worked both ways so I too was lying on someone's dining-room table). That was what he sold me on, the fact that I was a lawyer

10

working for a reputable firm, and also that I was tall and quite fair-skinned, but he omitted the fact that I had one humungous scar down my left arm and that I couldn't really cook.

By my parents' standards, twenty-seven was far too late to be getting married, and my mum was truly baffled by it, saying to my father that I was one of the prettiest girls on the circuit and there was a queue of men waiting to marry me. But I had managed to fend them off so far by telling them that things were changing and men were looking for women who were settled in their careers; it wasn't like the olden days when they just wanted to know your height, complexion, and if you had long hair down to your back. It was, however, getting to a stage where this argument was wearing thin. As my dad said, at this rate I would be heading towards retirement: hence more and more weekly CVs.

"What?" he shouted.

"I said I had a headache."

"I thought you said redundant."

"No, just a headache."

"Thank Bhagavan," he sighed, glancing up to one of the many incarnated god statues.

My mum came out of the kitchen, rolling pin in one hand. "What headache, beta? It's because you are not eating properly."

"I think I'll just go to bed, I'll be fine, Ma."

"Not eating with us?" she asked, looking over at the dining-room table and fixing her gaze on it. "Rajan

Mehta. He's thirty-one, an accountant. He's got his own flat in Victoria . . ."

My heart sank. I turned my back and began walking up the stairs as she shouted, ". . . three bedrooms and two bathrooms."

I couldn't put off the inevitable. I had to tell them about Jean Michel, and tell them soon. He was away on a business trip in New York and as soon as he got back we had to sort something out. I picked up the phone to call him and put it down again; he was having back-to-back meetings so it probably wasn't the best time to call. I flicked through my address book to see who else I could phone. I had friends, of course, but nobody I could open up to. Since Ki's death I had kept all my other friendships on a superficial basis: nobody knew what was really going on inside my head as I refused to go through that kind of closeness again only for it to be snatched away. I flicked through the pages once more. No, there was no one, no one who had an inkling that anything was wrong. Anyway, where would I start? The fact that I did not allow myself to cry, that I was desperately missing Ki, that I hated going into work, or that I didn't know whether to marry Jean Michel?

Suddenly, a thought occurred to me.

"Did you send that Guru for me, Ki? Is that what you meant when you said you'd speak to me? Was he a sign?"

I pulled out the leaflet and read: "Guru Anuraj, Psychic Healer, Spiritual Counsellor and Friend."

I dialled the number. He gave me an appointment to come and see him the very next morning. I had a shower and went to bed.

It was five-thirty in the morning when I drove to the address he had given me. I didn't want to tell my parents that I was going to see the Guru as it would have sent my mother's thoughts propelling into all kinds of directions and that was dangerous. So when she spotted me up and about very early in the morning I told her I was driving up to Leeds for a client meeting; the lie, believe me, was for her own protection.

I know it was an odd time but my mum always said that, supposedly, between four and seven in the morning are when prayers are most likely to be receptive — that's when she annoyed all the neighbours with her howling and chanting.

"Kavitha, why you can't you learn to sing like the Cilla Black?" my dad would ask her.

"I *am* singing."

"This is not the singing, see, neighbours have written letters doing complaining," my dad said, producing letters that contained handwriting which appeared remarkably similar to that of his own.

"This is all for Nina, so she will find a good man, coming from a good family," my mother replied.

"No, only man who comes will be police."

But she continued unabated by threats of the council charging her with noise pollution. Because, for her, if it produced the desired result it would all have been worth it.

When I arrived I knocked on the door as instructed. A short man opened it and took me to the dining room where he asked me to take a seat. He said that the Guru was with someone and would see me shortly. I was nervous and excited; seeing the Guru was the first positive step I had taken in a long while. Admittedly, I was also feeling slightly apprehensive, not about being in a stranger's house but about what the Guru might say, so I focused on the decoration in the dining room and, like Lloyd Grossman, studied the clues and imagined what sort of family lived there. Half an hour later the man came back and led me to another room. I knocked on the door and went in.

Warm jasmine incense and soft music and candles filled the room, and on pieces of colourful silk stood statues of gods in all different sizes. The Guru acknowledged me by nodding his head and asked me to remove my shoes and take a seat opposite him on the floor. I did so nervously.

"Date of birth?" the Guru asked swiftly.

"Fourth of September, 1972."

He proceeded to draw boxes, do calculations, and then, like a bingo caller, he reeled off some numbers which, he said, were the key events that had marked my life: aged six, an accident with the element of fire which had left deep scarring. I looked at my right arm; it was well covered, how could he have known that? He continued: aged eighteen, a romantic liaison which did not end in marriage. At this point he raised his eyebrow. Aged twenty-five, another. I saw how this could look bad to a holy Guru who believed in traditional values and the sanctity of just one arranged marriage so I avoided eye contact.

"A Western man?" he questioned.

I nodded.

He shook his head. "It is being serious?" he asked.

I nodded again.

"Parents knowing?"

I shook my head.

"Parents not arranging anything?"

Parents were very busy arranging things. Last week the hot favourite was a twenty-nine-year-old investment banker, this week it was thirty-one-year-old, five degrees accountant Raj, the letters behind his name rolling off the page.

The Guru stopped at age twenty-six, with the death of my best friend.

"It will all change," he promised. I fought back the tears and then he touched the palms of my hands and they began to tingle, a warm glow that made his words feel safe.

"Stagnant life now, unable to move forward, unable to take decision. See this," he said, nodding at my palms, "this is now flow but too much negativity in body for flow. Let it go. Let it all go." And that's how the whole coconut-over-bridge routine came about.

It sounds bizarre now but he performed a ceremony that morning, asking permission from the gods to be able to treat me. The coconut he used in the ceremony was meant to represent me and he stained it with saffron. He did the same with my forehead so that the coconut and I were united. The river was supposed to represent new life. After mumbling a prayer, the Guru asked me to return after I'd thrown my coconut self off the bridge. I could have chosen anywhere where there was water, even the canal near where we lived, but I didn't want the coconut to sink to the bottom and find a rusty bicycle, a portent of doom if ever there was one, so I chose London Bridge.

"There will be a big change in you, Nina," he said as I left, coconut in hand. "Come and see me later this evening."

After I hurled the coconut off the bridge I felt immensely relieved. I wiped the stain off my forehead and went to work, ready to caress Boo Williams' ego. I got to work only to be told that Boo was too upset to get out of bed and would be in the following day instead. Still, I was unperturbed.

Richard, one of my colleagues, commented on how well I was looking.

"I'm getting engaged," I replied.

When the coconut had left my hands all my decisions seemed so clear. I wanted to phone Jean Michel right away to tell him that I was going to marry him. I started to dial his mobile number but decided to wait for him to come back from his trip the next day and tell him in person. Everything that day at work was effortless. I knew I wouldn't have to be there for long: once Jean and I were married I could think about other options. And my mum and dad? What would I do with them? If I looked at things optimistically, Jean could charm my mother — he could charm anyone, he was

16

incredibly charismatic — and my mum, in turn, could work on my dad. Together we could make him come around.

Jean called me later that afternoon and I had to stop myself from blurting it all out.

"I can't wait to see you, ma cherie."

"Me too. When you're back it's all going to change. I love you, Jean."

All I had to do was wait one more day and all the pretence could stop.

The Guru had given me the energy to make all obstacles appear surmountable and later that evening I returned to thank him for what he had done. He prescribed one more session for the following day, just to make sure I would keep on track. How I wish I had stopped there.

The next morning the Guru's door was slightly ajar so I knocked on it and walked in. He had his back to me and was lighting his candles, humming away and swaying to Sting's "Englishman in New York", which was playing loudly. It got to the alien bit when the Guru turned around. He looked startled when he saw me and immediately stopped the tape recorder, saying that he was sampling the music that was corrupting the youth of today, and promptly changed the cassette to a whinging sitar.

"Sting is not a corrupting force," I said. "In fact, he's against deforestation."

The Guru glared at me when I said deforestation like he didn't know what the word meant, but now I think about that look — eyes narrowing, brows furrowed — it was probably more that he remembered he had a job to do.

He signalled for me to sit on the floor and held my hands. They tingled with warmth again as he whispered kind words and then he began humming and chanting. Then the Guru asked me to lie down and he proceeded to touch me, moving slowly from my hands to other parts of my body, my neck, my feet; incantations and gods' names being chanted all the while as he healed the negativity that shrouded me, asking me to let it go. As he unbuttoned my clothes and took off my top, his breath became rhythmic, his chanting louder, his beads pressed against my chest. I closed my eyes, wanting to believe that I was lost between the gods' names and that none of this was really happening. It couldn't happen; a holy man wouldn't do this, he couldn't do this, this wasn't supposed to happen. His beard brushed against my skin, his fingers circled my mouth, I pretended that my trousers had not come down.

I have often asked myself why I didn't get out of there sooner and how I had got myself into such a position. I didn't want to believe what was really going on, because if I did, nothing whatsoever would make any sense — and the only thing at that point in time that I had left to hang on to was my belief. I didn't want to believe what his dry, filthy hands were doing because I would have had to concede that whoever was responsible for sending me signs had sent this Guru, who was into an altogether different kind of spiritual feeling. Nobody could be that cruel.

As he placed his salivating mouth on my lips and pulled up his robe, I smelled him, and it was this that made something inside of me snap. He smelled of coffee. I kicked him, pushed him off me and managed to get out from under him before he used his magic wand.

"No," I shouted.

"You're cursed," he screamed as I ran out of the door. "Cursed, and I will make sure of it."

How I had sunk to such depths still remains a mystery but, essentially, that is where my journey began. I was confused and desperate, feeling wholly inadequate, riddled with self-doubt and dirty. I wanted to call Jean Michel and tell him but he would kill the Guru. So I tried to block it from my mind and pretend that nothing had happened.

The train I was on stopped. Some old man with the same rotten teeth as the Guru got on. It's funny how that happens; reminders of the things you are trying most to forget. He smiled at me and I felt physically sick. My hands began to shake. "It didn't happen," I kept saying to myself. "It's all in the mind, it didn't happen," and I reached into my handbag to get a mint. While I was fishing for it I found an envelope that was marked urgent.

It was a contract that I had looked over for a client, and which had been sitting in my handbag for the last two days. I had promised to send it back the next day and had completely forgotten. But today it was all going to change. I had to hold it together.

"All change here," announced the driver. Although running late I was determined to buy a stamp, find a postbox, and personally post this letter. Posting it myself would be symbolic of my commitment to getting my life back on track. But, wouldn't you know, there wasn't a postbox in sight.

"You're cursed," I kept hearing, and the more I heard it, the more adamant I became that I would find a postbox and put everything behind me.

My boss, Simon, was slightly concerned when I arrived late. I was *never* late.

"Is everything all right, Nina?"

"Fine, just fine," I said, making my way to my desk.

I turned on the computer and looked out of the window. The buildings were grey and dreary and set against a grey winter sky. So many times I had sat looking out of this window, imagining the sky to be orange, wishing that I could soak up the rays of an orange sky, fly out of the window and have the courage to do something else, something that gave me meaning.

I had been working at Whitter and Lawson for the last three and a half years, representing all kinds of artists but mostly those who had issues over copyright or needed contractual agreements with galleries drawn up. I read somewhere that people work on the periphery of what they really want to do so that they don't have to cope with rejection. So, someone who harboured desires to be a racing-car driver would be a mechanic on a racetrack but not actually drive the car. It was like this for me in a sense: I'd always wanted to be a painter and so I worked with artists. But my job wasn't really about art, it was about making money, dealing with boosting egos. Feeling increasingly cynical and secretly thinking that I could do much better. But I couldn't — it wasn't really rejection I feared, it was disappointing my father and sabotaging his investment in the *Encyclopaedia Britannica*.

I'd known I wanted to be a painter since the age of six. My brain had always had difficulty engaging with my mouth and I was unable to fully articulate any emotion except on paper. So anything I felt, I produced in a swirl of finger-painted colours that nobody could quite manage to understand. When I found out that my sister wasn't coming back I did more of the same. My parents didn't hang the pictures on the fridge door with a magnet — they didn't know that that is what you were supposed to do with the nonsensical pictures that your children produced. They didn't even lie and tell me how good they were. Instead, the pictures were folded up and binned while my father would sit with me and read me bits from the *Encyclopaedia Britannica*, extracts that even he didn't understand. He was preparing me for a career in law, or "love" as he mispronounced it.

His career choice for me was not based on any long-standing family tradition. He was a bus driver and I think he just wanted to give me the best possible start, and make sure I would not have to face the instability that he had suffered. That's why when the encyclopaedia man came round when I was young and sensed the aspirations my father had for me, he blatantly incorporated me into his sales pitch by saying that the books would set me on course for a high-flying career. My dad bought the whole set, which he could clearly not afford, taking on extra jobs like mending television sets so he could buy the entire set and receive the latest volume, year after year.

At sixteen, when I expressed a desire to go to art college he went ballistic and didn't speak to me for weeks. When he did it was to say, "Nina, I have not sacrificed the life so you can do the hobby, the lawyer is a good profession. Not that I am pressurising you, not that I came to the England to give you the good education and work every hour and make sacrifices."

Put that way I could clearly see his point. So I did an art A level without him knowing about it — just in case, by some miracle, he changed his mind. He didn't and so I went to university to study law.

Whitter and Lawson was where I did my training, and I worked incredibly hard so that they would give me a job after I had finished; at least that way I could be around artists and connect with their world. Everyone around me said it was impossible, there were hardly any Indian lawyers representing artists and it was a place where contacts mattered. People said that I would need a miracle to be taken on by the firm but I busted my gut and worked every single hour I could, going out of my way to prove everyone wrong.

I remember making promises that I would do a whole series of things if I got the job, like give away ten

22

per cent of my future earnings to charity and buy a *Big Issue* weekly. To whom these promises were made I couldn't really tell you; maybe just to myself. So I should have known that the first visible signs of wanting out was crossing the road, making out like I hadn't seen the *Big Issue* man when he was blatantly waving at me. But I pretended, pretended that I was lucky to have a job and make lots of money and be in that world. My dad always said this was what life was about — working hard, being disciplined, making money, surviving in a "dog eating the cat" world. But then my best friend Ki died and none of that made sense anymore. An uneasiness began to set in.

Felicity, the PA, called me to say that Boo Williams was waiting for me in reception.

Ki disintegrated rapidly at twenty-five. She had felt a lump in her leg while she was away travelling but decided it was nothing. By the time she came back it had spread throughout her whole body. There was nothing anyone could do. I pretended it would be fine; didn't even see the head scarf and the dribbling mouth and the weight loss. She whispered lots of things to me and I made a whole heap of promises to her. I'm not sure exactly what I said, I wasn't really there so couldn't remember any of it. Not until that moment, the moment I sat at my computer thinking about how I'd not taken responsibility for anything.

What I had promised her was that I would live my life passionately and do all the things I really wanted to, not just for me but for her.

The day she told me about her condition she dropped it in like it was something she forgot to mention on a shopping list. Ki had got back from Thailand a couple of weeks earlier, and we had spent virtually every day together since. That day we were off to Brighton, and her dad was in the driveway cleaning his car.

"It's hot weather, na?" he asked.

"Good, isn't it?" I replied.

"Makes me want to go and visit some bitches."

I looked at him as Ki came out. He continued, "Na, beta, saying to Nina we must visit some bitches."

"It's beaches, Dad, beaches. Yeah, we'll visit loads and we'll make sure we do it soon."

I remember thinking that comment was strange as she normally took the piss out of his mispronunciations.

"Yours is into bitches, mine thinks I'm into porn," I said walking back in with her.

"What?"

"I didn't realise that the Sky box downstairs was linked to the one upstairs, and I was flicking through it and lingered on a few porn channels and this lesbian talk show."

She looked at me.

"It was just out of interest, didn't know I was interrupting Mum and Dad watching their Zee TV. Then in the morning I heard my dad tell my mum to talk to me, to have a word, maybe marriage would straighten that out. So she just left a couple more CVs on the table."

"When will you tell them about Jean?"

"Soon," I said.

"Tell them soon, Nina, it's not worth the wait. Do what makes you happy. You'll make sure you're happy, won't you?"

I looked at her. Where did that come from?

"I've got cancer, Nina, and it's bad. Phase three, that's what they called it. Don't think they can do much with chemo but they'll give it a go."

She said it just like that, like she had bought some new trousers from French Connection and had forgotten to tell me.

She hadn't told her parents. Outside, her dad was blissfully ignorant; bucket in one hand, sponge in another, cleaning his shiny silver car and talking about bitches, unaware that shortly his life would change forever.

I deluded myself that chemo would sort it. I knew if I bargained hard and made a whole series of promises, it would be all right. Right until the last minute I believed that. Even when she died, I held on to her, not letting go. Her dad had to pull me off her.

The phone went again. "Ms Williams is waiting for you in reception, Nina."

"I heard you the first time," I snapped.

My colleagues turned and looked at me. I never lost it. No matter what, I was always calm. Calm and reliable Nina, who worked twelve hours a day if necessary. Calm and dependable Nina, who did what was asked of her; who went to the gallery openings that nobody else in the firm wanted to go to.

I got up and went to reception to meet Boo. She was dressed in black and wore bright red boots, the colour of the dried tomatoes she had put into Venus de Milo's sockets.

"Sorry to have kept you waiting."

"Quite," she replied.

And that was it, the word that tipped me over the edge.

"Quite," I mumbled.

"Yes, I've got better things to do with my time," she replied.

"Like make apricot statues?"

Felicity looked up from behind the reception desk, shocked.

"I don't like your tone, Nina," Boo said.

"I don't like your work, but there's nothing I can do about that, is there?"

"Nessun dorma", which was playing in reception, seemed to be playing unusually loud in my head as Boo started ranting. I wasn't really listening to what she was saying but just gazed blankly at her, watching her lips move and hearing the Guru's words telling me again and again that I was cursed. The only thought I had was to get out of there.

"Boo, Nina has been under the weather recently, haven't you, Nina?" Simon said, hearing her shouting and coming out of his office to try to placate her.

26

"Yes, under the weather, under a cloud, a dirty grey sky. I have to go, I have to leave."

There was silence: the kind of silence that is desperate to be filled.

And Simon didn't stop me. Over three years at the firm, sweating blood, pampering over-inflated egos and making him money and he didn't even say, "Come into my office, let's talk about it."

Maybe if he had I would have stayed, because all that I needed was some reassurance that I was worth something.

"Right," I said, getting my coat. "I'll come back for the rest of my things later."

"I'll make sure Felicity sends them on to you," Simon replied.

I splashed through puddles, wandering aimlessly, feeling numb. I should have been elated, relieved at least that I had left work; but the way it had happened was out of my control, he was essentially showing me the door. After everything I had done, that's how much I meant. What would I say to my parents? Not only would I crush them by saying that I was marrying Jean but now my dad's biggest fear of me losing my job had come true. Perhaps it was better to break it to them all at once: if I didn't have a job I couldn't go through with their list system anyway so that didn't matter, and at least I had Jean. Jean would be there no matter what. He would return home later that evening and between us we could find a way to break it to them so that it wouldn't completely crush them. Things weren't that bad, I tried to convince myself. I'd just attempted to put the whole Guru thing behind me — there were good things to look forward to. Jean and I could finally settle down. I felt excited at the thought of seeing him again, having him wrap his arms around me and reassure me that everything would work out. As I had time on my hands I decided to go to his flat, make us dinner and wait for him: he was due back around six.

A short time later, my shopping basket was bulging with colourful vegetables. I had no idea what I was going to do with them but anything that had any colour went into the basket. Jean liked chicken so I decided to throw one in and figure out how to cook it later. I picked up a recipe book, some wine, flowers and candles and made my way to his apartment.

I smiled at the concierge as I entered the building, but instead of smiling back he glanced down at his feet.

"Busy morning, John?"

"Yes, miss," he replied, calling for the lift. I could sense that he wasn't in the mood for chatting so I waited in silence for the lift to come down.

The tiles and mirrors reflected the huge ceilings of the apartment block and the lift was rickety and had an old-style caged door. I had always thought I'd get stuck in it. Before Jean Michel went away on his trip he had stopped the lift as we were halfway down. I had panicked. "I'll take care of you, cherie," he said. "Always, you know I will. Nina, I want you to marry me."

And although I was overwhelmed the first word that came out of my mouth wasn't "Yes" but "Dad". All I could see was my dad's face, so absolutely crushed.

Jean tried not to appear disappointed. I asked for time to think about it. He said he understood, but now my head was clear I would have a chance to make it up to him.

We had met two years earlier at a party. The moment he walked in half the women in the room turned to look: he was six foot two, with blue eyes, jet-black hair and a big smile. I watched his every move from the corner of my eye and my heart jumped with disbelief as he made his way towards me.

"Are you OK?" he said in a deep, confident voice, as if he had always known me.

I turned to check that it was me he was talking to and that I wasn't mistaken: out of all the women in the room, he had chosen to speak to me.

We talked for hours and as I left he said he'd call. The days seemed interminable as I waited and my stomach did all sorts of things each time the phone rang. He called two days later, said he had wanted to phone straightaway to see if I got home safely but had held out as long as he could. There was something very solid about him: he was confident yet also excitingly passionate and spontaneous. There was no routine in our lives, no planning; things just happened.

He whisked me away from the world of the semi, Croydon and list systems, away from practicality and duty, and made me feel beautiful. He had all the qualities I lacked and when I was around him I never felt inadequate. Ki said he was what I needed; that he made me see things differently, beyond the values and concepts that had been drummed into me.

She, like Jean, was also a risk-taker, but ended up with someone who seemed safe, reliable and predictable . . . although he didn't turn out to be in the end. Ki was laid out in her coffin in her red bridal sari. Her boyfriend, who was supposedly madly in love with her, hadn't wanted to marry her, but her mother insisted that that was the way that she wanted to be dressed. Had she known towards the end that her boyfriend's visits had become more and more infrequent? He didn't even manage to make it to the funeral and three months later he was seeing someone else.

Jean Michel saw me through that period. Although my way of coping was just to get on with life and try not to think about things too deeply, I knew if I needed to talk he would listen. He always listened; he always tried to understand.

I turned the key to Jean's flat and it wasn't double locked.

"Careless as usual," I thought. "Goes away for four days and forgets to double-lock the door."

I carried the shopping into the kitchen and thought I heard a noise. Maybe the cleaner was in, although it wasn't her usual day.

"Hello," I shouted. Nobody responded so I began unpacking the shopping. The fridge had half a bottle of champagne in it along with some pâté. There was another noise.

"Hello, is anyone in?" I said, going towards Jean's room.

Jean suddenly came out, making me jump.

"Jean, I didn't know you were home. When did you get in? Didn't you hear me? I've got so much to tell you."

He looked very pale.

"Are you ill? What's wrong?"

His bedroom door clicked closed.

"What's going on? Who's in there? Who is it, Jean?"

"No one, Nina," his voice sounded odd. "Don't go in there."

I went in and saw this woman emerging like some weasel out of a hole. She had a mass of red curls and was half-dressed.

All I could think about was the concierge, party to as many secrets as he was keys. He could have said something like, "Miss, don't go up there, the gas men are seeing to a leak, come back in a few hours." I would have listened.

I stood there, completely frozen, trying to comprehend an obvious situation. There were no clichés like, "It's not what you think" or, "She's not important." In a way I wish there had been because in those moments of silence I understood that he could not possibly love me and that he loved himself much more. He expected me to say something, to do something, but I just stood there in silence, staring at him. And then I walked away.

I ran down the stairs and out of the building, cars beeping as I flew recklessly across the road, not caring if they knocked me down. I ran like I never wanted to stop but when my sides began to ache I couldn't go on any more. Stumbling on a bench in Green Park, catching my breath, the tears began to trickle down my face.

The only other person apart from Ki who knew me inside out was Jean. I had showed him who I truly was and he had rejected me. Was I not good enough? Was that it? Was I fooling myself that he loved me? Did he mean it when he asked me to marry him? Did I make that up too? Was it because since Ki's death I had been distant, or was it because I made him wait? He said that he would wait for as long as it took.

My arm and my chest, the ugly blotchy creases — he had pretended that they didn't matter? Did she have ugly blotchy creases that he ran his fingers down while whispering that he loved her, every single part of her? Was that it? Was he touching her, saying that he was there for her, while the Guru was touching me? Did he pretend to love me because he pitied me?

Tears streamed down my face.

"Help me, Ki, please, I need you. Show me a sign if you're around. You said you would. Please. Are you seeing all this? Are you?" Nothing came. "You lied to me. You said you would always be with me but how can you be? If you were with me you wouldn't let any of this happen. None of this. But you're dead and dead people can't do anything, can they? I trusted you and you lied. I let you give up because you promised you would always be with me, but you deceived me just like everyone else."

32

The rain began falling. I sat on the park bench thinking that there was really no such thing as fate: imagining providence having a hand was just a way of not feeling alone, a way of making sense of a pointless journey. "I'll give you one last chance. Speak to me like you said you would. Go on, I'm listening now. Do you want me to beg? I'll beg if you want."

I crawled down onto my hands and knees. "See, I'm begging you. Please."

Still nothing came.

Clutching at the blades of grass I fell forward on my knees onto a patch of muddy wet grass and began sobbing my heart out, oblivious to who was watching me. I looked up at the grey, miserable sky and the bursting rain clouds. "Fall harder, go on, is that the best you can manage? I don't care what else you throw at me, send someone else to feel me up, go on, I don't care any more. You've taken everything, everything. Do you hear me? You probably don't even exist, do you? All made up, all of it, lies."

I sat back on the bench and was aware that I was making an awful gut-wrenching sound. The wailing came from feeling cheated by the death of my closest friend, cheated by love and the injustice of being touched up and having my faith simultaneously taken away. Unable to fight any more, I let the rain pour down on me. It soaked through my coat as I sat there continuing to think. I thought about the nature of love and how that too was a lie. Ki's boyfriend had left her to die. Jean Michel had fooled me into believing that it was possible to love. All along my parents had been right. Life wasn't about emotion, emotion was for people who had nothing better to do with their time. It was about coping and easing the struggle, being practical and realistic, that was what my dad was trying to prepare me for. Their ideas about love were practical, they left no room for emotion and no room to be hurt, let down or disappointed. They were right: romantic airy-fairy notions of love did not exist, and if they did they were impractical and could only lead to disappointment. Life was all about survival. Trust no one as everyone was out for themselves, have no expectations: that way you could not be let down.

Eventually, when I could take the cold no longer, I made my way to the train station.

I was soaking wet so that each time I moved slightly the seat made a sloshing sound. Water ran down from my hair into my face and then dripped onto my coat, which was covered in mud. A scummy dark mess of brown on a brown coat; dirty on the outside, dirty on the inside. The commuters desperately avoided eye contact with me and tried not to look when I emitted that erratic sound; that noise when you can't quite control your breathing. By the time I got to the High Street I had assimilated the day's events. I managed to go into McDonalds and clean myself up a bit and by the time I reached our road I had tried to pull myself together. When I got to the blue front door of our semi, I even managed a fake smile.

My mother was in the kitchen making rotis and my father was in the sitting room, snoozing under his newspaper despite the Hindi music blasting out of the television. Their world rotated the same way it had done since 1972 when they came to London. In the evenings, Mum rolled out the rotis and made sure they were perfectly circular. During the day she worked at a tailor's and sometimes took home extra work making Indian garments. My father had been on the same route for twenty years and wasn't taking retirement until he saw me married; something else he succeeded in making me feel guilty about.

Although I could see the connection between retirement and marriage, he managed to find a connection between marriage and most things, and if it didn't provoke a response in me he would bring out the death card. "Tell me, who will look after you, Nina, when I die?" And if he wanted to provoke an extreme response he would say, "Are you going to do the same as your sister?" This, however, was rare, as he did his very best not to mention her.

My sister Jana had left when she was eighteen. Her departure deeply wounded my parents as she had gone off to live with a "white boy". They decided the best way to handle it was to pretend nothing had happened and not to talk about her, exiling her into the recesses of their minds. The jewellery my mother had saved for her wedding was safely packed away in the hope that at some stage it could be used for me. So I knew it was madness going out with Jean Michel because it couldn't lead anywhere, but he convinced me that everything would work out and that he could win them round. Foolishly, I believed him.

Outwardly my parents hardly ever showed signs that Jana's departure had affected them, and in those intervening years many things happened but their routine remained the same. At exactly seven o'clock they would eat and by eight they would both be in bed, flicking between Zee TV and ITV.

"Didn't you take your umbrella, beta? What has happened to your coat?" my mother asked, putting down her rolling pin and handing me a multi-stained tea towel to wipe myself down with.

"I fell over."

"Go and get changed," she said, picking up the rolling pin and pointing it at me.

"Ma . . ."

"Hmmm . . ."

"About Raj, Ma, you know, the accountant man."

She put down her rolling pin again and turned to look at me. Her eyes lit up like all her prayers had finally been answered.

"I'll see him. You can call his mother to arrange it."

Why exactly these words came out of my mouth remains a mystery; perhaps it was easier than, "Ma, I've been touched up by a Guru, I've lost my job, found my boyfriend with someone else and have accepted that Ki is dead." Or maybe it was just that I was finally ready for the kind of stability they had: a gale-force wind could descend upon them, or an earthquake that measured eight on the Richter scale, and they would still be unaffected. In the words of my father, "This is what the routine and the discipline are both bringing."

I went to have a shower, vigorously scrubbing every part the Guru had touched until it hurt while I began figuring out ways to break the news to my dad that I no longer had a job.

He was sitting there in the front row when I graduated. That's when he really got into power dressing — wearing red and looking like Santa. It also gave him a certain amount of status in the community to say that his daughter was a lawyer and he would often get out the graduation photo and tears would form in his eyes.

That's why I couldn't tell them when I went back downstairs. He munched through his rotis asking if I had had a good day, not really stopping to listen for an answer but telling us about some rude passenger who had refused to pay full fare and how he "bullocked" him and how he was tired of the "riff-raffies" on his bus. Mum had put Raj's CV safely to one side and kept looking over at it and touching her heart as if to tell me that it would break it if I went back on my word. I couldn't eat anything so told them that I had had something after work, had had a long day and needed to go to bed.

Unable to sleep, I had lots of questions with no answers and an aching feeling of emptiness and solitude, compounded by the fact that I wanted to scream and scream out loud and not stop. But I couldn't. The day had begun with the Guru's hands touching me, his fingers circling my lips, and ended with me covering my mouth, making some pathetic, muffled sounds under the duvet so that nobody could hear.

That weekend I didn't get out of bed. I was running a temperature and was in a state of complete delusion. I could hear my mum faintly in the background, pottering about, bringing food to me, mumbling something about not taking an umbrella, but I slept through it in a blissful state of illusion, imagining that I was married to Jean Michel, that everything had been a nightmare. It was only my dad's voice that managed to penetrate through my dreamlike state.

"You'll be late, Nina. Don't want to get the sack, get up, you're better now, no?"

Waking up that morning, when every part of me wanted to remain in a heap, was hell.

"You'll be late, Nina," my dad shouted again, and then I heard him say to my mum, "When I was her age I had to get up at five o'clock every day, even when I was sick. And I was married." He said it like marriage had been a double punishment but my mum wasn't listening. Her mind was still on her future son-in-law.

Dad married Mum under a fog of controversy. It was controversial in the sense that he felt he had been duped. The story goes that he had a chesty cough and went to a chemist, well not really a chemist as you would expect but a shop somewhere in Uganda and that this beautiful woman served him. He was, at the time, searching for a wife and was utterly taken with her. He made a few enquiries as to her eligibility but it turned out that she was already married to the man who owned the chemist's. In true Indian style, not letting an opportunity go, the woman said she had a sister who lived with her parents in India who would be perfect for my father.

My dad, impetuous as ever, agreed to marry the sister without checking out the goods — if she was anything like her sister she would be snapped up pretty soon. When he saw my mother on the wedding day he tried to hide his disappointment but then I think he really grew to love her. That's what arranged marriages were like; you learned to fall in love. "I was the fooled," he joked in front of her. "See, Nina, you're lucky, you can meet these boys and see if you likes them: me, I had no choice." And despite the fact that he said he had no choice, they were really compatible and I could never imagine one without the other. It was hardly fireworks between them — more like a Catherine wheel which failed to ignite in the rain but then unexpectedly fizzed about a bit — but it worked for them.

I could barely open my eyes as they felt so sore. I dragged myself up, managed to have a shower, put on my suit and made out as if I was going to work, creeping down the stairs so they wouldn't have to see me. Just before getting to the front door, I shouted, "Bye, Ma. Bye, Dad."

"You'll be home early this evening, nah, beta? I've told Raj's mother to get him to call you at seven-thirty," my mum said, pouncing on me from nowhere. "Oh, what's happened to the eyes?"

"Allergy," I replied. "Anyway, I'll try not to be too late," I continued, thinking of all the places I could go to kill eight hours.

She handed me an umbrella and saw me out.

My head was throbbing and my body ached. I went to a café and sat there drinking endless cups of coffee, trying to make some kind of a decision as to what to do. What was going to happen to me without Jean — he was there to cushion all the blows. What was I going to do about work? Thank God my dad had drilled it into my head about being careful with money in an attempt to prepare me for "the days of the flooding". Most of what I had earned was put aside. He was right: life was all about trying to make yourself as secure as possible so nobody could come along with any surprises. After hours of sitting there and thinking, I decided to drag myself to the Tate.

For a Monday morning it was busy, with people flocking to see the wardrobe stuffed with worldly possessions. Thankfully there was a Matisse exhibition on. I always liked Matisse. He also studied law and his father was furious when he said he wanted to give it up to paint. He was a great painter and didn't begin to paint until after recovering from an illness. They say it was providence that sent him that illness to set him on a different path, that only looking back do we know exactly why things have happened.

It had been almost ten years since I'd picked up a paintbrush. I could have continued to paint as a "hobby" after I began my law degree but it was always all or nothing with me. Even when I was angry or sad and had a desperate urge to splatter the emotion across a blank canvas, I resisted and picked up my books and studied instead. Studied and did what everyone else wanted me to do, and became who others wanted me to be.

The rooms where Matisse's pictures were displayed were not as busy as downstairs. But as soon as I walked in I could feel the warmth. His pictures gave me energy, their raw emotions expressed with an explosion of pure, intense colours. There was no option but to stare at the paintings, to feel them: violets to stir feelings placed next to sunny, optimistic yellows, vibrant oranges against laconic blues and sober greens floating among a sea of passionate cerulean red. When I stared into Matisse's colours I could see other colours that weren't really there; realities that were invented; somewhere I could escape.

Matisse's paintings carried me into his world without me even realising, making me forget who or where I was. He painted windows that let you fly in and out; bold strips of colour like the green that ran along his wife's nose and made you feel you could balance on it, look at her every feature and see what he saw; hues of reality next to splashes of imagination. I wandered around for hours, drawn into his world, lost in the depths of his colour, soaking up every ray, searching for the shadows that he had skillfully eliminated. In every painting, I found peace.

I went to have lunch in the cafeteria and found that my thoughts had become calmer, and because I didn't want to think any more deeply I concentrated on the noise that the cutlery and crockery were making, watching the tourists, many of whom had pulled out their guidebooks to see which exhibitions they would visit next.

Before leaving the Tate I visited the shop and picked up a book on Matisse. I randomly flicked through the pages and stopped at one of his quotes:

"In art, truth and reality begin when one no longer understands what one is doing or what one knows, and when there remains an energy that is all the stronger for being constrained, controlled and compressed."

I put the book back. It wasn't a sign — dead people were unable to speak.

With a few more hours to kill before going back home, I decided to take a walk in Green Park. Jean Michel didn't live too far from there and sometimes we had gone walking together. It was an effort to drag him out as he really didn't like walking. He didn't really enjoy staying in and watching videos, either, as I did. He liked finding new restaurants and eating out; he would drive halfway across the country to find a good restaurant. He loved going to the casino and betting all his money on one number. I was intrigued by his boldness, but looking back I should have known then that I would never have been enough — life with me was probably boring, with my constant refusal to go away with him and rushing off home to my parents instead. But he said we were good together, that I brought calmness to his life; but then he said many things, most of which probably weren't even true.

I switched my phone back on and the message box was full. All of them were from him, frantic messages, every one saying how much he loved me. I so desperately wanted to believe him, to speak to him and have him put his arms around me and tell me that there had been some terrible mistake, that he could explain it all, but instead I made myself delete the messages one by one. Time, that was what I needed, time to sort out my head. I bought a coffee, sat on the park bench and thought more about the quote before setting off for home.

No sooner had I turned the key, my mum was waiting anxiously, rolling pin in one hand, telling me that Raj would be calling at seven-thirty.

"You already told me that before I left," I said.

"Good day?" my dad asked, turning back to watch the television before I had replied.

What was I supposed to say? That Henri Matisse had given me some much-needed peace.

"Yes, good day."

I went upstairs, quickly had a shower, and bang on time the phone rang. No unpredictability there, then.

"Hi Nina, it's Raj."

"Hello."

There was a moment's hesitation and then he took control.

"I hear you're a lawyer and working in the city?"

"Yes, and you?" I asked in a half-hearted attempt to deflect the conversation away from myself.

"No, I'm not a lawyer," he laughed. Well, it was more of a grunting sound. And why did he laugh? I mean, if the man thought that was humour we might as well put the phone down now.

"No," he said, gathering himself together, "I work for a consultancy firm as an accountant."

There wasn't much to say to that.

"So what do you like doing?" he began again.

There was no stopping this man; he careered straight past the silences and kept on going.

Be kind to him, Nina, talk. It's not his fault, none of it is his fault. What did I like doing? Suddenly I felt a sense of panic. It was the realisation that my life up until that moment had revolved solely around Jean and work. I had to say something, and so, like an eight-year-old, reeled off a list of hobbies. "Reading, cinema, watching TV, painting."

"Oh, painting? What do you paint with?"

"A paintbrush," I replied.

He laughed again. "Very good, that's very good, I see you too have got a sense of humour. I've dabbled in watercolours but I'm not very good," he added.

Then there was another silence.

"Seen any good films?" he asked.

I said the first thing that came into my head. "*The Matrix.*"

"I saw that on the plane to Japan."

For the first time he had my attention. Japan? What was he doing in Japan?

44

"Japan?" I enquired.

"Yes, I have to travel for work and so I extend my stay wherever possible. I love to find out about other cultures. It's important to expand the mind."

"Where else have you been?"

He listed practically half the countries in the atlas but not in a pretentious way. I stopped him at Chile and asked what it was like, and for the first time I sensed he was being himself.

"I've always wanted to go there," I said, and to my surprise he did not come out with a cheesy line like, "I'll take you" or, "Maybe you'll go there soon." Instead, he said it was beautiful.

There was a pause but now it wasn't awkward.

"Perhaps you'd like to meet up?" he asked.

I had images of my mother, a protagonist in an Indian film, wailing and beating her chest in despair at the thought of me saying no, so I said "Yes". It would be just one meeting and then I could say it didn't work out.

"For dinner or a movie?" he asked.

Movie? Before I made a comment on his use of the word "movie" I thought twice. It was only the Croydon multiplex and I wouldn't have to talk to him that much if we were seeing a film. "Yes, a movie sounds good."

"Great, I'll pick you up on Saturday, about three?"

"All right."

"See you then, Nina."

My mother was downstairs, eagerly waiting for me. I could hear her pacing. As soon as I came down she pretended to look disinterested, resuming the rolling-pin position. She turned around for a second and her right eyebrow signalled as if to say, "Dish the dirt." The other eyebrow said, "He's a good boy, got a good job, coming from a very good family, now tell me you have arranged to meet him."

"Three o'clock on Saturday," I said.

"OK, OK," she muttered as if she wasn't bothered, but when she turned back to her perfectly circular rotis I could feel her beaming.

Knowing that my parents were distracted with the whole Raj scenario, I felt less guilty the next morning about putting on a suit and pretending to go to work. Jean Michel had left three more messages. I wanted to listen to them but again deleted them one by one. Then I went back to see Matisse, the only person who I could turn to at that moment in time.

I bought the book I had seen the day before. It told me about his life and each of the paintings. It also included a commentary by critics on what he was trying to achieve, saying something about his search for chromatic equilibrium. How did they know that anyway? Maybe he wasn't trying to achieve anything except to express his feelings? Did it matter what they thought he was trying to do? What mattered was how the paintings left you feeling, not a skewed interpretation on what he did or didn't want to do. I searched the book for his own words and came across another quote: "There are always flowers for those who want to see them."

"Are there, Matisse?" I wondered aloud.

The cafeteria was full again at lunchtime and I found myself having to ask if I could sit next to a girl with long, mousy-blonde hair.

"Sure," she replied in an Australian accent, smiling away. When she spotted that I had bought the same book on Matisse as her and commented on it, I nodded and kept my head down. I wasn't in the mood for chitchat.

But she continued. "He's just great, isn't he? And I love the quote on flowers."

Ordinarily I might have taken this to be a sign, having just read the exact same quote, but in my jaded state I took it to be some lonely traveller who probably had no money and was trying to strike up a friendship so she could ask if she could sleep on my sofa. I imagined my dad finding her on his Land of Leather sofa in the morning.

" 'There are always flowers for those who want to see them,' " she continued out loud, just in case I wasn't familiar with it.

"And weeds," I wanted to say, but remained looking down, eating in silence.

"Nice meeting you," she got up to leave.

"Yes," I replied as she went off.

I sat there for a while reading. Some Japanese tourists signalled to the seats next to me to ask if they could sit there. They seemed really grateful that I said yes. I nodded, relieved that they couldn't speak any English and turned the page.

The last bit I read before heading off to Green Park was about the nature of creativity. Matisse said that creativity took courage. My dad would say creativity took a lot of lazy people who had nothing better to do all day except to waste time. The Turner Prize did nothing except confirm his perception: "See, they fooling people and making the money. Maybe I should get Kavitha to make some patterns with her samosas and send them in." I closed the book and caught the tube to Green Park.

Creativity takes courage.

Does it? I don't think I can take a leap of faith, not on my own, anyway. I don't trust myself. Does that make sense? I've never really done anything on my own. I'm used to doing things for other people, that's what makes me feel secure. I'm used to being someone's daughter, someone's girlfriend, someone's lawyer. I'm not used to being me. I don't believe that I am big enough to make this all better. If I'm myself, I don't think I'll survive. Don't worry, I'm talking to myself, not you, Ki. Wouldn't want you to think that I'm asking you or anything. Wouldn't want you to rise from the dead or do something complicated like that.

I sat on the bench for a little while longer, then wandered around the back of Mayfair looking in gallery windows before going home.

"Good day, Nina?" my dad asked.
"We got an important client today."

"Very good," he said as he delved back into his newspaper. He didn't really need to know the ins and outs of "love", just to be occasionally reassured that I wouldn't unexpectedly be made redundant; hence the addition of new clients every now and then.

It's not my natural inclination to bend the truth. I wasn't one of those types who went to school with a long skirt and rolled it up on the way there. Truth-bending is something I have learned to do out of necessity, and not necessarily to protect myself but my parents. When I was with Jean Michel I always said I was seeing Jean or staying there, but they jumped to the conclusion that he was a she and I let them believe it.

"Bring this Jeannie round," my dad would say.

"Yes, we would like to meet her. I'll make roti and paneer," my mum would add. It went on like this till I couldn't make any more excuses, so I got Susan, one of my friends, to stand in as her.

My dad liked "the Jeannie" as he referred to her. After ascertaining what Susan's parents did and estimating their combined annual income, he thought she was a good person to mix with.

Now I looked at my dad, took a deep breath and said, "Dad, the office is experiencing some difficulties with the phone, so if there is an emergency ring me on my mobile." They never rang the office, but just in case.

"Hmmm."

"Did you hear me, Dad? Fire, flood, office, call me on my mobile."

"What fire in the office, it's not burned down, no?"

Now I had his attention. "No, I'm just saying, in case of an emergency or if you need to speak to me, call me on my mobile."

"Nothing is wrong, no, Nina?"

That was the moment to confess and, believe me, I wanted to, but he looked at me like he wanted reassurance that everything was OK and I just didn't have the strength to tell him.

"Everything is fine."

"They need someone to come and fix it?"

"Fix what?"

"The phones. I can come and sort out problem."

"No, Dad, but thank you."

My mother was in rolling-pin position and asked me the standard questions: what I'd eaten for lunch, was I ready to have dinner, if I was going to go up and have a shower. As she returned to her rotis, I stared at her. Where was that other person she had unleashed when she raged at my sister? Did she ever think of Jana? Did she worry about what she ate and what time she was going to take her shower? She must have, I know she must have. Once I caught her unpacking the jewellery box she had packed safely away, emptying its contents and crying, but she never said anything to us, me or my dad. Instead she kept it all inside and carried on with her routine. And many times when I tried to speak to her about my sister she would turn her back to me and walk away.

After I came out of the shower, the phone rang. It was Raj.

"Hi Nina, I know we're meeting on Saturday but I just thought I'd give you a call and see how you are."

"I'm fine," I heard myself reply politely. It was quite a relief to talk to someone who didn't really know me, who wanted to talk about superficial things like what films I watched; someone who was unable to affect me in any way and didn't require any depth of conversation.

"How are you?" I asked.

"Good. Had a busy day. I am just going to read now."

"What are you reading?"

"*Seven Habits of Highly Effective People*."

"Right. And is it working? Are you being effective?"

"Hope so. What are you going to do?"

"Going down to eat and then hopefully get to sleep early. I haven't been sleeping well."

"Don't eat too late," he said. "I've heard that causes insomnia because the food isn't digested properly."

"It's not the food," I heard myself saying. "It's just there are lots of things going on at the moment . . . lots of . . . lots of . . ." I searched desperately for the word I was looking for but the best I could come up with was ". . . contracts."

"Are you busy at work, then?" he enquired.

"Yes. Very busy."

"I'll leave you to it, Nina. I just wanted to say hello, that was all."

"Thank you," I said as I put the phone down.

And that was the first time that I really warmed to him, because practicality brought a certain amount of stability that did not require much of me.

It was time to get a new mobile phone as I was finding it increasingly hard not to listen to the daily messages from Jean. After buying the phone I went back to the Tate and back to Matisse.

The blonde girl from the cafeteria was there again, studying the paintings. She smiled when she saw me. I smiled back and wandered off into the next room before she could ask me for the sofa. She followed swiftly behind me.

"Excuse me," she whispered.

I pretended not to hear her.

"Excuse me," she repeated.

I turned around.

"You dropped this." She handed me my Matisse book.

"Thank you," I said, taking it. "I didn't even hear it drop."

"It's what Matisse does to you. Sometimes you can just be lost in his colours."

That's exactly what I had thought. "I know what you mean," I replied. "Is he one of your favourite artists?" I found myself asking.

She nodded.

"Mine too," I said, wanting her to ask me another question.

But she didn't ask me anything else, just smiled politely and left.

My feet took me effortlessly around the room as I tried to see the flowers in his paintings. Even in his down-times he painted light, he painted with bold colours. Maybe that's what he meant when he said, "Creativity takes courage", that every day he showed up and painted no matter what else was happening in his life.

The cafeteria wasn't that busy as it was late afternoon. I could see the blonde girl sitting and eating a sandwich and although there were other empty seats I could have sat at, I went up to her and asked if the seat beside her was taken.

"No," she smiled. "My name's Gina by the way."

"I'm Nina."

"Nina, Gina," she laughed. "Pleased to meet you, Nina," she said, shaking my hand.

"I liked that quote too," I found myself saying out of nowhere, trying to make up for my previous unfriendliness.

"The one about seeing flowers?" she asked. "It's beautiful, isn't it? It reminds me of my mum."

"Is she in Australia?"

"No, she's dead."

I put my own sandwich down. "I'm so sorry, I really am, I didn't mean to —"

"No, it's OK, really. That's why that quote means so much."

I wanted to ask her if she spoke to her, if her mother responded, if she looked for signs.

Instead, I asked, "Are you on holiday?"

"No, I live here now. I'm an artist. How about you?"

"I am — was — a lawyer but I'm thinking about painting again."

"Well, if you need a studio, I know of one going. Or if you know of anyone who needs one, let me know. I'm desperate to find someone who'll take mine for three months so I can go back to Australia."

She said she wanted to surprise her family and escape the winter months but hadn't managed to find anyone who was interested in subletting her studio despite placing several ads. We talked some more, mainly about Matisse, and I took her number just in case I came across anyone who needed a studio.

Later, I sat in Green Park trying to convince myself that it was not meant for me.

"Ki, Matisse talks about seeing flowers when there are none. I want to see them. Even if you're not there and you're not listening it doesn't matter. I want to believe you are. Sorry about what I said to you the other day. There's a studio that has become free. Do you think it's meant for me?"

Silence.

"That's what I thought too. What if I just tried it out for three months tops? Haven't really got anything else to lose."

I began to feel almost excited when I thought about the possibility of having my own studio and being able to paint. The only problem with having a studio was that the level of deceit would escalate even further. I had never intended to lie so blatantly to my parents. I didn't want to; the days I was going to the Tate were just to get my head straight. Perhaps I would try broaching the subject of renting a studio with my dad. I would say that the firm had given me a three-month sabbatical so I could understand the work of my artists better. It wasn't that far from the truth, really.

My dad was upstairs in the spare room, fiddling with one of the many television sets he had, when I arrived home.

"Can sell this one for fifty pounds. Newsagent wants it for tomorrow."

"Right. That's great." I thought the best way of bringing up the studio subject was by telling him what Matisse said and then at least I could start talking about painting and lead on from there. "Dad, what do you think of this quote?"

"What?" he shouted.

I had to rephrase the sentence. "An artist who is worth a lot of money said that there are always flowers for those who want to see them. What do you think about that?"

"He's your client?"

"Sort of."

"Very good quote."

"Really, do you think so?"

"Yes, that is why he is the rich. Wastes no money buying the expensive flowers from the petrol shops and saves the money that the flowers are taking. Not giving the peoples the flowers every time he is seeing them."

I wanted to bury my head in my hands in despair. He would never understand. Even if I sat down with him and explained in great detail why it was so important to me, he just wouldn't get it.

"Thought about what you are going to wear to see Raj?" my mother asked later at dinner.

"No, I have had other things on my mind."

She made some suggestions that I pretended to listen to. The only way I could possibly escape it all was to paint. My decision was made.

The next morning I phoned Gina to tell her that I was interested in looking at her studio. She told me to come by whenever I could that day.

It was located at the back of London Bridge, in an alley with cobbled stones that led nowhere in particular. The sign read "Forget the dog, just beware if you disturb the artist at work". I knocked on the door and Gina pulled it open.

"Good to see you again, Nina. Well, this is it."

The studio was a converted garage, bright and airy as it had a skylight. There was an enormous table in the centre of the room and a smaller one on the side which had a kettle, a toaster and a blow heater that were all attached to one adapter.

"It's safe," Gina said as she saw my eyes rest on that spot.

The walls were covered with pictures of Sydney Harbour in different sizes and forms.

"Homesick?" I asked.

"I don't think there's anywhere more beautiful than that view."

56

The floor was concrete grey, splattered with colours that had managed to jump off Sydney Harbour.

"What do you paint?"

Where was I supposed to start? I couldn't say I didn't know so I said, "Birds."

"Any particular kind?"

"Just the flying ones."

She laughed and moved towards her easel, remarking that that was where the light fell best. "I'm leaving that here but if you've got your own and you want me to put it away then that's fine."

"You mean I can really rent this studio from you?" I asked.

"If you want it, it's yours. The only thing is can you give me cash instead of a cheque. Other than that, you can have it from Monday. That gives me time to pack up my stuff but if you want to drop your things by before then, just give me a call."

When I got home there was complete chaos. The garments my mum had made were stuffed into black binliners and there were about twenty television sets on the landing. My dad was up a ladder, screaming at my mum, telling her to pass the sets to him quicker so he could put them in the attic. She was huffing and puffing and looking as though she was going to pass out.

"What's going on?" I asked.

"Inland Revenue man is outside. He's been watching the house for the last two hours. Fukkus, Kavitha, fukkus."

"It's focus, Dad, focus."

"Yes, I know this, this is what I am saying to her. Why you telling me, tell Kavitha, she is almost dropping the television. She doesn't know what a big problem this is."

I looked outside the window and to my horror saw Jean's car. Jean was making his way towards our house.

"Oh God," I muttered.

"I know, I know, that's what I thought. Help us, Bhagavan. Hurry up, hurry up, Kavitha," he shouted.

"I'll get rid of him, Dad," I said, running down the stairs.

As I opened the door, Jean was standing on the doorstep. I closed the door behind me and pulled him away from the house.

"What the hell are you doing here?"

"Nina, I had to see you, your phone is dead and you haven't answered any of my letters."

"There's nothing to say except it's over."

"Can't we at least talk about it?"

"No, not here, not now."

"When, then?"

"I don't know."

"Tomorrow," he said. "Come round to the flat."

"No," I said. "Just go, Jean."

"I won't let you go," he said, "not like this. I love you."

"OK, OK, I'll call, please just leave."

I went back into the house.

"I've got rid of him, Dad."

"Thank Bhagavan."

"I told him he wasn't within his rights to wait in his car and watch out for illegal activity as there was nothing illegal going on, and if he continued to wait in his car I would make an official complaint. I don't think he'll be coming back." The lies were getting bigger, and the frightening thing was they were getting easier to tell.

"See, Kavitha, all those years to make Nina study 'the love', all worth it," he said coming down from his ladder. Then he hugged me.

Dad never hugged me. I could count the times he had on one hand. When I went to hold him he would do this ninety-degree rotation so I got the back of him and then he would walk out of my embrace. My mum never knew how to respond when I held her and would stand there like a statue, waiting for the hug to pass like it was some massive tidal-wave that would knock her over.

The next morning, I went to the bank. My dad took £300 a month from me as part of my wedding contribution. I always thought that if I married Jean this fund would cushion the blow slightly as he could keep the amount he had built up and console himself and my mother with a holiday or a new car. Mind you, they never went on holiday, but they would have had to go somewhere for a couple of weeks until the scandal died down. When my Uncle Amit's daughter began living with Roy who was black, "the honchos" had endless rounds of secret talks to confer so they could sort out the situation. Pressure was put on my Uncle

Amit and his wife; they were bombarded with CVs of every single male specimen on the planet who could be a possible replacement. When this didn't work, one of the honchos leaked the news to the wider community. I thought Uncle Amit and Auntie Asha would have to emigrate but they stood firm, attending family functions, ignoring the whispering and gossip and being shunned by certain members of the community; but they never managed to live it down. But Uncle Amit was different from my father, he didn't need the approval of the community or that sense of belonging.

"Parents taking modern approach, what can you expect?" had been my dad's first reaction to the news. Though in my dad's case this wasn't strictly true: he hadn't had a modern approach but my sister had still left. I didn't correct him. "This is not looking after the children. What will happen to this girl? He will leave her, she will have baby, nobody will want her. Parents will die, she will live alone, nobody wants her or baby."

So a happy life, then. "He might not ever leave, Dad, they probably really love each other," I replied.

"Two years I gives them. The love is not enough, Nina, you must understand this. Everyday living with someone is hard. See your mother and me, she knows me, I knows her. She is not thinking that she will one day wake up and find the Bra Pitt."

"Brad?"

"Yah, yah, him. I knows I will not wake up and find the Cilla Black. This is life. Kavitha understands me, I understands her. We have the family, the culture, the traditions, the security. This is what is making the

60

marriage. This is why I am working for you, I want you to have what I have with Kavitha."

Thinking about him doing two jobs for me made me feel incredibly guilty for taking money from the bank to pay for the studio. It would only be for a month or two, just to sort my head out, just to get it out of my system.

The man at the art shop was of no help to me as I stood looking at the rows and rows of brushes and paints, and the different types of paper and canvases. When I used to paint I painted in oils best, so I went over to the oils section only to be confronted by more tubes in different colours and sizes. I hesitated for a moment. Painting with oils was not going to be practical. My mum had a nose like a bloodhound and she would smell the linseed and turpentine on me. I walked over to the acrylic section and chose the paints that I needed, and bought a dozen primed, stretched canvases and brushes. I called Gina to see if the material could be delivered to the studio later that day. She told me to come by whenever I wanted.

When I arrived she was taking down her paintings and wrapping them in brown paper.

"So have you been painting long, Nina?"

"No. I'm just experimenting. I'm not an artist or anything. I used to paint when I was younger and then I had to stop."

"Why?"

"Family stuff," I replied. "But I'm taking time off just to find out what it is I'm supposed to be doing." I didn't know why I was divulging such information but

61

she had something about her that made you want to tell her things.

I desperately wanted to ask her about her mother. "How long have you been here?" I asked instead.

"Eight months. I went to art school in Sydney, did a few exhibitions over there and have been going to college here, but it's hard to break into the circuit, unless you know someone or you get spotted. I do love London but sometimes it can be a really cold and lonely place."

"I know what you mean."

"You got family here?" Gina asked.

I nodded.

"See, that makes all the difference," she said. "You've always got them to fall back on if things don't work out."

"Not if you have a family like mine," I said. "What about you?"

"My dad is back home with my little sister. I want to surprise them for Christmas."

"Do you believe in signs?" I suddenly blurted.

Instead of giving me the strange look of incomprehension I expected, she answered, "Why do you think I said the quote aloud?"

There was an instant understanding that passed between us at that moment, and we didn't even have to say what it was.

"How did she die?" I asked.

"Skin cancer," Gina replied.

"I'm sorry. My best friend died of cancer too."

"It's the pits, isn't it? I promised my mum that I'd come to England. What did you promise?"

"That I'd paint again and everything I did I would do passionately."

"This would be the work of my mum, you know."

"What?" I asked.

"Getting you and me together. It's got her name all over it. Maybe your friend and my mum have got together up there and said, 'These two, they need to meet.' What's your friend's name?"

"Ki."

She looked up at her skylight. "Ki . . . Mum . . . Thank you."

And when she did that it was the first time that I thought I wasn't losing my mind. There was someone else in the world as crazy as I was.

Gina told me she had been teaching English in Japan before her mother had fallen ill. She wasn't told how bad it was so didn't hurry home until the final stages, and then when she got home she couldn't bring herself to leave Australia again. It had taken a huge leap of faith to come to England, and she said with leaps of faith came the call to adventure. I wouldn't know about that — the biggest leap of faith before my foray into painting was going out with Jean Michel and look where that had landed me.

She said she wasn't giving up on England, just needed a rest from the rain and from trying so hard to make things work. I understood this: if I had had an Australia to go to, I would have gone there too.

The delivery men came with my paints and canvases later that day and as Gina helped me unpack we talked about death, not in a morbid way but in a way that both of us understood. I didn't want to leave the warmth of her studio. I wanted to tell her more, tell her about the Guru and what had happened, but it was getting late and she still had lots to do.

"Nearly done," she said, unwrapping the last canvas.

"Thank you, thank you so much."

"I've hardly done anything. If you need to use any of my stuff, like brushes or whatever else you need, just go through those boxes."

And though I hardly knew Gina it felt as if she had always been my friend. I wanted to hug her and tell her that it would all be all right, and that she would come back to London and find that it wasn't such a lonely place. As I was thinking this she wrapped her arms around me and told me that she was sure I would find what I wanted through my paintings. She was as generous as Ki was and I desperately wanted to believe that our meeting had been orchestrated by the two people we loved.

On the way back home, I thought of the money spent on renting the studio and buying canvases and paint, of how one thing had led to another. Then I thought about managing the deceit. Perhaps it was better to say nothing, to stop adding new clients and blatantly lying.

As I walked in the door, my dad put down his paper and pointed to a box.

"Nina, why your work send you this big box?"

Oh God, it was my things, work had sent me all my things. Don't panic, breathe deeply, remain silent, say nothing, do not lie.

He looked at me, waiting for a response. "Why they doing this?"

"Didn't I tell you, Dad, we're moving offices."

"No problem in the company?" he asked, putting down his glass.

"No, no problem. Actually, we've got more clients, we're expanding so we need to move to bigger premises." That would account for the change in telephone numbers and the technical difficulties we were experiencing.

"Doesn't make sense to me."

"What, Dad?"

"Why they're not sending box to the new office? Why they're sending it here?"

"Feng shui." I said the first thing that came into my head.

He looked at me, puzzled.

"Because they want us to have a clear-out of our files and our personal belongings so we don't bring old things into the new office. It's feng shui."

"He's the office manager?"

"No, feng shui is an idea about clearing space and bringing new energies in. When you get rid of something old, something new comes in its place."

"I always know this," my mother shouted out from the kitchen. "I'm telling you, since we tidy television sets and put them all in attic there is change, maybe energy will bring Nina's marriage. To bring them down, it's unlucky. Bhagavan will tell you." See, even she was prone to a bit of truth bending; nowhere in the Gita did it say, "Thou shalt keep broken television sets in the attic" or, "Broken television sets left in attic will lead to daughter's marriage."

Dad mumbled that they wouldn't stay in the attic long, just for enough time to stop the taxman snooping around, and then he muttered, "I have to fix the television sets and drive the bus for a living, but Fongi Shu, he tells the peoples any rubbish and he makes the money. He's not Indian, no?"

"No, it's Chinese, I think."

"The Chinese peoples, they are the clever, very clever."

My resolve not to tell lies was obviously not working, and seeing as I'd just told one, another one wasn't going to be so bad.

"It's been a really busy day at work. That new client is very demanding and I might have to be a bit more hands-on."

As I heard myself saying the words I knew he wouldn't understand, but these were the only words he latched on to. He put his newspaper down again and looked at me, probably imagining me hugging my clients and them doing ninety-degree rotations away from me too.

"What I mean by hands-on, Dad, is helping the client a bit more: so, say if he is organising an exhibition in Mayfair, I might go and help him in his studio."

I knew it made no sense but my dad only chose to hear words that he liked, hence Mayfair.

"Good, good," he mumbled.

My mother was listening from the kitchen. "Ma, I was just saying to Dad that one of my clients is going to want me to help with an important exhibition he has so I might have to help him a bit in his studio."

I knew it was volunteering far too much information but I had to get her bloodhound nose off the trail.

"Has Raj called?" she replied.

"What!" Here I was trying to set her off the track and she was going on about the accountant. As I went back into the hall to take off my coat she followed me.

"Why don't you call him? You are seeing him tomorrow, no?" she said before giving me a chance to reply.

"I'm not calling him, why should I?"

"We don't want him to forget you, Nina. A boy like that probably has a hundred girls to choose from."

I wanted to ask her if she was ever disappointed; disappointed at the way her life had turned out, if she ever felt passionate about anything other then her circular rotis. But instead I said that I was seeing Raj in twenty-four hours and I was sure that if he wanted to speak to me before then, he would call.

No sooner had I said that, the phone rang.

"Hello Nina, it's Raj."

"Just a moment." I turned to my mum. "Ma, is that burning I can smell in the kitchen?"

"No, beta, I switched off the gas."

"I think Dad's calling you."

"I'm not," he shouted.

"Ma, can I speak to Raj on my own?"

"Sorry about that Raj," I sighed as my mother reluctantly shuffled back to the kitchen.

"That's OK. Nina, I just wanted to know if you were still all right to meet tomorrow?"

"Do you feel like going to a gallery instead?" I asked. There was a pause. "I mean it's all right if you don't want to, we can go to the cinema, it's just that I was thinking that . . ."

"No, no, a gallery is fine. Shall we meet at the Tate?" he suggested.

I liked the fact that he suggested the Tate. Maybe he wasn't so bad after all. "There's a Matisse exhibition on at the moment."

"I know," he replied.

I was impressed. "Around three o'clock?"

"Three o'clock is fine, Nina. Shall we meet in the café?"

And he knew about the café.

I told him I'd meet him there.

I went upstairs to call Jean.

"Thank God, Nina, I have to see you to explain."

"Do you know that there's a Matisse exhibition on at the Tate?" I asked.

"What?"

"There's a Matisse exhibition on at the Tate."

"Is that where you want to meet me?"

"No. I just wanted to know if you knew that?"

"No. Will you meet me, Nina, just to talk and listen to what I have to say?"

"Will you promise to leave me alone if I do?"

He said he would and so we agreed to meet the next day at seven.

I woke up very late the next morning. It must have seemed like an eternity to my mum who was hanging about outside my bedroom door.

"Yes, before you ask, I'm going to see some paintings with him."

"Paintings?" she repeated.

"Paintings?" my father interrupted as he was passing. "If you want to see paintings you can see the paintings here . . ." He indicated the numerous pictures of incarnated gods on the landing, hung on Seventies retro wallpaper.

These were the moments when I wanted so desperately not to be related to him.

As I got ready to leave for the Tate, my mother stopped me.

"You can't go like that," she said, thinking about the hundreds of girls dancing before Raj — the competition. I was wearing a pale blue polo-neck, jeans, a long black coat and had no make-up on.

"What will he think when he sees you?"

"He will think he hasn't been the fooled. Fooled, I tell you," my dad shouted from the sitting room.

"Put at least a bit of colour on your lips. I know you don't need the make-up. I know that Bhagavan has given you a very pretty face, but it is to show you have made some effort."

"It's not about looks, Ma, it's about what's on the inside." This was half the problem with the list system; for me it was all too superficial. Everything was to do with the outward appearance — what you looked like, how much money you had, what job you did. Also, it wasn't as if you could go on hundreds of dates with a guy to get to know him and then say no, you didn't like him. This would be another red mark against your family name.

"But please, beta, do this for me."

"It's the weekend, Ma," I said and then, feeling a little guilty, I went back up and put some lipstick on.

Raj was already sitting at a table waiting for me when I got to the cafeteria. I knew it was him by the way he was fidgeting with his cup. As he looked up I didn't think, "wow" but it wasn't a heart-sinking disappointment either like it could have been, and I could see how the other ninety-nine women would find him attractive. As I walked closer to him his aftershave smelled stronger and stronger. He got up to greet me and it was slightly awkward as we didn't know whether to shake hands or kiss each other.

"Hello, Nina, how are you?" he asked, missing my cheek and kissing my ear.

"I'm fine, thank you."

His height at over six foot had been greatly exaggerated. He was slightly smaller than me and had a gap in between his front teeth, which I was sure that my mother would say was symbolic of good fortune. He'd also overdone it with the gel in his hair and it made it look greasy.

"You're very tall," he commented.

I didn't know what to say to that so I smiled.

"I'm always nervous about doing this," he said.

And then he went on at great lengths about how he felt. I caught the first part of it which was that he had now got a system in place when meeting the prospective date but then after that I wasn't really listening to what he was saying, and I knew it wasn't right but I was comparing him to Jean. Jean's eyes sparkled, Raj's didn't. Raj's lips were much thinner; Ki said she never trusted a man with thin lips. It was the occasional grunting laugh that brought me back to the conversation.

"So how about you?" he asked.

How about me what? I had missed that first part of the conversation. "Well, as you know, I'm a lawyer, as you know . . ."

"You're funny, Nina. I meant how many times have you done this?"

"Done what?"

"Meeting, on the arranged system?"

"Ohh, this?" I wanted to tell him about all the weirdos I had to see before meeting Jean, and about Jean, but I didn't as I knew if word got back to the honchos who were responsible for matching up the CVs, mine would be marked with a red pen and my mother's reputation tarnished forever. "A few," I replied.

"You're very beautiful, Nina, I would have thought you would have been snapped up just like that," he clicked his fingers.

There it was; cheesy line number one. Only one person in the world had ever made me feel truly beautiful on the inside and out; what did he know? Raj sensed my irritation. "I'm sorry, I didn't mean it like that. It came out wrong . . . nerves . . ."

Feeling guilty at taking my frustration out on Raj, I replied, "No, it's OK. Thank you."

It transpired that he really had no need to be nervous as he had been on about twenty dates, had got as far as two engagements, but for one reason or another, neither of them worked out. His perseverance was commendable.

"Third time lucky," I said like a fool.

"Indeed," he replied, smiling.

We talked about each other's jobs, families and interests, and on paper the honchos seemed to have done their job well — he was a suitable match in the eyes of my parents at least. Raj then asked if I wanted to see the Matisse exhibition. I didn't want to say that I had visited it all week.

"I would love to. Do you like Matisse?" I asked, surprised.

He nodded.

As he got up I was distracted by the T-shirt underneath his blue jumper. It was on inside out so that the label was showing. It was probably nerves, haste or just clumsiness, but I found it almost endearing. I was definitely warming towards him, almost despite myself.

"'Creativity takes courage,'" Raj said as we entered the room.

"How did you know he said that?" I replied, astounded. Was this a sign? No signs all year and then a bloody shower of them.

He laughed and this time I didn't hear the grunting sound. "There's a lot about me you don't know, Nina," he said confidently.

"Can I ask you a question?"

"Ask as many as you like," he replied.

"If you went to a casino, would you put all your money on one number?"

"I wouldn't go to a casino."

"But if you had to, what would you do?"

"I would cover all eventualities — put as many chips on as many numbers — that way you can't lose."

We looked at the paintings together and his favourite was *The Red Studio*, the same as mine. To my surprise I found I could have spent much more time with him, but I was aware that Jean Michel would be waiting for me and that I was already running late.

"Is there somewhere you have to be, Nina?" he asked, spotting me checking my watch.

"Yes, I'm really sorry. But I'm sure we'll meet again."

"Look, Nina, I've met lots of people and I know that I like you and I'd really like to see you again. Tomorrow?" he asked, pinning me down with a date.

I took a moment to think about it: I did want someone who was calm, who knew what they wanted, someone who was practical yet could understand me on some level. Above all, someone who was the total opposite of Jean. And how did he know that about Matisse?

"Is it OK if I call you and let you know this evening?"

"You can call me whenever you like," he replied.

I had said I'd meet Jean at seven but it was seven-thirty when I got to his apartment building. The concierge opened the door for me and smiled. I took the lift up and rang the buzzer.

Jean answered the door. He looked tired and just for one fleeting moment I wanted to forgive him and tell him that I had really, really missed him.

"I thought you weren't coming. I'm so happy to see you, Nina."

Be strong, I kept telling myself.

"Come in, cherie, come in," he said, coming to kiss me. "Cherie" sounded stupid. I turned away so he caught part of my ear.

The lights were dimmed, candles were lit and he had made dinner.

"Why didn't you use your key?" he asked.

"Well, I don't know, let me think . . . because I might find someone else here?"

"Nina, I'm sorry, I was drunk. We got a deal with . . ."

I couldn't believe what he was telling me. "Drunk . . .? Drunk . . .?" If he had said he was angry with me and wanted to hurt me, maybe then I could listen, but drunk?

His eyes searched mine for something he could tell me that would make it better but they couldn't find anything. He reached out his hand to touch me.

I wanted to tell him about my week, giving up work, finding a studio, but didn't know where to begin and, besides, I felt I couldn't pour my heart out to him any more.

"Do you know that it takes courage to be creative?"

"What?" he replied, perplexed.

"Creativity takes courage."

"Does it?"

"I don't know."

He grabbed my hand, told me that he loved me, that he was sorry and would do whatever it took to make it up to me, that it would never, ever happen again. That we could start over. He said he would do absolutely anything to make me happy. And I wanted to believe every word of it, I wanted to believe it was all going to be all right, but I couldn't because it wasn't all right. And what if my dad was correct? What if love was fleeting and understanding was what was really important. If Jean understood me, I mean really understood me, he wouldn't have done that. What if in a few years he found someone else again? I took a deep breath, moved my hand away from his.

"You'll need these back," I said, handing him his keys and then heading towards the door.

"Nina, I love you," he shouted.

I closed the door behind me, fighting back the tears. The sad thing was I loved him too, but it wasn't enough any more.

When I got home my mum was sitting downstairs with the contents of the jewellery box sprawled across the floor.

"All for you, when you get married," she said glancing up at me. "Raj's mother called to tell me it had gone very well."

"Yes, it went well, Ma."

I didn't need love, I decided then, I needed understanding; so I called Raj and asked him if he wanted to go for a walk in the park with me.

I wished I had had the luxury of a whole string of dates with Raj before having to make a decision but arranged introductions didn't always work like that; well, especially in our family they didn't. So if you see someone twice, especially in the space of two days, it's a given that you'll be walking around a fire with them and feeding each other sickly sweets on your wedding day, unless, that is, you want to deal with a distraught mother who says you have brought shame and disrepute on the family.

But how exactly events precipitated themselves that Sunday is beyond me. The walk in the park had gone well and by the end of the afternoon Raj wanted to know if there was possibly a future for us. At that time I couldn't answer the question but by the evening I was somehow engaged to him.

76

It started in my absence when my dad was going through my things looking for my car insurance papers. He had taken my car out and bumped it, and true to his impatient nature couldn't wait a couple of hours for me to get back and sort it out. While rummaging through my things, he came across letters from Jean. Letters that had been sent earlier that week, telling me how sorry he was and how much he loved me.

Putting together the fact that I wasn't married at twenty-seven, the Zee TV lesbian talk-show incident, and believing Jean to be a woman, he almost had a heart attack as he finished reading how much Jean loved me.

He screamed at my mother, calling her to witness the evidence, and told her it was all her fault, that she had spoiled me and let me get away with "the murder". They were both pacing the house, waiting for me to get home.

Raj had given me a lift back and, thank God, I hadn't asked him in. My dad opened the door before I had even had a chance to put the key in the lock.

"We've found out about you and the Jeannie," he shouted. "It is shameful. How will I hold my head in the community if anyone finds out?" he ranted as I walked in.

My mother was weeping in the corner, refusing to look at me.

"You don't understand, Dad . . ."

"No, Nina, you can not deny it," he said, pulling out the letters from his pocket and throwing them at me.

"It's not what you think, it's . . ."

"How can you do this to us, after everything we have done for you, it's . . . it's . . ."

"It's a man, Dad. Jean is a man. You met Susan, my friend Susan, who was pretending to be Jean who's a man."

My mother wailed even louder, the wedding sari ripped to shreds in her mind.

"Don't worry, it's finished, and anyway, if it wasn't why would I be seeing Raj?"

As they took a moment to think about this the doorbell went.

My dad answered it.

"Hello Mr Savani."

"Oh Bhagavan, what more today? My daughter told you I have paid all my tax bills."

Oh God, Jean, I thought.

"Nina," Jean said seeing me by the door. "Who was that man who dropped you off?"

Dad looked confused as my world caved in around me.

"Nina, I love you," Jean shouted.

My dad looked over at my mum who had gathered herself together. "Kavitha, the taxman is saying he is in love with Nina."

"He's not the taxman, Dad, he's Jean, 'the Jeannie'." I turned to Jean. "What will it take for you to leave me alone, Jean?"

"I won't, not until you tell me that —"

"I'm marrying someone else," I blurted.

My mother looked at me, wiping her tears with the end of her sari.

"His name is Raj and he's an accountant," I continued.

Jean looked at me, incredulous. "The man in the car?"

I nodded. And then he walked away. And soon after I'd said it, I wanted to shout out, "Don't go, Jean, it's not true." But my mother had somehow managed to wrap herself around me and was weeping with delight.

Dad thankfully thought that Jean had fallen in love with me the day he had met me at the door. It was understandable, he said, as I got my looks from his side of the family. Mum said that we'd have to keep it all quiet so as not to disrupt the wedding plans. But then she would say that as she kept a lot of things quiet. And me, I called up Raj later that evening to ask him if he felt he might be lucky the third time around.

My dad was right: in life you can't have everything you want — it was better to make it as pain-free as possible.

The next morning I woke up feeling very dazed, and for one moment I breathed a sigh of relief thinking that agreeing to marry an accountant and being an unemployed owner of a studio had been a nightmare. The moment I realised it was true, I wanted to smother myself with the pillow.

"What a bloody mess, Ki, suppose you're unable to help me out here?"

She would be laughing at the mess, telling me to get out of it and give Jean another chance, but it was too late — wedding plans were already being put into action.

My mum was like a contestant on *The Price is Right* who had just found out that her name had been called and was running down the steps in a state of delirious excitement. "Get up, beta, and go to work and then you can come home early," she said bouncing into my room. "We have so many plans to discuss, so many things to do. Come on, beta, we've done it, we've done it."

She pulled back the duvet and I dragged myself into the shower. Part of my job was getting artists out of contracts that appeared watertight, but this was something else: verbal agreements in the semi were binding.

I got changed into my suit, pulled out my sports bag and packed a change of clothes, a few jumpers, a dirty pair of trainers, towels and an old bed-sheet. Should I be caught I was prepared with the answer of the forthcoming charity jumble sale that the firm were holding.

"So you'll try to come home early? We have the engagement party to think about."

"I don't know, I might go to the gym after work," I replied as she was eyeing my sports bag.

"But the party . . .?"

"You just decide, Ma, call whoever you want. I'm running late."

"Thank you, beta, thank you. You have made me the happiest woman on this earth and you know —"

I left before she could finish.

★　★　★

It was freezing cold but it wasn't raining. All the units adjacent to the studio were closed. Just outside the studio door was a grubby pair of boots. I put them to one side, unlocked the padlock and went in. The studio looked bare with no Sydney Harbours looking down over it and the emptiness heightened the absurdity of what I was planning to do. Blank canvases were stacked against the wall and one hung on the easel with a note. "Good luck with the birds — play the tape if you get stuck."

I stood in the centre of the room looking up at the skylight. "You crazy, crazy woman, Nina, what have you gone and done? What are you thinking of?" I said to myself. I changed out of my suit and into my jeans and jumper, tied my hair back and put the suit on the suit hanger. The heater was already turned on full blast. What was I supposed to paint?

Tubes of paint had been laid on the table in an orderly fashion. It wasn't my natural inclination to be orderly but I had to be that way at the firm. I had to be a lot of things at the firm. I stared at the blank canvas for what seemed like hours, thinking about my family, Jean Michel, about Ki and the deep insecurities the Guru had touched. It was as if I were looking at myself in the mirror and seeing all the parts that hurt. I picked up the paintbrush with my right hand. I wasn't even really right-handed but from being a child my dad had insisted on me using it, as in our culture it was considered bad manners to do anything with the left hand.

"Chi, Chi, Chi, dirty girl. Not with that hand, Nina, what will the peoples say if they see you?"

But now I rolled up my sleeve and put the paintbrush in my left hand. All down my left arm was scarring, blotchy skin that revealed my deepest inadequacies. I could have had the prettiest face in the world but it wouldn't have mattered; inside I felt ugly and worthless; inside was a gaping hole that had been left by the people I had loved the most. The Guru had found his way into that place and confirmed what I already believed. I heard his words again: "You're cursed."

This was the arm that I hid from everyone, that I tended not to look at. This was the arm I covered, pretending that everything was fine, but here in the confines of this space there was no deceiving myself — this was the arm I wanted to paint with. Nobody here was telling me what to do or how to do it; I could reveal everything about myself and nobody would judge me. I stared some more at the canvas and started to see black. The optical illusion of colour was like the optical illusion of life: stare at something hard enough and eventually you see what you want to see.

Blacks, that's all I saw: black hole, black deceit, burning black, black at the funeral, empty black nights waiting for my sister to tuck me into bed, the Guru's black teeth, his dirty black fingernails. Thick ivory black squirted from the tube directly onto the canvas. But there wasn't a hint of ivory in this black, not one shade of another colour, and with the thickest, hairiest brush I frantically covered the entire canvas with this black.

82

I swept my hand across the meticulously placed paints and went to get the pair of grubby boots that I had seen outside. They looked so miserable — maybe they belonged to a tramp who had rejected them. They had no laces just holes as if they had been deeply wounded. I hurled them onto the table and watched them land defeated. One fell on its sole, the other on its side.

While the paint was still wet I took another black and smeared the paint on with my fingers. I could not stop. Molten anger bubbled to the surface as I pounded the canvas with my hand and fingers, smearing black onto black, trying to find the shape of the boots on the canvas. My hand and my arm ached but I kept on pounding frantically, finding the ugly creases and the lacklustre holes where laces didn't even want to go through, until eventually I had to stop and sit on the floor.

When Ki left she took a huge part of myself with her, the part that made me believe I could be anyone or do anything, Jean Michel took away a bit more and what was on the canvas was the part that had stayed with me.

As I hoisted myself up to go and knock the boots off the table, a shaft of light reflected back from them, wanting to tell me something else.

I stared at the boots in this light. They had walked for miles and miles and had been bought at a time when people saved up to buy things for special occasions. Maybe a man had saved up for weeks to buy them for his wedding and had proudly walked down the aisle. He'd also kicked a football in them with his son. When they had been chucked out years later, he searched all over the house and every subsequent pair he bought was in a vain attempt to replicate those cherished boots.

Perhaps a woman in a charity shop had picked them out just before they were put on display for the customers. She felt that they would fit her husband and had bought new laces that matched. Polishing and wrapping them up in newspaper, she had handed the boots to her husband, swearing it was a stroke of luck that she had found them as it wasn't her turn to empty the bags that day. Shortly after that he was promoted. He would have wanted to be buried in his boots when he died but his son hadn't known that and they were discarded along with the rest of his belongings.

Finally, a tramp had come across the boots quite recently after rummaging through some bin liners. He had also come across a decent suit. In a drunken state, he had taken them off and forgotten where they were. It became his mission to find them and every day he would search a different street.

Putting the canvas I had been working on to the side, along with the dirty black brush, I cleaned my hands, took a new brush and another canvas. Without mixing the colours I thinned paint with water and washed the canvas in a sea of cerulean blue. While I waited for the paint to dry, I put on the tape Gina had left me. It was Puccini's *Madame Butterfly*. Opera wasn't really my thing but I listened to it anyway. Carried away by the waves of emotion, I sat staring at the blue and then I suddenly saw something.

84

Dampening a rag with water, I looked at the spot two-thirds of the way down and wiped the space. I picked up an ochre yellow from the floor and oozed a buttery mass onto the empty space. The bristles on the paintbrush swirled the pigment into two rotund shapes that resembled the shape of the boots. I didn't feel as if I were the one who was painting as the strokes were rhythmic and disconnected me from all my thoughts.

Pockets of green came through where the blue paint hadn't come off, and these were effortlessly worked into the painting. Confident red-iron laces were added and where the yellow met the red a hopeful orange shone, the same orange as the soles; the same orange as the sky I had envisaged while sitting at my office window.

The bright colours made the painting look vibrant and full of life. For the first time in a very long time, it made me feel optimistic. Is this what Matisse meant by seeing flowers when there were clearly none? If painting could create an illusion, if it could make you feel things or see things that weren't there, then this was what I wanted. At that moment I was certain of only one thing; that this was what I wanted to do with my paintings. I wanted to see magic and paint it even if it couldn't tangibly be seen. I wanted to put bold colours together, see colours that hadn't been painted and bring inanimate objects back to life.

I took white paint, squirted some onto the palette, thinned it with water and in the left-hand corner I painted the words "For Ki". Looking at the space in between the words and sensing that there was a great distance between them, a distance that shouldn't have been there, I inserted the letter "u" so it read, "Foruki".

I cleaned the boots with a damp rag so that most of the grime disappeared. There was string in the cupboard along with brown paper, both of which I placed on the table. I cut two long pieces of string and put each of the strings through the lace holes, and when I had finished I packed them both in brown paper.

I washed my hands with soap and water but couldn't get my nails clean and kept scrubbing my fingers until they felt raw. After my brushes were cleaned and the paints neatly organised on the table again, I got changed into my suit, sprayed myself with perfume, glanced at the canvas one last time and smiled. I picked up the boots, switched off the lights and locked up the studio.

The boots were left where I had found them and then I switched my phone back on. There were two messages from my mum and one from Raj asking how I was and to give him a call back whenever I could.

On the journey back home I prepared to condense my world back into Croydon, to squeeze it back into the semi. No sooner had I walked through the door than my mum cornered me.

I panicked, thinking that she could smell the paint or would spot the state of my fingernails, and so I tried to get away from her.

"Where have you been, beta, you're very late? Have lots of things to tell you," she beamed.

"Let me have a shower first, Ma, I've had a really busy day," I said quickly.

She followed me upstairs and talked nonstop through the bathroom door but I didn't want to hear a word of it.

"So it's OK, then? Two weeks' time, so December twenty-sixth and second of April?" she asked, shouting through the door.

"What's OK?"

"The engagement and the wedding."

I opened the bathroom door in disbelief. The second of April was less than four months away — what was she thinking. I hardly knew this man. "What?"

"I spoke to the priest today and he said that was a good date and then I called up Raj's mother and she too agreed. We're all so happy."

"It's too soon," I shouted.

"Soon, soon," I heard my dad shout from downstairs. "We have waited twenty-seven years."

"But I've phoned people and made arrangements now, beta."

"Unmake them."

She took out her sari-end from her midriff and before she even began sobbing, I left her there.

How could she just do that? Engagement, priest, wedding, all within four months.

There was nobody I could talk to about it except Raj so I returned his call.

"Am I glad you called, Nina. I've just heard about the engagement and the wedding date, and I didn't want you to think that it was me pushing you. Far from it, we don't even really know each other."

"That's exactly what I was thinking." This man was growing on me more and more.

"Anyway, when you get to find out some of my really bad habits you might want to delay it indefinitely."

"And they are?"

"Well you'll just have to find out, won't you?" he flirted.

I giggled pathetically. This was what happened when you spent hours in a room full of paint and had no one to converse with.

We talked about his day at work, his colleagues, his friends, he asked me lots of questions but I diverted the conversation so we spoke mainly about him. I didn't want to lie so I tried to find a way of broaching the painting-by-day subject.

"Do you believe in magic?"

"Black magic?" he replied.

"No, things like coincidences. Coincidences, and also when you take a leap of faith that other things happen almost as if you have no control over them, as if someone is helping out." I was thinking about my transition into the art world but he took it to mean us.

"I never thought about it but I suppose in a way I do. I took a leap of faith with you and it feels right and it's all moving along almost like we have no control over it."

Did I feel that way about him? Well, no. But there had been a sign.

"What about signs?" I asked.

"What do you mean?"

"A sign is an indication that you are doing the right thing."

He didn't say anything.

"The sign between us," I continued, "was that for days, even before I met you, I was thinking about the Matisse quote — you know, the one about creativity — and then you said it to me. Out of all the things you could have said, you gave me that quote."

"I can see how that could be a sign," he answered diplomatically. "It's nice to think about things that way but I work on gut feeling, Nina, and I know I'm sure about you."

Yes, that's what I liked about him. His certainty and practicality: there was no spontaneous, impetuous behaviour, no way on earth that I would ever find him with a red-headed woman.

"So what do you think?" he asked.

"About what?"

"About getting engaged in two weeks?"

Carried along by his sense of certainty and convincing myself that all the doubts I had were not about Raj but about the superficiality of the list system, I said yes.

My mother couldn't stop kissing my forehead when I told her I'd agreed to the dates, and my dad hugged me. It was getting to the stage where I could use both my hands to count the number of times he had done that. But I knew I had made them proud; the kind of proud that studying law couldn't even come close to, and before I knew it they were on the phone, calling all their friends and relatives telling them that their daughter was getting married.

"See," my mother said to my father after she had made the last call. "Cleaning the house of old televisions has brought Nina a husband."

And although he didn't want to, he begrudgingly conceded that the "Chinaman Fongi" might well be on to something.

Early next morning, I was woken by the sound of my mum singing her heart out with prayers. Singing, though, is probably not the right word, more of a howling noise. My dad began protesting but she sang like nobody could stop her.

The journey into the studio that morning took less than an hour and somewhere during that time the sun had risen. By the time I got there it was eight o'clock. The musty smell of paint lingered in the air from the day before. After getting changed I sat in front of the easel looking at the painting of the boots. I took it down and leaned it against the table leg and put a new canvas on the easel. I sat staring at the blank canvas for hours before looking again at the black, ugly canvas from the day before. It wasn't black I saw now but grey; grey like sad skies that have the promise of another colour above them; grey like the two stone-carved elephants we had in our sitting room, brought back from Uganda. They had changed hands from the craftsman who sat on the beach making them for tourists to my tight-fisted uncle who had resold them to my father. These carved elephants were what he asked relatives to bring back every time someone returned, and despite the fact that he could now afford to go there himself, he never did.

I left the easel, put the tape on, reached for Paynes Grey and squeezed it out into an empty paint-pot. My parents had lived in East Africa after they were married and my dad took care of one of his uncle's tea plantations. Years later, when his uncle died, everything was left to my dad. The story from here on changes depending on who is telling it: my dad says that he built up the plantations across East Africa and had amassed a fortune, whereas his cousin, my Uncle Amit, says that he ran the business into the ground and the extent of the debts he had run up were not discovered because Idi Amin came to power and made all the Indians leave.

My father, having amassed a fortune or not, was told to leave it all and go. My parents' lives were turned upside down when they, along with thousands of others, were told to leave. We were bundled into a van, my dad holding my mother who was clutching onto me — her baby — and my big sister. It must have been hard: one day they were surrounded by fields, the next they were looking out onto lonely pavements.

Our world shrunk to a two-bedroom flat above an Indian restaurant in Croydon which we had to share with my dad's brother, my Uncle Nandan, and his wife, Auntie Leena. Mum and Dad had to get jobs straightaway and they took the first thing that came, out of desperation. My mother worked in a factory and my father got a job with London Transport. It must have been hard for him because he had to exchange everything he had for a bus. I don't think he ever dared to dream bigger, just in case someone took those things away too; or maybe the fight for survival in England precluded the luxury of dreaming. Whatever it was, he remained trapped in his double-decker and pinned all his hopes and aspirations onto his two girls.

At that moment in time, one of his daughters was thinking about painting elephants and the other . . . nobody knew where she was. I left the grey paint and took out the tube of Cadmium Red. It was the colour of my dad's double-decker, the colour of his favourite shirt, the colour of his pride, his sadness and his anger. Most of the canvas was covered with it except the space where I wanted the elephants to go.

My dad was close to Jana. His face lit up when she walked into the room and this must have hurt my mother because she had never had that effect on him. Jana was beautiful and had a mass of black curls. When she used to collect me from school everyone said that I had a very pretty mother.

"She's my big sister," I would say proudly, correcting them.

Taking the pot of grey and thinning it slightly with water, I outlined an elephant shape and then painted it.

When I was little I had an obsession about cutting sheets of paper and gluing them back together. Jana was the only one who knew this, in fact she was the only one who knew most things about me as she was always with me. I loved to either cut and glue or play in the middle of the kitchen floor with my collection of Matchbox cars. Jana would watch me play while cooking for the others and waiting for them to all arrive back from their jobs.

One day, as she was making dinner, the phone rang. She told me to stay where I was, saying she would be back in a minute. I'm sure she was gone for more than a minute and I only wanted to help her. I took a chair, put it next to the cooker and stood on it so I could stir the dhal. The spoon dropped to the side just next to the blue flame and as I went to get it my sleeve caught fire. Blue quickly turned to orange which turned to black. At first I just watched the flames; they rapidly spread up my arm across my chest, and as I watched it was almost as if I wasn't there. It was the smell that brought me back — a charred, burning smell — and then I felt excruciating pain and began to scream and scream. My sister got to me in seconds but just at that moment my mother came back from work.

She took a towel, soaked it and threw it over me, and shouted at my sister to call an ambulance.

Jana was crying.

"Do it," my mother shouted.

The rest I remember vividly not just because of the pain but because I have never seen my mother so angry. Even today I have never met again the woman she turned into that day.

"Look what you've done to her," she screamed when my sister came back. "You can't even look after her for five minutes, always thinking of yourself, you're so selfish. You've always been selfish. It would be better if you —"

"Ma, it wasn't my fault, I only —"

"It's never your fault, nothing is ever your fault. Go and speak to your boyfriend, don't think I don't know, go speak to him again and let her burn."

Then my mother fell silent as she looked down at me and continued rocking me in her arms. "It's OK, beta, mummy's here. Mummy will look after you."

The ambulance men came and Jana was told to stay behind and wait for my father.

Later that night when I was asleep in the hospital bed, I had this strange feeling that Jana came to visit me. She told me that it was time to leave and kissed me, whispering that she would always love me.

When I got back home from the hospital she wasn't there. My dad said she had gone on holiday, and each time I asked she was still on holiday. It made no sense to me — there were no letters or phone calls — and when she'd been gone for three months, my parents said she had decided to stay where she was. One day I heard my mum and dad talking, and my dad was sobbing when my mum told him what had happened and about the "white boy". They both agreed never to mention her name in the house again and for the purpose of the list system — to avoid any controversy and avert scandal — she was erased.

I know it broke Dad's heart when she left and so all his attention went on me. Now when I walked into a room his eyes lit up. Everything he did, he did for me, and I tried my very best not to disappoint him. It made me feel even more guilty for the lies I was now telling him on an ever-increasing basis.

A few inches to the left, just beneath the grey elephant, I painted a smaller elephant in white. Both softened the red background in which they were set.

The tape had stopped a while ago but I hadn't noticed until I put the brush down. I played it again and sat for a while eating chocolate, packets of crisps and drinking Coke that I'd bought from the newsagent's on my way to the studio. I never ate junk but in my studio there were no rules; everything was made up as I went along.

When the tape had stopped again I decided it was time to go home. Why I took the tape of *Madame Butterfly* with me I have no idea. Maybe because the studio felt like another world, somewhere where there was peace and nothing else existed, and I wanted to bring something of this world into the semi.

The moment I walked through the door my mum put her rolling pin down and came at me with a list of plans and things that needed to be done.

"I'll go over it after I've had a shower."

"Yah, but don't forget most important thing is to invite Raj home day after tomorrow. Call him now to ask him."

"Good day, Nina?" my dad interrupted.

"Yes, you know, same old thing."

"Good, good," he said, returning to his newspaper.

"You'll call him, no?" my mum insisted.

After coming out of the bathroom my mum was still shouting up the stairs, making all sorts of suggestions for the engagement. I put the tape of *Madame Butterfly* on to drown her out, turning it up louder and louder with every question asked.

Dad came up to my room, banging on the door.

"What are you trying to do to me, Nina? Kill me? I have to listen to Kavitha in the morning and now you make me listen to this. Why is that lady screaming like that? She got no job or husband?"

"She's found out she's been deceived," I replied calmly. "Fooled," I rephrased, using his terminology.

"No, Nina, you have been the fooled, buying such music. People they buys anything these days. Maybe I should put Kavitha on a tape and make the money. Turn the lady off or make her more quiet."

I switched the tape off, called Raj, and went to discuss the preparations with my mum.

When I left home in the mornings it was dark and when I came home it was dark. Everything was artificially lit by streetlamps, deceitful night pretending to be day and daylight cut short prematurely and swallowed up by night. In these hours of darkness I found myself on the train, preparing myself to go from one world to another, and it was only at these times when I actually thought about the insanity of what I was doing. As I climbed up the underground steps and walked to the studio, it didn't seem so insane. And when shafts of light entered my studio it was the only thing that was real; painting was the only time I could be myself and totally free. In the studio there was no pretending to be anyone else other than who I was, no wedding, no expectations, nothing. Yet, ironically, whole realities that did not exist were created with colour. Around evening, when I looked up at my skylight and saw the grey clouds encroaching, it was time to prepare myself to be someone else.

As my train arrived at London Bridge, I put all wedding plans and what would happen out of my mind. By the time I got out of the station my thoughts were consumed with what to paint next. No one had reclaimed the boots, which were still outside, but someone had unwrapped them. The table in the studio was a mess with empty Coke cans, chocolate wrappers and crisp packets. I left it all on the table, got changed, put the elephant painting against the wall, switched the tape on and sat in front of my easel. I turned around to stare at the canvas and the little elephant.

White; white like the writing on the Coke can, the sling that protected my arm, the gobstopper Ki had once given me all those years ago, the sheet that she was wrapped in to be laid to rest. White, like innocence, anticipation; the start of something new.

On the way home from school, Jana always made sure we stopped off at the newsagent's and bought me sweets. I wasn't allowed to tell Mum and Dad this because the money she was given for housekeeping wasn't supposed to be spent on confectionery, but every day we got something and she sat me up on the wall outside while I ate. Sometimes her friend David came and sat with us. He worked in a garage across the road but I wasn't allowed to tell anyone this either.

That's how I met Ki. Ki was the newsagent's daughter and one day I saw her in his shop behind the counter. I recognised her from school and smiled. She didn't smile back; she probably didn't need any more new friends as she already had loads of them, all of them huddled around her at break-time when she got out her assortment of sweets. That's the kind of power a packet of cola cubes had back then. She had big round brown eyes and I remember thinking that my eyes would be as round as hers if my dad had a sweetshop.

The sweetshop girl ran from the counter and went to balance on a broom. I held my sister's hand like I too had something to be proud of. We saw her most days after school and that was all she did, run and balance on her broom head as if it were her most prized possession, but she never said anything to me there or at school, not even hello. But my sister spoke to her and she spoke to the owners of the newsagent's; Jana could talk to anyone.

Not until months later when I had been off school for a while and had my arm in a sling did broom girl come and talk to me. She came up to me one playtime shortly after I had returned to school and offered me some gobstoppers.

"You don't come to the shop any more," she said.

Like she really cared. After my sister went on holiday, my mum stayed at home to take care of me and didn't know about the sweetshop. I glanced at the packet of gobstoppers being tempted at me. I said nothing. No one could buy me like that.

"What happened?" she said pointing at the sling, her cheek bulging in the shape of a round ball.

I shrugged one shoulder and she thrust the packet in my face again, took out a gobstopper and placed it in my hand. The information was worth one gobstopper.

I tried to explain the sequence of events but it must have sounded confusing, and as I got to the part about my sister I began to cry.

"Here, take them," she said trying to console me, handing the whole packet over. And then I found her looking out for me every playtime.

The canvas was painted white.

"Do you want to be the witch?" she said when my arm got better and all that was left was the scarring. At the time, being the witch was a privilege, but I didn't know this. I assumed it was because she thought I was ugly and the scars could add to the character portrayal. But when we played with the other girls there would always be a fight as to who would be the witch and if any of the girls said anything about my arm, she'd beat them up. Those were the roles we fell into; she took care of me and I let her. I still missed my sister desperately but I grew to love my new friend.

A year later, my sister began sending letters to me at Ki's sweetshop. I don't know how she knew I'd get them, maybe she didn't as she began each letter with, "I don't know if you'll get this, my little one." Ki's mother secretly read them to us. Jana was living in Manchester with her friend David but didn't leave an address at the top so I could write back to her. Every birthday and Christmas she sent me a card but that all stopped abruptly when I was twelve. Every day after school, without fail, I would go into the sweetshop hoping for a letter that never came. Ki's mother would shake her head and cuddle me. Her family became mine.

Around this time, Mum and Dad bought their own house, and it was round the corner from Ki's. If I wasn't in her house, she was in mine, but I preferred to be there as her parents let us do pretty much what we wanted. If my dad was at home we couldn't really run about as he would track us down and make us sit at the dining-room table while he read bits from the encyclopaedia or *The Reader's Digest* which he'd begun to subscribe to. On Saturdays, Ki's dad would let us help him out while he went to the cash and carry. We could unwrap all the packets of sweets, drinks and crisps and then her mother would give me a carrier-bag full of stuff to take home. I'd draw her lots of pictures as a way of saying thanks. Ki's mother put them on her fridge door although I bet she wished she hadn't done that because week after week she got more and more garish pictures.

Ki and I didn't end up going to the same secondary school but it didn't matter, because after school we were inseparable. She was very popular at her school but I didn't have a gang as I was shy, very self-conscious of my scar, and was forced to wear this awful grey oversized anorak that my dad had got down the market. On top of that, I had the misfortune of having to sit next to Rita Harris, who was the class babe. One day Rita drew up a list where she paired up the girls and the boys. She decided to leave my name out as she said none of the boys would want to be paired up with me. When I told Ki about this, she came to our school at lunchtime and beat Rita Harris up and made her say sorry to me in front of everyone.

Shortly after that, things turned. I got rid of the anorak, made new friends and began to believe in myself a little more. Even my Uncle Amit who hadn't seen me in years remarked on the change and said I had turned into a swan, though at the time I had some difficulty understanding this as he pronounced it as "wone" — it was only after further clarification when he mentioned the ugly duckling that I knew what he was going on about.

The only time Ki and I didn't speak for weeks was when I said that she was being dumb leaving school to do a secretarial course.

"God, Nina, you've been spending too much time with your dad."

"But you can go to university."

"Have you ever thought that I might not want to? I don't do things to please other people."

"You don't have to."

"At least I don't spend my time creeping around pretending to be someone I'm not. Why don't you tell your dad you're doing an art A-level. It's spineless."

"Spineless?" I repeated. "You're just spoiled. You've always been a brat. Anything you want, just go ask daddy." And as soon as I said it, her eyes looked as if I'd dropped the heaviest rocks in them.

Normally after an argument it was me that went quiet, but I couldn't handle her silences; they were of a different kind — they could completely freeze you out. Even so, every day I went to her house as normal, watched videos and listened to her tapes despite the fact she wasn't speaking to me, and chatted away with no response. Then one day, as I was telling her how I had caught my dad blowing the television a kiss when Cilla Black was on, I could tell she wanted to laugh, so I threw my arms around her.

"You're such an idiot, Nina," she laughed.

"Dad and Cilla can always break you down."

It was a given that we'd always be there for each other and forgive each other anything.

Ki worked for the same travel company for years. When I started at Whitter and Lawson she got into a pattern of temping and travelling until she met her boyfriend Sanjay. Her trip to Southeast Asia was to be her last before she got married.

She bought me a buddha from a market stall in Bangkok. She was in Thailand and was meant to go on to Australia, then Sanjay was going to meet her and together they'd go to South America. But Ki came home early with the pain in her leg that kept getting worse. The buddha was bought for me in haste as a souvenir.

Every time she went somewhere she got me something, as if to entice me out of my life in London. Some of the things she brought back wouldn't have got me out of Croydon.

Towards the end was the only time when I looked after her, but I had to, I had to make her fight, not let her go. She pretended she was getting better, that she was getting stronger and I believed this because I wanted to. If you stare at something long enough you can see whatever you want to.

The canvas was still blank. Where was she now? What would she be doing? Where did an energy like that go? It couldn't just dissolve into nothingness. I dented the Coke can with my fist, first in one direction and then in another; things were really so fragile. Taking thick, bright red I painted a buddha in the colours and shapes of the Coca Cola tin, adding white so there were different hues of red. It took hours and hours to replicate the detail and the dents of the can and when I looked at my watch it was seven o'clock; time to go.

Exhausted, I sat back and looked at the canvas. The painting was bright, vibrant and full of life without a trace of its fragility. Thinning the red paint, on the left-hand corner in bold capitals, I wrote "FORUKI". If I had to get rid of all my pictures but could keep one, it would be this one. It gave me a great sense of peace, an energy — her energy, her boldness.

I packed my things up, changed into my suit, put some make-up on and went to meet Raj.

It was on Raj's insistence that we met at Holborn tube station so he could meet me directly from work. I got there ten minutes late. He looked good in his suit, taller, and there wasn't as much gel in his hair. Raj

103

didn't quite know what to do when he saw me so I kissed him on the cheek.

"Sorry I'm late."

"I've just got here myself," he replied. "Where shall we go?"

"There's a nice Belgian restaurant here . . ." and then I stopped, thinking maybe it wasn't such a good idea in case I bumped into my old boss or some work colleagues ". . . but you normally have to book," I continued. "Let's go somewhere you know."

"We'll walk over to Covent Garden, there's a nice little Italian restaurant. You don't mind walking, do you, and you do like Italian?" he asked.

"Italian's good and I love walking," I replied. "If I could, I would spend all day walking."

"Me too," he said. "It helps me think."

I always thought that too.

"You know there's a theory that walking balances both sides of the brain's hemispheres," he continued. "When you have a problem, it's because you are predominantly using one part of your brain, so when you walk the physical act of walking makes both sides of the brain communicate with each other; that's why the problem seems less of a problem when you go for a walk."

"Really?" I asked.

"Yes," he replied, attempting to take my hand — he caught two of my fingers instead.

I laughed nervously.

His hand was moist and I could feel it throbbing. It wasn't like Jean Michel's grip that felt firm and safe.

104

"How did you know that? About walking a problem out?" I asked, feeling stupid for my childish laugh.

"I have a fascination with personal development and ways we are able to improve ourselves. You know we only truly use a fraction of our potential."

I understood all about not using potential.

Covent Garden had a real Christmassy feel; the streets were decked with lights and the shops were beautifully decorated. It was the first time in ages I felt there was something to look forward to.

"So did you have a busy day," he asked.

"Yes," I said. "I got quite a bit done. Did you?"

"Not much. I was just thinking about us and this crazy scenario."

"You can back out," I said hastily.

"That's the thing. I don't want to. It's never felt this right." He squeezed my hand tightly. "And I know my friends are going to love you, Nina."

I wanted to tell him about Ki, what had happened to her, but it didn't seem appropriate so I asked him about them.

He talked about each of them and then just as I felt he was going to ask me about my friends I changed the subject totally and asked him about the type of music he liked.

"That's what I love about you, Nina. I never know which way the conversation is going."

By the time we got to the restaurant we had covered music, film and travel, and then we got on to the family.

105

My mother had asked me not to mention Jana to avert any scandal. Under this list system any family scandal would be red-penned and circled by the honchos and used against us at a later stage. But I told Raj about her and sent Jana to Australia instead, where I said she was living, happily married, and that we hardly got to see her.

"It must be hard. You must miss her," he said.

I nodded. Later it would all come out, I thought. When I knew him well enough.

He told me that his parents were looking forward to meeting me. I checked if he was still coming around the next day to meet mine.

"I don't think I've ever seen them this happy," I said.

"I have," he replied. "I mean, *my* parents. Twice before," he laughed, with not one trace of a grunt. Raj reached for my hand across the table and it felt warmer and safer. Maybe everything would be all right.

"What's good?" I asked looking at the menu.

He ordered the food and wine for both of us. We ate, talked some more, and then it was time to go home.

He hailed me a cab and before I got in it, he kissed me. It wasn't a passionate kiss, more of a "this is going to be just fine" type of a kiss.

The next morning as I walked into the studio I felt incredibly optimistic. The red was striking and the buddha filled my studio with a different kind of warmth. After studying him for a while I sat cleaning my brushes, organising the paint and then reorganising

106

it. I painted one more canvas white, changed back into my suit and went to Green Park.

It was cold but I sat eating a sandwich and drinking a coffee and imagined what Jean Michel was doing, and then as I found myself thinking too much about him, comparing Raj's incessant need to fill silences with Jean Michel's ability to listen or say nothing, I got up and went around the galleries in Cork Street. It wasn't fair to Raj to compare them like that — his need to talk was because we didn't know each other. As I looked through the gallery windows I envied the artists who were able to display their work. Mine wouldn't even make it to a church fete. It was only three o'clock but I went home anyway.

"Why are you home so early, beta?" my mother said coming out of the kitchen.

"You told me to be."

"Yah, yah," she nodded fiercely.

"I'll have a shower and I'll come down and help you."

"No need," she said. "All done. You go and rest and then you can do your hair and make-up."

I wanted to say something but instead had a shower and watched *Countdown*. My dad came in from work but before he had a chance to say anything I said, "My boss told me to leave early today as I mentioned we had an important family function."

"Everything at work good, Nina?"

"Yes, Dad, it's fine." It had to be, this is what he'd sold me on, the fact that I was a lawyer with huge prospects. People like Raj's family wouldn't be interested in families like ours if it weren't for this one fact.

"Very good," he replied. "New clients?"

"No, as I said before, I'm just busy with one of our most important clients. He's got an exhibition coming up soon . . . in Mayfair," I added, so it would make him think about the first part of that sentence.

"Good."

"See, Dad, artists can earn a lot of money."

"What?"

I knew he heard the word money. "Money — I was just saying that artists can earn lots."

"They are the fools the people who buy paintings. Anybody can put paint on the paper. That's why the artists need you; people are taking them to court because they realise they have been the fooled."

Raj rang the bell promptly at seven-thirty. My mum had changed into her favourite green sari and my dad had his red shirt on. Kitchen activity had commenced the day before and an array of dishes had been cooked with the best cutlery and plates being taken out. Dad had wiped them all with a tissue and my mum had gone over it once again so fluff or marks that the tissue had left were totally eradicated. The television was off, there was no background noise and so the bell rang loud and clear. My mother and father looked at each other, then my mother got up to open the door but my father glanced over at her. "Wait, Kavitha. I'll go, don't want him to think we are desperate to see him." She nodded and sat back down, then my father waited a few seconds before he went to greet him.

"Pleased to meet you, Uncle," I heard Raj say.

There was a pause and then my father said, "Yes, good to meet the man who will make my Nina happy."

He showed him into the sitting room.

"This is my wife, Kavitha."

"Hello Auntie. How are you?"

She did her prayer-pose thing to which he couldn't quite respond as he had his hands full with an enormous chocolate box.

"These are for you," he said handing them to her.

"Thank you but I really shouldn't eat them." She patted her stomach, wanting him to tell her not to be so ridiculous; that she was fine without having to lose three stone.

"Don't be silly. You're fine, Auntie," Raj replied.

She beamed.

He then came over to kiss me on the cheek. My parents smiled at each other and my mother raised that eyebrow that could converse on its own.

"Drink?" she asked.

"Something soft, Auntie. I don't really drink."

Didn't he guzzle a bottle of wine yesterday? "We've got some wine if you want," I said mischievously.

"No, Nina, orange juice is fine."

"Whisky, Dad?" I asked. He nodded.

There was silence and then Raj said, "So do you still work, Uncle?"

"Soon I'll retire, when Nina is settled. I have my own repair business," I heard him say, conveniently missing out his day job.

"What kind of business, Uncle?"

"Repairing electronic goods. You are an accountant, no, Rajan? Very good. What accountant?"

"Tax," Raj replied.

"I was having the problems with the taxman. He came to the house and then . . ." I took the drinks and burst into the sitting room before he could say anything more.

"No, Nina, the taxman . . ."

My mum skilfully interrupted by asking after Raj's mother and family. He seemed confused at the different lines of conversation.

"See where you get it from, Nina," he laughed before turning to my mum and saying, "they're fine, Auntie, all waiting to meet you again. My mother says it's been far too long."

I remembered it had been too long because my dad had called her a "snub" and didn't want my mum to socialise with her, but now they were on their way to being best friends, family even.

"And your daughter, do you think she'll make it home in time for the engagement?" Raj added.

"Of course, Nina has to be there," my dad laughed.

"No, no, your other one."

There was silence. Mum looked shocked.

"Australia," I said, "Jana's in Australia."

"Australia. Couldn't take cold weather," my dad added quickly, "and then . . ."

"She got married," I continued, knowing that if my dad were left to his own devices he would lead everyone to a murky crocodile swamp where there would be no way of back-pedalling.

110

"Got married to a pharmacist. I've told Raj already, Dad, so you don't have to bore him."

"This girl," he said, pinching my cheek, "we will miss her."

Mum regained her composure and asked if we were ready to eat and led the way to the dining room. She pulled out her circular rotis, which she had kept warm in the oven along with all the paneer, dhals and shak she had made, and we sat round the table.

"You're a brilliant cook, Auntie," Raj said.

To which she promptly got up off the chair and served him another helping and a roti.

"Nina is not good," my father stated. "But she will learn now she's getting married — too much hi and bye to stop at home and learn good cooking."

"That doesn't matter, Uncle, I can help."

My dad was horrified. "Man is not supposed to cook," he instructed as if it were one of God's commandments. "Man is supposed to bring home bacon or . . . brinjals," he said, laughing at his own joke.

Raj laughed politely.

"Victoria is not far from here so you can come to eat whenever you like," my mother added.

After we got married we would be moving into Raj's three-bedroom flat in Victoria. Although he had bought it years ago it was vacant as he still lived with his parents. He had asked how I would feel about moving to Victoria the day before and I said it didn't bother me. Only when she made this comment did the reality

111

sink in. I had to live with a virtual stranger; I hadn't even lived with Jean.

Sensing my panic, Raj said, "You too, Auntie, come around whenever you want to see us. I don't want you to feel like you are losing a daughter. You're gaining a son."

That one sentence gave her enough voltage to illuminate the whole of Croydon.

"Thank you, thank you, my son."

Seeing how happy Raj made everyone I tried to convince myself that by the time the wedding came around he wouldn't be a stranger — he would be someone I loved . . . hopefully.

The rest of the evening went pretty smoothly. Raj smiled politely at my dad's comments and mum kept getting up off her chair and serving him some more. When it was time to leave Mum wouldn't let Raj go. She became the tidal wave she so feared would engulf her, wrapping her arms around him and hugging him in to her bosom so that there was no way out. "Thank you, thank you," she kept repeating.

"No, thank you, Auntie," he managed after somehow releasing himself.

"Thank you too, Uncle."

My father shook his hand and patted him on the back, except it wasn't a pat, more of a wallop. "We'll talk tax next time, son."

"I'll see you out to the front door, Raj," I said.

We got outside to the gate. "I'll completely understand if you want to back out."

"It makes me fall in love with you even more, Nina."

112

I was taken aback by the use of the word love. Love wasn't supposed to enter into the equation — not yet, anyway.

"Oh, right," was all I could manage and then he kissed me goodnight.

Over the next few days I painted six more buddhas on one canvas in different colours and backgrounds like an Andy Warhol picture, except it wasn't as good as the original. It was more an exercise in experimenting; placing contrasting colours next to each other and then seeing what that did to the painting. During that week I came to the conclusion that the relationship with Raj couldn't progress any further unless I was completely honest with him.

So on Friday, when I was due to meet him, I decided I was going to tell him about the other part of my life he knew nothing about. He would understand — he came across as an empathetic type of a person. Perhaps I wouldn't start from the very beginning but tell him about my three-month unpaid sabbatical which was helping me sort out my thoughts.

We had decided already that we would go to the cinema, but because Raj was running late he arrived slightly agitated and rushed and so it didn't feel appropriate to bring up the conversation on our way there.

"I am so sorry, Nina, this never normally happens."

"It's OK if we miss it, Raj," I said as he drove faster.

"We can't be late," he insisted.

"It's only the cinema."

113

"Yes but it's booked and paid for."

If it had been Jean Michel we would have gone and done something completely different — plans were there to be made and broken.

Somehow we got there on time, missing only the trailers. As we sat watching *The Matrix* he grabbed my hand and I leaned against his shoulder. Nobody would have guessed that two weeks earlier we had been complete strangers.

Throughout that evening it never felt like a good time to bring up the painting subject. Would he understand? Stability, and his need for having to know exactly what was happening when, was completely opposite to what I was doing.

"Just be yourself and they'll love you," he said as he dropped me home.

"Sorry?"

"When you meet my parents tomorrow all you have to do is be yourself, Nina."

The way he said my name felt as if he were talking to someone else. "I don't think they would," I replied.

"What do you mean?"

It was the perfect opening. "Do you ever feel that you can't really be yourself?"

"All the time."

"Do you really?"

Just as I thought we were getting somewhere, he said, "Except when I'm with you."

No, not a cheesy line. I wanted a story about deception, about secrets and untruths, but he didn't have one.

114

"I have something to show you," I said pulling up my sleeve so he could see the scarring. He had to ask me where I had got it and then at least we could start from the very beginning; the inability to express pain except on paper, the feelings of inadequacy, how painting made me feel that none of that really mattered because what I did with the colours made me feel good about myself as a person.

He was taken aback but then quickly said, "Is this what you're worried about, Nina? It doesn't make a bit of difference to me." And then I thought he was going to pull up his trouser-leg and show me a wound and ask where I got mine, but instead he gave me another cheesy line and said I was beautiful and he still couldn't believe how lucky he was to have found me.

Raj came the next morning to take me to his parents and as he parked outside in his black BMW my dad was jumping up and down asking my mum to look out of the window to see his car.

"I knew we made Nina the good match, he's a nice boy. Close the curtain now, Kavitha, he's coming to the door."

"Hello Uncle, hello Auntie, it's nice to meet you again. You know my mother and father have asked you to come around tomorrow?"

"Yes, yes, your mother called me to tell us," my mum beamed.

I didn't want Raj to sit down and never find his way out of the sofa so I said, "I think we're running late. Shall we go, Raj?"

"Not even stopping for a drink?" Mum asked.

"It's not good to be late, is it, Ma, especially when you're meeting for the first time."

"No, but remember, beta, you met Mrs Mehta at Auntie Leena's house."

I had been about nine and at that age one auntie looked pretty much like another: centre-parted hair in bun, red dot on forehead, lots of gold jewellery and all neatly wrapped up in a sari — the wearing of socks and sandals depended on how old they were.

"Yes, but still, best not to be late."

"Yes, Auntie, we really have to go."

She nodded, smiled at Raj, embraced him in her bosom thanking him once again, and then we left.

One hand was on the steering wheel, the other hand was holding mine and after much conversation from him, we got to Raj's house in Sutton. I say house but it was more of a mansion. His mother was waiting for us saying that his father would be back shortly as he had gone to play golf.

"I've heard so much about you, Nina. It's so lovely to meet you finally," she said, kissing me on both cheeks.

She was completely different from the bun and dot look I had envisaged for her. Instead she had a side-parted bob, lots of diamond rings on her manicured fingers and was wearing black chiffon trousers and a long red top.

"Nice to meet you too, Auntie."

"Come through, come through. You're even prettier than on the photo I was sent. Normally it's the

116

opposite. They do themselves all up, the mothers send the photos, and then they come here and you think dinner and dog."

"Dog's dinner" was the phrase she was looking for but instead I sensed that she wasn't a woman who took kindly to being corrected. "Thank you," I replied instead.

She led us into the sitting room, which was incredibly spacious with minimalist furniture on oak-wood flooring. I had tried to persuade my dad to get rid of the Seventies-patterned carpets we had, and to convince him to put down some laminate flooring, but he said that it looked cheap. I wondered what Raj thought about our sitting room stuffed with brown leather sofas and the elaborate chandelier that my dad had got off a man he knew down the market. It didn't work; not that much in our house actually did work.

"Tea? Coffee?" she asked.

"Nothing for me, thank you."

"Raju, will you get me some juice. Get some for Nina as well. Nina, you'll have some, no?"

I didn't get a chance to answer before Raj was sent off.

"So Nina, you're a lawyer I hear . . . for artists, no? You must come across some famous people."

"Some," I said.

"How interesting. Uncle and I know Ravi Shankar."

I said I didn't represent him.

She laughed. You can tell a lot about a person by the way they laugh and hers was an elongated "Ha", which sounded fake.

"We're all so excited about the wedding. I was speaking to your mother and we've both got it in hand. No expense spared. I don't mean to be rude but I want to give you both the best possible wedding and that doesn't always stretch to the modest wage of a bus driver."

"He's also an electrician," I added.

"Sorry?"

"My father, he's also an electrician."

"Yes. We were thinking the Café Royal, and if that was booked maybe the Hilton on Park Lane and definitely no plastic plates. I find that so crude."

Raj came in with the juice.

"No, Raju, I'm just telling Nina maybe the Café Royal for the wedding and reception."

"Whatever Nina thinks best, Ma."

"She has far too much to worry about with her career and this networking that they are all doing. It's agreed, then, your mother and I will take care of it."

I thought about the other two candidates before me who had fallen by the wayside and I was positive that she had had something to do with it.

Then his dad rushed in. A nice, quiet, sedate man, the only offensive thing about him being his chequered trousers.

"Pleased to meet you, Nina," he said shaking my hand. "Sorry I'm late."

"Wash your hands and get changed," Raj's mother ordered.

He went upstairs and came back down after a while and then we all had lunch. She'd thrown together a

118

buffet with quiches and salads. I thought that if she served this to my father he'd be violently sick on her rosewood table as he couldn't cope with "English food" and couldn't swallow anything that wasn't wrapped in a roti.

Raj sat next to me, occasionally squeezing my hand under the table while she fired out questions that she alternated by talking about herself. By the end of the afternoon it was decided that she would take charge of the preparations. With the speed she had us out of the door I was sure that she would be on the case that very moment.

"Nina, are you having second thoughts after meeting mine now?" Raj asked when we got outside.

And instead of saying yes I saw where the vulnerability that made him wear his T-shirts inside out had come from. Maybe I could look after him, maybe he could look after me, maybe we could take care of each other, so I said, "No backing out now," and squeezed his hand.

Though the days were getting a little longer the space between my two worlds was increasingly widening. I let others organise my life while I threw myself into my paintings. All the anxiety and doubts were splattered onto canvas and the more I needed to believe that it would all work out and that marrying Raj was absolutely the right thing to do, the more inanimate the objects I chose to paint became and the more I tried to bring them to life. One day it was a concrete brick painted on rough strokes of green grass; the next it was a red iron-oxide bicycle wheel on fresh white snow.

The following week I went through a phase of painting houses. Derelict houses whose colours and symmetry hid their state of disrepair, and then I painted houses in the style of rich sari fabrics set against grey backgrounds, and then grey houses set against rich sari-coloured backgrounds. When I got home, a selection of engagement saris were sprawled across my bed and my mother sat waiting for me asking me to choose. Every day it was the same routine. I would fold them away, not choosing any. She just thought I was playing a guessing game with her and this heightened her excitement.

The Christmas holidays came and I couldn't paint in the studio as it would appear strange that work had not given me the customary days off, so despite the fact that I yearned to be in the studio I busied myself shopping and buying Christmas gifts for everyone — not that we ever celebrated Christmas.

Every Christmas morning as a child I'd go around to Ki's house. My mum would drop me in the morning and collect me in the evening, and though Ki's mum invited her in she was always in a hurry to get back to the garments she had to stitch. Ki's parents were also Hindu but they would still put a tree up in the run-up to Christmas and a mountain of presents for Ki would be underneath. There would always be something there for me too. Ki would open her presents before I came, bar one of them, and we would sit and open these together.

When we were seven my dad told us that Santa Claus was an invention so that people could make lots of money, but when we asked Ki's dad if that was true he said that Santa was as real as people believed him to be. Weeks before Santa came, Ki's dad would sit and help us write letters to him and Rudolf. We had to think very carefully about what we put in these letters as they always brought us the number one item on our list. This year I couldn't face Ki's parents and put off going to see them yet another day. Instead, I handed my mum and dad their Christmas gifts.

"You should not do these things, beta," my mum said, ripping her present open. "We don't even celebrate Christmas."

"They're only . . ."

"Gloves," she said with a hint of disappointment, and then almost immediately she perked up knowing that they might only be gloves but this was no consolation prize; she could put them on and hug her real prize (her future son-in-law) in all weathers.

"Open yours, Dad."

"I know what it is, it's a CD. You can put as much wrapping around it but I cannot be the fooled."

He tore the wrapping open and his eyes lit up in a way that made my mother suspicious.

"Show," she demanded.

"*You're My World,*" she read. "*Thirty-fifth Anniversary Collection*. Cilla Black."

"Only the Cilla," he said, trying not to appear embarrassed. And then he completely changed the subject. "Why the English peoples are eating the ugly bird on this day? Somebody is probably telling them that this was the Jesus's favourite food and is making the money from this. They may not even be having this bird where Jesus lived."

"Dad, not everything is about making money, sometimes people do things because they love to and there's nothing else in the world that they would rather do. Take Cilla, for example, she sings because she loves it."

"No, Nina, she is singing because she is making the money."

"But before, when she didn't have any, she was singing."

He stopped to think about this and then said, "Don't talk about the Cilla now, Nina, you knows your mother doesn't like her."

Christmas passed as it did every year with my dad lying on the sofa waiting for the Queen's speech and then dozing off, looking like an exhausted, tanned Santa who had just come back from his holidays in the Bahamas. My mum was busy pottering about preparing for the engagement party that was to be held on Boxing Day.

I finally chose an orange silk sari with small gold-embroidered elephants. With anticipation, Mum picked out the jewellery, ironed the sari and brought it into my room.

"I never thought I could be this happy, beta."

"Me neither," I replied, thinking that the only other way I could make them any happier was by producing a child a year after the wedding. When I went to bed she came to kiss me on the forehead. The last time she did that I was six.

Early next morning the bell rang. It was the make-up lady. I couldn't believe Mum had arranged for a lady to come.

"What's the point of wasting the money trying to fool him? He already knows what Nina looks like."

For the first time ever I agreed with my dad but Mum seemed to derive some kind of pleasure watching my hair being put up in ringlets and my skin being plastered with foundation. After I put my sari blouse on, the lady attempted to patch up the scarring on my arm with powder, and that's when I lost my temper.

"If they can't cope with seeing that they can stuff the wedding. Is that why you asked her to come, so she can cover that up? There are some things you just can't cover up, Ma," I shouted.

Sensing that the entire wedding marquee she had constructed in her head was about to come crashing down, she made out as if it were all the make-up lady's fault and asked her to leave.

"I'm sorry, beta, I didn't tell her to do that."

"Didn't you?"

"No, I just asked her to put some colour on you. No need to be upset, it will all be OK."

My dad salvaged the situation with a diplomacy that I didn't even know he was capable of.

"This is for you, Nina, your mother and I bought this." He opened the box and pulled out a necklace — a simple silver chain, not at all like the heavy gold pieces I would have expected.

"Thank you, it's beautiful," I said as he put it on for me. "It's just nerves."

My Auntie Leena and Uncle Nandan were the only people from our side of the family who were invited to witness the actual engagement ceremony, but a whole collection of various family members and distant relatives were called to congregate at Raj's house later that afternoon for lunch. It was on Raj's mother's insistence to have it at her house as she said it was probably bigger. My uncle and aunt were both tearful when they saw me, probably because I had given them hope by agreeing to an arranged marriage — if I could do it, maybe their two younger daughters who showed absolutely no inclination would go the same way.

Raj's family came in their convoy at exactly eleven o'clock. "Don't look out of the window," my father yelled as he pulled down the net curtain. Two of the leading honchos responsible for the matchmaking also got out of one of the cars; they had come to preside over the proceedings. Their granny-like appearance and hobbled walk were deceptive: these women were capable of handling an AK47 and taking out any unnecessary obstacles in an instant. Raj's mother was in her full regalia and she instructed her husband to straighten out her sari as she approached our door. Behind them all was Raj, swamped in his new grey suit.

The bell rang and my father ran to open the door.

"Welcome," he said to them all. They began taking off their shoes and Raj's mother, bewildered at the state of the carpet, kept glancing at my father hoping that he'd tell her not to bother. She looked as if she'd never stepped foot in a semi and was staring at the Seventies retro wallpaper while leaning against the door which had some dodgy Christmas lights precariously suspended around it; my father had bought them from the market especially for the engagement. I was worried that she might electrocute herself if she moved her hand any further but my mum saved her from this when she asked me to go and touch their feet. Once they had all assembled in the hall, I had to bow down to the honchos and my future in-laws. Insisting I did not need to go all the way down was also part of the whole routine but no one except my father-in-law-to-be did this.

Raj and I smiled nervously and were quickly ushered into the sitting room and asked to sit on the floor next to one another. Those who could find space made their way into the Land of Leather showroom. Raj's mother sank into her seat and had difficulty getting up when it was her turn to place before me the gifts they had brought. The honchos were getting impatient and began coughing and spluttering; it was taking too much time, they needed to be fed.

From a bag, Raj's mother took out a red sari, gold necklace, silver anklets, a nose ring, some bindi and lastly a hairy saffron-stained coconut and gave it all to me. There it was, the fated coconut finding its way back; once thrown hastily over a bridge, now participating in an engagement. How events had precipitated since that day — back then I was certain that I was getting engaged, but not to a complete stranger. Jean: what would he be doing right now as I sat with this family accepting a ring from my future husband.

"It's a family heirloom," his mother said as Raj slipped it on my finger.

It was enormous and I wondered if the candidate before me had sausage-shaped fingers. It was also very ornate, with clusters of diamonds set around a huge emerald, not at all like the single solitaire Jean had produced.

"Such thin fingers you have, Nina," she commented. "And I meant to ask you earlier, what happened to your arm?"

My mum, bewildered that the proceedings had taken a diversion, hastily added, "Nina had an accident with fire when she was little. The ring is beautiful."

"Show," my dad indicated. As I lifted my hand to show him, the ring fell off. There was a gasp from one of the honchos — perhaps she felt it was a sign of foreboding. No one paid her any attention. Dad picked up the ring and studied it closely. "Very good. You can see good quality diamond don't go black."

The ring he had bought my mother under duress for their twenty-fifth wedding anniversary had turned a funny black colour and had left ugly stains on her hand.

126

"I paid a lot of money for that but I was the fooled," Dad had said to Mum.

I wanted Jean to come and rescue me — to get me out of there. Raj's mother instructed Raj to get it altered as soon as he could.

Raj and I were then fed sickly sweets and that was it — we were officially engaged.

"I am the proud," my father proclaimed, closing the ceremony. They were all given tea and savouries and then it was time to make our way over to Raj's house.

His family left first and we followed half an hour later. Everyone was talking excitedly in the car but I didn't feel like I was there with them; it felt as if it was all happening to someone else as I sat in silence looking out of the window. We parked in the drive along with a fleet of other cars and then I participated in a foot-stepping ceremony before entering his home.

Red bindi mixed with water in a bowl waited for me on the porch. My sari was lifted up as I placed my feet in the bowl. My right foot had to enter his house first and just by the door was a white sheet so that the stained footprint could tell everyone that I now belonged to Raj's family. They all clapped and cheered as my red footprint left its mark. I was now one of them. It was too late to back out.

Crowds of people came up to us to wish us well; endless streams of uncles and aunts who fed us even more sweets. Then, after lunch, a group of uncles got out their thablas and started singing and a chorus of aunts joined in. Some, like my mother, wailed; others clapped. As their clapping grew more and more frenzied, people felt that they had no option but to get up and dance. Raj sat by my side throughout it all, watching. He needed taking care of as much as I did and although we didn't know each other that well there was some level of understanding. After being fed more tea and sweets it was finally time to go home.

My parents and I got back about seven o'clock. I ran inside, grabbed my car keys and immediately went out again.

"Where are you going?" my mother shouted.

"There's something I've forgotten."

Without getting changed, I got into my car and drove to Ki's house. I sat in my car outside her front door for ten minutes before getting out, overwhelmed with sadness. Sadness because it was Christmas and she wasn't around, sad because she wasn't there to stop me getting engaged, sad because there was only one light on at her parents' house. It had been at least six months since I'd seen her mother. Despite the fact that the house wasn't well lit, I knew she was in. "Auntie, it's me, Nina. Open the door," I shouted through the letterbox. She came to the door, opened it, and tears welled in her eyes when she saw me. I could barely bring myself to say hello. She held me and the two of us stood in the hallway for a while, understanding the other's pain in a way that nobody else could. It was dark inside, no Christmas tree, no lights.

She didn't ask me why it had taken me so long to come round but just wiped her tears with the end of her sari, wiped mine and then cupped my face in both her hands and whispered, "You look beautiful."

"I'm sorry I didn't come yesterday, Auntie, I wanted to."

"It's OK, beta, you must be busy."

"I'm getting married, Auntie, and I wanted to ask you and Uncle to the wedding."

I looked over at Ki's dad. A man once so full of life, now reduced to flicking television channels like a zombie, hoping that someone, somewhere might give him some answers. He couldn't even bring himself to turn and look at me.

It was a stupid question but I asked her if she was all right. I wanted to ask her lots of other things, like if she ever had doubts, doubts about getting married, doubts if Ki was out there somewhere. Most of all, I wanted to ask her if she had lost her faith along with her daughter. But I didn't ask her anything; nothing important, anyway.

Auntie said she was glad that I was getting on with my life and then she asked me if Raj was a good man.

"I think so," I replied.

She nodded.

"Is it OK to go up?"

I had lost count of the amount of times I had asked that question. Every day, without fail, I had visited Ki, no matter how late it was or how tired I felt.

"What's changed in the world today, Nina?" Ki would ask, waiting for me. And throughout the day I would collect in great detail things that I could tell her. The way the light had fallen, if someone had made me laugh, the people I'd come across, the food I'd eaten. If nothing had happened, I'd just made it up.

"And tell me how it's going to be?"

"I'll find a way to tell Mum and Dad about Jean Michel and marry him. We'll move out of London and then at some point I'm going to paint pictures."

"What kind of pictures?"

"Bright, colourful ones on huge canvases."

"Where will you live?"

"Maybe in the country or by the sea. We'll have one of those old farmhouses and I'll learn to cook."

"And?"

"You'll come to visit."

"Yeah, I'll come and see you there. I'll always be with you, Nina, I know I will, and I'll talk to you."

Whenever I needed to change the subject so we could avoid the topic of death, I'd ask, "Where are we going next?" That's what we did on the weekends. We'd pretend we were in one of the countries she hadn't yet travelled to. I'd get the appropriate food just so it smelled vaguely like the place, put some music on even if it didn't correspond exactly with where we were meant to be, and then I'd lie next to her and read to her about it from travelogues.

She died on the day we were in Chile. She died in my arms while I was reading to her about Patagonia; salsa was playing in the background.

I went up to Ki's room. The walls were light green and everything was in the same place as it was the day she left. Her scent still lingered. It was as if she would walk back in and resume her life at any moment. Her patchwork quilt was thrown over the bed and on top of it was a tatty dolphin. The television was still on the dresser with the remote control on the side table next to her mirror, along with her make-up box and photos.

"I'm getting married. I don't know what you think about it, you haven't said anything and if you don't think it should be him I suppose you would have let me know by now. It's still lonely without you. I didn't think it would be like this but it is. What else? I'm painting. Did a buddha for you the other day, don't know if you've managed to see it yet but I thought it would make you laugh. I'm sorry I haven't seen your mum for so long. It's been . . . well, there isn't really an excuse. Miss you, but then I know you know that."

I blew her a kiss and went back downstairs.

"I'll make sure it's not as long next time, Auntie," I said as I held Ki's mother and kissed her goodbye.

New Year passed without much excitement. Raj and I had dinner together to see it in. He made a toast to the first of many. Jean had sent me a card wishing me every happiness and part of me felt furious with him; if it hadn't been for him I wouldn't have been in this situation . . . and how dare he wish me luck, did he think it wasn't going to work? I was eager for the holidays to end so I could get back into the studio and forget. Forget Jean, forget the wedding, forget everything.

There was a postcard from Australia waiting for me at the studio when I arrived on my first day back. "Sending you Sydney sunshine. Hope you are finding what you want. Gina x"

Was it what I wanted or was it all happening way too fast, as if I had no control over it? But through painting I was finding something; it was giving me a sense of peace, especially the buddha. My studio was full of dead objects brought back to life and overseeing it all was my happy buddha, breathing life into the studio. He needed to be framed. Every day I thought this but every day there was some excuse not to leave the safety of my haven. But after seeing Ki's mum I wanted her to have him: the buddha would bring light to the dark corners of her house and I knew even if she didn't like the picture she would hang it somewhere and he'd watch over her.

I started painting a left footprint on icy grey pebbles but framing the buddha was on my mind; I left the painting and wrapped up the buddha so I could take it into the frame shop around the corner. A shiny black Bentley with tinted windows was parked just outside the shop. There was an argument going on inside between a very well-dressed man and the framer: "Mangetti won't be happy with this, you said it would be ready. He waits for no one, he'll be furious."

I knew the name.

The framer was trying to pacify the angry man who was huffing and pacing up and down. A young apprentice swiftly came up to me and asked how he could help. I told him I needed my canvas framed. Instead of just unpacking the canvas, I balanced it on the counter and ripped it open. The ripping sound brought all eyes to the counter. The angry man glanced at me and at the buddha.

As the young apprentice went to get some sample frames out I could feel the man staring intensely at the buddha.

"Anyway, tell me how much longer you will keep us waiting?" he shouted at the framer.

"It should only be a few more minutes," the framer replied.

The apprentice brought the frames out and I chose a silver-plated one. I was shocked when he told me the price but then it was for Ki's mum so the cost didn't matter.

Sensing my initial apprehension, the apprentice said, "We are specialists, used by some of the best gallery owners," and then he lowered his voice. "I would say to ask Mr Mangetti's assistant but now is probably not the best time." He smiled, signalling the angry man with his eyes. I left my name and a deposit.

Tastudi Mangetti was Director of the Fiorelli Gallery in Milan and also had several high-profile business interests in London. I had come across his name when representing one of my artists who was having an exhibition at the Fiorelli and his paintings had been damaged in transit. Mangetti refused to accept liability; he was just awful to deal with. What would he be doing having paintings framed in London Bridge when he could have them framed anywhere in the world? I passed the Bentley again on my way out, and seeing as I was out already I decided to go and buy myself an engagement card and a present from the people at work. It would keep Dad happy and also distract me.

The shop assistant at Selfridges was really helpful and I spent a long time debating whether we'd like a vase or a lamp. After I opted for the vase I went back to the studio and dabbled a bit with the red on the footprint, then wrapped up the vase and wrote the card out to myself, and then wrote out a card that I had bought for Gina. I was going to enclose a letter telling her how I had got myself engaged but then I thought it wouldn't make any sense to her as it didn't make any sense to me, so instead I said I hoped she was having a nice holiday and that she would have a fantastic year ahead of her. It was time to go home when I stopped to ponder what my year ahead would be like.

Both my parents immediately spotted the huge carrier from Selfridges.

"Engagement present from work," I said holding up the bag. One lie turned into another and then another and then it didn't matter how many I told as I had become totally immersed in it. As soon as the painting was out of my system, maybe before the wedding, all the lies would stop and then I could stop feeling like such a fraud.

"Show," my dad signalled, reaching for the carrier. He pulled out the vase and looked disappointed and I waited for him to voice it.

"This is all they could whip the round?"

"It's a really nice vase, Dad, by Marcela Lonecroft."

He read out the card which was stuck to the wrapping paper.

"Congratulations, wishing you all the very best, Felicity, Richard, Seamon . . ."

Before he went through the whole list of names I stopped him at Simon. "Simon is the senior partner, Dad."

"Very good, invite them to the wedding," he replied, returning to his newspaper.

"We don't have to invite them to the wedding. I know we are restricted on numbers," I panicked.

"No, no, plenty of room for the peoples at work," he replied.

Raj came around for dinner and my dad asked me to show him the vase that work had bought us. He said that his colleagues hadn't got him anything as he hadn't told anyone this time around; didn't want to tempt fate. It wouldn't have mattered if he had as I knew there was no way that fate could possibly be tempted — this was a wedding that was going to happen no matter what.

A few days later the framed picture was waiting for me and I went along to collect it.

"This painting that you brought in by Foruki," the framer began.

"No, no, that's, 'For you, Ki,'" I replied.

"That's what I said — Foruki," he repeated. "Japanese name, isn't it?"

He didn't wait for my answer and just as I was about to tell him that it was a dedication, he continued. The framer said that Tastudi Mangetti's assistant was so impressed with my painting that he went back to the

Bentley and called Mangetti to come and have a look at it.

I stared at him in disbelief. "What?"

He continued, "We do a lot of work for Mr Mangetti and he came out of the car. He said it was original and was intrigued by Foruki's bold use of colour and the way he signed his painting."

"Did he?" I asked astounded.

"He did, and he doesn't come in here for nothing. Are you Foruki's assistant?" he asked.

"No. You see it's a bit of a long story," I began.

"You're his friend?" the framer interrupted, indicating that he didn't want to hear the long story.

"Well . . ."

"Tastudi has left his card and has asked your friend Foruki to call him."

I thanked the framer and took the buddha back to the studio, utterly amazed at the turn of events.

"Tastudi Mangetti," I laughed out loud, "interested in my painting." Looking at the signature I could see why he had thought Foruki was the artist's name. The "F" and the "K" were written in a sharp, elongated way that made it appear slightly oriental. I sat thinking what I would say to Mangetti if I had the courage to call him.

I couldn't say to Mangetti that it was a painting done by me; he wouldn't possibly buy any pictures if he knew it was me — a complete unknown — and anyway, I didn't have the confidence to say, "I'm Nina, the artist." I wasn't an artist — not in the true sense. How could he possibly be interested in me? Mangetti wasn't

136

just anyone, he set trends, but if I could just sell him one painting then I could prove to my dad that it was possible to make money from something you loved doing. What would be the best way? If I said that I was Foruki's agent maybe that would work; that would create a distance between me and the work. Besides, Mangetti might be more receptive to talking to me if I said I was the agent. Planning what I was going to say, I picked up the phone and then I panicked and put it down again.

"Breathe, Nina. Relax, distance yourself, it's not your painting, it's done by a man called Foruki. You're not selling yourself, you're selling someone else. It's not that difficult."

I dialled the number again. My heart was thumping. His assistant picked it up and asked who I was.

"Breathe," I kept telling myself, "act as though Foruki is your client."

"I'm Nina Savani. I represent Foruki."

"Foruki," he repeated.

"Yes, Mr Mangetti showed some interest in his buddha painting."

After a few seconds he transferred me to Mangetti.

"Tastudi Mangetti."

My heart was beating faster. "Just be bold," I thought, "show no hesitation."

"Nice to talk to you again, Mr Mangetti. It's Nina Savani, I represent Foruki."

"When did we speak last, Ms Savani?" he asked.

"I used to represent Françoise Dubois, she had an exhibition at . . ."

"Yes, yes, I remember," he said dismissively. "I'm interested in buying the buddha piece."

No, he couldn't have that one, it was for Ki's mother. Maybe I could persuade him to buy another one.

"I'm terribly sorry. That particular one is not for sale."

"Has it been earmarked already?" he asked.

Yes, that was it, it wasn't for sale because it had been earmarked. "Yes," I replied, trying to sound confident.

He said he had never heard of the artist and began asking me lots of questions about him. I wasn't prepared for all these questions and in an attempt to halt them in a seemingly confident manner, I tentatively suggested we meet for lunch.

He was taken aback by the suggestion. I was beginning to lose my nerve.

"Why would I want to meet you?" he asked.

Why would he want to meet me? And at that moment I knew how Jean Michel felt when he was losing and decided to bet all his chips on one colour. I sat upright in my chair and said with certainty:

"He's about to hit the London scene. I'm sure you'll be intrigued by what I have to say about him." People in the art world loved to know that they had made a discovery; they loved all that hype.

Mangetti said that he might be available Thursday lunchtime and asked for Foruki to be present. He said his assistant would call later to confirm the meeting.

My hands began to tremble as I put the phone down. "You're a lunatic woman," I said to myself. "You lied and you did it so blatantly. What's happening to you?

What kind of person are you turning into?" And instead of sitting down and finding the answers to these questions, I got up with a rush of energy feeling completely exhilarated. Getting changed, I went to meet Raj.

I was buzzing when I met Raj at Lazio's, the Italian restaurant in Covent Garden. He noticed and asked me what had happened. I was going to tell him all of it, explaining the painting scenario from the beginning, just missing out a few details like the coconut, Jean Michel and the signs. To spill everything out in one great flood would have been such a relief and then I thought about the vase that was a gift from my colleagues; where could that fit in? And all the times I sent him to Holborn tube station to meet me after work because . . .?

My mobile rang and I wanted to get it in case it was Mangetti's assistant.

"I'm sorry, Raj, I have to get this," I said, and then spoke into the phone. "Hello."

"Tastudi Mangetti here."

"Hello Mr Mangetti," I said getting up from the table to go outside.

"Yes, I would like to meet Foruki. It's my particular interest to bring new talent to the fore. I'll meet you both at one o'clock, Thursday, at the restaurant in Brown's Hotel."

Before I had an opportunity to say anything, he hung up.

I switched the phone off, taken aback. Where was I going to find a Japanese man who looked the part? My grocer was Japanese but he wasn't old — in my mind Foruki was old and, anyway, the grocer didn't look right — he had streaks in his hair the colour of his plums. That left three days to find a Japanese man. What was I supposed to do? Filled with panic, I went back to the restaurant, doing this neck-jerking thing I did whenever I was nervous or had something to hide.

"You were going to tell me what happened to you today, Nina."

"Er . . . yes, well . . . we . . . I, I got a new client today. Except he isn't a real client. What I mean is . . ."

"He's not signed on the dotted line yet." Raj had a habit of interrupting me. "He will, I'm sure you'll charm him. You know, Nina, it's so refreshing to see someone who is as into their career as I am."

"What?" I asked, seeing the opportunity to tell him pass me by.

"I'm so proud that your career is important to you too," he said. "It gives us more common ground."

Forget ground, I was skating on thin ice. "Ice," I vocalised the last word.

Before I knew it he was calling the waiter to get me some. He was like my dad — he only acted on the words he chose to hear.

"So my career is important to you?"

"Definitely. I'm so proud of what you do," Raj replied.

140

My stomach felt tight, I didn't feel hungry any more. "Tell me about your time in Japan," I asked, trying to find a distraction.

He happily talked about his trip to Japan while I wondered what had possessed me to ask Mangetti for lunch and about the web of deceit I was weaving — it wasn't me.

Pay attention to what he is saying, Nina, I kept telling myself; it might come in handy as research. But my thoughts were consumed by how important my career was to Raj and where I could find an old Japanese man within seventy-two hours who could be relied upon to say very little.

The next morning I got up late as I had supposedly taken the day off work to run some errands for the wedding.

"Good," my mother said. "Maybe you can help me with a few things. Wedding is less than three months away."

"I've got some people to see."

"What people?"

"The florist," I replied.

"I thought Raj's mother was doing that."

"No, we are."

"OK, I'll come with you," she said grabbing her coat.

"Ma, I can do this by myself seeing as you've both pretty much organised everything."

"I'm only doing it for you, beta."

"Are you?" I wanted to ask. This was all her disappointments cancelled out by one big wedding; her wedding, the wedding she never had, the wedding she couldn't give my sister. But I didn't say anything as she had turned around and put her coat down.

"And have you asked work for the time off to come to India with me?"

She was planning to go to India to do a whole wedding shop. And as much as I knew that if I went with her it would make every single one of her dreams come true, I couldn't go. I could not leave the studio for two whole weeks. Even if it meant that on my wedding day I'd be wearing garish colours and jewellery like BA Baracus from the A-Team.

"Ma, I don't think that work will give me the time off, not with the honeymoon and everything."

"I will pray they give you the time — Bhagavan has listened so far."

"Better go," I said, feeling guilty and not wanting to involve Bhagavan in the whole proceedings.

"I see, beta, maybe want to go and have lunch with Raj after," she said, smiling.

The grocer had some flowers; well, some dehydrated chrysanthemums. Perhaps I could buy a bunch and then ask him if he had any elderly relatives. I got in the queue and after he got an old lady her tomatoes he turned to me and asked what I wanted.

"A bunch of yellow chrysanthemums please."

"Coming right up, miss."

Not long before I'd be a Mrs, I thought.

"Anything else?"

142

I couldn't do it so I bought the flowers and walked away.

Where else could I find old Japanese people?

I stood back in the queue again.

"Forgotten something?"

"This is going to sound very strange but I'm doing some research into Japanese culture, things like cuisine, and I was wondering if I could possibly speak to your father."

"My dad's dead," the grocer replied.

"I'm so very sorry," I said, turning away, wanting to run off.

"But you can speak to my mother if you like," he added.

I imagined Foruki as an elderly woman — no, it had to be a man, but I couldn't suddenly say that his mother wasn't good enough after raking up the death of his father.

"That would be very helpful," I answered.

"You can go and see her now if you've got time. She doesn't really go out that much so she'll be happy to see you. What did you say your name was?"

"Nina."

"I'll give her a call and let her know you are coming around. What was it you wanted to know about again?"

"Japanese fashion, cuisine and art."

I didn't expect him to call up and ask her there and then. I didn't expect her to say yes so eagerly either but he gave me her address and said she was waiting for me.

Three hours later I was still in Mrs Onoro's sitting room, looking at the porcelain cats she had everywhere, drinking green tea, thinking that I had a wedding to organise and an elderly Japanese man to find in forty-eight hours, but instead I was sat listening to Mrs Onoro's life story.

I had to interrupt her at some point so I asked if she knew any men.

"You want marry my son?" she enquired.

"No, no that's not what I meant. I'm getting married soon," I replied quickly, thinking I should have phrased the question better.

Then she blushed. "I seeing Hikito, he is a good man, but my son, he don't know."

"Hikito?" At last, an elderly Japanese man, this was sounding promising. "Where did you meet?"

"Hikito, he is Reiki master, met at Japanese Association talk."

It was just getting better, a whole association to pick from!

"Would it be possible to come to this association with you, so I can get a man's perspective on Japanese culture."

"We meet next week."

No, next week was too late. "What about Hikito? Maybe he can help me."

"He don't speak much good English."

"Perfect," I thought. An old Japanese man who said very little — just what I was looking for.

"Can I meet him?" I asked.

"You want Reiki session?"

I didn't quite know what Reiki was but I agreed, thinking that Hikito was the one — he was potentially my Foruki.

Mrs Onoro went off to make a phone call and came back saying that Hikito could see me in an hour and that she would come along as translator.

A short while later we made our way to his house. A Japanese man came to the door. If Mrs Onoro hadn't told me that he was seventy-four I would have thought he wasn't a day over fifty. His skin was smooth and unlined and he had twinkling brown eyes that shone with wisdom. There was no mistake: here before me stood Foruki. He took Mrs Onoro's hand and he kissed it, then he looked at me and nodded.

"Take off shoes," he instructed. They spoke in Japanese and when it went quiet I tried to ask him if he was free on Thursday afternoon but he put his lips together and his index finger to his mouth, indicating silence.

He led us to his sitting room. The curtains were drawn, there were lighted candles everywhere and the smell of incense. In the centre of the room stood a massage table that he pointed to.

What was going on? I shook my head. There was no way in the world I would let this man touch me, not after the Guru incident.

Hikito said, "I don't hurt you."

Tears were welling in my eyes. For some reason I had this overwhelming need to tell them about the filthy, dry hands that felt me; the Guru's heavy, rhythmic breath that made everything seem much slower and

145

more intense; his smell. How he made me believe in him, took away whatever I had left and made me feel dirty and worthless inside. I started to cry, uncontrollably so.

They stood silently for a few minutes. Hikito gave me a tissue. "I understand," he said. "Lie down," he indicated, pointing to the table.

"I stay here," added Mrs Onoro.

I reluctantly got on the table. "Close eyes," Hikito instructed.

Half-closing my eyes, I watched what he did. Hikito had his hands six inches above my head. He made a sign with his palms and then his hands went around my body from one part to another without touching it.

"Close eyes," he repeated.

He had his hands at the soles of my feet and I could sense heat, warm heat. He slowly moved up to my solar plexus and as I experienced more and more heat I had to open my eyes to make sure he wasn't touching me.

"It's OK," Hikito reassured.

He moved from my solar plexus to my heart and I felt someone safely holding my left hand. I wanted to open my eyes but I couldn't just in case the feeling left me.

It was the same kind of feeling that I had had as a child when I was in hospital and I thought Jana was there; warm and loving.

"Your friend here," Hikito said. "She say you doing good. That she always hold your hand when you think you by self and you think you by yourself a lot."

146

Tears streamed from my eyes and at that moment in time there were no questions I needed to ask or anything else I needed to know. I felt completely and utterly secure, as if things were exactly as they were meant to be.

"She tell me to tell you that Chile is beautiful."

Hikito's hands stayed over my chest and not only did I see the most beautiful colours, I held them in my heart as if they were a part of me. Indescribable hues of indigo, violet and blues, colours beyond indigo that I could not possibly describe, all of them dancing within me, making me feel safe, and then as he moved towards my head I fell asleep. A deep, undisturbed sleep that I thought had lasted for hours.

Only an hour had passed when I woke up and Hikito gave me a glass of water.

"Drink lots of water," he said. "You do good."

I had no questions; I understood none of it yet somehow everything made perfect sense.

Mrs Onoro was sitting on the sofa in tears. She got up and held me, saying something in Japanese. I wanted to give her flowers but she deserved more than the miserable-looking chrysanthemums that I had.

"Thank you," I whispered.

I couldn't bring myself to ask Hikito to be Foruki; it didn't feel right to bring him into the web of deceit, so I paid him, thanked them both again and left. As I turned to wave they had gone in.

I arrived home in the evening, still with the dreary bunch of chrysanthemums.

"Hope they are not from the flower shop where you ordered wedding flowers," my mother said, looking disdainfully at them.

"No. Couldn't find any good ones, Ma, so I'll just leave it to you."

"All day out to look for flowers and comes back with this," she gestured to my father.

Surprisingly, he didn't comment. Just peered up from behind his newspaper, peered back down again and then said, "There are the flowers always for peoples who wants to see them."

"What, Dad? What did you just say then, Dad?" My heart leaped. Maybe finally he had understood. It had been a truly magical day; maybe something that I was unaware of had happened.

"Why we need flowers there in the wedding? Peoples can see them like your client who is not wasting money buying them from the petrol stations."

"Bhagavan, help me with this man, of course we need flowers; and beta, you didn't even go and see Raj. You said you were going to have lunch with him and I told him that when he called."

"Why?" I shouted and then I fell silent. There was no point in arguing, we were worlds apart, not even the biggest bridge would join the two worlds together. They would walk into mine and not see paintings, a Japanese healer, not notice any difference; because to them my world appeared exactly like theirs: stuffed with Land of

Leather sofas, dodgy television sets, rotis and potential husbands.

"Because that's what you said. He's waiting for your call," she replied calmly.

The sense of peace that I felt — that everything was exactly as it should be — quickly dissipated. It wasn't right, none of it — not Raj, the wedding, the lies, none of it. What I felt for Raj was a brotherly type of love, it was nothing compared to what it was like with Jean. There was never any real inclination to touch Raj; maybe to take care of him but not to touch him or to run my fingers through his hair. My dad said that attraction grows the more time you spend with someone and that he hardly noticed now the fact that my mother had "the buckhead teeth". Maybe it was a gradual thing. I dialled Raj's number.

"Hi Nina, Mummy said that you were coming to see me today." He had started calling my mother that the day we got engaged. It niggled at me but my mother touched her heart every time she heard it. I couldn't quite get my lips around that for his mother so I continued to call her Auntie.

"No, she just got a bit confused."

"What have you been doing then?"

I couldn't bring myself to tell him any of it: the search for the Japanese man, the Reiki healer. He'd be more interested about hearing how the wedding preparations were going so that's what I told him. "I went to find a florist to do the flowers."

"We could have done that together, baby," he replied.

Baby? Now that did irritate me. "No, it's best if we do other things," I replied, meaning practical things like arranging where the guests sat and food sampling.

But instead I'm sure I heard him grunt, not laugh. "We'll have plenty of time to do that."

"Do you want to go and see a movie tonight?"

"No, I'm really tired but I'll see you after work tomorrow night?"

"Tomorrow, then. I can't wait to finally put the ring on your finger," he replied.

"Yes," I said. "I'll speak to you tomorrow."

"Miss you. Do you miss me?" he asked.

"Yes," I mumbled.

Putting all thoughts of finding a Japanese stand-in out of my head, I ate some perfectly circular rotis and went to bed.

I got to the studio early the next morning and the boots had gone — I felt glad that the tramp had found them at last; perhaps it was a sign. Maybe they had disappeared days ago and it was the first time I had noticed them missing. I got changed, pulled out the dying bunch of chrysanthemums from my sports bag, put them on the table and took out the canvas that had been painted white all those many weeks ago.

I sat for hours thinking about the colours I had seen the day before, and when the light fell I began mixing paints. I mixed several colours in two palettes trying to replicate the tones in some way. Hours were spent doing this, trying to re-create warmth. Taking the chrysanthemums, I gently pulled off the petals and heaped them into a pile.

Before painting, I sat with my palm open. "I pretended to believe, Ki, every day, even when I couldn't see. I pretended it was you but you know that, don't you? Sorry about the things I said. I'm seeing Tastudi Mangetti tomorrow and I'm scared, really scared. It's something you would do, not me. You were always far braver. Did you orchestrate that? Did you do all of this? Did you make me meet Gina? If it was you, you couldn't have chosen a nicer person. Did you send me Raj? Is there something I'm missing there? I mean, don't get me wrong, he's kind and everything but I can't quite see you putting the two of us together. Is it about not having any expectations? See, if it's that, it doesn't make sense because you always told me not to accept second best. That sounds awful, doesn't it? That makes Raj sound like a consolation prize. It's not what I meant. It's not as though I want to go back to Jean either. I don't know, maybe it's because it's all happening too fast.

"I've been up for most of the night thinking about all of this deceit; although I am lying to paint, painting makes me believe in myself again — I can't remember the last time I did. During the time that I'm here in this room, the world looks like I want it to, and when I am painting I am me, the me that you know.

"All I ever wanted was to believe that you were around so I wouldn't have to do this on my own. I didn't have the strength to do this on my own. And when it was hard, really hard, I pretended you were

151

there and that's how I got through it. Now that I know, really know, I don't have that need to believe any more. Do you understand that? I want to let you go. It's not that I don't need you because I do, more than ever, but I want you to rest knowing that I love you very much and whenever I want to see you or hear you laugh, all I have to do is close my eyes. See, you've got me going again. I'm turning into a wuss."

Wiping the tears, I outlined an enormous handprint on the canvas and then took the petals and individually painted them onto the handprint with hues of indigo, just as if they were lines running along a palm. Death and wastage stuck together with thick colour. I dipped my hand into the rest of the paint and covered the handprint with my palm. Then I slowly peeled the petals off one by one, leaving nothing but spaces of calm white light among a storm of indigo.

I met Raj briefly that evening for dinner and instead of yet another outright lie, I told him about an artist who painted hands.

"You can tell a lot about a person just by their hands. It's one of the first things I look at."

"Me too," he replied, taking mine.

"Do you?"

"Yes."

I told him about the artist who had done a huge imprint of a hand and all the lines running across it were painted from chrysanthemum petals.

"Really?" I couldn't work out if the "really" was out of interest or because he didn't know what else to say.

"It was a big palm. What do they say? The bigger the palm the more generous the person. The fingers were long and delicate. This palm looked as if it should have longer lines but it didn't."

"I love the way you get so involved with your clients' work, Nina."

When he said that, the urge to tell him about my painting didn't seem so important. At least he appreciated that I cared about art.

"Sometimes it doesn't feel like work," I replied.

"Every day seems like work, you're lucky."

"Do you ever feel like you'd like to go off and do something different?" I asked.

"Not really, I don't know what else I would do except travel, but even then there is only so much travelling you can do before you start getting homesick."

"I would love to paint," I added, answering my own question.

"If you were to do it for a while you'd enjoy it, but then it's like most things: once you have it, it becomes boring."

This comment struck me as odd. It didn't seem to fit in with the way Raj operated.

"Boring?"

Sensing my tone he answered quickly, "I am just being practical."

I didn't feel the need to broach the subject about Mangetti and so I moved on to our wedding plans. His mother had asked us to check a whole load of details like the size of the mandir, the short-listed musicians and the selection of mementos for the guests to take away; so this is what we did for the rest of the evening. After dinner he dropped me home and kissed me goodbye. It was our first proper kiss and it bothered me. It was a suction-type movement where Raj engulfed the whole of my lips and hoovered them up with his mouth. Maybe it was wrong of me to think about how Jean kissed but they couldn't have been more different so I couldn't help it.

As soon as I crawled into bed I fell asleep and dreamed about paintings, Japanese waiters and boats, along with many other things that made no sense. When the alarm went off I lay there thinking about my meeting with Mangetti.

"Get up, you'll be late," my dad shouted.

I was immobilised by fear. What was I thinking of doing? It was ludicrous, Mangetti was a huge player in the art world. Word was that he was going to be one of the judges for the Turner Prize. He wasn't stupid. I wasn't a real artist or an artist's agent; surely he would be able to spot that.

"One day early, one day late. Twenty-five years I've been on time," I heard him shout to my mother.

"She has a lot to think about with the wedding."

"What's there to think?"

"Lots of things. Girl has a lot to think about before she takes a decision like that."

She was right. It was a big decision. What if it didn't work out? What if Mangetti suspected that it was me who did the painting? He had the kind of power to make sure that I didn't step foot in the art world again, as a lawyer, an agent or even selling paintbrushes.

"It is the easy. She doesn't have to think, just do it, like me and you, Kavitha, we just do it."

"Yes, get up and just do it, do it like you have nothing to lose," I told myself, getting up. What about Foruki? He was still expecting Foruki. What could I say about that? It was a mess, he would see right through all of it. Think; think it through carefully.

"What is that girl doing up there? This far we make her come, we give good education and what does she do? Taking it easy now she's getting married; having the lie in. Nina, what you doing there? Enough of the lie in," Dad bellowed.

The word "lie" reverberated around my head. Not just a simple bending of the truth; this one was going to be one big whopper. I got into the shower and began planning. Foruki wouldn't turn up to meetings, he wasn't like that, he didn't listen to what other people said, didn't do what they wanted. He was his own person, an artist who valued himself and his work, and if he didn't feel like showing up, he wouldn't, and nobody, not even Tastudi Mangetti, could make him.

I got changed into my best suit — the suit I wore for important days at work — and while putting on my make-up tried to steady my hand. This was it — all I had to do was to act professional and it would be fine. I went downstairs.

"We didn't see you yesterday, beta. Did you eat anything?"

"Yes, had something with Raj."

"Have the breakfast."

I couldn't eat anything or I would be sick.

"Have to go, I'm running late."

"What? No breakfast?" my mum asked.

"If you get up earlier then no need for this hi, bye," my dad interrupted.

"Wish me luck, I'm dealing with an important client today."

"Nothing to do with the luck, just hard work. When I made my money in the plantations . . ."

I left before he had a chance to go over that story again.

Mangetti was more conservative in his approach to art and his interest was more in paintings than installations, photography or sculptures. I sat in a café near Green Park planning meticulously what I was going to say about Foruki. All I had to do was pretend he was a very important client, and how hard was that going to be? I had pretended for the last three and a half years with clients I didn't even believe in, bullshitted about liking statues built with dried fruit, put all my emotions to one side and remained calm and professional.

Raj had once told me that in every meeting he had he visualised good outcomes, something about the body sending out chemicals that gave off positive vibes, so over and over again I imagined Mangetti agreeing to buy a painting.

It was one o'clock when I made my way nervously to the restaurant. Brown's was busy, but as soon as I walked in I knew who he was, and when I told the head waiter that I was there to meet Mangetti I knew very well where he was going to lead me. Mangetti was tall, immaculately dressed in a black polo-neck and black suit and appeared to be in his mid-forties. His nose was crooked and extremely prominent so I thought if at any time he made me nervous I would just focus on it and stare hard. My heart beat faster as I went over to meet him.

Taking a deep breath, I smiled. "Nina Savani, pleased to meet you, Mr Mangetti," I said, holding out my hand.

He gripped it solidly. "Mr Foruki?" he indicated at the empty space next to me.

"I'm terribly sorry but Foruki is unable to make it. He's very introspective and doesn't like attention so he's hired me to conduct all negotiations here in London."

I focused on his nose while I waited for him to leave. "Really?"

I nodded.

He gestured for me to take a seat and then sat down himself.

"It's strange I haven't come across his name before."

"It's taken me a long time to persuade him to share his art. He's only done a very limited amount of exhibitions in Japan. He doesn't do them to sell his paintings. He doesn't need to." *You're talking too much, Nina, there's no need to go into so much detail. Let him ask the questions.*

"Come now, Ms Savani, you hardly expect me to believe that?"

Of course I didn't expect him to believe any of it. Was he going to put his napkin down and walk off?

"You're expecting me to believe that a man who signs his name so boldly on a canvas doesn't want to be known?"

"He doesn't want to be known but he wants his work to be respected. There's a difference; he has his reasons for signing so boldly," I said, surprising even myself by how convincing I sounded.

"They are?"

Yes, what were they? "His upbringing . . ." Oh God, what kind of disturbed upbringing was the poor man going to have to go through. *Don't go there, Nina, get back on track.* ". . . but I'm not here to talk about that," I replied assertively.

"Is he British? Japanese? How old is he?" The more I refused to go into Foruki the more he wanted to know. That's how people in the art world worked; elusiveness equalled more hype; give it to them on a plate and they didn't want it. My boss used to term this as "whispers", leak a little information and then act all vague and elusive so they would be left craving more.

"He's in his early thirties, was born in Britain to a Japanese mother and had to return there as a child. Hence the fact that he doesn't speak English." Having not had the heart to ask Hikito, I thought if I was desperate my grocer could step in and keep his accent under wraps.

158

"Every day I come across talented artists, there are thousands of them. But this one, he seems interesting. Tell me about his concepts."

The waiter came to take our order. Mangetti ordered a bottle of wine that cost as much as my father's chandelier and his Land of Leather suite. I imagined my dad keeling over if he knew the price of that bottle. I worried about the bill — it wasn't looking good. We ordered our food. I chose the cheapest thing on the menu.

"I'm sorry, you were talking about concepts," I said, composing myself and deflecting the answer back to him.

"Yes, when I saw that buddha painted in the form of a red Coca Cola tin, I was struck by Foruki's critique of how far the fusion of East/West culture had gone. And the juxtaposition of the subject and material — highly original."

What was he going on about? Hardly juxtaposition, more memories of Ki's sweetshop and her souvenir. I smiled, thinking she would be laughing at all of this. Just go with it, if that's what he wants to hear, tell him that.

"Yes there is an element of social critique there but his particular interest is resuscitating inanimate objects."

He nodded, waiting for more.

"He attempts to infuse inanimate objects with magic. All part of the upbringing, as I said, which I am not at liberty to divulge."

159

"Intriguing. And the painting of the buddha, how much is it?"

"As I've said, it's been earmarked," I replied.

The food came.

"Surely you can sell it to me. Everyone has a price, Ms Savani?" he said, looking at me directly in the eye.

He was asking me to name a price, any price. This is what I wanted — to sell a painting — but he couldn't have that one, that was for Ki's mum. Don't buckle; don't buckle. I focused on his nose. "I'm afraid not," I replied.

He seemed like a man who was used to getting his way but surprisingly he didn't insist. Just as I was about to say that there were other paintings he could buy he asked, "And where do you come into the picture?" He took a sip of wine and laughed at his pun.

"Mr Mangetti, I have come across many artists but very few have actually managed to really captivate me and lose me in their paintings. It's rare. A year ago, I was in Japan and I came across his work. I was so inspired by Foruki that I tracked him down and convinced him to come to London. There are few times in life when I have had this gut feeling so I've brought him over so his work can be shared." *Keep going, keep going, Nina.*

He listened intently.

"I gave up a good job at Whitter and Lawson to back Foruki: I don't give up the luxury of working for a firm like that for backing people I don't completely believe in — and with Foruki I've never believed in anyone more."

160

"As you know, Ms Savani, it's my particular interest to bring new talent to the fore. I'd like to see more of his work."

I had prepared myself for this eventuality; this for me was very-best-case scenario and I honestly didn't believe it was going to happen.

"I am trying to persuade him to hold an exhibition."

He nodded.

We finished the main course and he asked if I wanted dessert. I declined, thinking about the mounting bill; at this rate I'd have to take out an overdraft and I just wanted to get out of there while I was on a roll, but he ordered something for himself along with dessert wine.

Putting my chips again on one number, I said, "Give me six weeks. My new cards are being printed but I'll call you with a concrete date, Mr Mangetti."

He gave me his card. "So you won't sell any more of his paintings until I have had an opportunity to see them all first?"

"I'll see what I can do," I replied.

He ended the conversation by telling me that he was going to Italy on business and that he would wait to hear from me soon.

"It was a pleasure meeting you, Mr Mangetti," I said as he left.

"Call me Tastudi and the pleasure was mine."

By that time I was so excited and relieved at how the meeting had gone that I didn't care what the bill came to, and after I had paid it I ran to Green Park.

"Yes, yes, I bloody did it," I screamed, jumping up and down, punching the air. "I did it."

People stared but it didn't bother me, nothing at that moment in time bothered me, not even the fact that I had never organised an exhibition.

After getting over the initial excitement and beaming at everyone on the tube, I went back to the studio, put my painting to one side and sat in front of a blank canvas. The reality of what I had done started to dawn on me. I had told an outright lie to one of the major players in the art world and now had to organise a successful exhibition in six weeks. That was two weeks before my wedding. If it was shoddy and if Mangetti found out that I had deceived him, he had the power to make sure that I never worked in the art world again.

Don't panic, I kept telling myself, opportunities like this never came along and I could make it work. I had to make it work. But how the hell was I going to find a venue and then make sure people turned up? I needed journalists and people from the art world. Foruki, he had to have a past, galleries in Japan that he had exhibited at — he couldn't just suddenly materialise from nowhere. What about a mailing address? Invitations? It suddenly all seemed far too much for one person. And how was I even going to begin to think about the wedding.

Do it step by step, don't panic, you can do this, you can make it work, just hold your nerve, I reassured myself. Take another leap of faith and go for it. And though I knew I was way out of my depth, and was nervous and scared, there was a certain part of me that felt totally exhilarated and alive.

162

I took some black paint and on the canvas I made a list.

Find venue
Office space? (Computer, phone, mailing address)
Stationery (invitations, letterheads, brochures)
Invent Foruki — will the grocer do? (Past? Profile?
    Concepts?)
Talk to all art contacts/hype to other artists
Enough paintings for exhibition? Do more?
COST???????

Money wasn't going to be too much of a problem as my dad had asked me to stop paying my monthly instalments into the wedding fund. He had also given me a three thousand pound rebate; a sort of bonus disguised as a wedding gift. Feeling that he'd better share his good fortune of finding both a groom and a mother to pay for most of the wedding he handed me a cheque: "Wedding gift. Buy a sofa for your new house, Nina. You never lose the money on good leather sofa. I will come with you when you buy it." His obsession with sofas had started with a flippant comment that my Uncle Amit made years ago about a man not making his mark in England until he owned a Chesterfield. This stuck in my dad's psyche and he dreamed of owning Land of Leather.

I took out a sheet of paper and elaborated in more detail on what exactly I needed to do. Treating Foruki as if he were one of my best clients I drew up a strategy. I would email Gina and ask her about galleries in

163

Japan — she said she had lived there and so she would know. I didn't have to go into what exactly I was intending to do.

I went to the library to do some research on Japanese art and art galleries in Japan. A lot of Japanese paintings were about relating big flat areas of colour together using flat shapes. I was astounded to read that Matisse had been influenced by the Japanese style, when I — rather, Foruki — was heavily influenced by Matisse. Was this a sign? A sign that my paintings really did have Japanese influences without meaning to? Is that why Mangetti readily believed that the painting had been done by a Japanese painter? I read on. It was plausible and it didn't seem that far-fetched when I looked at some of the pictures in the books. After I felt I had enough information to make it all hang together, I moved on to logistical planning.

The search engine threw up hundreds of names after I'd typed in "office space, London Bridge", "hot-desking, London" and "printers, London Bridge". Reading through each one carefully I wrote down contact names, numbers and addresses and then I went to Green Park, sat on my bench, took a deep breath and started calling people who rented out desk space in offices, making arrangements to see them the next day. Before I knew it, it was five o'clock and time to go.

Raj was leaving work early and meeting me at Chancery Lane so we could pick up my engagement ring, which was being altered.

164

He kissed me. I wanted to tell him how well the meeting had gone and so did it in a roundabout way. "We got a really important client on board today. I said I'd help him with his exhibition."

"Who is he?"

"A Japanese artist by the name of Foruki."

"I think I read something about him recently."

"Did you?" I asked, astonished. He couldn't possibly have. Was he prone to truth-bending as well or had he confused the name with someone else? "Where did you read about him?"

"I can't remember but his name sounds familiar."

The ring was still too big so we left it at the jeweller's and then went to Raj's mother's house.

His mother had wedding invitations sprawled across her table and was bursting to tell us that she had booked the Park Lane Hilton. "What do you think?" she said, thrusting an invitation into my hand. "Four hundred guests, maybe more."

"I don't think we even know two hundred people," I replied.

"*We do*," she interrupted. "So, what do you think?"

The one I was holding was embossed in gold and very simplistic. "Which printer did you use, Auntie?" I asked, thinking maybe he could do Foruki's invites, perhaps even the other stationery.

"One of Uncle's friends. He's done some work for the Queen. Which one do you think, then? This one, no, Raju? Do you want to use our printer to do your invitations too, Nina?"

"Thank you, but we've found a really good one," I lied, only because I wanted to do something that she had no control over.

"He said it will take only four days to print so by the end of this week we can send them out. When is your mother going to India, Nina?"

My mum was going off to India on her own, disappointed that despite all the praying and singing Bhagavan hadn't managed to wangle it so I could go with her. Her imminent trip would make it slightly easier for me to organise the exhibition, though, and I was relieved that she would soon be gone.

"This weekend," I replied.

"OK, OK, so we all agree on this one," she said taking back the invitation that was in my hand. "I have sorted out all the catering. At the Hilton they have a select list of caterers who they use so I've asked them to send me a fusion menu — you know, a mixture of East meets West — as a lot of our friends are English."

Caterers, that was a point. Would I need food at the exhibition? What about the drink? I hadn't even thought about the drink. "The drink," I mumbled.

"All arranged too. We'll have an open bar. Your mother was going to take care of the flowers but if it's too much for her to do before she goes away we have an excellent florist." Raj's mother indicated a huge vase that had some swirling twig-like arrangement going on.

"Thank you, Auntie, but I'm sure she'll be able to sort it out." What was the point of making Raj and I wade through her endless lists if she had it all planned.

"OK then, let's have dinner," she said.

166

She summoned her husband who was sitting quietly in the next room with a piercing screech, and served a concoction of curried puff-pastry followed by apple crumble and cream. My dad had suffered indigestion when he and my mother had first gone to meet the in-laws and he had made sure he ate well the next time they went to see her, muttering, "This is why woman must know how to cook or she will kill man."

Both my mum and dad were in bed when I arrived home.

"Beta," my mum whispered out on hearing my footsteps. "Beta," she called out again in between my dad's snores.

"What is it, Ma?" I said, going into their room.

"You've eaten something?"

"I had something at Raj's house."

"How it went?"

"His mum's got it all under control."

"No, not wedding plans, work. Your important client?"

I was taken aback because she never asked about the specifics of work or clients but she seemed genuinely interested for a change. "It went well, Ma, really well."

"Good. Only today even, your father and me, we saying how proud we are of you."

Thank God it was dark and she couldn't see my face riddled with guilt. "There's no need to be, Ma."

I wanted to go over to her, hold her, unburden myself and confess.

"Every need. You make us so proud."

In a couple of months it would all be over. I would be married and then there would be no more deceit. I would have hopefully got it all out of my system and I would endeavour to be a good wife to Raj.

"Good night, Ma."

"Sleep well, beta."

I went to see three offices in southwest London and settled for the last one in Westminster as it had a desk with the use of a phone and computer along with a shared receptionist who would take messages in my absence. It was £200 per week and I signed the contract for six weeks. There was no going back now and I felt a sense of excitement once I had made the commitment.

The desks were separated off with huge barriers so you couldn't see what people either side or in front of you were doing. It wasn't particularly busy but those who were there had their heads down, lost in their work.

"What's your company name?" the office manager asked.

"Sorry?"

"Your company name — when you get phone calls how would you like the receptionist to answer?"

I thought for a moment. If the receptionist said Nina Savani Limited it would make the company seem small — when I called people up to hype Foruki I had to make it seem as if it was a busy, cutting-edge company.

Frantically looking for inspiration, I noticed a picture of a brown owl behind her signed Kendal. It had a solid ring to it.

168

"Kendal," I replied. "Kendal Brown."

"There's also a divert system on the phone — I'll show you how to action that. Here's a set of keys and the pin number to use the phone. All calls are itemised and are charged separately. You choose your own computer password and let me know what it is. That's all you need to know really . . . oh, there's a kitchen area to your right so you can help yourself to tea and coffee and the toilets are just around the corner. Any questions?"

"No, not really."

"Well, if you put your full address there and sign here, you can start using the office . . ." she looked at her watch ". . . as of now."

I gave her the studio's address and took all the paperwork she handed me.

Sitting at my new desk and switching on the computer, the first thing I did was fiddle about on the screensaver typing the words "GO NINA" in capitals. I laughed at my own craziness but inside I desperately wanted to succeed. I wanted the exhibition to go well. What I wanted beyond that I really didn't know, maybe just to feel as happy, as crazy and as alive as I did on seeing the words dance boldly in front of me.

Pulling out a contact sheet from my folder with names and telephone numbers that I had drawn up, I divided up the list of people on the basis of how well I knew them and how they could help. There were artists, gallery owners, curators that I had met at my time at Whitter and Lawson, some of whom I knew very well. I would begin with them and would say that I had left

169

the firm to dedicate more time to artists I felt passionately about.

The first thing was to find a venue. None of the major galleries in London would exhibit an unknown, especially not in six weeks. Impression was absolutely everything and Foruki had to look big as well as different. Somewhere obvious wouldn't do. I thought about who on my list could help specifically with venues, then reflecting on what Raj had told me about confidence, I took a deep breath and began calling them; almost as if they were obliged to help. Raj had got this from one of the many books he had read and said that if there was a level of expectation and confidence in a person's tone then people would be more likely to be receptive.

Despite having many contacts it was harder than I thought it would be. There were few leads but eventually a promising one came from a PR company who I hyped Foruki to. The lady said she was dealing with a restaurant chain called Artusion. They had restaurants in Tokyo and New York, and were opening their first restaurant in London soon. The concept was simple: a modern Japanese restaurant and a gallery where up-and-coming artists were exhibited. It sounded almost too good to be true. The PR lady said she could arrange a meeting; I left her my details. A restaurant/gallery was an unusual place to hold Foruki's first exhibition in London but Foruki was different. It would be an ideal venue.

I rang the artists whom I had once represented just to tell them that I had left Whitter and Lawson and

170

casually dropped in that I was spending my time representing an up-and-coming Japanese artist. The more influential people who had heard of Foruki the better.

A few of them wanted to know if I would represent them too. I had to say that there was a clause in my old contract which stated that I was unable to take old clients with me, but I thanked them for their support and hoped that they would be able to make it to Foruki's exhibition. Later that afternoon my boss Simon called me up, curious about what I was doing.

"I'm sorry about what happened, Simon, with Boo and everything. It was inexcusable."

"Quite out of character for you, Nina, but I suppose you had your other plans in mind."

Is that what he thought? That I had orchestrated a departure so I wouldn't have to work my notice? I wanted to tell him that it wasn't like that — that there was no planning or scheming involved — but how else could it all be explained besides telling him the truth. "All I can do is apologise again for being so unprofessional."

He asked me what exactly I was doing and I talked about the artist that I had brought over from Japan and invited him along to the opening night. It was better to keep on good terms with him. Simon could make trouble for me, he could say anything about me; that I had lost it at work and was near-enough sacked.

Once he had established that I couldn't possibly be any kind of threat to him, he dismissed me abruptly.

"There's another call waiting. I wish you the very best in your endeavours, Nina," he said with a touch of sarcasm.

Maybe I was a nobody in his eyes and it was a mad idea, but this made me resolve to make Foruki as big as I could.

The PR lady called back saying she had managed to fix up a meeting for the following day with the owners of Artusion. I then took a walk to see the stationer. Taking a copy of Raj's mother's wedding invite, I showed them the type of style I wanted for all my letterheads and business cards and for Foruki's exhibition invites.

"Kendal Brown just across there like that, and the contact details here."

"Costly," the printer kept saying, "especially in that style. Gold doesn't come cheap, especially if you want it embossed." So I picked out a much cheaper version for my own wedding invites seeing as all my uncles and aunts would only need to read it once to make sure where and when exactly they were being fed. The invite would then, inevitably, be discarded or used as a coaster.

Foruki's invites couldn't be done at that time seeing as the printer didn't have all the information he needed but he said that I could pick the rest of the stationery, letterheads and so on, on Monday. When he presented me with the bill I slipped in the fact that I would give him more business, adding that I was in charge of ordering all the company's stationery, and hc gave me a discount that would have made my dad proud.

My mum was busy cooking when I got home. My dad was not all that impressed with the discount when I told him, worried more about who from work would be attending the wedding.

"Your boss will come to the wedding?"

"Hopefully, if he's not away; but Simon's said that he'll give me a few days off before the wedding," I added, thinking that logistically the whole suit routine in the run-up to the exhibition might prove a bit difficult.

My mum rushed out of the kitchen. "So you can come with me to India? Oh, Bhagavan, thank you."

"No Ma, it's just in case I have to do last minute things here."

"Your father will do them."

He pretended not to hear her.

I imagined Dad running about organising the exhibition. "No, it's only really me who can arrange it all."

"Bhagavan has other plans for you, it was not meant to be. Never mind. I am doing all the cooking for your father. All you have to do, beta, is defrost the food in the morning and heat it in the microwave in the evening," she said pointing at the many plastic containers. "So, beta, try not to come home too late because he doesn't know how the microwave works."

It wasn't going to be possible to get in for seven every day, not with all that I had to organise. "I know I'll be late, Ma, it's really busy at work and they've already given me time off and, anyway, Dad's an electrician, of course he knows how it works. Don't you, Dad?"

"What?" he said, peering from behind his paper, pretending again that he hadn't heard a word.

"The microwave, you know how it works. It's just that I know I'm going to be home late and I don't want you to starve."

He muttered something.

"Alternatively, I can ask Raj's mum to send food parcels over. I'm sure she would be happy to help, I mean she loves organising people."

The newspaper was flung on his chair as he stormed into the uncharted territory of the kitchen, and before you knew it he had mastered the microwave, hob, and found out where the freezer was located.

The three of us sat and had dinner together and my mum commented that it had been a while since she had seen me this happy — and I did feel happy, happy and excited for Foruki and for me, I suppose. She talked about the kind of sari she would bring back and described the jewellery in great detail. My dad dropped a random comment in about *An audience with the Cilla Black* being on ITV the following week and I was thinking about what I would say on Foruki's invitations. And although the three of us were each in our separate worlds, we had never been so close; all bonded by a prevailing sense of excitement.

The next day, I prepared to meet with the owners of Artusion and the PR lady later that afternoon. To calm

174

myself I went into the studio early and began to paint a portrait of what I thought Foruki looked like. Having him there on canvas would make him seem more real. I painted an abstract face in oranges, reds and yellow with only a slight hint of white. I didn't get time to finish it but he seemed as though he would be the kind of man I would have liked to work for; peaceful and not at all temperamental. "I'll try and do my best for you, Foruki," I said to the man on the unfinished canvas. Washing my hands and changing back into my suit, I made my way to the restaurant.

Situated in Mayfair and literally just around the corner from the wedding venue, Artusion was due to open in a fortnight. As soon as I stepped in I heard *Madame Butterfly* playing in the background. This was most definitely a sign. It was spacious, elegant and minimalist, designed in black, white and red. The manager, Christophe, introduced himself and led me to an office, saying that both the owners were in town and were keen to meet me.

"Emanuel Hikatari and this is my business partner Michael Hyland. I deal with the restaurant, Michael deals with the gallery."

They both appeared to be in their early thirties. Emanuel Hikatari was tall and lean, while Michael Hyland was even taller and robust; he had a very gentle smile and a perfectly symmetrical nose. For a moment I felt like I was in one of Matisse's paintings, balancing on this man's nose and seeing every single feature: large round eyes, unusually long lashes. What were his hands like?

He held one out to shake mine; it felt warm and confident. "Pleased to meet you."

I couldn't quite place his accent.

"And Emily Bruce-Williams you know, of course."

He was introducing me to the PR lady. I'd only spoken to her, never met her before, but I held out my hand as if we were life-long friends.

"Hello again, Emily."

After the introductions Emanuel Hikatari got straight to it. "Emily tells us you're representing a Japanese artist. His name?" he asked coldly.

"Foruki," I replied.

"Surname?"

He didn't have a surname. "That's what he likes to be known as." Why was he being so hostile? Could he see through me?

"I'm half-Japanese, I've never heard of him and it is an unusual name."

"It's a pseudonym," I replied.

My hands felt sweaty. He turned to his colleague. "Have you heard of this, this pseudonym?"

"No, but that's not necessarily a bad thing," he answered. His eyes were infinitely warmer than his partner's and his voice was not arrogant. "Where has he exhibited?" Michael asked with interest.

I couldn't lie about the Japanese galleries, they would know. So I said I discovered him in Japan and then reeled off a list of well-known artists I had represented to add credibility to what I was saying.

"Where in Japan?" Emanuel Hikatari asked.

"Tokyo, I discovered him in Tokyo," I replied assertively. I turned and directed my answers towards Michael. "He isn't famous, he doesn't want to be famous, I had to persuade him to come to London; and for his first exhibition here I want to find somewhere that reflects his personality — innovative yet understated."

Emanuel interrupted, "Can you guarantee press coverage? That's what I want to know."

"Yes," I said looking at him confidently, with absolutely no idea of how to get press there.

"I'll leave it entirely up to you, Michael." He excused himself, saying he had another meeting to go to, and left.

As soon as Emanuel Hikatari left the room, the PR lady suddenly stirred to life and began twirling her long blonde hair; she too had felt the thaw. Once again, she explained the concept of Artusion and how it was important for them to find the right artist for the exhibition. She went on to say how they were maximising coverage by opening the restaurant with an installation done by the Turner Prize winner, alias wardrobe man, Maximus Karlhein.

"But after the initial PR, I want the first real exhibitor to be a painter. I don't mind if he's not famous — it's about the work. Have you brought any slides with you?" Michael asked.

"No, but I can get some to you." I should have thought about slides but I had thought it was going to be much easier than this; it was hardly as if I was trying to get Foruki into the opening exhibition of the Tate Modern.

"Let me show you around the place," he said getting up.

He towered above me and we walked towards a spiral staircase. He let me go first and I had a strange sensation of being able to feel his presence even though he was two or three steps away from me. It was making me nervous and I just focused on trying not to trip or fall down those stairs, and as we reached the top he glanced at my face to see my reaction.

The staircase led to an opulent yet minimalist gallery. The walls were white, it was bright and spacious with large arc-shaped windows that overlooked London. The floor was intricately done in mosaic with Japanese letters. It was perfect.

"It's not finished yet but it will be soon. I do apologise if my partner was a little short with you, it's just that there is so much left to do and so little time."

I knew the feeling.

"So what style does Foruki adopt?"

"Abstract." I kept the conversation to a minimum in case I said the wrong things, and although I had become something of an expert I didn't want to lie to him. He had the kind of eyes that made him incredibly difficult to lie to.

"And you, Nina, how long have you been an agent?" He didn't call me Ms Savani as he had done in the room downstairs. Was he trying to catch me off guard, did he think that I didn't sound competent? I didn't want to blow it now.

"I was a lawyer in the art industry for almost four years and gave it up recently to represent Foruki."

178

There, almost the truth. I wanted the conversation to end there because he was making me feel nervous and I too wanted to play with my hair like Emily Bruce-Williams.

"So you'll drop the slides off by tomorrow?"

"I'll courier them over to you," I replied, trying in vain to sound professional. Then I looked at my watch, thinking that I'd have to find someone who would have the slides ready for the next day. "I have another meeting to go to but it was a pleasure and I would be grateful if you could contact me as soon as possible once you have reached a decision."

"I certainly will," Michael Hyland replied, smiling.

I rushed off and finally managed to find someone who would take pictures of the canvases and develop them into slides for the following day.

After the man had left I attempted to finish Foruki's portrait, but saw nothing except fiery hues of red in large bold strokes so that is what I painted. His eyebrows appeared to be the only thing salvaged from this fiery storm. I couldn't stop thinking about Michael Hyland. Yes, OK, he definitely had something about him and was attractive, but that was it. Engaged people could still find other people attractive, that was no crime. Married people found other people attractive — Dad and Cilla, for example. "She's the dynamite," he had accidentally blurted when he first saw her many years ago on *Blind Date*. Ki and I had split our sides laughing as my mother disgruntledly went to attend to her rotis.

Later that evening, Ki had probed further as to his fascination with her.

"I know she's good-looking, Uncle, is that why you like her?" she had sniggered.

"No, not just the looks. I respects her. She is just like me, coming from the humble beginnings, taking a risk and coming to London, also has the funny accent but this did not stop her, she still worked hard and made it."

"But Uncle," Ki had said trying desperately to control her laughter, "Cilla's not an immigrant, Liverpool's not that far."

"It doesn't matter how far, she came in a boat with only a suitcase."

"A ferry?"

"Ferry, boat, all the same, Kirelli. I understands her."

Understanding; understanding was what mattered and Raj and I had this. OK he didn't know about the paintings so on this basis we couldn't have a full understanding but maybe it was time to tell him.

I stared at Foruki's face; it had gone from calm and sedate to fiery. If it was an omen, it wasn't a very good one.

Raj phoned a while later to say he couldn't meet up as we'd planned because he had to take important clients who had come over from the States to dinner. I desperately needed to see him that evening, to have him put his arms around me and to know that surely attraction could grow. I wondered who else I could talk to and thought about going to see Mrs Onoro but I couldn't just turn up, and besides, I didn't want to go and see her empty-handed. Raj's mother phoned to check that the flowers were still being organised by my mum and then she wanted to speak to her to make doubly sure that all was going according to plan and on schedule. It was all on track, running smoothly, she had made sure of that; there was no room for error, none whatsoever — and especially not from me.

The next morning I went to the office and began making a list of people who could help me with PR. There were only two people on it. One of them was a freelance journalist, the other was a PR director, both of whom I'd met at exhibitions. I called up the PR man first and I almost fell off my chair when he told me how much it would cost to run a campaign for Foruki. I didn't have that sort of money and so I called up the journalist who asked me to send him a press release. Not even sure what this was exactly, I agreed. What I needed was a step-by-step book that would tell me about PR. I added this to my list of things to buy, put everything back in my folder and then went to collect the slides.

I thought about calling a courier but it was another expense so I took the slides to Artusion myself, planning to just drop them off to Christophe. When I got there, however, Michael was in the restaurant area, talking to some workmen. I thought he hadn't seen me but just as I was leaving he called out my name.

Having made up some flimsy excuse about being in the area, he invited me to have a coffee with him and I agreed, thinking that maybe I wouldn't be so tongue-tied and could make a better job of convincing him to exhibit Foruki if I spent more time with him informally. Michael asked how long I had known him and what was so special about him that I would want to leave Whitter and Lawson to represent him exclusively. And instead of giving him the same rehearsed bullshit, I talked about Foruki as if he was someone I really, truly believed in.

"There's a vulnerability about him which he doesn't show, you can't even detect it through his paintings but I know it's there and I know this by what he paints. Mostly he paints inanimate objects and tries to see magic in them, even when it's not there; and he uses bright colours if he can, or colours that seemingly don't go together." Lost in the analysis of my own creation, I continued, "Sometimes he contrasts dead objects with something that is alive, hoping that . . ." Realising I was getting carried away, I ended the sentence with, ". . . Yes, hoping that it will work. This is my interpretation of what he's trying to do, he might tell you something completely different. Actually, come to think of it, he won't tell you anything at all. He's a complete recluse."

Michael laughed. It was a gentle sort of a laugh. "So you say you gave up working at the firm to represent Foruki?"

"Yes, because I believe in him and it is the first time I've really believed in any of my artists. And how about you? How long have you owned Artusion?"

182

"Five years. Emanuel and I started from scratch with nothing except my passion for art and his for food."

"Who are your favourite artists?" I asked.

"Postmodernists like . . ."

". . . Picasso and Matisse," I said, finishing his sentence.

"Yes." He held my gaze intently and I quickly changed the subject, looking away as I did so.

"So why the installation by wardrobe man? I mean Karlhein."

"PR. Everyone's talking about him at the moment, sometimes you have to play the game to get the attention and then you can do what you want."

He understood about the game. Maybe he would understand that sometimes you have to bend the rules in order to play, even if you really didn't mean to play in the first place. Half an hour had passed in an instant. We talked more about the art world and I could have talked to him for hours but I had work to be getting on with and so I thanked him and left. Michael said he would be in touch soon.

I went for a walk along the back of Cork Street, taking in the pictures displayed in the gallery windows. What if mine was in there one day? Mine couldn't be but what if Foruki's was? What if he was a success? What would happen then? Would I have to continue to be him? I couldn't suddenly switch and be me — Mangetti could never find out. Don't get carried away, Nina, it's a sabbatical — remember that — and then you get back to reality.

Raj and I met later that evening and I stared at him, wishing that he would just hold my gaze for once and not feel the need to fill the silences with inane chatter.

"So, baby, tell me about your day?"

I began by telling him about Artusion but he wouldn't let me finish. He interrupted me by saying that he had read about it in one of the papers but didn't think the concept would take off in London because the last thing people wanted to do after a meal was to look at paintings.

"There are people who can see paintings anytime," I responded, surprised by his comment. "Anyway, you love paintings too."

"Yes," he said, attempting to backtrack, "but I like to know what I'm doing. If I'm going to a restaurant, I want to have dinner; if I'm going to a gallery, I want to see art."

His argument didn't make any sense: it was such an odd thing to say for someone who liked art. "But if you're going to a place where you know you can do both, all the better."

"Not left your lawyer-head at work today," he said patronisingly. "Anyway, baby, why do we care if it's a success or not?"

And then I lost it. "I care," I shouted, "and I care because it's original and it's bold to do something different and not follow the pack like sheep." Maybe I subconsciously meant us, being herded from list to engagement to marriage, but he stopped me from going any further and tried to calm me down.

"This is our first real argument, baby."

"No it's not, because if it was an argument you would be shouting back at me. What are you passionate about, Raj, tell me?"

"You, Nina, you. I love you."

And hearing those words made me realise how deeply we had gotten into this. There was no turning back — love had entered into the equation, for one of us at least. How could he love me? He didn't even know me. Maybe it was me who expected too much; I expected too much and therefore was always so disappointed. There was no room to be disappointed with Raj because this was who he was; he was uncomplicated; he liked to know that a restaurant was for eating in and a gallery was for seeing art. Why was I getting so worked up? No expectation, no room for disappointment, just stability.

"I'm sorry," I said. "It's just been a long day."

"I understand," he replied.

He couldn't understand. Michael Hyland had crept into my psyche in a way that nobody, not even I, could understand.

There were hardly any people on the train when I made my way to the studio early the next morning, not even waiting for the light to begin painting. There was an energy bubbling away inside of me that worked its way onto the canvas, balancing the red hues on Foruki's face. *Madame Butterfly* was playing as usual while I was working so I didn't hear the knock on the garage door until it turned into a bang. It was ten o'clock in the morning and nobody ever came to the studio, so I kept silent, hoping whoever it was would go away.

"Anyone there?" There was another bang on the door.

"Who is it?" I asked, clutching my paintbrush in case I had to stab an intruder.

"It's Michael, Michael Hyland."

Bloody hell. What was he doing here? I put down the paintbrush, thought quickly about grabbing my proper clothes but it was too late, he had already pulled the door open.

"Hi," he said.

I didn't even have time to roll down my sleeves; my arm was exposed. He could see the scarring. I fumbled with the sleeve, trying not to panic, trying to find some kind of explanation as to why I would be standing in a studio clearly in the midst of painting a portrait of someone who did not even exist.

"You left this at the restaurant," he said handing over my folder. "I thought it might be important so I looked inside for an address, hope you don't mind."

I hadn't even noticed the folder was missing. Oh God, he must have seen my scribbled notes and the plan. "Thank you," I replied, not knowing what else to say and willing him to leave.

"Even more impressive than on the slides," he commented.

"Foruki was kind enough to let me use his studio for the morning. I just dabble," I said, flicking white paint randomly on the canvas.

186

He stood studying the pictures.

"Thank you for bringing back the folder. Was there anything else?" *Leave, please leave*, I willed.

"I saw the slides yesterday evening but this, this is something else. He's good, isn't he, very good. There's a tremendous warmth that comes from these pictures." Then he turned to me, "So do you paint here often?"

Go, just go, I thought.

"Is that him?" he continued, pointing at Foruki.

I nodded. He would know if I had done the self-portrait, I would have done the rest. He wasn't stupid. I had to get him out of the studio before he finally put two and two together. "Like I said, Foruki has let me use the studio for the morning. I don't mean to be rude but I don't get that much time to myself so if there isn't anything else." I signalled towards the door with my eyes.

"Why are the lines not longer on that palm?"

"What?" I replied, thrown by his question.

"That painting there, the lines are so short."

"Because everything about the picture is so alive and the only way I . . . Ki . . . Foruki could capture the nature of death was by the length of the life, heart and fate line."

"Did he experience the death of someone close?"

"His best friend."

"Died young?"

I wanted desperately to tell him about Ki but nodded instead.

There was silence.

187

"Anyway, I mustn't keep you. I just wanted to tell you that you — Foruki — can exhibit at Artusion. There will be no charge for the food or the drink but come around when you are not so busy so we can finalise the other details."

He knew. I knew he knew, he knew I knew he knew, but I couldn't say anything except, "Thank you."

"If Foruki needs help with PR, let me know and I'll tell Emily to get on to it," he said, glancing at the canvas behind me with the list of things to do so prominently displayed.

"I'll tell him," I said. "Thank you, Michael."

A splattering of white had hit one of Foruki's eyes and it looked like a stream of tears. I know how he felt. What was I going to do? How would I explain it? What if he told someone? No, he wouldn't, he would have said something now. Out of all the people in the world, why did it have to be him? Why wasn't it Raj? I left the canvas, anxious after Michael's visit. He had seen me, me in my studio, and accepted it with no questions? Why? He understood about the lines on the palm. I had had this overwhelming need to tell him about Ki; I didn't even have this with Raj.

Raj had to come and see the studio and the pictures. Raj would restore a sense of normality but at the same time I also had to tell him everything. It wasn't right that Michael, a virtual stranger, knew; and Raj, the man I was about to marry, remained in blissful ignorance about this part of my life. I called him up and said that there was something I wanted to show him and asked him to meet me at London Bridge when he finished work. Raj wasn't good with surprises and wanted to know what it was. "Just meet me at six-thirty," I insisted.

It was the perfect opportunity to tell him about Foruki but I needed to see his reaction to the paintings first without telling him it was me. Deep down, I wanted him to just look at the pictures and guess. I tidied up the studio, took down the canvas with the list of things to do, packed away anything that he would know was mine, changed back into my suit, and feeling very excited I went to meet him.

"Hi baby," he said as soon as he saw me. "What's with the big secret?"

"It's not a secret, Raj, it's just that Foruki has left me with the keys to his studio and I wanted you to be one of the first to see his work."

"Do we have his permission?"

"He won't mind, just come see it with me. We won't get another chance to see it together like this."

"If it means so much to you baby, let's go," he said, grabbing my hand.

"Were you very busy today?"

"No, not really, what about you?"

"It was a strange day," I said. "I forgot some important documents at a restaurant and the owner came by to drop them off."

"Right. Why was that strange?"

Yes, why was it strange? I was going to say that Michael could have sent Christophe or one of his staff with the folder, that he had 101 other things to do when his restaurant was about to open, and then when he came . . . "You know, when you expect someone to behave in a certain way and they don't."

"Is that a good thing or a bad thing?" Raj asked.

"I don't know, that's why it's strange. Anyway, Foruki wants the exhibition held there — it's Artusion."

"We're here," I said a few minutes later, stopping outside the studio.

"What, here?" Raj asked surprised, looking at the building. "You'd think that he could afford somewhere better."

"It's about what he does with the space inside, not what it looks like from the outside," I said, unlocking the padlock and pulling the door open. "Let me just put the lights on. So, what do you think?"

He stood as if he were taking in the atmosphere. "It's amazing how people can work in such places."

"What?" I asked, irritated.

"I mean what he is able to do with such space and the paintings are . . . the paintings are . . . interesting. Yes, look at that buddha. You can see there how he is trying to make a point."

"Really?" I asked.

"Yes, baby, see there again. Andy Warhol did a picture like that about the nature of fame. This guy Fuki is trying to say that even religious concepts in today's era go through a fashion."

I was dumbfounded. What was he going on about? "I don't think that's what he meant . . ."

190

"He's obviously got some Indian influence here," he pointed at the derelict houses painted in the colours of sari material.

At last, I thought, thinking that surely he must recognise the orange house with the delicate elephant print — the pattern of my engagement sari.

"Again, social commentary. Maybe about how cultures have fused."

By then I was exasperated by Raj's words.

"Then this footprint," he continued, analysing the painting of the red footprint on pebbles. "It's possibly the mark he wants to leave, the red boldness is what he has to offer. See, all his paintings are bold and expressive."

"It's my left foot that wasn't captured on the white sheet, the one that doesn't belong to your family," was what I wanted to say. But instead I asked him what he thought about the palm.

"See the contrast in colours between the palm and the foot, the palm is . . ."

I wanted to save him from himself and from what I would say if he continued any further so I threw a rope to help him. "That's the palm I was talking to you about, Raj, you know, when I said I felt the lines should have been longer but they're not."

"Yes, I see what you mean. They could have been longer. He seems an interesting guy this Fuki. Is that him?" he glanced over at the portrait.

"Yes it is, and it's Foruki." I tried to hide my disappointment. There was no moment of revelation, no spark of recognition, no comprehension of who I really was. Maybe after the exhibition I wouldn't even tell him that it had been me, and we'd just get on with our lives like normal people, living normal lives in a normal world.

"Now, baby, I've got a surprise for you too."

"You have?" I asked.

He put his hand inside his pocket. "I've been waiting all day to do this." He pulled out the ring. "There," he said, putting it on my finger. "It fits and it's beautiful just like you. Don't you think so?"

"Yes . . . beautiful."

"And thank you for sharing all this with me, baby, I can see how it's important to you."

"It is," I said, switching off the lights and putting the padlock back on the door.

I didn't sleep all night, thinking about Raj's reaction, thinking about Michael coming to the studio. They had both seen me and my work and reacted in different ways. Raj didn't want to see me in the pictures, it was about him — how much he thought he knew about art. But then that was unfair of me to do that to Raj — if I hadn't built Foruki up so much to him, I'm sure he would have seen that it was me.

It must have been about seven o'clock on Saturday morning when my mum came into my bedroom, mumbling something about Raj's mother telling her that he had given me the engagement ring. I pulled my hand from under the duvet and waved it at her. She gasped, seeing again the size of the rock, and then tried to get me up so we could all organise who was coming to the wedding. It had to be done that day as she was leaving for India that evening. I couldn't wait to have ten days where I could just concentrate on the exhibition.

My mum lifted up the duvet and practically dragged me out of bed. I went to make a cup of tea and she followed me just in case I got lost.

My dad was sitting downstairs in his red pyjamas. He was busy drawing up the guest list. Seeing several red marks across people's names I said, "Just invite whoever you want, Dad, don't worry about my friends."

"No, Nina. Come, sit, see what I've done. These here," he pointed, "they won't appreciate Hilton. We'll have a party for them here later."

My Uncle Amit and Auntie Asha were also crossed out.

"Don't you want them to come?" I asked. "Is it because of —?"

"No, not because of the Raw," he interrupted.

"It's Roy, Dad, Roy."

"For two dickheads I suffered," he shouted.

Dad went through a phase of picking up phrases on the bus; sometimes he didn't quite get the gist of what they meant. Anyway, Auntie Asha was inoffensive and my Uncle Amit was lovely; he owned lots of factories and had helped my dad financially when we first came to London. I would never have called them that. Maybe I hadn't heard him right. "What?"

"Two dickheads and they did nothing."

Imagining Raj's mother keeling over upon hearing these words, I thought I'd better check to see if he knew what he was saying. "Do you know what that means, Dad?"

"Yes, it means twenty years with no help from them."

"Oh . . . decades."

"Yes, dickheads, what I'm saying. Two of them, struggling to make the ends meet when he could have made me the boss in one of his factories."

"He did ask if you wanted to be supervisor."

"They're not coming," he said adamantly.

We went through everyone on the list and the guests were chosen on the basis of who had done what for my dad and whether they would be significantly impressed with the venue. At some point there was some crossover as some of the guests had wronged my father considerably but he wanted to show them how far he had come and so they were included. My mother just insisted on the key honchos being present.

"All done. You'll write out invitations when they come?" he said two hours later.

I went to buy my PR books and then on my way back I saw a porcelain cat that reminded me of Mrs Onoro so I bought it for her and went around to see her.

"Sorry I haven't come around sooner. I have been meaning to but it's been so busy," I said as she led me to her sitting room.

"World too busy today," she commented as I sat down. "You better now? I make you some tea."

She came back with a tray.

"This is just something I bought for you to say thank you."

"Oh, it beautiful," she said opening it. "You good girl."

No, I'm not. I used to be but now I'm turning into this serial liar, is what I wanted to tell her. "I saw it in the shop window and I thought of you," I said instead.

Her son, the grocer, came downstairs. "Ma, have you seen my . . .?"

He stopped when he saw me in the sitting room.

"No, Rooney, why you no marry a girl like this? Look what she bought me." The cat was thrust into his hands.

"How's your research coming along?" he asked.

"Oh, the research, yes. I've decided to specialise in Japanese painting at the moment."

"I don't know anything about art."

It was then I decided that Foruki was not going to be present at his exhibition. The grocer didn't look right; he had these awful maroon streaks in his hair.

"Ma, do you know where my green shirt is?"

"I ironed and put in your cupboard. It there only."

"Anyway, nice to see you again." He said something in Japanese to his mother and went back up. Probably said something like, "Why are you letting crazy women into the house bearing gifts of porcelain cats?"

"He good boy really. You marry soon, no?"

"Two months."

"He good boy?"

"Yes. I think so."

"Only think so?"

"He is. I don't know him that well. I mean it was sort of arranged but he's nice. Talks a lot, interrupts me at

195

times, but he's nice and he's kind. Mrs Onoro, when you married your husband, did you know he was the one for you?"

"I too young to know anything but now I can tell if person good by looking in eyes. He got good eyes?"

They were small but that was if I were comparing them to Michael's eyes, and they didn't sparkle but there was nothing bad about them.

"I glad when my husband died. He was no good man and now I free. You make wrong choice you no free."

She left me to think about that as she went to get the tea. The irony was, despite the fact that I was marrying Raj who was solid and reliable, I had never felt freer or bolder within myself — I was bordering on reckless. It had been me who was solid and reliable with Jean Michel. How was it possible to change in only a matter of months?

Mrs Onoro came back.

I enquired after Hikito. She blushed, telling me he was well and then she said, "I wait fifty years to find a good man."

I wanted to tell her about Michael, how he threw all my feelings into utter confusion, but I looked at my watch. Mum was going to India, I had to take her to the airport.

"I have to go."

"You come back soon?"

"I will."

My mother and father made it work. Although it wasn't the best marriage in the world they were still together and in their own way, they loved each other. Raj was a good man and this was the most important thing. He was practical, stable, kind, and he loved me and would never do anything to hurt me.

He came with us to the airport to see my mum off.

"See you soon, my son," she said engulfing him. "Look after them both, beta."

"I will," I replied.

There was no way out of this. I couldn't break their hearts. I just had to accept that and then maybe things would get easier and then there wouldn't be such a conflict inside myself.

The next day I spent with Raj's family and somehow found myself calling his mother "Mummy", just as he did. Surprisingly, it was quite a pleasant day, or maybe that is the way I chose to see it. Either way, I vowed that as soon as the exhibition was over there would be no more lies and I would do my very best to be a good wife.

It was good that my mum had gone to India because when she wasn't in the house there was no more talk of weddings and it made it seem less real. I also took my engagement ring off, justifying it to myself by saying that I didn't want to get paint on it.

And Michael Hyland, I put him to the back of my mind; that electric thing he did to me whenever he was around. It had no effect on me, it couldn't — it was wrong, I was marrying Raj, that was that, it was time to focus now on hyping Foruki. All my energy had to go into making this exhibition work — it was only a month away.

I needed a strategy and a plan. I had read through the PR books. Confidence; it was all about confidence and believing in the hype. I drafted a press release and reread it and then I sat at my desk, psyching myself up to call the list of art correspondents. I dialled the first number and hung up.

"Pitching" was selling an idea. The more confident you were about a product the easier it was to sell. I believed in Foruki, I just had to make others believe in him. I dialled the number again.

"It's Nina Savani from Kendal Brown. I have . . . er . . . an artist by the name of Foruki who has his first exhibition in London coming up."

"What makes this one unique?" the journalist asked abruptly.

"Er, his style."

"What about it?"

I froze, not knowing quite what to say about his style and I just wanted to get off the phone, so I said I had another call to attend to and hung up.

It was a complete disaster and so unprofessional. I didn't know quite what to say and the journalist must have known that I was a fraud. It wasn't working. Maybe I should just call up Michael and ask for the help he offered. It would be good to speak to him and share the experience with someone. No. No Michael. I sat in front of my computer and the words "GO NINA" danced in front of me. I smiled and closed my eyes and imagined Ki laughing at my half-hearted attempts. Inspired by the thought of her splitting her sides, I picked up the phone and started again.

With each call I made it got easier, and I learned more and more while making them.

"Hello, Nina Savani here from Kendal Brown. We met at the ICA last month and you asked me to let you know as soon as the Japanese painter Foruki was exhibiting." This was the first thing I learned. Give them the impression that they already know you; they were much more receptive if they thought they knew you.

Despite the fact that they had no recollection of the meeting and maybe hadn't even gone to the ICA, most of them acknowledged me, perhaps embarrassed by their poor memories.

"Well, he has a press launch on the twenty-second of March and he's specifically asked me to send you an invitation."

More often than not, they asked for a press release along with the invite, just to refresh their memories.

And so it went on like that until I had contacted most of the journalists on the list.

The most audacious thing I did, surprising even myself, was attending every major opening in London that week despite not having any formal invitations. While at Whitter and Lawson we received invites regularly and more often than not I had to attend these functions to network and build contacts. It was the same arty crowd, mostly talking nonsense; artists making stains on serviettes which some fool would buy for a couple of thousand pounds. There would always be one or two people who looked like they didn't belong there; they were more often than not the only ones who were worth talking to.

I put on a smart black dress, caught the tube part-way to the function, then caught a cab so I felt like I hadn't just walked off the streets. My heart leaped as I prayed that the door person would not turn me away. I acted as if I had misplaced the invite or rummaged in my handbag, and, amazingly, they'd let me through. If I was lucky, someone I knew would call out my name and that didn't make me feel so bad. At the exhibitions I mingled, handed out my business card, talked about Foruki and his up-and-coming exhibition and sought out the journalists and spoke to them. It was as if I were a different person with an inner strength, poise and social confidence that even I didn't know I possessed.

There was a woman at one of the events who I really clicked with and we had a very good conversation about the artists being over-hyped and everything these days being about celebrity and not necessarily about the work. It transpired she was a producer on Radio 4 but had previously been an economist. I was desperate to share my experience of my own career change but instead listened attentively to her. We got on very well on a personal level and before she left, she asked me for my contact details.

Another thing I did were Simon's famous "whispers", telling a few artists who I was on good terms with that Foruki was going to be the next big thing and being as elusive as I could. They, no doubt, would make enquiries with their agents, who would in turn make further enquiries. And so it went on like that for the rest of that week, talking to people, hyping to a select few, going to exhibitions until late in the evening, participating in the theatrics that went on behind the scenes. Consumed with the overwhelming desire to turn Foruki into a success, I was absorbed in the world that I was creating for him. Part of me enjoyed the challenge and I wanted to show these people that it was possible to be a nobody and play the game as they did.

Because I had been so busy I hadn't seen Raj all week. I was relieved because I didn't have to think about the wedding plans, Raj, or if my dad was surviving on his frozen-food rations. By the end of the week my wedding invitations were still lying on my desk. On Friday I sat writing out Foruki's invites and after I had done that, I quickly scribbled out my wedding invitations.

In the midst of the chaos, Michael called.

"Kendal Brown. Nina speaking."

"How are you, Nina?"

I took a deep breath as I recognised his voice. See, he could phone me and there was no electric thing going on.

"I'm fine, just incredibly busy organising everything."

"That's why I'm calling. Can you come in this Sunday. We can sample some food for the launch and finalise the details of Foruki's exhibition. I've put Emily onto the PR as well so we need to talk about the best way to handle that too."

"There was no need for that, we've got it all organised," I said, not realising that I might have sounded ungrateful — and why had I said "we"? This

201

multiple personality thing was being embedded in my psyche.

"I thought you might need a hand."

"Thank you."

"So one o'clock then?" he asked.

Raj and I had planned to go for lunch and then to the cinema that day. "It's a bit short notice."

"It's the only time I have available before our launch and we really need to get everything tied up."

"Sunday it is, then."

Before I went home I made one last call, possibly the most important call yet. I spent twenty minutes psyching myself up, convincing myself that it would all work out. I dialled the number and hung up before I actually spoke to Mangetti. After composing myself, I redialled.

"Mr Mangetti, it's Nina Savani."

"Nina. How are you?"

Absolutely sick with nerves, I can't sleep at night because the level of deceit has just snowballed out of all proportion and now, well now I'm just running with it. That's how I really was. I sat upright in my chair and said, "I'm very well, thank you. How are you?"

"Yes. I'm well."

"I just wanted to let you know that Foruki's exhibition is on the twenty-second of March."

"Let me just check my diary," he replied.

My heart began thumping. Please be free, I thought. I'm doing all of this for you, please tell me you can come.

"Yes, that's fine. I look forward to meeting both you and Foruki."

I thanked him and hung up.

I couldn't believe it. I wanted to cry with relief and had to leave my desk because I was so overwhelmed. "He's coming, Ki. I've done it. He's going to come." I posted both sets of invites on my way home.

That Saturday morning when I woke up my dad began grumbling about the starvation diet that I had subjected him to.

"Days, I tell you. I haven't eaten for days. Waiting for you, no sign, no call, nothing. Why didn't you put me in a home? At least I would have been fed."

"I told you, Dad, I would be working late, doing overtime so I can have time off for the honeymoon."

"This is all you are thinking about, the holidays, not if your father is well."

"Believe me, the holiday is the last thing on my mind. Anyway, when we go to the Hilton today I know there aren't going to be any rotis, Dad, so don't start arguing about the food. Raj's mother is paying for it so we'll just let her choose."

He grumbled something about murdering the guests with the "poffs". Admittedly, Raj's mother did have a thing about puff pastry but I assured him she wasn't the one cooking and I managed to convince him to agree with everything she said. The total cost of the wedding if she didn't pay for it was the key influencing factor.

Raj and his parents came to collect my father. I wanted to meet them there but Raj had insisted on driving us.

"I've missed you, baby. It's been such a busy week."

"For me too," I replied as he opened the car door for us.

"Raj, we're going to have to meet up later on tomorrow. It's just that I've got some bits and pieces to do."

"I'll help you."

"No," I said too quickly. "I mean it's just some things for work and then I'll meet you after."

"That's my girl," my father shouted. "Always working, even in the weekends, very top in her job."

Raj parked just across the road from Artusion. *Why?* I thought. It would be a nightmare if I bumped into Michael while holding Raj's hand with the whole family in tow.

"Isn't that the place where your Japanese artist is having his launch?" Raj asked.

"Yes, that's it. It's almost two o'clock, we'll be late," I said, getting out of the car quickly and trying to hurry everyone up just in case we bumped into anyone.

"What artist?" Raj's mother asked.

"Oh no one in particular, just a Japanese artist who I'm representing at the moment."

"You'll have a party there for him?"

"It's not really a party. It's an exhibition."

"Lots of interesting people go to these functions, no, Nina? I go to music things you know, when Ravi Shankar has something on, but I've never been to an art thing," she replied, obviously angling for an invite.

204

I ignored her.

"Mummy would really love to go along to something like that. You can get her an invite — it's not a problem, is it, baby? You are organising it, aren't you?"

It was a huge problem, and what was an even bigger problem was we hadn't seemed to get very far out of the car and the "baby" thing was really starting to annoy me.

"Full of boring art-world types. You'd hate it, Mummy," I said quickly. "I mean, I only go because I have to for work."

"Yah, but just for the experience, Nina, I'd love to come."

"She'll be fine, baby, I'll bring her."

Raj wasn't invited either.

"I'm going to be working," I said, trying to remain unfazed, "so I won't really get a chance to speak to you. You know how it is when you're working."

"It will be nice to see what you do, baby, and you won't even know we are there."

It was hard to keep coming up with objections.

"Agreed then," his mother asserted. "What date is it?"

"Thursday twenty-second. Won't you still have lots to do for the wedding?"

"All done by then. You'll come as well, no?" she said, turning to my father and asking him out of politeness. "Dillip can't come, he normally has his golf committee meetings on Thursday evenings, no, Dillip?"

Her husband nodded.

About to have both my worlds collide and destroy each other, I quickly said, "Dad's not really into exhibitions or art."

"What?" he grunted.

Please God, please make him say no. You can't do this to me.

"To see Nina's Japanese painter. You'll come? It's on a Thursday night."

"Can't see Japan man. *Astitva Ek Prem Kahani* is then."

That's right, he never missed that, eight o'clock Thursday on Zee TV. He was in front of that box regardless of whatever else happened in the world. Thank you, God.

I took Raj to one side.

"Raj, it's a really important artist and I can't lose him so when we're there, you've got to act like you're not my fiancé. Work doesn't like it if we bring our family along to these events."

"Completely understand. You won't even notice us, if you want we'll pretend we don't know you."

What a nightmare. This was all I needed — his mother screeching at the exhibition. There was no way she was going to pretend she didn't know me.

"Promise me, Raj, that you'll speak to her. It's very, very important."

"I promise, baby. We'll be invisible."

We got to the restaurant and the waiter showed us to the table and handed us our menu. There were a selection of hors d'oeuvres to begin with followed by curried vegetables and potatoes on a bed of filo pastry drizzled in olive oil, or pan-fried fillet of salmon with mint and coriander sauce. The only thing that could really pass off as Indian were the desserts: kulfi ice-cream, gulabjam or rasmalai.

My dad sat studying the menu. "No samosa, paneer, chana dhal, roti?"

I kicked him under the table.

"OHH . . . no samosa, paneer, chana dhal, roti. Good, good, all the greasy foods makes peoples fatties."

We tasted it all. It was fine. However, several times Dad looked as if he would be sick but remained unusually quiet while he ate.

"Delicious," Raj's mother exclaimed.

"It's a good menu, isn't it, Dad?" I asked when we had finished.

"Yes, it was the good. Very good," he managed.

The heated towels came at the end and this was the part I was dreading. Dad took the towel out of the plastic wrapper and instead of just wiping his hands, he flannelled his face, rubbing it vigorously and making sure he did behind his ears.

Raj's family looked at him completely bewildered and then looked at each other.

"Ah, good, very good," he said, handing the towel back to the waiter.

Then Dad asked him if he had any paan. The waiter didn't have a clue what he was talking about. "Just give me the mint and water to wash the taste," he said.

They dropped us back home. My dad headed straight for the freezer, defrosted another container in the

207

microwave and heated it up. He sat in the sitting room waiting for *An Audience with Cilla Black* and I hovered around hoping for an opening where we could just sit and talk. There was none and so I waited for Cilla with him. When she finally came on, he clapped. Clapped really hard, knowing that my mum wasn't there to hear his adoration for her.

"Oh, the Cilla, the Cilla," he repeated as he stood up clapping as if he were part of the audience.

She took the mike and opened by singing, "Surprise, Surprise . . ."

He bellowed along with her as if he were on stage singing a duet: ". . . the unexpecteds hits you between the eyes . . ."

"I'm not a lawyer any more, Dad, and I'm having mega doubts about marrying Raj. There, I've said it."

"Shhhhh, Nina, let me sing with the Cilla."

The trees in Green Park seemed happy that spring was finally on its way; winter had seemed endless. The benches were occupied by couples enticed out by the unexpected sunshine. I know it was something that I shouldn't have done, but I put my engagement ring in my pocket before arriving at Artusion. It slid off almost too effortlessly and I justified it in my mind by thinking that I wanted to keep both worlds completely separate.

I was expecting to find it heaving with people ready to sample food but it was quiet, and then I thought it wasn't the kind of establishment like my Uncle Nandan's restaurant, where people queued for miles if you said anything was free. The restaurant was

208

shrouded in darkness and appeared to be closed. I rang the buzzer and Michael came to open the doors.

"Come in, Nina."

He was dressed informally in a black T-shirt and jeans. It was really nice to see him again.

"You're looking well," he said.

I acted like I didn't hear the comment, as "well" was far from what I was looking; it had been yet another sleepless night worrying about Raj's mother's presence at the exhibition.

The restaurant was empty so I commented on that instead. "And the others?" I asked.

"What others?"

"I thought that there would be a few more people." Maybe I had misheard him when he invited me or I was getting into my dad's habit of just hearing things I wanted to. I mean, I saw what I wanted to.

"No, it's just you, if you'd like to sit here," he said, pulling out the chair. I caught myself glancing at his hand to see if he had a ring and as soon as I found myself doing this, I diverted my thoughts. Michael went into the kitchen and brought out a platter of Japanese canapés. I couldn't believe he had gone out of his way to sort out the food just for me to try; it was a very kind gesture.

"The chef came in this morning to make them. This is maki, and this is nigiri, katsu . . ."

"I'm not really familiar with Japanese food," I replied, adding quickly, "I mean the first time I ate it was when we were in Tokyo."

"You really were in Japan, then?"

It was the first true acknowledgement from Michael that he knew Foruki's real identity.

He waited for my answer and I didn't lie.

"No, I have never been to Japan."

"It's the name of a restaurant?"

"No."

"Help me out here, Nina — how have you been to Tokyo if you've never been to Japan?"

I wanted to help him out, but if I did, I would involve him in the deceit. And although he already knew, it wasn't spoken about, so therefore it didn't matter. And why him? Why couldn't it be Raj who I was about to spill my heart out to?

"Nina?"

The way he called my name like that, so softly, made me feel even more desperate to tell him.

"My friend Ki and I were in Tokyo. Not Tokyo as you would know it but in her bedroom. That's what we did, she loved to travel and we pretended we were in some part of the world, not in some back bedroom that smelled of raw fish and Domestos staring at cheap red paper lanterns. It didn't matter at that stage anyway, she was ill, really ill, and she couldn't eat any of the food, couldn't swallow, and I was trying to make things better for her but I couldn't." And though it must have sounded like the ramblings of a mad woman, he let me continue, without interrupting, without needing to add his comments.

After I'd told him all about Ki, I glanced up at him, tears in my eyes.

"I'm sorry," I said. I didn't know what I was sorry for: sorry for unburdening myself, sorry for deceiving him, sorry that I was in tears, sorry that it wasn't Raj sitting there.

"How old was she when she . . .?"

"Twenty-six."

"I'm sorry too," he said simply.

The warmth in his eyes was sincere and I wanted to tell him all of it — all about the plan which had spiralled out of control.

"This all started because I promised her I would paint again. I never meant for it to get this far, you know I've never really lied, not on this scale anyway."

"You don't have to tell me."

He was right, I didn't have to tell him a thing, but I began at the beginning with leaving my job; Matisse's quotes; the serendipitous meeting with Gina; the suit routine; going to the framer's; Mangetti's interest in the buddha painting; setting up the office. With each piece of information it felt as if a huge burden was being lifted from me. The only bits that I missed out were Raj and the wedding, because at that moment it didn't seem part of my life. That part was like it was happening to someone else and I didn't want him to know that I was getting married.

Michael looked dumbfounded. "And you haven't told anyone else? How have you managed to keep it all in?"

"By pretending it was happening to someone else, maybe? Pretending that Foruki is real, that it was all going to somehow come together and I could pull it off if I really focused. It is the first time in my life that I have taken a risk on any scale."

"Might as well start big then," he smiled.

Michael knew Tastudi Mangetti, he knew most of the major players in the art world and he told me to be careful. Mangetti was renowned for being ruthless and getting his own way; if he ever found out he would make sure I would never work in the art world again. He asked me what my strategy was but there was no real strategy, just to get Mangetti to buy a few paintings and to sell the rest so I would have made a sizeable amount to tell my father about, and then I would kill off Foruki. By then, the art world would have moved on to the next artist.

"And what about you? What happens to you, Nina?"

"I haven't allowed myself to think beyond the exhibition."

He was surprised that there wasn't more calculation to it. But that was the point, it wasn't ever meant to be calculated; I had taken one step and events had escalated and I went along with it all because it was the first time I had ventured outside my comfort zone and also because it had been a very long time since I had felt passionate about something. And now it had got to a stage where it had become a personal challenge and I needed to know that I could pull it off.

Michael told me how he had gone to art school in New York but knew early on he would never make money from his work so he looked for another outlet to express himself through. He teamed up with Emanuel

Hikatari whom he had met through a friend and together they had gradually built up a reputation for finding new artists. They had taken risks with many unknown artists who were later spotted and made into commercial successes. I knew he was taking a huge gamble with me because if it ever came out in public that he knew Foruki was an invention, his reputation would be ruined.

"I'll understand if you want to back out, Michael. Really I will."

"No, I'm not even thinking about that. I want to help you. What you're doing takes guts."

I didn't know about guts, stupidity maybe. "Do you think creativity takes courage?" I asked.

"I would say that not being creative also takes courage. It's hard just to go through the motions and not do what you really want to do."

I hadn't thought of it that way.

My phone began ringing. It was Raj. I looked at my watch. I'd completely lost track of time; he was probably waiting for me outside the cinema.

"I'll be there in half an hour," I said, answering quickly.

"You have to go?" Michael enquired.

"I'm sorry to leave in such a rush, Michael." I hadn't tried any of the food, we hadn't talked about the contract, the exhibition or any of the PR. "We'll talk again soon."

He said he would do whatever he could to help me.

"Thank you," I said getting up, "you're very kind." What I really wanted to do was throw my arms around him and thank him for really listening to me but I couldn't bring myself to, so I shook his hand and left.

Raj was waiting at the cinema and seemed irate, pacing up and down. I'd never seen him like that before.

"Where have you been?" he shouted.

"I'm sorry, I was at Artusion, trying to plan the exhibition."

"On a Sunday? Anyway, the film has already started; we'd better go in."

The film was *The Green Mile*, and despite really wanting to see it I couldn't concentrate as I was thinking about the conversation I had had with Michael. It had been a relief to talk to him, to feel unburdened . . . and then, feeling incredibly guilty, I held out my hand and took Raj's.

He squeezed it and whispered, "I'm sorry if I shouted at you earlier, baby."

I spent most of that week in the office, making more phone calls, sending out press releases. Michael called every day to see how things were coming along and if he could offer any assistance. I really did try to keep our conversations strictly professional but at times the conversation would veer off to other realms and I would find out things about him, such as he lived in New York but was in London until the restaurant was up and running. But it was the little details about him that I loved finding out about. Like how much his family meant to him — how he would try to get back to Ireland as often as he could to see his niece and nephew; that he liked to drink cinnamon coffee every morning and in this time would plan his day. Jean hadn't been too concerned about seeing his family; Nantes wasn't far at all but he only saw them twice a year and he never sat and planned anything in the morning. He had always been rushing around, spontaneous and impetuous. I didn't even know what Raj was like in the mornings. And in these moments, when I caught myself thinking about three different men, I would seek refuge by burying myself in my work, and in Foruki.

Michael called to say that he was sending someone over to the studio to take pictures of the paintings for a brochure and he would come by the studio himself at some point, drop the contract around and help me pick out the paintings to exhibit. I also had wedding jobs to do like call around and find a wedding cake as this was the only thing Raj's mother had entrusted me with, but I couldn't work up the enthusiasm to do it.

On Wednesday I received an RSVP from my Auntie Shilpa accepting Foruki's invitation to see his work. At first I didn't understand but then at the bottom she had put, "Will food be available in the canapé?" Then it dawned on me that when sending out the invites there must have been some kind of mix-up — I had sent exhibition invites to the wedding guests. With visions of my relatives turning up at Foruki's launch, I began to panic; all this work only to have relatives come and cause havoc. I rushed home to retrieve the guest list and my dad's address book.

"Who's a there?"

"It's me, Dad. What are you doing at home? Aren't you supposed to be at work?"

"Feeling a bit sick," he said, listening to Cilla's CD. "And you?"

"I've forgotten some important documents that I brought home to read and the client needs them sent off today."

He wasn't listening but I needed to get him out of the sitting room so I could get the address book that was by the phone along with the guest list.

"Dad, is that the bathroom tap I can hear?"

"Go switch it off, no wasting water here," he indicated with his hand.

I went upstairs. It would take a burglary to move him.

"Oh my God," I screamed.

"What?"

"No!" I gasped.

"What?"

I remained silent while he made his way up, huffing and puffing.

"Have we been burgled?" I asked, looking around his bedroom.

"The burgled where?"

"Here."

"Don't be the fool, Nina; this is the mess. You are not cleaning in the house, you doing nothing so I wait for Kavitha and then she . . ."

Before he had an opportunity to finish I ran downstairs, grabbed the address book and shouted, "Got to go, Dad, will see you this evening."

I got back to the office and began calling up all my relatives asking them if they had received an invitation to Foruki's exhibition. Most of them didn't know what I was talking about and congratulated me, thanking Bhagavan that I was finally getting married. Others who had received invites to the exhibition wanted to know why they couldn't come after all. It was a lengthy process to sort it all out and took the rest of that day — hours that I didn't have.

That evening, my dad and I had been invited to Raj's house for dinner but he said he was sick with a stomach bug and didn't want to make it worse. Raj's mother had her checklist and itinerary out and asked if I had managed to organise the cake.

"Yes. Raj and I will go and see them on Saturday."

"I've organised a band to play at the reception," she said.

"Indian music?"

"No, no, none of that. A good band, play at Daddy's golf functions. Latest pop songs."

"If Nina wants Indian music I'm sure we can arrange it," Raj insisted.

She ignored him. "Pretty much all done then. When is your mother coming back from India, Nina?"

"This Saturday."

"And she said she was speaking to her priest, no?"

"Yes, I think she's already done it but I'm not too sure."

"Just in case he can't do it, I've organised someone. Our priest can step in at the very latest moment; Daddy and I know him very well."

She knew everyone very well: should my mother's priest be taken ill she had a stand in; there was a stand in for everyone except the bride and groom. This wedding was going to happen no matter what.

The next morning I went into the studio to try and sort out which paintings to put in for the exhibition. There were only eight paintings which I felt were good enough to be included — I couldn't put just eight paintings into an exhibition. I had more than that but the others were experiments, some dabblings. Perhaps the best idea was to lay them all out and that way I could see how far Foruki had come.

I moved the large table to the side and laid all the pictures out on the floor in the order that I had done them, beginning with the grubby pair of black boots and ending with the hand print and then the portrait of Foruki. It went from darkness to light and in between were shades of vibrant colours; the reds from the buddha and the background of the painting with the elephants. If it were really my exhibition, I would have laid them out in this order, as each painting had a part of me and my story to tell: from the blackness and need to escape the grubby hands of the Guru to the red footprint of committing to a marriage; the inanimate bricks and stones and the constant need to believe and to keep believing and the many houses that despite being vibrant with colour still made me feel alone. But

218

it wasn't about me any more, it was about trying to turn an unknown Foruki into a success. I began rearranging the pictures.

From Obscurity to Light, I thought. That was a good title for Foruki's exhibition, not just to describe his work conceptually but also his feelings about entering the art world from the point of being a recluse and not wanting to be known. I thought about painting a black shadow on a grey background to go alongside the picture of the boots — this could be Foruki's feelings back then and then I could end the exhibition with his vibrant self-portrait alongside the handprint.

There was a knock on the door. It was Michael. I invited him in and tried to make him feel welcome by tidying up the clutter on the battered chair so he could sit somewhere, but he said he was fine standing.

"Completely understandable. Don't want to get your suit dirty."

"No, no, it's not that, I want to help you arrange your paintings," he said, taking his jacket off. He was wearing a pale blue shirt with faint white pinstripes that were hardly noticeable. His shoulders were broad; they looked like they could carry the weight of the world and still remain strong.

"Before I forget, here is your contract. Get a lawyer to check it over," he smiled, handing it over to me.

He had sturdy, dependable hands; hands that were . . . I had to stop myself thinking about them.

"Thank you," I said, taking the envelope and putting it to one side.

We discussed what each of the paintings would mean to Foruki and he helped me rearrange them.

At times our hands brushed past each other's and I had to tell myself to get a grip as I felt like a coy protagonist in an Indian film; thinking all that was missing was the wet sari, the rain scene, and a tree for Michael to pop out from behind and for us to dance around.

"So when are you thinking of going back to New York?" I asked.

"When I'm happy that the gallery is in safe hands."

I hoped it would take him a while to find someone to run it.

"Don't your family miss you when you spend so much time away?"

"My family are based in Ireland." I knew this already but I wanted to know if he would say the word girlfriend. He had to have a girlfriend in New York.

"Where in Ireland?" I asked, trying to escape my thoughts.

"Galway. Have you been there?"

I told him I hadn't, missing out the fact that I hadn't really been out of London much. My dad didn't believe in holidays: "Peoples, they pay to see anything. If I paint the house pink and put 'Taj Mahal of Croydon' they'll come, you'll see that, Kavitha," he said to my mum once after she hinted that she would love to go somewhere.

Michael began to describe Galway; rugged countryside and rough seas: "You can't help but be captivated by it. It's one of the most beautiful places to paint. Even in

220

winter it has something special. People say that winter is when it's at its most depressing, but when everything is seemingly dead, that's when all the elements really come together."

Michael asked me where I was brought up. I thought about Croydon and its elements, most notably the tramp and his dog who sat on the corner of the High Street each day; and it was hard to make it sound as exciting, more so in winter, so I said London.

He told me his family had always supported him and allowed him to do whatever he wanted, even when he chose to go and study art in the States. The struggle, therefore, when he had finished was entirely with himself and trying to make a go of it alone. "You're fortunate and they must be so proud," I replied, thinking of my dad preparing me for my career with the *Encyclopaedia Britannica*, the path he had chosen for me and the list of men I was presented with. Perhaps it's harder when you have the luxury of choice and the struggle is internally and not externally. If Dad had said to me, "Goes on, Nina, be an artist," where would I have ended up? It would have come too easy. Would I have relished every moment of painting as I did now?

We could have spent hours more talking but I was aware that he had a launch to prepare for and many other things to do, besides helping me, so I thanked him for his time and said I could manage on my own. He looked surprised and I realised it sounded ungrateful and had come out all wrong but I was too proud to say that what I really meant was that I wanted him to stay for as long as he wanted to.

I understood what my dad meant when he said Cilla was like dynamite. He clearly felt attracted to her but admired her from afar, in his world of fantasy. That was what I felt about Michael. It was hard not to admire him, to be intrigued by him, but it was safe to admire him because I knew nothing could come of it; he probably just felt sorry for me and thought that I needed all the help I could get. He was probably attached — there was no way a man like that would not have been attached — and anyway he would be going home to whoever was waiting for him and I was getting married.

After he left I tried not to miss his presence and began finding things to clean. I didn't have to be someone else when he was around; he saw me as I was, in my space, and accepted me. When I'd cleaned the brushes for the fifth time I decided to open the envelope and sit and read the contract. For some reason there were two contracts. One was for the artist Foruki, who was represented by me. I skimmed through it — the terms and conditions were standard and it stipulated that Foruki's work was to be exhibited for four weeks. And then I flicked through the other contract thinking that it was an addendum of some sort. My name jumped out at me where it said "Artist's Name". It didn't make any sense. Thinking that there had been an error I went back to the beginning and read word by word, line by line, and almost fell off my chair by the time I got to the end.

The other contract was for me; for me to have my first exhibition as myself in a year's time with Artusion.

222

I couldn't believe it; nobody except Ki had shown that much faith in me. I read, savouring each line, each paragraph, marvelling at the possibility of having my very own exhibition, being able to share my work freely. Feelings of elation quickly returned to sobriety as a year seemed a long time away. So many things were going to happen in between now and then and having my exhibition seemed the least likely.

Stunned at his gesture, I changed out of my clothes and into my suit and went to Artusion.

Emanuel was by the entrance, giving instructions to Christophe. He stopped when he saw me. "Michael tells me the publicity is going well."

"Yes," I replied.

"Good, that's what I like to hear."

I asked to speak to Michael.

"Is there a problem, Nina?" Michael asked when I walked into his office.

"I can't accept this invitation to exhibit. I've been thinking about it and I don't want you to get into any trouble. What if someone finds out that you knew all along that Foruki doesn't exist. It's your business we're playing with and I can't do that to you."

"If it happens, I will deal with it, Nina."

"And why have you drawn up this contract for me?"

"Why not? You can hold your own as an artist, you don't need to hide behind anyone else, and in a year's time when this is all over and people have forgotten about Foruki's exhibition, I want you to come and

223

exhibit with us. I mean, we are getting something here — exclusivity."

I wanted to tell him then that it was highly unlikely because I was marrying someone else, someone who didn't even know about my need to paint or that part of my life, but instead I thanked him for his generosity and faith in me.

"Come for lunch on Sunday," he said as I left. "We can go over things properly then."

"But you're not open . . . and won't you be busy with your launch?"

"We always make time for our prospective artists," he replied.

Something had changed; someone else totally believed in me. Foruki's exhibition *had* to work. I went to the office to respond to all the telephone calls and enquiries Foruki had received. Apart from the invitation mix-up it was going well; people had begun responding, confirming that they would be there. A few journalists called to ask me to reveal his real name as I had told them all that Foruki was a pseudonym. But I refused and then they wanted specific information like how old he was and where he had exhibited: the more vague I was about him, the more they wanted to know. So I just made things up that I thought they'd like to hear: tragic childhood, substance abuse, a man who had cleaned up his act and who was ready to share his talent. The gallery details Gina had given me for Japan when I'd last spoken with her were so obscure that I knew they wouldn't bother to go and check his previous exhibitions. With what remaining time I had I worked on new canvases with a different kind of light and optimism, buoyed up by Michael's faith in me.

On Saturday morning Raj came so we could go and see wedding cakes. His mother had come with him so I didn't really get a chance to sit and talk to him like I wanted to. In fact it was pointless the both of us going because she already had her heart set on a five-tier cake with a tacky couple on top who had been made from brown marzipan.

"Cute, no?"

After a few hours of shopping with them I decided I would prefer to go with my dad and collect my mum from the airport, so I rushed off.

The plane had arrived early and we spotted my mum from a distance as we entered the arrival hall. She was wearing a sari, an overcoat and some thick woollen socks and was mopping her brow with a Kleenex. Although we were waving frantically at her and my father was bellowing out her name across the concourse, she stood at the exit squinting her eyes, clutching on to her trolley and obstructing the other passengers from meeting their relatives. The trolley was stacked high with three suitcases, two of them tied with string to fortify the contents. No doubt these contained the bridal outfits. My father and I made our way over to her.

"Ma," I said, hugging her.

My father patted her on the back.

"Raj?" She gasped, staring at the empty space between my father and I.

"He's just sorting out some bits and pieces. I'm sure he'll come around later."

She breathed a sigh of relief.

On the journey back home, my dad told her how he had had to sort out his own food as I was always too busy. He invited her to comment on his weight loss but as he seemed heavier she made a comment on how healthy he appeared given the fact that she had been away. Not satisfied with her response, he expressed his concerns about what would happen if she were to die first and wondered how I would look after him in his old age as I was never there. Before you knew it he was protesting, refusing to be put in a home.

"This is the way now, Kavitha. Old, take their pension, their house, and put them in the home."

She ignored him.

"So how are you, beta? Everything going well?"

"Yes, it's more or less all organised."

"Very good," she smiled.

My father interjected and told her about the food tasting he had had to endure and said she was lucky she hadn't come back a widow. My mum wasn't listening; her mind was on those suitcases. Eager to unwrap the goods she had brought, she asked my father to drive a little faster.

He swore pretty much at every driver who overtook him and at times didn't bother to indicate. It was moments like these I wondered how he'd survived on the buses.

"It's the woman. They should stay in the kitchen and be banned from the road."

We didn't comment. My mum was thinking about which saris would be best and I was thinking about what names to give the paintings.

As soon as we got home Mum went into the kitchen, got a knife and cut the string, unlocking the cases. She didn't even bother to take off her coat.

"What do you think, beta?" she said, pulling out an ornate red sari and then placing one hand to her heart.

Ki had been dressed in a beautiful, plain, embroidered wedding sari for her funeral. I wanted to cry. She would laugh if she could see this, she probably could see it and would say that it looked like something a drag queen would wear. It had sparkly bits everywhere with a kitsch gold pattern.

"It's pretty," I said.

"And here, here are the bangles and the rest of the jewellery . . . And then I have bought this one for later," she said, pulling out a gold thing. "Go, go try it on."

"I'll do it later, Ma."

"Half the way around the world I've gone for you and you can't try it on?"

"All right, I'll do it now."

I went up and got changed. Maybe it wouldn't look so bad if we could take some of the tassels and sparkly bits off. After I got changed, I went downstairs. My mum burst into tears when she saw me; my dad began to sob. Red, after all, was his favourite colour.

"The beautiful," he cried.

Raj came around later and my mother sat close to him all evening.

"Nina has all her clothes," my mum said, "looks very beautiful."

The BA Baracus/drag queen look was hardly what I'd call beautiful but if it pleased them then that was the main thing. "And you, Raj, everything is done?"

"Yes, though I don't think I'll look as beautiful as Nina but everything is pretty much arranged. Mummy is happy with it all and now I just can't wait to go for it."

"Go for it?" she repeated, more as a question about what that meant precisely.

"Yes," he replied, "I certainly will."

"Meeting Raj?" my mum asked as I was sitting by the mirror putting lipstick on.

"No, just a client."

"On Sunday?"

"It's the artist I was talking to you and Dad about."

"It's a woman?"

"Yes," I replied uncomfortably, sensing that this was what she wanted to hear.

Michael had invited Emily to join us, and in a way I was relieved. It was too tense and charged when were alone. I gave her a list of people who I had contacted and we talked about concentrating only on Foruki's artwork as opposed to his personal life.

"Are you sure we can't take any pictures of him? He'll be much easier to pitch if we have a photograph."

228

"No, he's an enigma, he won't allow any."

She found this fascinating and I had to give her the whole back-story that I had made up about him.

"It's fascinating," she said. "It's all material we can use."

"Emily, I think at this stage all we want is an awareness, no features, so if you bring up his name to people that you speak to that would be really helpful," Michael said.

"Of course," she replied and then she went through the coverage she had lined up for wardrobe man.

We had lunch together and then she had to dash off somewhere.

"I'd better be going too," I said.

"Someone's waiting for you?" Michael asked.

I should have said yes, I should have told him about Raj, but again, I didn't.

Despite having every intention of leaving Michael there, I found myself walking in Green Park with him and then sat with him on the bench where the whole episode had really started. The grass that had been yanked out all those months ago had grown back, while winter had taken me through a bizarre series of events. Now everything had changed again. Those insecurities and doubts had gone and others had replaced them as I sat pretending that I didn't feel anything for this man. I felt strangely uncomfortable because I was myself with him and I hadn't been truly myself for a long time. It was effortless — the days I didn't know how to be me or how to express what I felt, I threw myself into my work and painted. But here I was articulating

229

everything that had ever meant anything to me. If only things were different and I wasn't marrying Raj.

"What's wrong, Nina?" he asked, seeing the thoughtful look on my face.

I told him about the time I sat on this bench after seeing Jean Michel. He then told me about his fiancée who had left him a month before they were supposed to get married. A few months later she was married to someone else.

"Did you love her?" I asked.

"Like I've never loved anyone," he replied.

I was going to ask him how long ago it had happened and then I answered my own question. "Five years ago?" The single-mindedness with which he had built up his galleries could only have been fuelled by a passion that had been redirected.

He nodded. "Did you love him?"

"Loads."

"Do you still think about him?"

"Yes, but it's getting better." I didn't know if it was getting better because of all the distractions I had in my life or because of the months that had passed since Jean's betrayal, but it had been a while since he had occupied the major part of my thoughts.

"It's hard to put your heart on the line and trust again after something like that," he replied.

"It's better not to," I answered. "It's all about expectation; the bigger the expectation, the harder the fall."

230

"Is that why you're hiding behind an artist who doesn't exist?"

"I don't think I'm hiding. It just happened that way."

He said that everything is planned; that we subconsciously instigate every situation we bring into our lives.

I didn't agree with that because I couldn't have planned any of this, not even subconsciously. "If that's the case you won't believe in signs, then?"

"Signs?"

"Oh, forget it."

"No, tell me."

"Maybe another day." Signs were dangerous territory. If he suddenly came out with a Matisse quote at that moment, I wouldn't know what to do.

He asked me about the scar that he had seen on my arm and I told him about my sister and how she had left.

"You never tried to find her?"

"I went to Manchester a few times, but nothing." The more I spoke to him, the more uncomfortable I felt. It was as if he was unravelling layer upon layer and eventually he would get to the real me.

"Come on, let's go, it's getting cold," I said.

We left Green Park, walked along Cork Street looking at pictures in the gallery windows, and then I felt it was time to go home; back to reality.

There were four messages from Raj, each of them sounding more and more frantic. I switched my phone back off and eventually called him when I got back home.

"Where the hell have you been, Nina?"

"Out with a friend."

"Your mother said you went out with your artist. Did you?"

"No, I went out with someone who's helping me put together Foruki's exhibition. You don't know them."

"How can I if you don't introduce me to anyone?" he shouted.

"Well it's not like you've introduced me to your friends."

As soon as I said those words, I knew what he was going to say.

"When do you want to meet them? Wednesday? Are you around then or are you going to be consumed with your Foruki."

"Are you jealous of him? There's no need to be, really."

And then he calmed down. "Baby, it's just that I hardly get to see you these days and I thought the weekends were for us."

"They are, but today I went out and I had my phone switched off . . . and that's it."

"I'm sorry," he said. "So Wednesday, is that good for you — and I'll get everyone together."

"It's fine."

"You can bring your friends along too."

"No, I'll let you meet them another time."

"Really missed you today, wanted to talk to you," he said.

"About what?"

"About nothing. That's what makes it feel so special; that I need to talk to you about nothing."

"Well, I'm back now. Don't think I'll be going anywhere."

And that was the sad truth, it was never going to go anywhere with Michael and not just because I was marrying Raj. Even if I wasn't I don't think I would have had the strength to love again or go through any of that, not after Jean Michel. Everything I had could be put on the line for my work, but not for my heart.

On Monday I went in early to the studio, put the music on full blast and began working on a new canvas. If I had to paint deception what colour would I give it? I slapped on some dark greens. What's worse, deceiving yourself or someone else? Red came to mind and so I picked up the red paint-pot. If you start by deceiving yourself, you inevitably end up deceiving other people. What if you didn't really mean to deceive anyone and found this big massive whopper of a lie in front of you and then everywhere else you looked there were more and more lies all created because of the need to be what other people wanted you to be. Red found itself on most of the canvas. There was no escaping it: the facts were that I was getting married to a man who I did not love and was organising an exhibition for a man who did not exist, and both of these lies had to work because there was too much at stake for them not to. If I tried and just stayed focused for a few more weeks, I could get through it. The thought of what lay ahead was more than I could handle right now.

I put my suit on and went to the office. Raj called to say that he'd fixed Wednesday evening with his friends and then Michael called to check if I could make it to the restaurant's official opening the following day; there would be an array of people from the art world. It would be another opportunity to spread the word about Foruki.

"Beta, priest is coming to talk to you tomorrow, make sure you are home early," my mother said when I returned home.

"But I can't."

"You must. Raj and his family are coming as well. You can tell your boss you need to leave early — you're working very hard, he will understand, just say for your wedding."

I had to be there for the launch. There was no other option.

"Can't we make it another day?"

"No, all arranged, he's coming at seven o'clock. Make sure you are here."

I went around to Mrs Onoro's house.

"Nice to see you again, Nina. You good girl. You promise to come see me soon and you come. I make tea."

We sat drinking tea and talking about her family back in Japan and about Hikito.

"Mrs Onoro, when you first met Hikito, did you know he was the one for you?"

"We good friend first, we no do no pankie."

"Pankie?"

"Hankie."

I wanted to laugh.

"But there definitely something first time I saw him, but I no want man then I want friend."

I knew how she felt.

"A friend of mine is opening a restaurant tomorrow and I wanted to ask you if you could write something that conveys luck."

"You want me to write good luck?" She looked bemused.

"If there's a way of saying it in Japanese or if there is a Japanese character you can use."

"I see . . . let me think." She went to find a pen. "Here," she said handing me a piece of paper. "More or less that say 'Go for it' in Japanese, no point in writing proverb. No one remember that. Which friend this for? It man friend?"

"Yes."

"Oohhhh."

"It's not like that."

"What it like?"

"We're good friends."

"I see. You happy with man you marry, no?" she asked suspiciously.

I nodded.

"I not sure you happy."

It was time to leave before she delved any further.

"Mrs Onoro," I said hugging her, "I'm happier for seeing you. Thank you very much for this."

The following day I covered a small canvas with a red background, and once it had dried I painted the Japanese characters Mrs Onoro had given me in black. Signing the painting with my own initials, I wrapped it up in brown paper, got changed back into my suit and went to the restaurant.

Christophe was rushing around and said Michael was upstairs in the gallery. I went up and he was dealing with wardrobe man and his agent. The agent was arguing with Michael because wardrobe man wasn't happy with where his installation was placed. It was supposed to be an enormous replica of a Bonsai tree made of wood, with cups, saucers, plates and cutlery hanging off it. The agent was arguing because it wasn't bang in the centre of the room.

"As I said it's a critique of how things that are seemingly small have a huge impact, and that's why it's got to go in the centre, not the side, not here, but in the centre."

They turned to look at me when I walked in.

Michael introduced us. The agent gave me the once-over when Michael said I was representing the Japanese artist Foruki. Wardrobe man was polite enough and shook my hand.

"If you'll just excuse me, gentlemen, for one moment," Michael said, leaving them.

We went next door to his office.

"I came because I can't make it this evening."

"Why not?"

"Family engagement that I can't get out of but I brought this for you." I handed him the parcel.

His poise and professionalism momentarily left him as he ripped it open like a child and then he laughed. "A Japanese character, not signed by Foruki but you."

"You know it's my first painting signed as me."

"It's very, very much appreciated that you've given it to me," he said, kissing me on the cheek.

It felt as if there were a hundred butterflies in my stomach. "You'd better get back to the bonsai tree," I said hastily.

"Nina, please come back later and stay for one drink if you can," he said. "It would be a good opportunity for you to meet people and introduce Foruki's exhibition."

And it was ridiculous but I was annoyed that he had said to come because of Foruki.

After tidying up my studio I went back to Artusion and on the way called my mum to say that I would be slightly late. She went hysterical and made no sense, so I asked her to put my dad on the line and I explained to him that I had to do something for an important client and my job depended on it. Nothing could come in the way of my employment, not even a priest. He told me not to worry and that he would keep the guests entertained. That was what was worrying me but maybe it wasn't such a bad idea to further expose Raj's mother to my dad. It might make her think twice about the family she was allowing her only son to marry into.

Artusion was packed with guests. The PR lady was running around Emanuel Hikatari; they were both trying to coordinate the press who wanted pictures of wardrobe man next to the Bonsai tree. There were several influential personalities from the art world present as well as celebrities who made their way into the press shot of wardrobe man on the pretext that they thought his work was fascinating and needed to tell him. I circulated among them all, listened to the chitchat and brought up Foruki's name where appropriate. Michael was extremely busy. He appeared very charismatic talking to his guests and came over to greet me when he saw me; and though I knew I could have mingled for a while longer I thought it was time to leave; they would all be waiting for me at home and Michael had guests to see to.

It was totally ridiculous. I felt jealous of all those beautiful women hovering around Michael. How silly to think that he would feel something towards me other than pity. That's probably what Jean had felt. Why was I thinking like this anyway? I wished there was a little button in my head that said stop. Stop thinking about him, you're getting married. By the time I got to the semi I had pushed all thoughts of Michael to the back of my mind.

Everybody had already congregated at home when I arrived forty minutes late. Raj's mother was furious at being kept waiting and held up her watch. My dad gestured with his hand as if to say he had done a good job in keeping them all entertained.

"I'm so sorry, the tube was stuck in a tunnel and I couldn't call."

The priest somehow managed to get up off the sofa and my mother signalled to me to bow down and touch his feet. He wore a type of loincloth and his bandy legs were exposed so while I was down there I caught a glimpse of the war wounds that he'd once told us about. Seeing as I was down anyway, I touched Raj's mother's pedicured feet, but my future father-in-law stopped me as was customary in that whole routine.

"Where's your ring?" Raj's mother asked.

Everyone turned to look at my finger. It was in my suit pocket. I had forgotten to put it back on. What could I say?

"Sometimes, when it's quite late and I'm travelling home, I take it off because . . . because I don't want to attract muggers."

"The muggers," my dad shouted. "Everywhere, even tried to take television set from me."

"We don't have that problem in Sutton," Raj's mother commented sniffily.

I reached inside my pocket and put the ring back on.

"And what's the red things in your hair, Nina?" Raj's mother asked.

"I don't know, Mummy." Oh God — had I gone to Artusion with paint in my hair?

My mother came over and had a good inspection. "It looks like paint."

"Paint?" my dad shouted.

239

"I was at an artist's studio today, it might have come from there."

"But how?" my mother asked, continuing the investigation.

"Dropped or splattered?"

"Were you with Foruki?" Raj asked suspiciously.

"No."

The priest continued slurping his tea. "Would you like any biscuits with that or some mix?" I asked in an attempt to get away from their questioning.

"We've asked him already," my mother said. "He's been waiting for you for the last hour."

"So let's not make him wait any longer."

Raj and I sat down on the floor in front of him and he explained what the wedding ceremony would entail, what he would do and what all the symbolism meant. Then he went off track slightly and started talking to us about a young couple who he had married the year before who were having difficulties. "It is not easy, but you must work hard. Western notion is romantic but it does not last. It is hard work, commitment and the understanding which do."

My dad nodded vehemently and glanced over at my mother to see if she were in agreement.

The priest then branded the word "affair" about saying that this was the Western way out of a problem and I promptly barricaded the thoughts of Michael flooding my head.

After wolfing down more savouries and declining the invitation to stay for dinner, he said it was time to go; he had to be off as he had taped *EastEnders*. My

240

mother helped him up and then we had to do the feet routine all over again.

"Such a nice couple," he said, pinching our cheeks. "I know you'll be very happy together."

This was my cue to put my hands together in prayer pose to thank him for the blessing and perhaps for Raj to slip some kind of donation into his hands for the temple funds.

"It is not necessary," he said, taking the money.

Raj's mother wasn't very impressed by him and after he had left she said she hoped he did not ramble on as some of her guests were English and they wouldn't understand him.

"The English they likes the rambles," my dad retorted. He then went on to tell us about a passenger he had driven that day who was carrying what looked like an Indian rice sack, which she had paid £30 for. "You have been the fooled," I told her. He turned to Raj's mother. "But now it's the fashion. Give them the rambles, they likes it."

Surely Raj's mother wanted to break down at some point and take her son back?

I had to organise a van to transport the pictures to Artusion; another addition to the list of things to do. What was becoming increasingly urgent was to find titles for the paintings. I sat for hours looking at a blank canvas, hoping that something would come, but all I felt were doubts and more doubts. How had it all got to this stage? There wasn't even the possibility of postponing the wedding; everything was pretty much organised and there wasn't a valid reason to delay things. I went to the office and sorted through the RSVPs and drew up a guest list. What if nobody came to the exhibition? I debated whether to chase the people who had not responded but then I thought it would make Foruki seem desperate: he was supposed to not care who turned up.

The phone rang. It was Radio 4; they were doing a series to coincide with the opening of the Tate Modern and wanted me to join a discussion about the relevance of the Turner Prize.

I was shocked. "I'm sorry to be rude but where did you get my contact details?"

"You do represent Fuki, don't you?"

"Foruki, yes."

"You were speaking to the producer about him and she said you were a good person to have on air as you were quite vociferous in your views. You said that the Turner was about hype, egos and personalities and that you represent an artist who doesn't even use his real name as he doesn't want to be known."

"Was it an exhibition?"

"Excuse me?"

"When I spoke to your producer? Was it at an exhibition?"

"I don't know."

I couldn't go on radio, people would recognise me, and anyway what would I say? "I would love to participate but I'm incredibly busy at the moment. Maybe another time?"

"It shouldn't take too long. Just half an hour of your time tomorrow?"

Maybe it wouldn't be so bad; the only people I really didn't want to listen to me were Mum and Dad and this was hardly likely as any radio programme they listened to had to have Hindi songs blasting out of it. And Raj would be at work. Thinking that it might be an opportunity for Foruki to have a bit of exposure before his exhibition, I reluctantly agreed.

Michael hadn't called. We usually spoke almost every day but I didn't bother to call him either. It was best for everyone if we kept our relationship strictly professional from now on. He was kind and courteous to me as he was to everyone; I saw that yesterday at the launch. It was just in his nature. What was I thinking of?

Later that evening I went to meet Raj and his friends. He had chosen our Italian restaurant in Covent Garden and I had got there early. I was absolutely dreading it and so had had a few drinks before they came.

Pinkie, Saf, Mel, Din and Hitin came in a group headed by Raj. I felt envious at seeing them all together and then felt guilty about feeling that way so I overcompensated with the friendliness. He introduced us all. Pinkie, one of the girls, had her arm around Raj. I wasn't jealous of this, not even annoyed; in fact I wanted her to tell me at some point in the evening that they were having a passionate affair and that she was madly in love with him but she didn't. I also wanted to dislike them but I couldn't as they made me feel very welcome in their group, going out of their way to include me in a past that I didn't share with any of them.

"Raj talks about you all the time, Nina. Are you excited about the wedding?"

"Yes." Realising that my answer sounded flat and that it needed to be resuscitated, I started talking nonstop about the dress, the venue and how I was trying to find out where Raj had booked for the honeymoon.

"It's a surprise, baby," he said, leaning over and kissing me.

And then we talked about how we met and what each of us felt when we first saw each other.

"I knew from the very first moment I saw her," he said. "You pretty much knew too, didn't you, baby? In fact it was just after the second date that we decided to get engaged."

I thought back to his gelled hair, his inside-out T-shirt, his strong aftershave, and then Jean Michel coming to the door of the semi.

"Sometimes things just happen," I replied.

By the end of the evening, after a few more glasses of wine, the girls were exchanging numbers with me, promising that they would call and we would meet without Raj.

On the way home, Raj suddenly asked, "There are no secrets between us, baby, are there?"

Only about a dozen or so, I thought. "What makes you ask me that now?"

"It's just that sometimes I get the impression that there is so much about you that I still don't know about?"

"Like what?" I asked nervously.

"Your friends."

"If you want to meet my friends I can arrange it."

"It's not just that; these last two weeks you've been distant."

"Only because this new exhibition means so much and there's so much to think about with the wedding. It's a big step."

"It will all be over soon," he said, squeezing my hand.

"I know," I replied. "I know."

On Thursday morning I made my way to Broadcasting House. How had I managed to get on to Radio 4? It just wasn't possible to instigate these things subconsciously, whatever Michael said. The other members of the panel were a Professor of Art from Goldsmiths College and one of Turner's distant relatives. I sat wondering what on earth I was doing there.

The presenter introduced the other guests first and then turned to me.

"We also have Nina Savani from the agency Kendal Brown who is currently working with an artist who doesn't want to be known; a bit of a contradiction in there somewhere?" she sniffed.

Why did she sniff like that? Didn't she believe he existed? Was there a problem? Remain calm, Nina, and answer the question like Foruki would want to, I thought.

"It's not that my artist doesn't want to be known, he just doesn't want to be bigger than his work and this is what is increasingly happening. More and more we are living in an age where it is about celebrity, hype and PR stunts, and the quality of the work is overlooked. I think Turner would be disappointed to what his name is now being associated with."

His relative was nodding her head.

"Turner was ahead of his time and he would be rejoicing at the fact that many of these artists are ground-breaking and that they have brought art into a new dimension," the professor interjected.

"I would hardly call a wardrobe ground-breaking," I interjected.

The professor then replied immediately, "Yes, but then he has added to the debate; one must ask the question, 'What is art?' Surely it's about having a seminal idea in history in terms of art culture?" And then he began giving some spiel about conventionalism and used long words so no one could really follow his argument. All that was going through my mind when he spoke were my father's words: "Gives them the rambles, they likes it."

Sensing that her boat was heading towards an iceberg, the presenter asked Turner's relative for her opinion. She quietly said she thought it was important to bring the subject matter back to paintings.

The professor was off again, saying that paintings were prehistoric and taking art backwards and I argued

246

with him about art being about self-expression as opposed to self-absorption. It sounded good and it would have sounded better if it were true and if I was actually there as the artist.

In the closing stages of the debate, the presenter turned to me and asked me about Foruki. "Does this mean your artist would be completely averse to being on the short list for the Turner Prize?"

"Foruki, and this speaks for itself as it is not even his real name, would not want to be bigger than his paintings. I think for him he feels he would have done his job if his pictures are taken for what they are and not who he is." The likelihood of Foruki being on the short list was as likely as my wedding being called off but it was good to make it sound as if it was a possibility; it added more kudos.

"He wants to express himself yet he doesn't want to be known?" the professor laughed.

Hold it together, Nina, believe in your argument. "Your point being, Professor Landstein?"

He was about to go off again when the presenter hastily stepped in and closed the debate with a few last words from each of her guests. The news bulletin mercifully cut off the professor.

That afternoon the phone did not stop ringing: Foruki was in demand, people wanted to know where they could see his work. Michael called to say that people were ringing up Artusion requesting invitations to Foruki's opening night. He asked me to drop some more around if I could so Emily could deal with it.

In the evening I went to Artusion and as Christophe greeted me I spotted Jean Michel sitting at one of the tables. A sense of dread and panic filled me: why of all places was he here, and tonight of all nights? He was with a group of people and hadn't seen me so I decided to make a swift exit.

"I've forgotten something, Christophe," I said hastily. At that moment Emanuel Hikatari stopped me suddenly. "Leaving already?" He had sprung from nowhere and had positioned himself so that he was obstructing the door.

"Yes, I was just saying to Christophe that I've forgotten something. Congratulations, by the way, on your launch," I said, attempting to leave.

"Thank you, we couldn't have expected more."

Then I heard his voice. "Nina, Nina, I thought it was you. How are you?"

My heart was beating incredibly fast. "Fine, thank you, Jean," I said, taking a deep breath and introducing everyone.

"Pleased to meet you. Hope you are enjoying your meal, Ms Savani, I must leave you. Michael tells me it's going well and that there has been lots of press interest. Good to hear." Emanuel left us.

Jean looked at me.

"We're having an exhibition here for one of my artists."

248

"But you've left Whitter and Lawson. I tried calling you there."

"I've set up on my own now, working for a Japanese artist," I answered almost too quickly. Would that have sounded odd to him? Wasn't I the person who procrastinated over every decision and had to weigh up the pros and cons.

"That's fantastic, you're looking really well. It's so good to see you, Nina," he said clasping the sides of my shoulders.

It felt very uncomfortable.

"You're looking well too," I replied, thinking he seemed to have lost half his body weight and needed to be fed. I almost felt sorry for him and had to tell myself that he had betrayed me; he had betrayed me when I needed him the most.

"Are you still getting married, Nina?"

"Yes, in a month's time," I said coldly.

"That's quick."

"Better to say yes quickly before you find them with someone else." And as soon as I'd said that I regretted it because it showed him that he still affected me and what I wanted was for him to return to his table and leave me alone.

"No more than I deserve. As long as it's not a rebound thing, you know, you can't have known him that long. All of . . ."

". . . A week," I replied. "It is possible to meet someone and feel you've known them a lifetime." And this was true — perhaps not in relation to Raj, but it was true.

"Are you in love?"

How dare he ask me if I was in love.

"Yes," I replied defiantly. "Anyway, I have to go. It was nice seeing you again. Take care of yourself."

"You too, maybe we can . . ."

I walked away before he could finish his sentence, trying to hold my poise as I went up to the gallery in an attempt to show that he had not affected me.

There were a few people studying the bonsai tree. The porcelain appeared so fragile hanging off the branches, as if should a huge gust of wind come unexpectedly from nowhere it would send the whole thing crashing to the floor. Perhaps it wouldn't be the wind but a careless waiter blown into the direction of the tree. Maybe in life you have to factor in the unexpected so there is no room for disappointment. That was what my parents did; they always had a sense of mistrust about the good things that happened because they knew that the wind wasn't far behind, and that was probably why they sought stability in the things that they knew; that was why their marriage worked.

The priest was right, romantic notions of love were fleeting. How was it possible to feel so strongly for someone and then have another person come into your life and feel the same in only a matter of months? Love was fickle, just as life was. Love led to disappointment. Raj was stable, he would always be stable and it would last because with him there was no room for disappointment; no room to get hurt.

I sat in a corner of the room watching the way the light fell and the patterns the cutlery hanging from the tree made on the floor. They were intricate patterns like the web of deceit I was weaving and I think I knew then that the biggest lie was the one I was telling myself — but then one lie led to another and everything had become so embroiled that it was just impossible to see clearly. I clung to the fact that Raj came into my life when I most needed him and there had been a sign that he was the right one.

Michael came and pulled up a chair opposite me.

I handed him the invitations.

"What's wrong?"

What could I say? That I was getting married in a month but was feeling angry that he hadn't called me earlier; that I was jealous at seeing all those women hanging around him at the launch; that I had seen Jean Michel downstairs and he had provoked feelings in me but they weren't as strong as the ones Michael did; that I was unable to do anything with these emotions except pretend that they weren't there.

"I don't think I can do this any more."

"There have been many times when I have felt like that but you have to hold your nerve and you'll get through it. You've come this far, don't let it go, Nina. I know it will be a success."

"You don't understand, people are going to get hurt, I can feel it, and it will be all my fault; it's just such a mess, a big mess."

"Who's going to get hurt? There's only me and if it goes wrong I can handle it. I only take on what I know

251

I can handle." It was time to tell him about Raj. I glanced over at the tree, trying to find the right words.

"They all went for it," he said, indicating the tree.

"I never thought I'd hear myself say this but it's not bad. All those patterns the light is reflecting on the floor."

"It still can't beat a good painting. Have you thought any more if you are going to get a Japanese man to stand in for your artist? Because if you need anyone, I know someone completely trustworthy."

"No, it's better if Foruki isn't present."

"It adds to the enigma?"

"No, no more lies," I sighed, and just as I was about to tell him about Raj he asked me if I'd eaten.

"No, but —"

"Let me go down and get one of the waiters to bring us up something."

"I've got something I want to tell you," I said as Michael came back.

"Me too," he replied.

I thought it was something about the PR or to do with my paintings so I let him go first, thinking that it was better to get the superficial things out of the way.

He was struggling with his words; I'd never seen him struggle with them. "I was thinking that if you . . ." he reached out for my hand and touched my fingers. My heart nearly jumped out and I felt as though I was going to be sick.

". . . It's just that I'm going back to the States after your exhibition but I can stay if you —"

And before I could stop him and explain, he was interrupted.

"Just came to say goodbye, Nina."

It was Jean Michel. I quickly took back my hand and had to introduce them both.

"Pleased to meet you," Jean Michel said. "I just wanted to wish you the very best for . . ." he stared at me.

"Please don't say it," I willed, expecting to hear the word "wedding".

". . . for the exhibition," he continued. "I'm sure it will be very successful."

And then he left.

Jean Michel had thrown me. What I felt when Michael touched my hand made me want to get up and run. The level of intensity could lead nowhere but disaster.

"I'm sorry, I have to go," I replied, collecting my things together.

Once I got home I called Raj. He didn't pick up the phone so I left a message. "Raj, shall we just do something spontaneous and get married tomorrow, just go to the register office and get married? Why not? Let's do it."

And then I went to sleep.

The phone rang early next morning.

"Nina, what is this about the register office? I know you can't wait, I can't wait either, but Mummy will go mad."

"I was tired and it was all getting to me. You know when you just want everything to be over so you can just get on with things. Not have to think any more."

"That's why Mummy has taken care of it, so you don't have to think; and baby, it's not long to go now."

"I know, I know, I'll get through it."

I went into the restaurant that morning with every intention of explaining to Michael but he was uncharacteristically aloof and wholly professional, wanting to discuss where the pictures would go and the labels that needed to be made up. Not once did he bring up what had happened the night before and when I tried he said he understood the situation perfectly and asked me to leave it. And maybe it was just better to leave it.

After going back to the studio I painted more blacks, greens and reds; a whirlwind of deceit that had to stop. And seeing the other canvases, the titles suddenly just came to me; I named them in the colour that was most predominant. The paintings would begin with black and end in indigo. The print of the hand would be called *Beyond Indigo*, colours that I knew existed but I was unable to capture. What lay beyond indigo I didn't know, but all I had to do was get through the opening night and the rest would work itself out.

On Sunday Raj's mother had invited me over for lunch so I could meet her friends before the wedding. The drive was like a BMW showroom with the personalised

254

number-plates giving me an indication as to who would be present.

"Hi baby," Raj said opening the door. He kissed me.

"Raj, it's not that I don't like you calling me baby but I love the way Nina sounds when you say it." If I nicely corrected the little things that niggled me, the other things would be fine.

"But everyone calls you Nina and you are my baby."

"But nobody says Nina the way you do."

His mother screeched out my name. "See," I smiled.

Her eyes gave me the once-over and she tried not to appear too disappointed in my choice of clothes and then blew two air kisses because she didn't want her lip-gloss or her foundation to smudge. Maybe it wasn't such a bad idea to have her at Foruki's exhibition; she would fit in well.

"Come in, come in, everyone is waiting for you. I've asked all the men to leave, Daddy has taken them to his golf club. Raj, you can go now too."

He obeyed her instructions. If Raj wasn't around her too much then perhaps that would make him change too. He said goodbye to me as she hauled me into her sitting room where a group of ladies who looked like they had been cloned were sitting, waiting in anticipation.

Raj's mother went round the room introducing them but they were all pretty much identical: dripping in diamonds, sporting matching handbags and Gucci sandals with pedicured feet, a far cry from my mum's friends who sank to the bottom of the Land of Leather sofas in their ample salwars, sandals and woolly socks, and their centre-parted hair and large red dots. One set compared the price of a Gucci handbag, the others haggled over the cost of a marrow. It was mind-boggling how the honchos had managed to arrange a union between the two families and how Raj's mother had accepted my parents without deporting them from her home for entry under false pretences.

"Nina's a lawyer and works with lots of famous people. In fact we're going to an exhibition next week that she's organising for a famous Japanese Emperor."

"What's his name?" one of them squealed.

"Foruki."

"Yar, Foruki, I think my son deals with his investments."

The conversation revolved around shopping, celebrities and beauty tips. They wanted superficial so I gave them superficial and even pretended to heed the advice of a pencilled-brow woman who suggested threading my eyebrows further back so that it would accentuate my eyes.

I almost had some depth of conversation with one of them who had her own personal Guru who was advising her on all matters spiritual. The Guru had also made her do that coconut-over-the-bridge routine.

"Is his name Guru Anuraj?"

"No, no, his Holiness is Guru Rama. You must come home one evening to meet him. He only deals with very special people."

"Do you pay him?"

"Only donations to the temple funds."

I told her to be careful but she took offence, saying that the problem with westernised career girls was they thought they knew it all, and then I was whisked away by Raj's mother asking me to describe my wedding outfit.

After lunch Raj's mother insisted on waiting for Raj so he could drop me home but I needed to walk and to think.

Would I be like these women in twenty years' time? Starting off with no intention of being anything like them and then finding myself looking back as one of them? There was no backing out now so it wasn't even worth thinking about. The biggest of my worries were not my parents not speaking to me but what Raj's mother would do to them if I called it off; at best they would be humiliated and never be allowed to step foot in the community. I went to my studio to paint; in painting there were always answers.

I hung up my sari in the suit holder and changed into my other clothes then began mixing colours. There was a knock on the door.

"Michael?"

The door was pulled open. First I saw a pair of boots and then long blonde hair.

"Not Michael," an Australian voice giggled.

"Gina! You're back early."

"Don't panic, you've still got the studio for another week."

"How was it?" I asked, putting down my brush and hugging her.

"It was the best." She looked around the room. "Far out, you've moved on from birds. This is bloody fantastic. Has anyone seen this stuff?"

"It's a bit of a long story but I'm in the middle of organising an exhibition for Tastudi Mangetti."

"Not *the Mangetti*?"

I nodded.

"No bloody way! Go on, tell me."

"It's a bit complicated."

"I want to hear; all of it."

So I told her everything, starting with the Guru and ending with the forthcoming exhibition at Artusion.

She had her mouth half-open with disbelief.

"Why didn't you call me? Even if it was just to unburden yourself?" she said.

"I thought about it but then if I explained it all to you and said it out loud and heard myself, I wouldn't have gone through with it — it would have just seemed too insane. And then there's the rest."

"Go on," she said.

"My parents don't know that I'm painting. Every day I've been putting on a suit, pretending to go to work, when really I've been coming here. To throw them off the scent I arranged to see this guy who they wanted me to meet. I'm getting married next month."

"No!" she exclaimed. "Do you love him?"

"I think I can grow to love him if I just focus on the good stuff. I know I can. He's nice, really nice and kind."

"Does he know about all of this?"

I shook my head.

"God, Nina, there's more to it than being nice and kind, there's honesty and . . ."

"I know, but you don't understand — the wedding is in four weeks; there are six hundred and fifty guests. It's all arranged. Mum and Dad are so proud of me. It's been the only time that I've done something that they're so proud of, and I have to go through with it, there is no way out."

"But what about the paintings? And Mangetti's interest? I'm sure if you tell them they would be proud."

"No, they'd be horrified. I don't know if they would be more horrified at the fact that I paint or that I have been deceiving them."

"And who's Michael?"

"What?"

"When I knocked on the door, you said 'It's open, Michael.'"

"He's . . ."

"Oh no, Nina, don't tell me you've got another guy."

"It's complicated."

I told her all about Michael, how he had come into my life from nowhere and what he had done for me.

"But I can't do anything, I don't know what to do. How I feel about Michael is how I felt about Jean Michel and look where that got me. The right thing and the only thing is to get married to Raj. You know, the first time I met him he gave me the Matisse quote, surely that's a sign?"

"Sometimes you only see what you want to see."

"What am I going to do, Gina?"

259

"Concentrate on getting this exhibition together, get through it and the rest will follow. Tell me what needs to be done — I'll help in any way I can."

After we talked some more, she left saying that she would be back in the morning. It was a relief to have her back.

Gina was sent; Mrs Onoro was sent — these were the only things I knew for sure.

Mrs Onoro was in her dressing gown when I went to see her later that evening.

"What wrong my dear?"

"Nothing, Mrs Onoro, I just wanted to have a chat, that's all."

She looked at her watch.

"I'm sorry it's late."

"No it not late," she replied, taking the watch off and banging it. "It just that it normally tick loud, must have stopped. Come in, I make you tea."

I sat in her lounge staring at the porcelain cats.

"There," she said putting the tray down. "It is about man friend who I write 'go for it'? He go for it but it not right."

I nodded. "It's just that I don't want to hurt anyone."

"Hurt, it part of life. Accept it part of life and it easier."

"What about stability? Making sure that things are secure."

"It not exist, you know that. It excuse for not doing things."

"What about doing the right thing?"

"There no right or wrong thing; there only best decision at that time; maybe good maybe bad but you make it based on heart. You make bad decision when based on head."

"What if you don't know what your heart is telling you?"

"You always know; sometime you don't want to listen."

I sat a while longer talking about the plans for Foruki's exhibition. She yawned and said she would do a special prayer so it would all go smoothly.

"I'm very lucky to have you." I told her.

"You good girl, Nina," she said as I left. "You welcome any time, day or night." She looked at her watch again.

Gina came early the next morning and we began cleaning the pictures up and attaching picture fasteners. She talked about that first day she had seen me in the cafeteria at the Tate and felt compelled to speak to me, despite the fact that I seemed so totally unapproachable and moody. I told her that I thought she was a traveller who needed a sofa for the night.

"And there was that quote. Complete lunatic," I laughed. "You're worse than me. Who goes around cafeterias spouting quotes to complete strangers? Definitely desperate, I thought."

Then she began mimicking the way I asked if Matisse was her favourite painter.

"And what's with that flowers quote anyway?" I asked. "I was only trying to see flowers when there were clearly none and now this whole bloody forest has sprouted out of nowhere."

Gina laughed.

"I mean what kind of crazy woman throws a coconut off London Bridge and expects a miracle?"

"Not crazy, just grieving," Gina replied seriously. "When my mum died, I went to a faith healer who blew all the negativity out of my ears."

We looked at each other and burst into uncontrollable laughter.

"Did it work?" I managed.

"Like hell it did."

"But you know, it isn't just about seeing what you want to see or seeing what's not there. I had the most amazing experience a few months after mum died. One night when I couldn't sleep because the decision to go to England was really weighing on me, I felt my feet being rubbed. Mum did that when I was little and nervous or anxious about something. She's always with me, I know she is, and it's not because I want to believe it."

I told her about the Reiki healer and Ki being there.

"So how can you still doubt, Nina?"

"I doubt to protect myself. For example, if I say that I doubt my feelings for Michael that means I don't have to make that decision, I don't have to risk anything. I don't have to fear he'll go and do the same thing as Jean. If I say that I know it's him, I just know, don't even ask me how but I do, it means an awful lot of people get hurt.

"How have I let it get this far anyway? It was one lie that has spiralled so out of control, and all because I wanted to sell a few paintings to prove something."

"I know, Nina, but you have to make the best of it. I mean, you've got Tastudi Mangetti's interest so you've got to focus on getting through the exhibition. Try to put everything else to the back of your mind; deal with that later and just get through this now."

Gina helped me for the rest of that week. Whenever I stopped to consider not going through with the wedding I heard my father's voice saying, "I'm the proud'; I saw my mother with the contents of the jewellery box sprawled across the floor; I heard the priest telling us about western notions of romantic love; I heard Raj saying how much he loved me; and I imagined what Raj's mother would do to my parents. All these thoughts were put to the back of my head as I focused on making Foruki a success.

The day before the exhibition we hired a van to transport the pictures to Artusion. Michael came down to the restaurant and arranged for the pictures to be unloaded and taken up. I introduced him to Gina. When he turned his back she pretended she was going to pass out and made some swooning gesture. The wardrobe man's bonsai tree had been removed from the gallery and in its place was an exotic Japanese flower arrangement.

Michael was polite and courteous but kept the conversation to a minimum. At times I could tell he wanted to laugh at some of the comments Gina and I made. We stuck to the layout Michael and I had discussed but after we had finished arranging the paintings it still didn't feel right. The colours seemed to clash with each other and even before I voiced this he said it, and so we had to rethink the whole thing. It was seven o'clock when Gina said she had to leave as she was about to begin her shift at the restaurant where she had just started working. I called my parents to tell them I would be late again.

There was an awkward silence between Michael and I that I was unable to fill. I thought about doing something drastic like pretending to fall off the stepladder so I could get his attention but on reflection thought that this was manipulative. Not that conning the entire art world wasn't, of course.

"Would you like something to eat, Nina?" he asked.

"Only if you speak to me."

"I am talking to you."

"Properly."

Later, Michael went around earmarking some of the paintings. "Just makes him more in demand."

"But I've told Mangetti that he gets first option on all of them."

"All the more reason to earmark them then."

"I think I'll be at a loss as to what to do after. You can just get so lost in it all; it's like another world."

"You'll paint more, you have an exhibition to do for us."

I wondered if that would ever happen. Would Raj understand my need to paint? I thought about being Raj's wife, having to produce the first grandchild soon after and painting the odd picture now and then. How would I cope? Would this be enough for me?

We ate and spoke about everything other than what we really wanted to. After dinner we got back to work.

"About the other night," I began.

"It's all right, Nina, totally understandable, you're not over Jean."

"No, it's not that . . ." Before I had a chance to explain Michael went to dim the lights so we could see what the gallery would look like for the exhibition. The room felt magical. Fiery oranges and reds balanced against sedate colours, bringing them to life. There were no shadows; only light.

"It's beautiful, I can't believe we've done this."

"You've done this," he replied.

"Thank you, thank you for everything, thank you for believing in me." I went over to kiss his cheek.

My lips lingered on his cheek for a second longer than they should have. He turned his head slightly and his nose brushed against mine. This overwhelming impulse just to kiss him took over me — not to think about anything else but to do it. He touched the back of my neck with his hand. It felt warm and safe. I looked up at him, held his gaze and then I let him kiss me.

And for a while nothing else existed in the world but the two of us.

"I've been waiting a long time to do that," he whispered.

I marvelled at how happy and safe I felt. He took hold of my left hand and kissed my fingers.

"I never thought that I would feel like this again," he said. And that's when the enormity of what I had done struck me.

"Me neither," I said, tears welling in my eyes. I knew that someone was going to get hurt and I didn't want it to be him.

"Don't cry, Nina, we'll be fine. I'll never do anything to hurt you."

I buried my head in his arms and we held each other for a long time. It was getting very late.

"Let me take you home," he said.

"I've got this big van that I've got to drive back home in."

"I'll drive you."

"No, I'll be fine. There are just a few things I need to think about, clear my head."

He nodded. "It's a big day tomorrow. Call me as soon as you get home."

Michael walked me to my van and began laughing at the state of it; it was a big, dirty, beat-up van.

"It's the only one they had."

He kissed me again.

All I thought about was Michael as I drove home. Raj didn't even enter into the equation until I got to our front door and stepped over the threshold of the semi. As soon as I got in I called Michael saying that there were things that we needed to talk about.

"After the exhibition," he said. "You just concentrate on getting through that."

And that's what I decided to do, sort the whole mess out as soon as the opening night was over. It was a relief to have actually decided on something.

My dad woke me up the next morning with his shouting.

"Nina, it's seven o'clock, you will be the late."

"Don't have to go in today until later," I screamed back. "What?"

I put on my dressing gown and went downstairs.

"Don't have to go in until later. We have an important exhibition on today — you know, for that Japanese man — so they've given me the morning off because I have to work in the evening."

"We haven't seen you for days, beta, everything all right?" my mum asked.

"Fine," I replied, thinking about the kiss, what I'd say to them, what I'd say to Raj.

"We've got new neighbours," my dad interrupted.

"Really?" I tried sounding enthusiastic.

"Yah, look," he pulled up the net curtains and pointed to my van.

Oh God, how was I going to explain the van? "That's mine, Dad."

He stared at me, completely baffled.

"As I said, we have this really important exhibition on and last night I helped transport the artists' paintings."

"This is not making the sense to me. You still a lawyer, no? Why you taking pictures in dirty van? Artist is so poor he not got anyone to do this job. How can he afford you?"

It was the perfect opportunity to come clean with everything but it was the day of the exhibition and one more day wouldn't make a difference.

"It's a favour. I went out of my way to help."

"It's a woman, no?" my mum asked hastily.

"Foruki, now does that sound like a woman to you?"

"Foruki," she paused for thought. "Yes, a woman," she replied.

"And you still have your job? And everything is good?" my dad added.

My stomach felt as though it was tied in knots. "What would I be driving around in a van for if I didn't have a job, Dad?"

"Everybody want the favours today, nobody want to pay. I say no when they ask me to repair the television for nothing. This is what I say. Don't drive in dirty van, Nina. You're a lawyer, what will peoples say if they see you?"

Later I called Gina to tell her what had happened with Michael.

"I'm just amazed how you waited that long — he's gorgeous! Have you told Raj and your parents?"

"No, not yet. I'm going to leave it all until after the exhibition; then I'll deal with it."

"Yes, you need to focus, put it to the back of your mind."

268

"How?"

"Think of the consequences if you don't."

But Raj and his mother were coming that evening. They'd see Michael — surely they'd sense that there was something between us. It wasn't right, Raj needed to be told properly. I called him up in a vain attempt to dissuade them both from coming to the exhibition.

"No, baby, I mean Nina, it's no problem."

"It's full of boring types and I know it's not going to be Mummy's thing."

"No, baby, she's really looking forward to it. So am I, I want to see this Foruki chap."

"He won't be there, he rarely turns up at his exhibitions."

"Well, we want to come to support you but you won't even notice that we are there. We'll act like we don't know you like I promised."

"Raj, there's something else you need to know. Can we make time tomorrow evening?"

"What is it, baby?"

"It's best if we sit down and talk about it tomorrow."

I went to the office to sort out all the last-minute enquiries. Raj weighed heavily on my conscience. None of it was intended, I never set out to hurt him or his family. Yes, his mother was controlling and domineering but she didn't deserve this. What about the wedding guests? I thought about Michael and the kiss and then about how to tell my mum and dad. They had already had their hearts broken with Jana. How could I do it to them again? How would they hold their heads up in the community? What would I say? Where would I begin? Was it worth giving everything up on the basis of one kiss. Focus, Nina, try to focus. Tonight is not about you; Michael has his reputation, Mangetti will be there, you have to pull it off otherwise it's all for nothing. One more day and then all the lying stops. Michael left several messages on my phone but I couldn't speak to him. He didn't even know about Raj. I had misled him, misled them both. It was a mess and although I tried I couldn't put it to the back of my mind.

In painting I always found a sense of peace, but that day there was none. Both worlds were no longer separate and I couldn't keep up the pretence. I went to see Mrs Onoro in desperation.

"Mrs Onoro, it's me, Nina," I shouted through her letterbox.

She came to the door. "Bell no working, I tell Rooney to fix it but he too busy. Maybe he find girlfriend. You think he find girlfriend?"

The association of Rooney not fixing the bell and finding a girlfriend threw me and I wondered why I was standing there when there were so many things to be getting on with.

"What time is it?" Mrs Onoro asked.

"Four o'clock."

"I make us some tea."

She came back with a tray. "What can I do my dear?"

"I needed some advice."

270

She smiled proudly as if I had come to the right place. "I know keep many secret."

"Mrs Onoro, I've told so many lies, and I've made a big mess."

"Big mess, like when pig give birth, or big mess like . . ." She struggled to find a comparison.

"Yes, a big mess, like a really big mess."

"To get out of big mess you stand in the centre and you accept it," she said as if she had received wisdom from a fortune cookie.

"What if I just put it all off for a day?"

"It no matter. Big mess is big mess, today or tomorrow. Important thing to accept it."

"Thank you, Mrs Onoro, thank you."

"You no drink tea again?"

"I'll come back. I promise I will. It's just that there is somewhere I have to be."

"Always running somewhere. That why big mess come. Better to stop."

"I'll stay next time. I will."

She was right, it didn't matter if it was today or tomorrow, the most important thing was to accept it. I went home to get ready for the exhibition.

My mum was in the sitting room waiting to talk to me when I arrived.

"Can't stop now, Ma, I'm running really late and the guests will be arriving soon," I said, running upstairs.

After coming out of the bath I couldn't find the hairdryer. It had been by the mirror five minutes ago.

"Ma, have you seen the hairdryer?"

"What?"

"The hairdryer, have you seen it?"

"I'm not allowed to come, then?" she asked.

"Come where?"

"To see the Japan man?"

I imagined her standing in the centre of the gallery, waiting like she did at Heathrow airport, clutching onto her possessions and obstructing the guests, and a sense of panic filled me. "But *Astitva Ek Prem Kahani* is on. You never miss that for anyone, and anyway it's a work function and full of boring people."

"Raj's mother is going there. You are saying now she is better than me?"

"Raj's mother is only going there because she invited herself. Didn't she, Dad?"

"No big thing, Kavitha, soon she'll be part of their family anyway," he shouted up.

"Ma, I promise you, I'll make it up to you if I can, I'll make it all up to you."

"You have a surprise for me for the wedding?" This is what happened, this is how the whole mess started in the first place. I would say one thing and she would interpret it the way she wanted to. "I knew it. I knew there was something going on. It's a very big surprise?"

"It's not what you think and I want you to know that whatever happens, I love you and Dad very, very much."

She wasn't listening and went into her bedroom, opened one of the drawers and pulled out the hairdryer.

272

"Thank you, beta, thank you, I know you will never let me off."

"Down, Ma, down."

"Yah, I'm going."

"No, the word's down, and anyway, about the surprise, it's not what you . . ."

She was halfway down the stairs, telling my dad about the forthcoming surprise.

Forget about letting her down, I was going to leave her in the recess of a quagmire she would never find her way out of — and my dad, what would I do to him?

"Good a the luck, Nina," he said as I was leaving.

"What, Dad?"

"Good a the luck. We know you been working very hard for this Japan man."

Guilt, angst and nerves all knotted in my stomach ready for one volcanic explosion, but all I had to do was to get through the evening.

I got to the gallery at six-thirty. Michael was there with Emanuel, organising the waiters.

"Ms Savani, all set?" Emanuel asked.

"Yes. Thank you."

"Nina, there are a few things that I need to check with you. Would you mind coming into my office for a moment?"

"Sorry about not answering any of your messages," I said once the door shut behind us.

"I figured you would be running about today. Come here, Nina."

"No, Michael, we have to talk."

"I know but let's leave it till later. I just wanted to give you this and to wish you the very best for tonight," he said, handing me a box.

It was a paintbrush with my name engraved on it. "For when you decide not to hide behind someone else."

Forget about hiding behind someone else, I just wanted to go and bury myself somewhere. "Thank you."

"Keep your nerve and you will be fine," he said, holding my hand.

Despite the soft music, the sound of wind chimes and running water, all I could hear was the thudding noise my heart made as we went back to the gallery. I had a sinking feeling in the pit of my stomach.

"Which papers did you say were coming?" Emanuel asked.

"They haven't all confirmed but we are expecting quite a few," I replied, trying to sound confident, as if I had it all under control.

Bonsai tree/wardrobe man's agent was the first to arrive, followed by Gina and a group of people.

"They're mostly art students and are just gonna go around hyping. Nina, I can't stay for long as my shift begins soon but come around tomorrow when you've done the deed."

I nodded, almost detached from everyone and everything, pretending it was happening to someone else.

Between seven-thirty and eight a steady stream of people came. They were regulars on the circuit who went from exhibition to exhibition, strutting in a panoply of colour as if they were trying to outdo the paint on the canvas. Most of them didn't come to see the paintings and made it obvious by wearing ridiculous tinted glasses that they couldn't possibly see out of. They were there to see who came into the room and who was watching them. You could tell them any old rubbish as long as you dropped a few important names in. A bit like my dad in this sense they had very selective hearing, but theirs was sometimes made worse because of the substances they had snorted.

A few "darlings" and air kisses blew across the room; some went around appearing to study the pictures as if they warranted a huge amount of intellectual thought and then added their pretentious comments. Others were fascinated by the fact that Foruki hadn't turned up to his own exhibition; I could hear all kinds of speculation as to who he was and what his concepts were.

"Emperor's descendant . . ."

"Prince . . ."

"One of the Mykoto sons . . ."

"That's his agent over there . . ."

I circulated among them all, people that I knew, people that I didn't, and told them whatever I thought they might like to hear about the artist. The professor from the radio show was in one corner of the room studying the foot-print. A few journalists came, asked questions, drank more wine, and photographers took

275

pictures. Emanuel greeted the guests he had invited. Michael circulated, talking to people and occasionally glancing at me as if to say everything was going well.

Drink flowed, the waiters took the food around and the sound of the river and chimes were drowned out as the room became more and more crowded. There were several influential people from the art world present, but no Mangetti. My boss, Simon, was there.

"Good turn out, Nina. Tell me again where you came across this chap?"

"Last year in Japan." I told him what I had told everyone.

"I can't recollect you going to Japan." He wouldn't as I never took holidays, just worked. "OK," I wanted to say, "OK, it's all made up. There, I've never been to Japan." But then I spotted Raj and his mother coming in.

"Excuse me, Simon, I've just seen some people that I have to say hello to."

"I'm sorry, baby, we're a bit late. Mummy had to get something done."

"Remember — Nina, not baby," I added quickly.

"My fingers," Raj's mum said, swishing her nails in front of me. "It took a long time to stick on the jewels." She pointed to some tacky sparkly bits. "But I'll know now for the wedding time to leave at least two hours."

"Where's your ring?" Raj asked, looking at my fingers.

"Some people here don't know I'm getting married. Remember what we talked about before?"

"You won't even know that we are here."

276

And then I heard a familiar voice. I glanced up and wanted to curl up in a heap on the floor. "What are you doing here, Jean?"

"I wanted to wish you luck."

Raj's mother lingered as if she needed an introduction.

"Raj, if you want to take Mummy around to have a look at the pictures."

"And this handsome man is . . .?" she asked.

"This is Jean, a friend of mine."

"So nice to finally meet a friend of Nina's," Raj said, extending his hand. "Raj Mehta."

"Jean Michel Duval. When's the big day?" Jean asked.

Raj looked at me, surprised; nobody there was supposed to know that I'd let my fiancé come along to the launch. Why had Jean done that? Maybe now Raj would let his guard down and tell people we were getting married.

"Please don't do this to me," I thought. "Please just go away, all of you."

"Next month," Raj replied.

"Mummy, Raj, there's someone I would really like you to meet," I said spotting Gina.

"Gina, this is Raj and his mother. Gina works for Ravi Shankar."

"I do?" She glared at me. "Yes, I do. Nice guy."

She led them off to another part of the room. Raj's mother went reluctantly.

"Nina, I know you don't love him. You were with . . ."

"You don't have the right to tell me anything and if you'll excuse me, I have guests to see to."

I wasn't enjoying any of it, trying to keep people apart so they wouldn't say the wrong thing, keeping an eye out for how much Raj and his mother were drinking so they wouldn't let anything slip, trying not to say the wrong things myself, waiting anxiously for Mangetti. It all felt like one long nightmare.

Michael was safely at one end of the room and I could hear Raj's voice booming at the other.

"See, Mummy, he probably had some Asian influence here. Maybe spent some time there . . ."

Gina came over to me saying she had to leave, her shift was about to begin.

"Definitely doing the right thing," she said, nodding towards Raj's mother.

"I just want all this to be over."

"It will be, soon," she replied.

It was half past eight, Mangetti still hadn't arrived and I kept glancing over to the entrance. Michael walked over to me as if to reassure me. He put one hand on my shoulder.

Raj was looking at me and was coming over. "God, please don't let this be happening," I thought. My head began doing the jerking thing.

"Nina, what's wrong?" Michael asked.

"Baby, Gina doesn't work for Ravi Shankar really, does she? She said he's doing some interesting work with sculpture at the moment."

"She does. Ravi's diversifying into other areas."

"But baby," he said again.

278

The room fell silent. All I could hear was the word "baby", amplified and resounding around the room.

"Gay," I turned and whispered to Michael. "Arty type."

But then Raj squeezed my hand. He had promised: no physical contact, no hand-squeezing, no terms of endearment — not while I was working — but no, there for all to see, he gripped it tightly.

Michael stared at Raj.

"Raj, this is Michael. Michael, this is Raj."

"Her fiancé," Raj said, holding out his hand.

Now two words reverberated around the room: "baby" and "fiancé".

"Right," Michael managed.

Then there was a pause that I wanted to be swallowed by. Michael looked at me with incomprehension and then his face hardened. "I've come to check how it's all going and if you needed anything but I can see that you have everything under control so I'll leave you to it." He turned and left.

"Very nice of him," Raj commented and began prattling about something else.

Just as I was about to stop him, Raj's mother staggered over. "Ravi Shankar is exhibiting next month, Gina said she'll send me an invite. Raju, you'll take me home now. Nina, wonderful evening."

"Thank you. Raj, don't come back for me. I'll get a cab," I said, thinking that I had to find Michael.

"No, baby, I'll drop Mummy — she's only staying at the flat in Victoria — and then I'll come back for you."

"There's no need, really. I'll be seeing you tomorrow."

As they were getting their coats, I ran downstairs. I caught a glimpse of Michael leaving, called out his name and then ran after him when he didn't turn around.

"Michael, I can explain. It's not how it seems."

He turned and looked at me. "Leave it."

"No, you have to let me explain."

He continued walking and ignored me.

Distraught, I went back up to the gallery. Mangetti hadn't yet arrived. Where was he? Maybe he was stuck in traffic. He couldn't not come; not after this. The guests were leaving.

"I'm always here for you," Jean said as he was about to leave.

The irony wanted to make me shout at him: at that moment in time, standing there in front of me, he was the only one who was there — but where had he been when I needed him?

He waited for a comment.

"Bye Jean," I whispered as he turned his back.

Half an hour later they had all gone. The room was empty with only the mess of dirty plates, empty glasses, beer bottles and scrawled up napkins. I sat in a corner looking at the buddha and I cried. All of it for nothing: the planning, the scheming, the lies, all for nothing. It had been a crazy idea, what was I thinking of? How naïve to believe that Michael and Raj wouldn't meet each other and to think that Mangetti would actually show up. How stupid to think that the mess I had created wouldn't unravel before me.

"Oh Ki, it's a mess, a big, big mess."

I could hear footsteps coming up the stairs. I wiped my tears.

"Michael?"

It was Raj.

"What's wrong, baby?"

"It was for nothing, all for nothing."

"It was a success, lots of people came. OK, Foruki wasn't here but you said you didn't expect him."

"No, it's all been for nothing. Creativity takes courage, remember, you told me that and that's all I did. I took a leap of faith, seeing flowers when there were none, that's all I did."

He seemed confused.

"Creativity takes courage. Henri Mattise. That's who you quoted the very first time we met."

"Did I?"

"Yes you did. You said it the first time we met, remember?"

"Oh yes, got that from a book I was reading on developing confidence. It said that . . ."

"But it was the sign, my sign, you and me," I cried.

He looked like he had absolutely no idea as to what I was talking about.

"What about hands?"

"What hands? What are you talking about, Nina?"

"You said that hands meant a lot to you. What do mine tell you? What does that picture on the wall tell you? Or did you just pluck that out of the air as well?"

"Nina, maybe you've had a bit too much to drink. We'll talk about this later, when you're a bit more rational."

"I'll never be rational. I'll never be who you want me to be, you don't even know who I am. This, all this, is me. ME."

"Nina, let's just get you home."

"I can't marry you."

He stood still. "What?"

"I can't," I cried. "I can't. I tried, I really did, but I can't."

"It's been a long day, you're tired, Nina, you're not making any sense."

"I can't go through with it. It's not you, it's me."

"Nina, be practical. The wedding is next month."

I sobbed.

"What about Mummy, the preparations? Listen, baby, it's nerves. We all have them."

"I'm so sorry, Raj."

"You can't do this to me," he shouted.

"I'm sorry, really very sorry."

He had his head in his hands.

I walked around Green Park in the dark; no Michael, no Raj, no Mangetti, nothing. All of it had been for nothing. I had left Raj feeling as worthless as I once had. We couldn't subconsciously instigate scenarios and bring them into our lives. I wouldn't have wished this on my worst enemy.

It was eleven o'clock when I arrived at Gina's house. She wasn't in. Michael wasn't picking up his phone; I had left countless messages. With nowhere else to go I made my way back home. What was I going to tell my parents? How was I going to break it to them? All their expectations detonated in one night.

They were sleeping when I got in. There was food left for me in the oven: three circular rotis with peas and potatoes. Both my parents were snoring peacefully so Raj's mother had obviously not called them. It could wait until morning; things always seemed worse at night.

I crawled into bed too tired to cry any more, too tired to reflect but unable to sleep.

In the morning, things seemed no better. My parents stirred at about five-thirty. That was the time my mother got up to do her prayers. Before she got started, my dad sent her downstairs to make some tea and when she brought it back up I thought it was probably best that I did it then.

My hands were shaking, my throat was dry.

"Beta, you're up already," my mum called out on hearing my footsteps. "Did you eat anything last night?"

I went into their room and sat on the bed.

"Ma, Dad, I have something I want to tell you."

"What is it, beta?" my mother asked.

"There really is no easy way to do this and I want you to know that I tried, I tried my best to make you happy but . . ."

Mum put her hand to her heart.

Dad put his teacup down. "You've given up work, I knew it," he interrupted. "Please tell me it's not this, you could have waited until you were married. What if Raj's family finds out, then what?" he shouted.

"It's not that."

"Thank Bhagavan . . ."

"It's . . ."

"Oh Bhagavan, don't tell me she's not going to pay for the wedding. She was the one who . . ."

"I'm not getting married," I blurted.

There was a gasp from my mother.

"April the fool in March," my father laughed.

"No Dad, I've told Raj that I can't marry him."

"Hare Ram," my mother wailed, clasping both hands to her heart.

"What do you mean?" my father screamed. "Only two weeks left, you have to. The guests, the Hilton, all organised."

"I'm really sorry, I can't do it."

"No choice. I felt the same when I saw your mother but there is no choice and look how happy we are now." He grabbed her.

"I can't, I know I can't."

My mother began blubbering.

"Kavitha, tell her she won't find a good boy coming from a good family like that anywhere. Tell her, nobody takes girls who can't cook and she's getting old now. Tell her, make her understand nobody will want to look after her."

My mother was unable to speak.

"I'm not going through with it."

"Why?" he shouted.

"Because I don't love him."

"It's not about the love, it's about duty."

"Then I can't do my duty."

"Please, beta, please think, think what you are doing to us," my mother sobbed.

"Everything I did I tried to do for you, but I've realised it will never be enough — and you know why, because what you want for me is not what I want. I'm sorry, I never meant to hurt you, never meant to hurt anyone, but I can't pretend any more."

"Pretend? Nobody is asking you to pretend, just to marry him," my dad yelled.

"Every day I pretend. I paint. Do you know that about me? Every day I get up, put on a suit and go to paint?"

"Paint? And the love?"

"There is no law, there hasn't been for the last three months."

"The van," he shouted. "I knew this. Dickheads struggling and you telling me this? It's the Jeannie who has put the thoughts into your head."

"Nobody has. Did you hear me, Dad? I paint, I've given up work so I can paint and when I am painting it's the only time I'm me. I don't have to be anyone else but me."

"No, no, no," my mother cried.

"And I might as well tell you all of it. There's someone else."

At this stage my mum passed out.

"Jeannie," my dad raged.

"His name is Michael."

"Leave, leave my house," my father screamed. "Take your dirty van and go to wherever your sister has gone."

I went to pack my things together and they didn't even try to stop me. My father told my mother to let me go, that I was an even greater disappointment to him than my sister. The problem, he said, was that he had loved us too much and given us too much freedom. Maybe he didn't love us enough. If he did, he could have let us be ourselves.

Maybe loving us didn't even enter into the equation. It was all about keeping us clothed and fed and doing his best to do his duty and this was, for him, loving us. Seeing me married off was being a good father. No matter how much I argued that it was important to be happy, he wouldn't understand. Happiness was a luxury, an expectation, you weren't supposed to be happy, you were supposed to get on with it and try to make the best of every situation.

"See, Nina, you talks always about the feelings, if you talks about the feelings who will pay the bills. One day you can be happy, one day you can be sad, the feelings they comes and goes but the routine this never changes."

That is what they clung to and by doing what they wanted me to do and what was always done I would have made them proud, but by being me . . . the only way they could handle that was by telling me to go. I understood at that moment what my sister must have felt — a complete and utter disappointment to them.

Maybe that's what happens when you are forced to move continents and come to a foreign place; you become incredibly practical and don't get attached to anything again, not even your children.

I drove to Gina's house and rang the bell. It was seven o'clock in the morning. Nobody answered so I kept on ringing.

"Go away, there's nobody in," she shouted from her window.

"Gina, it's me. Will you let me in?"

"Bloody hell, Nina. What time is it?" She opened the door, half-asleep. "Jesus, what's happened?"

"I've told my parents everything and they've thrown me out. Can't find Michael anywhere, Mangetti didn't show and I've crushed Raj . . ."

"Slow down, slow down. Come in." She took my bags and led me to the kitchen.

"Your mum and dad have thrown you out and you've left that pretentious guy?"

"How am I going to manage? And Michael, he knows about Raj and he didn't give me a chance to explain. It's all gone wrong. I've hurt people, I've got no money, no job, no family, nowhere to go," I put my head in my hands and sobbed. "It was all just one crazy idea . . . mad . . . mad."

"Don't worry, sweetheart, I know it's not much but you've got me. If you don't mind sleeping on the sofa you can stay here until you get yourself sorted. Let's make you something to eat and you can tell me properly."

"I can't eat. You know he just told me to go. They both did, and when I went to speak to them they just closed the door and asked for my keys back. My mum was crying hysterically. What have I done to them? All for what? For nothing."

"They'll come round, you'll see. The first thing you gotta do is have a good sleep, you can't think straight like this. Then have a shower, get dressed, and go find Michael."

She made up the sofa, made me some tea, and sat down and listened to me ramble until I exhausted myself and fell asleep.

It was five o'clock in the afternoon when I resurfaced. My dad would be arriving home from work, my mum would be in the kitchen making rotis. Sleep didn't make things feel any better. I got ready and made my way to Artusion. Michael wasn't there. Emanuel Hikatari came down from his office to thank me for the successful coverage Foruki had received. I enquired after Michael but he told me that Michael had already left for New York.

No, he couldn't have gone, not without giving me an opportunity to explain, not like that.

"But I need to speak to him, about the exhibition," I added, trying not to sound desperate.

"The gallery manager, who I believe you met yesterday, will be taking over the day-to-day running; so if he can be of help?"

"It was really Michael I needed to speak to."

Emanuel gave me the numbers for Artusion in New York and said that he would tell Michael that I needed to speak to him.

As I stepped out of Artusion my phone rang.

"Michael?"

"No." It was Raj's mother. "It's true, you don't want my son?" She was incredibly calm considering she had six hundred and fifty guests and no wedding.

"I'm so sorry, Auntie, I never meant for any of this to happen."

"Tell me, why?"

I wanted to be as honest as I could with her. "I don't love him."

"When does love come into it? Just marry him; these things will come later."

"I didn't mean for this to happen."

"Then how else has it happened? You can change it."

"I'm sorry."

"There is nothing I can say to make you change your mind?"

"No."

She turned on me. "I knew from the first time I set eyes on you that you were cheap. Look what kind of family you come from. One could hardly expect better."

"It's got nothing to do with Mum and Dad. Don't take this out on them."

"They raised you," she shouted. "What can one expect these people to raise? You cheating housie." It was inappropriate to tell her that the word she was looking for was hussy so I let her vent.

"Who is this Michael? You're leaving my son for him? Don't think I won't make you and your family suffer for this."

And then the words flew out: "Maybe if you didn't spend half your life trying to control your son's life he would be happier, and maybe, just maybe, the others wouldn't have left."

"What?" she screamed. "I'll make sure you won't be able to set foot anywhere without people knowing how cheap you are, and I promise you, I will make you pay for this."

I cut her off. It was probably the wrong thing to do but when was I ever good at doing anything right?

Gina wasn't home when I got back. I called home. My dad picked it up and as soon as I spoke he put the phone down. I called once more and he did the same. I waited by the phone for a few hours and tried again. My mother answered and I could hear my dad shouting in the background, "If that is the unemployed fooler, tell her if she says there has been some mistake and that she will marry Raj she can come back."

"You'll marry him?"

"No, Ma, but listen to me, please."

She hung up.

I left a message for Michael. "Michael, it's me. I never thought it was possible to fall in love with someone just like that. There, I've said it. I'm not marrying Raj. I had my reasons. Can I explain? Please, just pick up your phone and hear me out."

He didn't call back.

It was dark; I went to the studio and stared at the blank canvas. The only thing that reflected back at me was emptiness and the bits that hurt. Taking out the blue and black paint, I mixed them together in a tin pot and then dipped my hand in it. An explosion of bluish black paint was thrown on the canvas and I swirled it around with my fingertips. Nobody cared if I returned home with dirty fingernails, nobody cared if I had paint smeared across my face or in my hair. After I'd finished I sat desperately trying to find some light in the painting but there wasn't any. No spaces between the movement that I could paint white. I stared hard.

"I know you're still there, Ki. I haven't come this far to believe you not to be but I've made such a mess of things. A really big, awful mess. I should have told him, I know I should have, but I never found the right time. I didn't even want to begin to think it was love because that kind of love hurts. It's safer not to really love someone, Ki, because they go, don't they?

"And Mum and Dad, I held on to them because I didn't want them not to love me any more, so I tried, I really did. I don't know what to do now."

I lay curled up on the floor, crying. Paint was sprawled everywhere, across my face, hair and clothes. I must have fallen asleep there because I was woken by the studio door being pulled open.

"Hell, Nina, it's not that bad. It isn't, look, look what they've written about you." Gina crouched down beside me and read from the paper she was holding.

" 'The enigma of Foruki. Foruki manages to capture the sense of obscurity to light on so many different levels as to be beyond simple explanation.' Another one here, look. 'This is a collection that must be seen to appreciate the conceptual diversity and the bold use of colour . . .'

"Nina, are you listening? What do you think?"

"I don't care any more."

"I know, but Imogene Bailey has also given the exhibition a brilliant review. She doesn't write anything good about anyone, so it doesn't matter if Mangetti didn't turn up; all these paintings are going to sell."

"It doesn't matter any more. Just lies; all of it."

"You can't give up, not now. Come on, Nina."

"What am I supposed to do? Michael's gone. He's not coming back. I have no family, no home, and a whole load of pictures done by someone who doesn't even exist."

"Keep believing, maybe? Believe that it will all work out? That's what you say, isn't it?"

"I can't see the light between the spaces," I cried. "The only place I have been able to see it is on the canvas. Even when it hasn't been there."

"We'll paint some, look," she said, picking up the white tube. "Let's pretend it's there and paint. Come on, Nina, get up and start again. We can do this."

She oozed the entire tube of white into a tin and mixed it with water and dipped her hand in, and then held it out to me so she could help me up. The paint dripped from our hands onto the floor.

"You ready?" she asked.

Together, we pressed our palms onto the canvas and covered every part of it with our white prints, and after we had finished Gina washed my hands for me with soap and water.

"Tomorrow we'll paint flowers there. Come on, Nina, let's get you home."

It had been incredibly hard going back to school after my accident: everything hurt, my sister had gone, she didn't drop me off or pick me up any more, there was no one or nothing to be proud of. The other children at school, perhaps sensing my self-pity, stayed away and didn't play with me. I watched from the sidelines feeling inadequate and alienated, completely unaware that someone was watching. Ki took me from the sidelines to the centre of every game, she saw something in me that was baffling even to myself. That is what Gina did too; she made me want to leave all the questions behind and start all over again, even though every part of me hurt.

The following day, like children, we went into the studio together. There wasn't really space for the both of us but Gina made it feel like ten people could fit in. We painted what we wanted to see and not what was there — huge, colourful flowers absorbing sunny optimistic colours, eliminating any signs of shadows.

Despite the fact that I had virtually no money left and was supposed to hand the studio back to Gina, she said I could share it with her for as long as I needed to. After we painted, she went to the flat and I went for a long walk in Green Park to try and sort out my thoughts. This had begun because all I ever wanted to do was paint, and that was what I decided I was going to continue to do. I would work part-time like Gina did. If even a few paintings sold from Foruki's exhibition, I would have enough money to rent my own studio and flat. I sat on the bench making plans. For the first time I could see myself being my own person, completely self-sufficient.

The phone rang while I was sitting writing notes on the bench. There was a fuzzy background noise. It sounded long-distance.

"Michael, is that you?"

"Tastudi Mangetti here."

"Oh, hello," I replied disappointed. It was ironic; if he had called me a week ago I would have been jumping up and down, but now, impressing him was the thing that mattered to me least.

"Nina? Nina Savani?"

"Yes it's me. How can I help you?"

"I saw Foruki's work. I prefer to see work in the starkness of an empty room. That is when you see if it holds its own. What can I say? Interesting? Original? The use of colour is impressive."

"Right." When had he gone to see it? He wasn't there at the exhibition.

His tone suggested that he expected me to be more enthusiastic. "Right?" he repeated.

"I mean, yes, I know — so how can I help you?" I asked, trying to focus.

294

"Foruki is good, very good. That was you I heard on the radio, wasn't it? I agreed with what you said about art now being more about the artist and moving even further away from the subject matter."

"You did?"

"Yes. This is what I like about Foruki's work, his focus on the subject matter. I was told he didn't even turn up to the opening."

"That's right, he didn't. He's media shy."

"There is something that I would like to discuss with him and it is of a delicate nature. When can we set up a meeting?"

What did he want to talk to him about? Did he want to buy a painting? If he did I could rent my own studio but I couldn't produce Foruki, no more lying. "Could you give me an indication as to what it is about?" I asked calmly.

"The Turner Prize. I want him to be entered in for it but I'd like to discuss a few things with him first."

I nearly fell off the bench. The Turner Prize? He was having a joke. Foruki and the bloody Turner Prize? Hold it together, Nina, say it's not possible — you can't pull that off, you're not lying any more. "Mr Mangetti, I have to let you know now it may not be possible to convince him to meet with you." I didn't want to lie, even if he was handing me the crown jewels on a plate.

"I'm sure you're skilful enough to persuade anyone, Ms Savani, and it would be to our mutual benefit. One more thing, why are all those paintings earmarked? You said you would give me first option. Are you saying that those paintings have been sold and that the buddha is still not for sale? Surely you can persuade Foruki to sell it to me?"

I felt overwhelmed. He could buy all the paintings if he wanted but not the buddha.

"That particular one is not for sale."

"Surely you of all people could manage something? Persuade him to meet with me and I will make sure it is worth your while."

I needed to end the conversation, I needed time to assimilate what he was saying.

"Mr Mangetti, I will call you back once I have had an opportunity to speak to Foruki."

"I look forward to hearing back from you soon," he replied.

What was going on? It was complete madness, Foruki being entered for the Turner Prize. No, I couldn't go that far; it was ridiculous. That wasn't supposed to happen. Mangetti hadn't even turned up to the opening night. How could he want Foruki to be entered for the Turner? It wasn't making sense.

I thought about it on the way to Gina's house. If he was being serious I just didn't have the strength to pretend any more. He would have to take me as I was.

Gina was back at the flat, about to leave for work.

"Did you sort out the stuff in your head?" she asked.

"Sort of . . ."

"And?"

"And then Tastudi Mangetti called," I replied.

"What did he want? Did he apologise for not turning up?"

"He wants Foruki to enter the Turner Prize."

She spat out the cornflakes she was eating. "Bloody hell! No! What? And what did you say?"

"I said I'd call him back."

"Why the bloody hell did you say that?"

"Because I don't think I can lie any more. It was never meant to go this far. People get hurt. What if someone finds out Michael helped me? I can't do that to him."

"No one is going to find out — if it ever comes out, Michael can deny it. Nina, you can't let this go. It's the bloody Turner. You've got to keep going and then when it's all over you can come clean. Think about it . . . Foruki going in for the Turner."

"I'm not sure."

"What's there to be sure about? Just go for it. Play them at their own game. Most of them are just full of crap anyway. When I went to the opening of Hutton's new exhibition you know what he did? He made a sculpture with cigarette butts and a few empty cartons and some idiot bought it for two thousand pounds. What kind of madness is that? Your paintings are original, Nina, it's the artist who's a fake. I've got to go to work now but please tell me that you'll think about it."

"It's all I've been doing."

"So think about it some more."

It was like Ki making me take centre stage. At first I thought she didn't understand, I didn't want to be humiliated any further, but she just wanted to make me stronger.

After Gina left I called my mum and dad.

"Have you changed your mind?"

"No, Dad, but . . ."

"The fooler." He hung up.

I then left one last message for Michael.

"Michael, Mangetti wants Foruki to go in for the Turner. I don't know what to do. What if someone finds out that you knew all along. Will you call me? Can we talk?"

An hour later Michael's secretary called back saying he would have no reservations with Mr Foruki entering the Turner Prize and wished him the very best with his career. That was it, nothing more.

I went to see Mrs Onoro.

"Oh Mrs Onoro," I said hugging her, "I don't know where to start. I've left my fiancé, my family won't speak to me and my friend Michael has gone."

"I make you tea and you tell me properly."

She made us some tea and I told her everything and then I asked her if she had ever pretended.

"I pretended for long time I happy when I not — at least you no have to pretend. You be yourself. Lots of people they not self because they pretend they happy when they not."

"What about truth?"

"Hikito say you find own truth. Nobody tell you what right or what wrong. You find your own way, you do what you think is right."

I asked if I could speak to her son, thinking that at that moment what was right was to finish what I had started and to see it through to the end with conviction.

298

"Ah," she smiled. "You want marry him?"

"No, no. Maybe he can help me with a job I'm doing?"

"Rooney supply fruit and veg everywhere. No job too small. You wait, he come home soon."

We talked about her childhood in Japan, how she came to England, what she wished for Rooney, and together we waited for him. Two hours later he came home. In that time I had managed to convince myself that asking him to stand in as Foruki made perfect sense.

"What's for . . .?" He stopped when he saw me, he probably thought I was stalking his mother so I could get to him.

"Rooney, Nina wait for you."

He looked at me suspiciously and said something in Japanese to his mother.

"No, she want big order for vegetables," Mrs Onoro replied in English.

"It's not exactly vegetables I wanted to ask you about."

Mrs Onoro showed no sign of leaving us alone so I could talk to him privately about being Foruki.

"Mrs Onoro, could I have some more tea please?" I asked, thinking she'd go off and make a fresh pot.

"I pour for you." She poured the cold tea into my cup, sat comfortably back in her chair and waited for me to begin.

"Well, well the thing is I'm a painter, well, I was a lawyer before that and I sort of fell into painting. When

299

I finished a piece, I dedicated it to my best friend Ki who died. It was because of her I started to paint again."

Mrs Onoro nodded vehemently.

"These paintings were spotted by a very influential man and he confused the inscription with the name of a Japanese painter."

"I no understand," she said.

"Well, he thought that 'FOR U KI' was a Japanese man and because he was so important I didn't tell him that it was me."

"Ohhhh," Mrs Onoro gasped. "You lie?"

"Yes, and now he wants to enter the exhibition he thinks Foruki has done for an important prize so he wants to meet him. I don't know any Japanese men except you, Rooney."

"Sorry, I don't want to get involved," he said quickly. If he needed confirmation that I was a lunatic, this was it.

"I'll pay you. Ten per cent of whatever I get from the exhibition. Say if I make thirty thousand pounds that's . . ."

"Three thousand, Rooney, he do it," Mrs Onoro said.

"You don't even have to say anything. Just talk in Japanese and a friend of mine will translate or I'll pretend to. You can think about it and tell me later if you want to do it."

"So I don't have to paint? Just turn up, talk in Japanese and you're gonna pay me for doing that?"

300

"I'll pay you if he goes for it and the paintings sell. If they don't I'll pay you three hundred pounds. Either way, you don't really have to do anything."

He took a moment to think about it and then he agreed.

"It so clever. Rooney he sell good," Mrs Onoro added.

I called up Mangetti to tell him that we could meet him the following week. He wanted to meet at Brown's but I mentioned that Foruki would prefer it if we could meet somewhere more private. Mangetti suggested meeting at his friend's offices in Cork Street. That left five days for Rooney to be primed.

Gina arrived home late. I couldn't find a Japanese restaurant near where she lived so I bought us a Chinese takeaway and had it ready for her when she arrived home.

"Tell me you've been thinking about it?" she asked. "It would be good to see one of us break the mould."

"How much Japanese do you speak, Gina?"

"Enough to get me by? Why?"

"Me and you have got a lot of work to do if Rooney is going to stand any kind of chance with Mangetti."

"That's more like it," she replied.

"I've been thinking all evening about this and I don't know how exactly this is going to work, but maybe you could act as Foruki's translator so Rooney doesn't have to talk about art. The only way I could convince him was by telling him he didn't have to do a thing."

"Let's get Foruki's profile right first, his background and his concepts, and then we'll deal with how we present it all to Mangetti."

Gina and I sat up for most of the night, eating Chinese food and expanding on the profile I had given Foruki.

Foruki was a pseudonym for Ronald David Onoro. He was born in London in 1973 to a Japanese mother and a British father. His mother, Lydia Onoro, was a descendant of a Japanese Emperor who came from a very wealthy family and she was a painter. Gina suggested making her good friends with Yoko Ono but I said it was a bad idea in case Yoko was tracked down for a quote on their friendship.

"You think it will go as far as that?" she asked.

"I don't know, but when we are doing this we have to try and think of every eventuality."

Foruki's father was Kenneth David, an archaeologist who had been sent on a project to Tokyo. Lydia and Kenneth met by chance on a bus, there was an immediate connection between them and they began talking (Lydia could speak some English). Just four weeks after their initial meeting, they married. I told Gina that it was a bit far-fetched that they married a month after meeting on a bus but she assured me that was what had happened to her parents.

The Onoro family were completely against the marriage and they asked Lydia to leave. So after Lydia married Kenneth they moved to London. A year later, Rooney was born. At this stage I wanted Kenneth to die so Lydia would be left penniless and alone with no alternative but to go back to Japan, but Gina suggested it was better if they were abandoned so there would be a whole range of emotions that Foruki could work with. I used my dad's example of what he envisaged happening to my Uncle Amit's daughter and Roy; and so their marriage disintegrated rapidly after the birth of their son, primarily due to cultural differences, and Kenneth met someone else. When Rooney was only two, Kenneth left them both. Penniless and with nowhere to turn, Lydia returned to Japan, thinking that her parents would soften on seeing their grandson. But when she arrived in her home town they refused to see her because she had brought disgrace on the family.

With no money, Lydia began selling fruit and vegetables and took her son to work on the streets with her. At night at home she would paint to escape her reality and if Rooney was awake he would enter her world of colour. There had to be this link to a fruit and veg stall just in case someone photographed him and came forward saying they'd seen Foruki down the market. We would do everything to keep him away from the press but there were no guarantees that they wouldn't track him down. If this ever happened, I could say that Foruki could do things that appeared completely eccentric like selling fruit and veg, but this was because before he started each painting he needed to re-create the joy found in the formative years of his youth. It was absolute nonsense, but as my dad put it, "Gives them the rambles, they likes it."

We spent a long time debating whether to kill off Lydia but essentially she had to go. Gina said the colours Foruki painted with were so bold and daring, almost as if they had been let loose from a place of tremendous angst. Therefore, Foruki had to have lots of pain in his life and be unable to express his grief except on the canvas.

Lydia died when Foruki was fifteen and he was left to fend for himself. After working the whole day doing odd jobs he would transmute his feelings onto the canvas. Feelings of despair, loneliness and sadness all poured out and were given colour and life. They were hopeful pictures, he wanted to see something else other than the starkness of his reality.

His life changed dramatically after an encounter with a wealthy Japanese widow who was taken by him and his paintings. She introduced him to an influential circle, moved him into her home and paid him money just to paint for her. After years of being with her she betrayed him and left him for another artist. A period of substance abuse followed, a period where Foruki questioned his self worth, anything he could snort was up his nose. That was until he found himself in the gutter and decided that the only way was up.

Foruki had several opportunities to exhibit abroad but chose not to, that was until I came along and found his work in some back-street gallery. I asked him to come to London because all that exuded from the canvas was energy and potential.

"What were you doing in Japan?" Gina asked.

"I had been feeling disillusioned at work for a long time and always had a fascination with Japanese art and so I made a preliminary trip where I happened to stumble across him."

"Sounds good," Gina interjected.

It was hard to convince him because Foruki wasn't an artist who could be enticed by fame or money and there was a nonchalance to his character. He was eventually persuaded on the premise that he could explore his feelings towards one part of his heritage that he had previously denied: his Britishness. Gina suggested that maybe he came to London because he fancied me but this suggestion also had to go; it was better if his feelings towards me were ambiguous, he had to concentrate on his art.

"We've got a few problems," Gina pointed out.

"And they are?"

"You said this Rooney bloke is Japanese; he's not half-English. Isn't that going to show?"

I thought for a moment. The Japanese thing; it only showed in his eyes as his skin was quite pale. "We'll have him wearing sunglasses. They help him see light in a different way, he only takes them off when he's painting so the light appears even brighter and this is reflected in his work."

"You're bloody mad, Nina."

We had Foruki's profile and back-story down to every minuscule detail, even what kind of aftershave he would wear. The next few days I spent going to the library and taking out books on personal development. Raj had talked a lot about Neuro Linguistic Programming and the art of empathy but I hadn't really listened. He had called me twice in an attempt to persuade me to go back to him and both times I took the calls, trying my very best to explain to him my reasons for doing what I did. The last time his mother caught him in mid-conversation with me and I could hear her shouting at him to hang up "on that cheating housie", which is what he did. There hadn't been any more calls since. In contrast, Jean Michel left several messages asking me not to go through with the wedding, that I was making a big mistake. I had already made the biggest mistake by not being honest with both Raj and Michael. There was still no news from Michael and I knew that at some stage soon I would have to give up hoping.

In two days I devoured books on NLP and learned about empathy and how you could appear to be on the same wavelength as someone. The way the books were written did not make it sound manipulative, which it patently was.

"This bit talks about the importance of body language. He's got to mimic Tastudi's gestures but so subtly that Tastudi doesn't notice a thing. This guy also talks a lot about eye contact but that's going to be difficult with the shades, but maybe if you're translating you should do the eye-contact thing with him," I said, holding the book up. "And also speaking in the same tone."

"What time did you say we were going round there?" Gina asked.

306

"Around eight."

I wanted to go and see Mum and Dad who didn't live too far from Mrs Onoro but it was too soon, I couldn't face the door being slammed shut in my face. And anyway, Gina was coming with me to Mrs Onoro's house to try and ascertain the extent of the work that needed to be done on Rooney.

"Come in, come in," Mrs Onoro ushered us in.

Gina greeted her in Japanese and Mrs Onoro was mesmerised.

"Oh you pretty girl," she said to Gina. "And you speak Japanese."

"Mrs Onoro, this is my friend Gina."

"Pleased to meet you at last, Mrs Onoro. I've heard a lot about you."

"And polite girl. You married?"

"No," Gina replied.

"That's very good. You don't marry until you find right boy. You engaged?"

"No."

"Rooney, Nina and her friend come to see you. Come down, put good shirt on." She led us into the sitting room. "I make you tea. Where you learn to speak Japanese?"

"In Japan," Gina replied. "I used to teach English there."

"Rooney put best shirt on," Mrs Onoro shouted up again as she went to make the tea.

Rooney came down in a black tracksuit. We only had four days left to transform him into a charismatic artist. "This is my friend Gina," I said introducing them.

When he went over to her to shake her hand I sensed that there was some raw material that we could work with; his eyes seemed to sparkle, his shoulders were pulled back so he appeared taller and confident.

"Tea here," Mrs Onoro came in with her tray.

"Gina's going to do the translation and maybe find some clothes that are more appropriate."

"I'm just kitting Foruki out, you know, the kinda clothes he would wear. So it would be good to know your sizes," she added. "And shoes, do you have any classy shoes? They are important," Gina continued.

"Go bring down shoes," his mother instructed.

"No," he replied.

Mrs Onoro sat back in her chair as if he had said something deeply offensive.

"It's all right, I'll take a look later," Gina replied.

I told him what we were planning to have him dressed in and how we were going to work on him. He objected. Mrs Onoro looked at him as if he had wounded her.

"I'll think about it," he replied.

Gina then read out Foruki's history.

"Kenneth bad man," Mrs Onoro shouted, fully recovered. "Good he dead. Why Foruki mother she have to die? She no good? How she die?"

"She was killed in a car crash, killed instantly so she didn't feel a thing. His mother was really nice, the best mother, but it was her time to go."

"So sad," Mrs Onoro replied.

"Anyway, that's his story. You have to imagine that I am Tastudi Mangetti and I'm going to ask you some

308

questions. Say the first thing that comes into your head in Japanese and try to copy some of my gestures."

"No bloody way," he shouted.

"Just work with us, Rooney. See how it goes and if it's not working, leave it, but at least give it a go," Gina said.

He seemed to respond to Gina better so I let her continue.

"Tell me what you want me to do again?" he asked.

"Answer Nina's questions by saying the first thing that comes to your head in Japanese, but when you answer try and copy her a bit. What she's doing with her hands or her head. The tone she's using. So if Nina talks softly, you answer softly. If she pauses when she's asking you a question, you pause in giving her an answer."

"So, Foruki, how long have you been in England?"

He said something in Japanese, moved his head forward and copied me.

"That's good but maybe don't exaggerate the gesture as much. Just make it slight. Now at this point you have to wait until I translate whatever you've said into English."

"How well do you speak Japanese?" he said.

"How well do you want me to speak it?" she flirted.

He glanced down, hoping nobody had spotted his embarrassment, but we all had, especially Mrs Onoro who had hawk eyes. She sat back in her chair and smiled.

"We're going to be talking about art and paintings so it doesn't matter what you say, just how you say it and the body-language thing. Mangetti will just be watching you but listening to what I say and I'll talk about your — I mean Nina's — pictures so you don't have to worry about that. What you do have to do is look at me intensely and nod at me as if you agree with everything. OK, Nina, try the next question."

Rooney seemed perplexed.

"It easy, Rooney. You copy way Nina move hand, tell her anything, then you look at Gina, wait, nod and agree," Mrs Onoro added.

He knew what he had to do, he just found looking intensely at Gina the tricky part.

"How do you think Britain influences your work?"

He answered in Japanese.

Gina translated. "The contrast in tones and colours are a constant source of inspiration. I can look at a grey building, set in a grey sky, and the luscious green tree standing next to it brings out the warmth of that building, a warmth that one cannot tangibly see. That is what I try to capture in my pictures."

He nodded away and then said, "What a load of bollocks."

"What did he really say?" I asked.

"Rooney, you no use such bad language. Not in Japanese either," Mrs Onoro interrupted.

He said, "*Well when it's really cold outside and it's pissing down, I hurry up and just try and shift more stock so I can go home.*"

"It's a good answer, it's how I feel when I'm in the restaurant trying to get rid of the last customers."

"You work in a restaurant?" Rooney asked her.

Fukkus, fukkus, I heard my dad's voice. "Focus," I said to both of them. "Who or what is your greatest influence?" I continued.

He copied my gestures and said something else to Gina in Japanese.

"I'm influenced by the nature of life and death, both seemingly transitory and disconnected. Life is supposed to bring joy, and death sadness, but for me life is death and death is life. They work in union with one another."

"Do you really like Clapton?" Gina asked. "Me too."

"What has Clapton got to do with anything?"

"Rooney said his greatest inspiration was music and his greatest influence was Eric Clapton."

It was working — sort of — if Gina and Rooney didn't stop every few minutes to ask questions about each other. She was taking the empathy bit slightly too far.

"And what about me influence you?" Mrs Onoro asked Rooney.

"Come here, sweetheart," he said cuddling her. "And of course there's you."

"See, Gina, how my son is good boy, maybe you want go up and see his shoes?"

"Haven't heard that line before," she laughed.

"It's all right, I'll bring them down," he said, trying not to appear embarrassed.

Rooney went to fetch his shoes. None of them were any good. Gina was thinking of a pair of black and white ones with a crocodile-skin look. "We're going shopping tomorrow for Foruki's clothes and shoes, come with us and then maybe you and Gina could go to Artusion to get a feel for the paintings," I said, sensing if they got all their personal questions out of the way they could focus more on the translating part.

"OK, I'll come," he said without hesitation.

"I spread word around in Japanese Association about famous painter called Foruki," Mrs Onoro said as we left. "Gina, after this all you come back have dinner with us. You too, Nina."

"What do you think?" I asked as we made our way home.

"You made him sound boring. He isn't boring. He's got heaps of potential."

"You flirting with him helped."

"I did not."

"You did and you know you did, Gina."

"Maybe just a little but he's cute, isn't he? Kinda shy but not, if you know what I mean."

He was cute in the way you appreciate a My Little Pony with all the matching accessories when you're eight, cute in the way that he had managed to match his hair to the colour of his plums. "In a purple, streaky kind of a way," I said.

"There's more to him, Nina," she replied. "You'll see."

After getting someone to mind his stall, Rooney spent the morning with Gina at Artusion while I went into a café and surfed the Internet. I read every single piece of information I could find about Tastudi Mangetti. What transpired from most of the pages was that he was incredibly well-respected and wielded an enormous amount of power in the art world both in Europe and the States. I knew this but reading it all in black and white made my stomach churn. What were we thinking of doing? If he found out, forget ever trying to exhibit in any sort of gallery, any paintings Gina and I did would be confined to craft fairs in town halls. And then my imagination began to run away. What if Mangetti was linked to the Mafia? What if he sent them to track us down after he found out that we had deceived him?

I imagined the Godfather knocking on the semi's door.

"Whatever you's selling me, I'm not interested, now get off." That was my dad's standard line to strangers who came knocking. It didn't bear thinking about.

"We can't do it," I said, meeting Gina and Rooney in Bond Street.

"Have you spoken to your dad? To Raj?"

"No, it's Mangetti."

"What, he's pulled out?"

"No, we can't mess with him. Gina, you won't be able to sell any paintings if he finds out."

"I'm not selling any anyway, so what does it matter?"

"It's not going to work; and what if he's got connections?"

"Connections?"

"Mafia," I blurted.

She began laughing. "This is what happens when I leave you for too long on your own. They're only paintings. It's not major, major; it's nothing he wouldn't do."

313

"What if Mangetti finds out we deceived him and it's a question of honour?"

"I'm not even going to answer that. We had a good morning and Rooney really liked his work."

I felt neurotic and stupid.

"It's good stuff. I'm up for it," he said.

Up for it? It wasn't a competition to see who had the best My Little Pony.

"Rooney, do you know what you're getting yourself involved in? It's deceit — out-and-out deceit."

"Sometimes it's best not to know, not to ask too many questions and get on with it. I want to help both of you."

He was right. I knew what he meant by not asking too many questions. When I was at the firm there were many things that we weren't technically supposed to do, like hide the provenance of a painting due to tax implications, but we didn't ask our clients too many questions and just got on with it. It was sort of a similar scenario.

Rooney made it sound so simple, they both did. "Take another leap of faith, Nina. We can pull this off if we do a bit more work."

The only way we could pull it off was if I held my nerve. "OK," I replied. "And we all know what we're getting into."

"Yes, and no more jitters."

The jitters had to be kept inside — they were putting their faith in me, I had to stay strong. "Let's do it, let's go and get some clothes for Foruki," I said, attempting to sound resolute.

314

We went mainly to the charity shops in the best parts of London, finding things that might be appropriate for him. Later, Rooney came back home with us to have dinner and to try on the clothes.

"I look like an idiot," he said coming out of the bathroom.

"Maybe we can lose the cap but you look great, just great," Gina insisted. "Those shades look amazing."

The sunglasses were enormous; they covered most of his face and he was dressed mostly in black, except for his jacket and shoes. The jacket that swayed down to his ankles was purple and the shoes had a snake-skin print. And though he looked the part, there was something missing.

"Does he need some jewellery?" I asked.

"Definitely not," Gina replied. "He's Foruki, not Liberace."

Being loaded up with jewellery for a special occasion was obviously an Indian thing that was embedded in my psyche.

"I know what it is," Gina said. "Rooney, you've got to let me dye your hair all black. It will just be for a few days and we'll dye it back. Go on, you've been great — I mean, you've let us do all this to you without moaning and it's just one last thing," she tried to convince him.

"Well, if you really need to."

Gina was like the Avon lady that came to our house, a person who could just convince anyone to do anything and then make them feel like it was their idea in the first place. Every time the Avon lady came to the door my dad stood with one foot behind it so there was no way she would be let in, but she always managed to get past him and convince him to buy bits and pieces for my mum.

"Kavitha, why you wasting the money, I know what you looks like," he would say as she stared longingly at the Avon lady's coveted products.

"Yes, but wouldn't you like your wife to have a touch of Cilla about her — you know, that glamour," the Avon lady would wink at my mum.

"You saying this is the lipstick that the Cilla buys?" he would ask, rummaging through her products.

"Sold the same one to her just last week."

She used the same line over and over, and he would fall for it over and over again.

I missed them both so much, even their routine and the comments they made to each other. Despite the fact they had their faults there was a safety that they provided. Jana must have found it hard to stay away. Did she just get used to being without us and felt that the best way was to cut everyone off?

It had been a long day. Rooney and Gina were engrossed in conversation. I wanted to leave them to it and go to bed but I didn't have a bed, just the sofa they were both sitting on, so I fell asleep in the armchair.

Early the next morning I woke up startled and with no recollection of going to sleep on the sofa. This was what my angst was doing to me; making me forget things, making me hallucinate. I had dreamed Raj was really Foruki but then Mangetti had found out Foruki did not

316

exist and was holding a gun to my head. I was frantically pointing at Raj, pleading with him to believe me, but Raj denied it and kept calling me a liar. I couldn't go back to sleep. It was 5.57a.m., in a few more hours I was supposed to be getting married. Raj would be feeling devastated today and my parents more so. My mum probably wouldn't even get out of bed, feigning a bad headache, and my dad would be fiddling with the television sets. Was it worth putting everyone through so much just so I could paint pictures and sleep on someone else's sofa? The sofa I so feared Gina would ask me if she could sleep on those many months ago at the Tate. She was one of the kindest people I had ever met, and Rooney, I had misjudged him. Why did they believe in me so much? Maybe it was better, as he said, not to ask so many questions; maybe then I could stop oscillating between doubt and fear and just get on with finishing what I had unwittingly started. So that is what I decided to do on the morning I was supposed to be getting married. I pulled myself together and resolved to see it through to the end. If it all went horribly wrong I would accept it, as Mrs Onoro said; I would stand in the centre and accept all of it and at least, deep down, I would know that I had given it my very best.

The phone beeped and I got off the sofa. It was a text message from Raj's mother that read, "HOUSIE YOU WILL PAY". I put thoughts about her, and about my mum sitting with the contents of her jewellery box, to the back of my mind and began making notes on all the things Mangetti could possibly ask and Gina's possible responses. I scribbled down what Rooney needed to work on and then I made Gina breakfast.

"Oh God, Nina, it's the day of the wedding. Are you OK?"

"Much better. I came to the conclusion that I have two options — to be Raj's wife or to do something extraordinary. Was it you who put me on the sofa?"

"Rooney. I took off your shoes and he picked you up and put you there before he left."

"He's a nice guy, isn't he?"

"And witty as well," she replied, "in an understated, not-witty way."

After finishing on his stall that morning, Rooney came round. Gina dyed his hair and got him to wear Foruki's clothes again. He appeared convincing.

"We've got to spend some time on refining gestures and mannerisms and you'll be perfect. When he asks you some questions that you think are difficult, make some erratic hand movements and mutter, like this. That's what I've seen some of these eccentric types do," I said.

Rooney laughed. He had a soothing, unruffled laugh.

We sat for hours rehearsing the kind of questions Mangetti would ask and what Foruki would do.

"When you don't know what to say, if nothing comes to you or you think it's a question that requires much thought, touch your heart, pause, lower your head as if you are thinking, and then answer."

After dinner Gina was getting out the wineglasses to show him how to hold the glass correctly, should he be

318

offered some, when Rooney spotted her acoustic guitar behind the cabinet.

"Do you play?" he asked her.

"Yeah, just a bit."

"Play us something," he said going over to it.

She picked up the guitar and then sang a Tracy Chapman song. Rooney asked if he could take the guitar from her and then he started strumming. First it was a chord here, a chord there, nothing spectacular. His fingers pressed firmly on the strings. They didn't seem like grocers' fingers, there were no muddy bits under his fingernails, no rough skin. He looked at Gina before tilting his head and then his fingers did their own thing. And the Rooney playing before us didn't seem like the Rooney who lived with his mum and asked her if his shirts were ironed; when he played he was a mass of potential and possibilities. He could have said he was anyone and we would have believed him. Gina's jaw dropped.

"Where the hell did you learn to play like that?" she asked in amazement.

"I was doing gigs before . . ." he stopped ". . . before my dad died, and then I decided to go back home, take over his stall and look after mum."

Gina and I looked at each other.

"What do you feel when you play?" I asked.

"There's just me and the guitar, the rest of the world doesn't exist."

He played us some more and we were in awe.

"It's bloody fantastic. OK Rooney, when you meet Mangetti, think about what you feel when you're playing, that it's just you and your guitar. Forget what I've told you about poise and posture; when he's asking you those questions imagine you're playing in your head and give him that look," Gina said.

By the end of the two days Gina knew every facet of my life; she knew what each of the paintings meant to me, what they would mean to Foruki. We spent hours discussing colours, influences, thoughts and feelings, and potentially what Mangetti might ask and ways of getting around questions. In the evenings Rooney came around and I watched the chemistry between them as I pretended to be Mangetti and asked the questions. He answered all the questions in Japanese, talking about his music or fruit and veg, but Gina skilfully converted his answers and made him sound as if he were an eccentric artist talking passionately about his concepts and influences. By the end of those two days I knew that there was nothing more we could possibly do; we were as ready as we would ever be.

The following morning I could hardly get myself dressed. My hands shook as I fumbled with the buttons on my shirt, trying to fasten them.

Gina was getting dressed in one of my suits.

"Aren't you scared, Gina, not even a little bit?"

"What's the worst thing that has happened in our lives?" she asked and then she answered her own question: "Death — so this is a drop in the ocean, it's nothing. OK we might be making someone see something that isn't there but this guy is responsible for making hundreds of people see things that aren't there. We're not hurting anyone. You can't go through life being scared or fearing what might or might not happen. You know that as well as I do, Nina, you take what comes knowing some things are inevitable. But what you can do is live every moment. The way I see it is that we've got a great opportunity here, there's nothing to be scared about — it's an adventure and we live it to the max, and whatever happens, happens."

Ki would have probably said pretty much the same thing. They were both incredibly optimistic, full of life with boundless energy and passion. They careered past obstacles and got on with things. One was looking out for me from somewhere else and the other was here; how could I fail?

Rooney came and we all sat and had breakfast together, though I couldn't eat anything. He didn't seem fazed either, it was as if it was just another day and instead of selling fruit and veg he was selling concepts. I sat thinking of all the last minute things we needed to do.

"OK, when we arrive do your greeting, you don't have to wait for Mangetti's prompt to say something if you feel like there needs to be a sentence in there somewhere."

"You've said that to me three times already, Nina, just chill," he replied.

"OK, but if you get nervous about anything, anything at all, focus on his nose. Stare at it hard. It's kind of prominent, you can't miss it, and I'm sure he must have a thing about it."

"Damn, we've forgotten something," Gina interrupted.

"What? What is it?" I panicked.

"Aftershave, he's got to have aftershave, it's important. We should stop off at Fortnum and Mason and spray something on him."

We caught the tube to Green Park and went to spray Rooney with aftershave.

"Remember," Gina said, "we have absolutely nothing to lose."

"Right, nothing to lose," I repeated seeing images of my dad being carted away by the Mafia.

My heart raced as we turned into Cork Street. "He's just a client, just a client," I kept saying to myself.

We walked into the main gallery and a middle-aged woman looked at us through her half-moon spectacles and asked how she could help.

"We're here to see Mr Mangetti. It's Nina Savani and . . ."

"Foki," she exclaimed getting up from behind her desk. "Delighted to meet you. Mr Mangetti is in the office, waiting for you," she said, holding out her hand. "Let me show you down there."

As her high heels went click, click, click on the parquet floor, my heart began thumping even louder.

"We have nothing to lose," I kept saying to myself. "It will be fine."

As he emerged from behind his desk, Mangetti looked smaller than I had remembered him.

"A pleasure to see you again, Nina," he said, shaking my hand.

"Tastudi, this is Foruki and his interpreter, Gina Walker."

Tastudi held out his hand. Rooney didn't take it. My heart began beating even faster and then Rooney bowed down and said something in Japanese.

Mangetti nodded and smiled and cast his eyes on Gina.

I introduced them again.

"As I said, Tastudi, Foruki understands English perfectly and he does speak some English but he would just feel slightly more comfortable if his translator is present to answer for him."

"Can understand but speaking English not very good," Rooney said with a strange Japanese accent.

"By all means, an artist always likes to express his work in his own language. Can I get you anything to drink?"

"Water," Rooney replied.

"Water is fine for all of us," I replied. I needed to sit down, my legs felt as if they were going to collapse if he didn't invite us to sit down.

"Leticia, some water please," he said to the lady. "Please take a seat." He invited Foruki to take a seat first.

There were enormous leather chairs that had probably cost a fortune; my dad would have been very impressed. He would be on his route now, shouting at all the customers who didn't give him the right change.

"I saw your work, Foruki. I'm sure Nina has told you what I thought of it," Mangetti began.

I left thoughts of my dad and focused.

Rooney paused, looked at me and said to Gina in Japanese, "*It's not mine but you believe what you want to. I'm actually a grocer, didn't think I'd end up being a grocer but there you go, you never know which way life is going to take you.*"

Gina turned to Mangetti and said, "She has indeed but I'd like to say that the artist is not the owner of the painting; he does not figure in the painting; he is merely the conduit."

That sounded good, we hadn't rehearsed that. I tried not to catch her eye and kept my gaze on Mangetti, imagining him being delighted with the answers Foruki provided. Mangetti appeared eager to follow up and was leaning forward in his chair.

"Interesting, tell me more," Mangetti continued.

Rooney leaned forward and said in Japanese, "*Well, I had a band. We were touring Europe when my dad died. My mum couldn't manage on her own, my dad was a bit of a control freak and never let her do anything, so I decided to go back and help her out for a couple of months.*"

Gina translated. "When I'm painting, I'm not present. I can't explain it, it's the time that I access parts of the self that I never knew existed. It is the only time when I feel the ego to be completely eradicated. At that precise moment in timc it's about the painting. Nothing else exists."

324

This was true; this was what Gina and I both felt. Painting was the only time when both of us felt we were truly ourselves and not pretending to be other people. Mangetti would understand this.

"That comes across. It's striking how you have managed not to allow your cultural background to permeate your work. I mean obviously the use of space and the flat surfaces would indicate a certain Japanese influence but this is not the overriding impression one is left with; I would go so far as to say that the paintings are unstilted," Mangetti responded.

Rooney paused and then replied, "*If you had any Japanese influence in the music, we'd only really sell in Japan. I know it's not all just about being commercial but you have to have some mass appeal.*"

Gina nodded as Rooney gave his answer and turned to Mangetti. "This is what I have discovered in Britain and that's why this particular collection is very close to me. It's not about being Japanese or British, or Indian for that matter. Art speaks a universal language; it's about conveying depth of feeling through colour and if at all possible trying to attain a neutrality or sense of peace through colour."

Word for word, this is what we had spoken about the night before. It was sounding fluid. Maybe this would be enough to convince him. I searched Mangetti's face for traces of doubt or hesitation but there was only eagerness to continue the conversation.

"Is that attainable?" Mangetti asked.

"*You've got to aim for something.*"

"Aren't we always seeking?" she translated.

325

I thought about interrupting and adding my own thoughts to the discussion but then without being prompted Rooney went off on his own direction. "*Most blokes would think it's weird that after all this time I haven't really achieved anything and I'm still at home. I've thought about it a lot. I don't think it is the comfort-zone thing, I think if I'm not there my mum wouldn't manage.*" He touched his heart.

Gina agreed with whatever Rooney was saying and turned back to Mangetti. "This is what my work is about; trying to find balance in an inharmonious world. Trying to find life among death, peace in turbulence and stillness in movement."

We hadn't practised that. I began to worry until Mangetti said, "And may I say you have done it admirably. This was exquisitely captured."

They were doing really well but it was dangerous for Rooney to go off on tangents, it wasn't something we had practised.

Gina waited for him to do something. She glanced at me.

Nod, Rooney, nod. Please don't say anything.

Rooney went off again. "*Don't need any admiration for it. If you met her, you'd know exactly why I do it.*"

She translated. "Thank you. And then of course there is the social commentary aspect."

What social commentary aspect? I thought. I began to panic — stop there.

"Take the buddha painting," she continued, giving Mangetti his own spiel about cultural juxtaposition — this is what I told her Mangetti had first said when he

326

initially saw the painting. "We live in a society where culture is increasingly becoming fused. I wanted to show that we are able to reach a middle ground, that both are compatible."

"These are my sentiments and indeed this is what your work conveys. A sense of peace, a sense of understanding. Is that what you would say?"

"*You have to understand what your customer wants: apples and pears, kilo there, kilo here, it's not rocket science, though, maybe it's the same in art, they want bullshit, give it to them,*" Rooney waved.

"Essentially the work is a search for identity; death being part of that identity, life being part of that identity. Confronting parts of the self that are ugly and transmuting light into them," Gina said and then added, "Identity is not about ego, and this particular collection — *From Obscurity to Light* — is the journey I took to realise this. It's almost as if the ego was left behind and the paintings were done by someone else."

Gina had a straight face and appeared deadly serious. I wanted to bury my head in my hands; surely he wouldn't go for it, not after she had said that, he had to know.

Mangetti leaned further across the table and seemed fully engaged. If the table hadn't been there to separate them he would have been in Foruki's lap.

"The handprint and the footprint is the only thing we have to leave; these are the only things that are alive," Mangetti added.

Nod, Rooney, just nod.

He nodded.

"Thank you, thank you," I thought, "We've done it."

Rooney turned to Gina and said something in Japanese.

Foruki would like to look at the work upstairs and give you a moment to speak to Ms Savani. This was just as we had rehearsed. As soon as they felt they had done their bit, this was what she had to say.

Mangetti turned to Rooney and said, "I completely understand but there's something I want to ask you before you leave. Foruki, I am not easily impressed. It's not often that I come across art like this that completely enraptures me. I want to enter you into the Turner Prize. I know what your objections will be, that you don't want to be exposed publicly, but please think about it."

Rooney nodded and said something in Japanese. If we were asked this question, Gina was going to say that he would need some time to consider it.

"I would consider it an honour," Gina replied.

NO!, I wanted to shout.

Mangetti appeared delighted. He called Leticia on the buzzer and asked her to come down. "Please take Mr Foruki up, he'd like to take a look at De Monte's work."

Rooney bowed before he and Gina went up with Leticia.

The two of us were left alone in the room together. I wasn't sure if I would be able to get through the rest of it without Gina and Rooney being there. My legs were shaking and I had to put my hands on my knees to stop them jumping up and down.

328

"Tell me again, Nina, where else has Foruki exhibited?" Mangetti asked.

I was telling myself to breathe and to treat him as if he were any client. "Client," I said out loud.

"Client?" Mangetti asked.

"Yes, client." How would I explain that outburst? "I was just thinking that Foruki is one of the best clients I've had. So unpresumptuous, that is what I liked about him when I first met him. Sorry, getting back to your question he's only exhibited in a few galleries in Japan and, even then, he's done that anonymously. As I said, exhibitions are not really his thing and he's only been ready to share his work in the last year."

"*From Obscurity to Light*. It was all done this year, wasn't it?"

"Yes, since he's been in Britain."

"And that has been?"

"Nine months," I said. After much debate, that is what Gina and I had settled on.

"Marvellous, he is such an original individual."

"Unique."

"I thought it would take much more to convince him to be entered into the Turner," Mangetti added.

So did I, I wanted to say.

"What he says about ego, the nature of fame and the search for identity is so valid. Between you and I there has been so much negative press towards the Turner Prize that some of the judges and myself feel that maybe this year it's important to have a slightly more traditionalist approach. I agree with what you said, it has become all about celebrity, all about hype, so

329

perhaps someone as noncontroversial as Foruki would bring something else to the table."

"Although he says it's an honour, I know he would want to retain his anonymity," I added quickly.

Mangetti nodded. "It just makes his point even stronger. The critics will have nothing to comment on this year."

That was one way of looking at it.

"One more thing, the buddha painting. I'll give you ten thousand pounds for it."

Though I was desperate for the money, I refused.

"Twenty?"

Twenty thousand pounds would have allowed me to paint for the entire year without worrying. "I'm sorry."

"I admire your integrity," he replied. "And those other paintings at Artusion which have been earmarked?"

"I'll have a word with Emanuel Hikatari at Artusion," I replied.

"Excellent. I would also like to commission Foruki to do a portrait. I'll call you to discuss the details as there's somewhere I have to be."

Mangetti led me back upstairs. Surely this wasn't it. It couldn't be this easy.

Gina was studying one of the paintings and Rooney was hovering, flitting from one to another.

"He's into comparison," I whispered to Mangetti.

"Foruki, it was an absolute pleasure meeting you," Mangetti said walking over to him.

Rooney bowed his head once again.

Mangetti thanked me and accompanied us to the door.

We walked round the corner of the street and like three lunatics who had managed to escape from an asylum we began laughing. I went over to them and put my arms around each of them.

"You did it, you were both fantastic. Thank you."

"We did it, I told you it would be a breeze," Gina replied.

"Weren't you supposed to say he would need much convincing to be entered for the Turner, that he would have to think seriously about it."

"Kinda got carried away there. Anyway, he's only using Foruki, he's got his own agenda. If they want noncontroversial, we'll give them noncontroversial."

"Can't believe we pulled it off," Rooney said.

"But I thought you didn't care?"

"I only said that, Nina, because you were nervous and at that time it's what you needed to hear."

I kissed him on the cheek. "Thank you, Rooney, for everything."

The paintings had all sold at Artusion. Emanuel Hikatari was delighted with the response and after the gallery had taken their cut I collected a cheque for £25,000.

"Dad, twenty-five thousand pounds," I put this in first so he would listen to the rest of my sentence. "Twenty-five thousand pounds, that's how much my paintings sold for."

He slammed the phone down.

★   ★   ★

331

We had dinner with Rooney and Mrs Onoro later that evening and I handed Rooney a cheque for £2500.

"Just for being Foruki?" Mrs Onoro asked in disbelief.

"There's more to it than just being Foruki," I answered. "Rooney was fantastic."

"Rooney available to be him any time. No, Rooney?"

"Any time."

"Well if we get short-listed for the Turner, and that is a really big if, we'll need him again, but for now it's all over, thank God."

"What are you going to do with the money?" Gina asked him.

"Buy a new guitar, maybe, then I'll start practising again. I've been putting it off with excuses of no money."

"Well if you ever want to do a gig let me know because on Thursday nights the restaurant I work at has live music and I can have a word with the boss," Gina said.

"Rooney, he do it," Mrs Onoro volunteered.

Just as we were leaving Mrs Onoro took me to one side.

"You good girl, Nina, you good to give Rooney a chance. He got confidence back," she said glancing at him.

"I didn't do that, he did; he was the one that gave me a chance."

"You see he think I need him, I think he need me. Maybe I tell him about Hikito."

"I think that's a good idea."

332

She hugged me as we left and I didn't want her to let me go as it had been ages since I felt that secure; they were like my family. "You come soon?"

"I will," I replied.

As Gina and I made our way home she said, "He's asked me to a concert on Sunday evening."

"And?"

"I told him yes."

One thing that has always been exceptionally hard for me to do is to let go, but then all the people who I loved the most were taken from me so I had no choice but to learn to let go. This time I wanted it to be different, I wanted it to be my decision and as much as I wanted to avoid the feelings of loneliness, it was time to stand on my own two feet and leave the warmth and security that Gina provided. With the money from the exhibition I decided to rent a studio and a flat of my own so I told her this once we had got home. Gina didn't want me to leave and said we could share both the flat and studio, but as much as I wanted to stay it was time to move on.

She helped me look and within a few weeks we had found both. The flat had one bedroom and it was just around the corner from Gina, and the studio was a converted warehouse in Shoreditch, split on two levels: downstairs was where I could stock all the materials and upstairs was where I saw myself painting. It was much bigger than I needed it to be and much more expensive but it felt right because I knew I would be spending most of my time there.

There was hardly anything to pack but Gina came with me to buy more paints and canvases for my new studio and helped me set up.

"This is for you," I said as she was leaving, handing her an envelope.

"What is it?"

"Two thousand pounds."

"I can't take this."

I had to insist that she take it.

"Oh Nina," she said hugging me, "it was never about the money. It was about breaking the mould and we did that."

"I know, but none of this would have happened without you."

Gina had once said that when you did something out of the ordinary, extraordinary things began to happen. The other thing she taught me was — and I don't know exactly how this one works, but — once you begin to see potential in someone else, even if they don't see it, they evolve into the person you envisaged them to be.

She was right.

After Gina went I was left alone in my studio and though I should have felt excited at the thought of being completely independent, I didn't. I had this huge pang of loneliness and sadness; it was as if she had taken everyone I had ever loved with her and left me alone with a gaping blank canvas. I thought about what I'd done to Raj and his family, to my mum and dad — all of that was because I was scared to be me, to show them who I was in case they didn't love me any more. Then I thought fleetingly about Jean Michel, how I could forgive him now for his mistake but things for us had moved on.

It was with Michael that my thoughts stayed. It was so wrong not to have been completely honest with him, but I was scared by the extent of the feelings I had for him, scared to expect too much, scared in case I was hurt again. My need not to be hurt overrode everything. Picking up my paintbrush I began to paint black silhouettes and wondered what Ki would make of all of it. When I had finished I put the paintbrush down.

"Did you see? Do you think it's all crazy? I can't quite get my head around any of it, how one thing has led to another and I'm here now, the place where I've always wanted to be. I can paint and there's no one to bother me or to tell me what to do but I still feel alone and I still miss you, there is no happily ever after, is there, Ki? You get what you want and you still think, 'Is that it?' I think all there is, is making the best of each day. When this exhibition is over I'll take the buddha over to your mum. Maybe she'll put it in your room. I want to mess your room up, take everything that's in it away. I wish I didn't still miss you like this. A big part of me wants it to stop."

Matisse's quote about flowers went around in my head. I thought about the new people who had entered my life in the last few months — Mrs Onoro, Gina, Rooney — and began painting colourful figures between the silhouettes, and when I had finished I didn't bother washing my hands or brushing my hair, I just went to an empty home.

★ ★ ★

Over the next few months I made several attempts to speak to Mum and Dad. I even followed my dad's bus route and waited for him at the bus stop but he closed the doors on me and drove off leaving the other passengers stranded. Being completely cut off from my family I threw myself into a world of my own, painting pictures that I had always wanted to paint, putting down feelings I was unable to express.

Mangetti had commissioned Foruki to do a portrait of him and because I couldn't go through with the whole sitting thing where Rooney would have to pretend to paint, I said Foruki didn't feel that a sitting was necessary as he worked from the vibration given off the subject matter. Despite the fact that Mangetti was paying £8000 for the commission I was unable to paint him and just kept painting flowers in all different shapes and sizes. Nothing came to me — the canvas was the only place where I couldn't fool myself.

There was still no news from Michael. Painting became everything to me; it was the only thing that I knew couldn't leave me and when I wasn't in my studio I spent time with Gina and Rooney.

Rooney began playing in Gina's restaurant and managed to find other venues where he could perform. Gina spent more time on her own work and the world revolved like this until the day Mangetti called and left a message asking me to call him at home.

I always had my phone switched off when I was working in the studio so later that evening I heard the message. I called him back, not even thinking twice about doing it, not like the first time I called him. His assistant picked up the phone and handed it to Mangetti.

"Hello Tastudi, it's Nina."

"Yes, Nina. How are you?"

"Very well, thank you."

"And how is Foruki doing with my painting?"

"It's coming on well," I lied.

"Excellent. I have some good news for Foruki," he paused. "We have short-listed him for the Turner."

I couldn't believe what I was hearing. There must have been some mistake.

"Nina, are you still there?"

"Short-listed?" I repeated.

"Indeed."

"That's very good news," I managed. The palms of my hands began to sweat.

"The judges were impressed with his exploration of darkness and light and his attitude towards identity."

"They were?"

"Yes, and they liked this whole idea of bringing art back to the subject matter and not the artist. Meaning no disrespect to Foruki but he makes his point in an understated way and we felt that this year this is what the Turner needed; a little more sobriety than the circus the media turn it into."

"Yes it does," I replied, not knowing what to say. If he was short-listed it meant press attention on a massive scale. What would we do? "To be honest with you, Tastudi, I'm not sure how he will take the news — you know, with the publicity and everything."

"We have taken this into account and have briefed the press office. The announcement will be made on June the fourteenth and they'd like you to come in to discuss how you'd like to handle this. So give them a call to arrange a time that is convenient."

"I will."

"Convey my regards to Foruki and I know he'll be very busy but we must do lunch soon."

"We will," I replied, remaining professional. "Thank you, Tastudi."

I hung up. I didn't know whether to scream with excitement or bury my head. This was serious. I thought it was all over. How were we going to pull this one off? I called up Gina.

"Gina, are you sitting down?"

"What's up, Nina?"

"Foruki's been short-listed for the Turner."

"No bloody way! . . . Roon, you've been short-listed for the Turner Prize."

"Is he there with you, Gina?"

"Yeah, he's here. Come round as soon as you can."

There was a bottle of champagne waiting on the table when I got to Gina's house.

"I know I should be happy but I don't know if I can go through with this once more. I'm only beginning to find some kind of stability and it means more lies and deceit."

"Nina, it's the Turner Prize. This just doesn't happen. It's a once in a lifetime opportunity and when

338

it's all over you can come clean or kill him off, it doesn't really matter."

"But Mangetti, I actually like him, I don't want to lie to him any more."

"We've come this far, you can't back out now. What will you say to him?"

"I'll tell him the truth. He might even understand."

"Think about this. Realistically, Foruki is not going to win. They've obviously short-listed him because he's not controversial and probably tempers all the other artists. They've done it for their own self-interest. They wanted someone with a traditional approach and you've given that to them — you're doing them a favour.

"When it's all over and if you feel the need to tell Mangetti, tell him — but just do this one more time. Do it for us."

"What if they find out?"

"They haven't up until now, have they? Artusion was a pretty big venue, nobody found out then, did they?"

"What if he wins?"

"He won't," Gina insisted. "They're just doing this to shut some of the critics up but there's no way he'll win, let's be realistic. It's fixed, they like all that circus stuff, they are not going to choose a painter."

"And if he does win?"

"Then that would be mad."

Rooney agreed with Gina and asked me to see it through as we had got that far.

The only reason why I would go through with it again was because I had become increasingly insular in

339

my own world and I wanted to feel the bond and the sense of excitement the three of us had created the first time we brought Foruki to life.

"Let's do it," I said, opening the champagne.

Kendal Brown's offices were reopened the following week and the phone line activated. I met with the Tate's press office to give them more information about Foruki. His résumé was brief and had the main biographical details and a list of some obscure galleries in Japan that Gina had put together where he had supposedly exhibited. The coordinator said that they needed more to work with. "The main point to stress about Foruki," I reiterated, "is his desire for anonymity and that the focus has to be on his work."

"It is going to be fairly difficult to maintain his privacy as the press always want to interview the artist and Channel Four do a six-minute presentation about the artist and their work which is aired the evening of the prize-giving."

"Is that obligatory?" I asked, stunned. How the hell were we going to do that?

"All the artists normally participate, even the ones who are media shy. We find the less information you give the press, the more they want, so I would advise Foruki to partake in the documentary."

How could I have Rooney on national TV talking about his concepts? "I'll try to talk him into it," I replied.

"It would be for the best as his privacy is so guarded you don't want him to stand out."

340

The press shots I handed over were photographs that Gina had taken of Rooney wearing a cap and enormous sunglasses. "These are the only shots he'll allow you to use," I said handing them over to the PR lady.

The day the short-list was officially announced, journalists began calling for specific details.

"The more I don't tell you about Foruki, the more you'll want to know; this is the point he's trying to make, that the artist is bigger than the subject matter." I was using reverse psychology so they would feel that Foruki was so up himself that they weren't going to bother finding out anything more about him. I also slipped in some personal details that would feed their insatiable curiosity, like his father abandoning him which had marked his psyche at a very young age, beginning the journey of the search for identity and the sense of self.

I tried to field their questions without sounding too evasive but there was a journalist called Richard Morris from the *Guardian* who was much more tenacious and wouldn't let it go.

"Miss Savani, the galleries where Foruki claims to have exhibited in Japan haven't heard of him."

My mouth went dry — of course they wouldn't have heard of him — but I was prepared for this question. "Of course they haven't heard of him. When he's in his own country he goes under different pseudonyms. It's never about him, it's his art. In fact he doesn't even like doing exhibitions and the only way he will show his work is to go under different names."

"So let me get this right. He has done no major exhibitions anywhere in the world and he suddenly decides to go in for the Turner, and this is a man who is media shy?"

"The only reason why he was persuaded to enter the Turner Prize was that it would be a platform for the statement he is trying to make on the nature of identity and celebrity in today's media-frenzied culture. Everyone is so obsessed as to who is behind the art that the art gets overlooked. He is trying to find authenticity in fakeness. Judge Foruki by the paintings he does and not the man he is. I have another call waiting, Mr Morris, I really must go," I said, trying to get rid of him. "If you have any more questions, give me a call." I put the phone down, incredibly nervous about what he might unearth if he dug a little deeper, but I put these thoughts to the back of my mind while I tried to concentrate on what exactly Foruki would put together for the exhibition at the Tate.

Richard Morris called again later that evening.

It's the weasel, I thought as soon as I heard his turgid voice. Didn't he have anything better to investigate?

"You say, Ms Savani, that you left Whitter and Lawson so you could bring Foruki over to London."

"That's right," I replied, sitting upright in my chair.

"Why is it that your former boss, Simon Lawson, says that he had to let you go because you were on the verge of a breakdown?"

Simon wouldn't have said that, I knew he wouldn't have, even if he wasn't impressed by my behaviour when I left. But how else would the weasel have known? What if Simon had said that?

"There was a conflict of interest between the two of us, he's hardly going to praise me for leaving." Yes, that was a good answer; that would cover it.

"And you say you went to Japan in May 1998 and that is where you stumbled upon your chap Foruki?"

Breathe, Nina, breathe. "That's right."

"Why is it that Mr Lawson has no recollection of you going to Japan at that time?"

I began to sweat. I took a deep breath and thought of the best thing I could think of. "It was hardly something that I was going to broadcast to my boss — what I do in my personal time has nothing to do with anyone else."

"So you're still not prepared to grant me the first interview with Foruki?"

"As I have said, Foruki doesn't court publicity and therefore I am unable to do this."

"Right," he replied.

The way he said, "right" made me feel incredibly uneasy.

"Is there anything else I can help you with?" I asked in a vain attempt to show him that he had not unnerved me.

"No, that's all for now," he replied. "No doubt we will speak again soon."

I called Gina straightaway. She told me not to worry, that all journalists tried it on; it was their job. But I wasn't reassured; he wasn't like the other journalists who I had spoken to. I got the sense that he could see through me; he made me feel as if he knew that I hadn't told the truth and was waiting to see how long it would take before I snapped.

Thinking about Richard Morris and what he might write the next day worried me and I was unable to sleep: he had the power to ruin us — not just us, but ruin Mangetti's reputation. Every time I wanted to call Mangetti and tell him everything, I called Gina instead.

The following morning, Gina and Rooney came around to my flat with the articles that had appeared. "See, nothing at all to worry about, Nina."

THE NONCONTROVERSIAL SHORT-LIST
The only thing that is controversial about this year's Turner Prize is its noncontroversy. The four short-listed are a sober mix of artists: Steve Carey from Leeds sculpts nudes with garden fences; Londoner Amanda Finley models still-life using fabrics; Foruki, a British-born Japanese media-shy painter, whose work is about identity; and finally, photographer Matthew Perring from Durham whose photography captures speed and motion . . .

ENIGMA SURROUNDING SHORT-LISTED ARTIST
The only thing slightly controversial about this year's Turner Prize is the identity of one of the short-listed artists. Foruki, a British-Japanese artist, refuses to reveal his real identity as a matter

344

of principle. Identity is one of the main statements he makes through his work and he is vehement about his art being at the fore rather than himself . . .

"It's just crazy," Gina said as she read.

"Are you having doubts?" I asked.

"Absolutely not," she replied. "There's so much we can do here."

My fears were allayed as I read on and nothing untoward had been written. Perhaps I knew it was naïve to think that he would let it go just like that but I wanted to be lulled into a false sense of security. I wanted to believe everything would work out because there was no time to dwell on what could potentially go wrong; there was only three months before the Channel 4 documentary was due to be filmed and I had a series of new pictures to paint for the exhibition at the Tate, all around the theme of identity. The biggest irony was I finally knew who I was but was doing one of the biggest exhibitions I would ever do for someone who did not exist.

For the next few months I was absorbed with my pictures. The first piece I did was a six-foot canvas with the famous image of Marilyn Monroe trying to hold down her white dress, but instead of using her head I painted a faint Japanese face. It was Mrs Onoro's face.

This piece took me weeks and after it was completed I took out another enormous canvas and painted it white. I was going to have an elaborate gold frame around it. In the middle I painted the words "self-portrait" in bold black letters and then signed it Foruki. On the next canvas I painted an abstract Rooney, changing his face slightly each time so by the fifth canvas his face completely dissolved and all that was left were segments of the colours used to paint the face.

The third canvas had an explosion of loud, vibrant paint. I was trying to capture the madness of what had happened in the last six months. The picture was of a rush-hour scene in the morning with a sea of commuters trying to get to work. Behind them all, on an underground poster, was a woman who was painting a picture of a man.

And the final piece in this collection was of an old man holding a newborn baby — only in these two phases of our lives do we not care who we are or what we have.

When the pictures were finally completed I let Rooney and Gina come to the studio.

"The first two are quite calculated. I thought we needed to make a strong statement about the nature of identity, and the next two . . . I don't know what they are about, it was just an emotion I had."

"They're absolutely beautiful, Nina," Gina said studying them. "Really beautiful."

The three of us spent hours discussing what each of the paintings meant and how to present it in a form palatable to Channel 4. Gina said she would prep Rooney and work on all his mannerisms so this would leave me free to take care of whatever else needed to be done.

The two of them had become very close: he was virtually living with her but he hadn't formally taken the step of moving in because he didn't want to upset Mrs Onoro, although I thought that she would have been delighted. They were good together — they joked about together a lot and he understood her. Being around Gina had changed Rooney considerably; he had become very self-confident and incredibly decisive. Gina also believed in herself a lot more because of the support he provided. Sometimes I was envious; not because they had found each other but because it reminded me of what I possibly could have had with Michael.

A few weeks before the curators were due to arrive I went into the office and dealt with all the admin and the queries from journalists all around the world. I did stop to think about the madness but when I did that I got the jitters and wanted to call Mangetti and tell him that there had been a terrible mistake. How I could class a blatant lie as a mistake I didn't know, and so the only way my conscience would allow me to reconcile the whole scenario was by treating Foruki as if he really were my client, and this being the case I endeavoured to do my best for him.

A few days before the curators arrived, Gina came to the studio with Rooney to show me how far she had got with prepping him.

"OK Roon, just make yourself feel comfortable with the paintings and then try to talk to us about them,"

347

Gina said. "Make like we're the camera crew or something, don't forget what I told you and, you know . . . that pose at the end."

"This is Marilyn Monroe," he pointed, "with my mum's head. She'll be dead proud, she's always wanted her face somewhere. This is my face all mixed up, suppose it's because no one knows who I am or who I'm supposed to be. Here you've got some tube scene . . . and anyone can see this old man and kid."

I despaired. If this was the best we could do we might as well have a banner on display telling everyone that we were a bunch of fakes. "We're not going to pull this one off. The viewers aren't stupid. Anyway, Foruki can't talk like that, what happened to the accent he was going to do?"

"Be serious, Rooney," Gina said.

"It's not going to work," I said, shaking my head.

"The whole question of identity is one I constantly searching for; is man a woman, is woman a man, what make him so? Is it society? Society tell us a lot of thing, make a lot of rule."

I looked up at Rooney.

"They turn people into celebrity; they give them an identity which is false. I try to find authenticity in fakeness. Look at Marilyn Monroe; it media who dictate who is she really; inside she might be old lady."

I smiled in disbelief as he continued. "My work is about trying to detract from artist and what to expect, the artist merely conduit. He is not painting. That is what I try to show here. Artist dissolves before picture," he said, pointing to the mixture of colour that had

348

become separated from his face. It not important who paint what but feeling and statement picture leave you with. This is human emotion," Rooney continued, indicating towards the picture of the old man and the baby. "Pure, simple emotion. It when human kind show their true self, no need to impress anybody."

I began to cry. "How . . . how did you do that?"

"Gina and me, we don't waste time. She's been teaching me how to speak. We want this to work for you, Nina."

"I haven't taught him how to paint yet," Gina said. "That's what we've got to focus on now, how he throws paint on a canvas and captures emotion. He doesn't have to learn the rest of it, just the initial paint-throwing bit."

Before the curators came Rooney had mastered how to appear to work in a style that Foruki would have been proud of.

We got Rooney ready to meet the curators. Foruki discussed at length in Japanese with the curators the work he wanted to display at the Tate while Gina translated. The curators agreed and together we decided how and when the pictures would be hung. We had a month left to practise as the paintings needed to be exhibited at the Tate by the end of October. Two weeks later the crew arrived from the production company to film Foruki at his studio.

"You're not allowed to take close-up shots of his face," I said to the cameraman.

"But you're hardly going to see anything with that big cap and those sunglasses."

"That is the idea, the press office told me that you have been briefed on the nature of what can be shown."

The director came over and said some close-up shots were required. Rooney threw a tantrum and said, "I don't know if I express myself properly but not me close up or I don't do this."

"Artists, very temperamental," I added.

"Quite," he replied. "Ian, no close-ups of the artist's face."

The presenter introduced Foruki's work first. "The paintings have such bold use of colour that they scream so loudly you can't ignore them; unlike the artist who wants to remain very much in the background."

There was a shot of Rooney pretending to be working away in the background. Gina and I had taught him how to look contemplative while putting the paint onto the canvas.

We'd also taught him another move, which was to pick up various paints erratically and dip his hands into the mixture while working in a frenzy. The cameraman got a shot of this and a close-up of his hands working away.

"Could you give us a commentary?" the presenter asked.

"He's unable to speak when he works," I added, "he enters a world of his own."

"We'll do a separate take with him talking later," the director shouted.

350

They took various shots of his hands and his feet moving, and of the studio.

"We need some sound bites now," the director instructed.

The presenter began asking Foruki questions.

"Foruki, why is it so important to you that the pictures appear in the foreground and the artist very much in the background, behind the work?"

We had rehearsed this question over and over.

"It's artist work that is important, not artist. People make judgements about my work when see me. I want them to look at work for itself, not for who painted it. I want them feel raw emotion."

"Cut, we didn't quite get what emotion that was."

Rooney had overdone the accent slightly so it sounded like "waw". "Raw," I repeated.

"Foruki, if you could just say that last sentence again, that is, 'I want them to feel raw emotion.'"

Gina had to leave the room as she began laughing.

Rooney did it again.

"Just talk to us about this particular collection," the presenter asked.

"This one is search for identity. People put value and judgement on thing so Marilyn Monroe, you expect her to be certain way, but maybe she not like that at all. Media age we live in is able to create celebrity but person they create does not exist."

He talked about each of the pictures. "This one here is when we show our vulnerability," he said pointing to the painting of the old man and the baby. "This is the only time we are truly ourselves, when we are vulnerable," Rooney stated.

"I think we have all that we need. Thank you very much, Mr Foruki," the director said. "Very interesting."

"When does this run?" I asked.

"It goes out on the night of the prize-giving between the live Channel 4 broadcast."

That wasn't too bad, I thought. If anyone recognised Rooney it wouldn't matter as it would be all over by then.

After having spent the entire day with us, the crew left. "Intriguing personality," the presenter commented. "Has something Michael Jackson-ish about him," he said sarcastically.

"Do you think we did it?" Rooney asked when they had gone.

Gina and I burst out laughing.

"You're an absolute star."

Two weeks later we were at the Tate gallery and the curators were assisting us and advising us as to where best to hang the collection. The other artists had already put their collections in the designated rooms.

As we were leaving I looked up at the high ceilings and the grandeur of the Tate. Rooney and Gina stopped. Each of us was struck by the enormity of what we were doing.

"What if we win?" Gina asked.

"You said it was highly unlikely," I replied.

"That was then."

Gina was the one who always reassured me. I pretended to hold my nerve and reassured her. "We see how it goes, we say nothing. Maybe Foruki has enough of all the publicity and emigrates, maybe he dies — I don't know. One step at a time."

"No, he won't win," Rooney said. "I just know he won't, that bloke with the garden fences is going to bag it."

The likelihood of Foruki winning was one in four. He couldn't win; he was just used to pacify some of the severer critics; the Turner Prize wasn't intended for artists such as Foruki, it was meant to court controversy. As Rooney said, "garden-fence man would bag it".

I couldn't put Tastudi Mangetti off any longer. He kept calling to see when he could see Foruki again. He came to Foruki's studio the day before the exhibition at the Tate opened to members of the public. Mangetti told Rooney how impressed he was at the new collection. Rooney spoke some English, some Japanese.

"But Foruki, you speak very good English."

Rooney nodded.

"But I know how it is when you are trying to express something that is in your heart . . . the depths of you," he gestured. "I feel the same way and want to speak in Italian. The work is just exquisite."

"Thank you, Mr Mangetti," Rooney bowed.

"And how is my commission coming along?" Among all the preparation I had forgotten that I was supposed to be painting Mangetti.

Rooney stared blankly.

"As you'll appreciate, Tastudi," I interjected, "Foruki has been extremely busy so it's not quite finished."

"Seeing as I'm here, let me take a quick look."

"No," Rooney shouted.

"What Foruki means is he never lets anyone see work in progress, it disperses the energy around the picture," I added quickly.

Rooney nodded. "Not good to see half man," he replied, "but you take this . . ." He pointed to a canvas that I had experimented on. "It not finished but when it finished it for you." Hadn't he just contradicted me as I'd said he never allowed people to see work in progress. I stared at Rooney, confused.

"How much is it?" Mangetti asked, staring at the red lines.

"No, it gift from me to you."

Mangetti was assuaged.

"Most generous of you, Foruki, and I accept it with the generosity with which it is given."

"Welcome, welcome." Rooney shuffled about a bit as if he had somewhere else he had to be.

"I know you are busy and thank you for sharing your space with me. It must have taken a lot and I appreciate it. Foruki, it has been a pleasure as always."

I showed Mangetti out. "A very affable character. Nina, do you know his paintings have doubled in value?"

I just wanted to get Mangetti out of there. "We'll talk about it later," I said. "When this is all over."

Mangetti climbed into his Bentley. "I will be in touch."

354

I went back into the studio. " 'Welcome'? 'Welcome'? You're getting too good at this, Rooney."

He laughed.

It was a hectic day; journalists were calling up asking if they could have an interview with Foruki and have pictures of him by his work. I said that he didn't do any interviews and the press office had pictures of him standing by his latest collection.

"But he has his back to the camera."

"I know. Can't you think up a title: 'Artist turns his back on fame', or something like that? It has been done this way intentionally," I said.

The journalist at the *Guardian* would not let it go.

"So where exactly did you say Foruki had studied art?"

"I didn't and he didn't. He learned from his mother who was a painter."

"And she is dead, is this correct?"

"Yes. It was through his paintings that he could come to terms with her death."

"Has he found the father he came looking for?"

"Sorry?"

"You said in our last conversation that he came to find his father."

I hadn't realised I had said that.

"Sadly, his father died a year ago."

"And what was his name?"

"Kenneth David."

"You've been most helpful, Ms Savani. Intriguing details you have given me, we'll be speaking again soon."

When he hung up I felt very nervous. Something didn't feel right. I didn't speak to Gina about it as she was getting as nervous about the whole thing as I was. I did what I knew best; put it to the back of my mind and pretended that everything would be fine.

The exhibition at the Tate was going well and my fears were allayed once more when nothing sinister about Foruki appeared in the press. Journalists just focused on interviews with the fence man who sculptured nudes, and also on how sedate and noncontroversial the Turner Prize nominees were this year. Articles did appear on Foruki, but mostly about his artwork being more important than the personality. Gina kept all the cuttings and would only let me read the good things that were said about him.

"Just one more month to go and it will all be over," I said.

"Nina, Rooney's moving in with me."

"That's fantastic."

"He's telling Lydia now. He's getting someone to watch over the stall part-time so he can concentrate on his music. So you don't mind?"

"Why should I mind? It's brilliant news. Mrs Onoro will be fine about it, you'll see."

"She's only got a bloke," Rooney said coming in.

"Did it go OK, what did she say?"

"She almost strangled me cos she was so happy and then she told me she's seeing a healer. 'For your legs, Ma?' I asked, and she said, 'No, for love.' Anyway, she wants us to go around for dinner on Saturday night and meet him. Come as well, Nina, she's been asking about you."

"I've got something to do," I replied, "but tell her I'll see her soon."

I knew I would have been more than welcome but I wanted to go and attempt to see my parents.

Mum and Dad hung up whenever I phoned so I got Gina to call up on Friday night to say that Dad had been selected in a special draw and the prize was two tickets to go and see Cilla Black.

I could imagine him asking her what draw it was, as he didn't believe you could get anything for free.

"Our representative will come and see you tomorrow evening at six o'clock and will explain everything clearly to you."

"What did he say?" I asked Gina as she got off the phone.

"He double-checked that she wouldn't try to sell him anything otherwise he'd tell her 'to get off'. When I said you wouldn't, he said he'd be waiting."

I didn't know what made me feel more nervous, meeting Mangetti or my dad.

I rang the bell and could hear him shout out to my mother that it was for him.

My heart was racing.

He opened the door. I put one foot against it.

"Dad, let me just explain."

"Get off, I'm waiting for lady."

"The lady with the tickets is me. Please let me in so I can speak to you and Mum."

"The door-to-door selling now, this is what you doing?"

"No, Dad. That was just to —"

"Dickheads suffering and now you selling door-to-door. Get off, I don't want nothing." He was jamming the door against my foot so I had to pull it back.

"Dad, please," I shouted through the letterbox. "Channel 4, I want you to watch Channel 4 on the twenty-eighth of November ..." and just for that moment I wanted Foruki to win because then he might be proud of me. Then it dawned on me that he wouldn't even know that it had been me behind Foruki, and what did the Turner Prize mean to him anyway? He thought my mum could win it by assembling a pile of her samosas in the shape of the Star of India; it was for a bunch of lazy people who had too much time and money.

I walked around to Ki's house. I just wanted to put my arms around her mum and sit with her. Despite shouting through the letterbox, no one answered the door.

The 28th of November descended with the heaviness with which it was anticipated. It was raining heavily and there was the odd thunderstorm. Rooney and Gina came to collect me from the flat. Rooney had got one of his friends to drive us to Tate Britain.

"It's going to be fine, Nina, and think, after today it's all over," Gina said. "Are you ready for this?"

"Can't be much more prepared," I replied nervously.

We had rehearsed what Rooney would do in the unlikely event that Foruki should win. He would say a simple thank you and depending on the level of media interest we would see what needed to be done. If we didn't win it would be fine as Foruki could just slip away into the background and nobody need know any different. I would sell some more of his paintings and he would return to Japan and probably die at some point.

I could see crowds as we approached the Tate. There were some anti Turner Prize protestors dressed up as clowns. One banner read: "We are the bullshit detectors." Another read: "Turner Prize for a bunch of fakes." My heart beat faster. They booed as we got out of the car and made our way into the gallery.

Several introductions were made in the foyer and Foruki was introduced to the fence maker who sculpted nudes and who was the bookies' favourite as well as the other artists'. They congratulated each other. Simon my old boss was there and congratulated me on Foruki's success. He said that if I ever needed a job again it was waiting for me complete with promotion. I thanked him politely. I didn't even know if Richard Morris was there but it didn't matter now anyway as this was the final hurdle and once we got through this it would all be well and truly over. Mangetti came over and introduced us to the other judges, lots of other people hovered around us and then it was time to take our seats at the table.

Gina and I sat on either side of Rooney. I looked up at the large ceilings and wondered how on earth we had got there. Drinks were served and then starters. My stomach was churning. A television camera pointed at us and we knew that we were going out live. Mrs Onoro would be at home watching nervously. I wondered whether my dad would flick the channel over from Zee and see me — maybe he would. There was a lot of hustle and bustle, people moving from their seats, nervous coughs, laughter, the sound of clinking glasses and talking which echoed loudly through the hall.

The Channel 4 presenter was trying to talk and move among the bustle and on several occasions nearly fell over. The director was introducing the fashion designer who was about to make the presentation and just as he was doing that a man with ginger hair walked over to me.

"Richard Morris, the *Guardian*."

It was an inappropriate time for introductions so I just smiled and waited for the fashion designer to open the envelope.

"Nervous tonight then, Ms Savani?"

"Nervous for Foruki," I said swiftly.

"One and the same," he replied.

He had my attention.

"Kenneth David does not exist. Lydia Onoro lives at Frith Road, her son is a Ronald Onoro, a grocer. Do you have anything to say?"

I could feel the blood drain from my face. I wanted to be sick. He couldn't do this to me, not then; he could have chosen any other day, any other moment.

"No comment," I stuttered.

360

I could see him go over to the judges. Please don't do this to me, not today. Tastudi Mangetti turned white, his eyes bulged, and then all I could hear was the crowd clapping and cheering and Gina saying, "Bloody hell, Nina, we've won, we've bloody won." Rooney got up. Mangetti stared at me. We couldn't publicly humiliate him. What was I going to do? I got up and went after Rooney.

"Think, Nina, think." We hadn't prepared for the eventuality that this would happen on the night of the prize-giving. I followed Rooney onto the stage and I was aware that cameras were pointing at us.

"Thank you," Rooney said, accepting the cheque. "Thank you very much."

The crowd clapped.

I had to say something, otherwise Richard Morris would make an announcement and Mangetti's reputation would be ruined. My legs were shaking as I leaned towards the microphone.

"There is one thing that I'd like to add." The crowd were silent. "There's a final piece to the collection at the Tate and he's here today — Foruki," I announced. The crowd were unsure as to whether they had to clap. "Take off your hat and glasses, Rooney," I whispered while a few of them were clapping.

"What, here?"

"Yes."

Rooney took off his hat and his glasses.

"I'd like to introduce you to Ronald Onoro. He didn't paint the pictures, I did, and I'd like to thank Tastudi Mangetti for his support in helping me with the

361

project. We wanted to make a statement about bringing art back to its subject matter and not the artist, so I thank you Mr Mangetti for allowing me to show my work behind the Japanese character we invented."

People were unsure of what to do and then they began clapping.

"Thank you," I said, smiling despite the fact I felt like collapsing and have someone take me away from there.

As we climbed down from the stage, camera crews, journalists and photographers surrounded us. "Nina, how did you come up with the idea?" "Did you do it because you are Asian?" "Nina, how do you feel about winning the Turner?" "Look over here." "Why did you feel the need to do this?" Rooney was accosted in the same way. "What do you do, Ronald?" "Are you an artist?" The Communications Director from the Tate rushed over to us and told them that all questions would be answered at a press conference at nine o'clock in the morning. He then turned to me: "Tastudi Mangetti is waiting outside for you both; it's best if you leave now."

Gina was across the room trying to get to us but there was no way of reaching her. We left. Mangetti's Bentley was parked outside, waiting for us. The clowns were shouting at us, "Bunch of fakes." We were, but not in the way that they meant.

The car door was opened.

"Get in."

Mangetti's assistant was sitting beside him.

"Were you thinking of ruining me?" Mangetti said very calmly.

"No. I'm so sorry, Tastudi. I didn't think we were going to win it."

"Is it true about Mr Foruki's occupation?"

"Yes," Rooney replied.

"But you came into my office and spoke passionately about your concepts; your art."

I shook my head.

"They weren't his concepts?" His eyes were bulging, his nose seemed even more prominent.

"No, Tastudi."

"I've been to your studio and seen your work." He was seething but trying to contain himself; his cheeks were florid.

"It was my studio. I'm really, truly sorry — none of this was supposed to happen, you see . . ."

"What about me?" he interrupted. "The press are going to have a field day with this. And me? What about me? Was it an attack on the establishment or just me personally?" he shouted.

"We can turn this around," I said trying to calm him down. "I know we can."

"Who the hell are you to tell me what we can and cannot do. I never trusted your sort anyway, you're all swindlers, cheap swindlers, stick to what you know best."

"Just hang on, Mr Mangetti, Nina meant none of this personally."

"Who are you anyway? A grocer?" He looked at Rooney as if he had just found him at the bottom of his shoe and then he turned to me, utterly disgusted. "Have my driver drop you wherever you want, I've got to get out. Be there at eight tomorrow morning or face the consequences."

Mangetti and the assistant got out of the car. Rooney and I got out of the car as soon as they were out of sight.

"Oh God, I'm sorry, Rooney."

"You've got nothing to be sorry about, in fact, I'm glad you did that to him."

Gina phoned to tell us not to go to any of the houses as the press might be camping outside. "They've been asking me all kinds of questions. I've said nothing but it's big. Nobody left, they were all waiting for answers and more press were turning up," she said.

We arranged to meet at a Travelodge near London Bridge and decided to stay there for the night. It was a nightmare; a complete nightmare. None of it was about making anyone look stupid; if Mangetti had given me a chance to explain maybe he would have seen that. And his threat — it didn't scare me, but despite the fact that Mangetti had been obnoxious I still wanted him to look good, then everything would finally be over.

Gina met us an hour later at the Travelodge and we spent hours with Rooney discussing all the possibilities and what we could say the following day. I went to bed at three in the morning. And though I was exhausted I was awake most of the night, unable to sleep.

I thought about the fact that I had won the Turner and it baffled me. How the hell did that happen? One of the biggest prizes in art was mine. Did I win it because they felt the paintings were good or because they needed someone and Foruki's unusual profile seemed to fit the bill? It didn't matter anyway, it was all subjective. Everyone was playing a game, it was just that some people were unaware of the rules. I had found myself in the midst of it all and made the rules up as I went along. How could I explain that it was as simple as that. All I ever wanted to do was paint and be me.

It was six o'clock when I hauled myself out of bed. As I came out of the shower I switched the television on and thought I saw a shot of my parents' house. It *was* my parents' house and there was a media pack outside.

"No, they can't do this to me." I held my hand to my mouth.

My mum opened the door, taken aback by all the flashing. She started calling out for my dad. He came to the door in his red pyjamas and had a microphone thrust in his face.

"Mr Savani, what do you think of your daughter's antics?"

Oh God, please don't let him say anything. "No comment," I willed. "Say 'no comment', Dad."

"Antics?" he shouted. "She doesn't have no furniture here, now get off." He made some erratic gestures.

I had my head in my hands.

The ensuing scenes were cut as they returned back to the news reporter.

"We seem to have lost the sound but I'm sure it will be a story that we will return to."

365

I called my parents but the phone was engaged. I kept trying in between drying my hair and after half an hour I finally got through.

"Dad, it's me, Nina, please don't hang up."

"Oh my daughter Nina," he said. "I can't speak to you now because we have the television peoples filming here."

"Is that Nina, Mr Savani? Could we possibly have a word with her?" A woman came on the line. "Nina, your parents are giving us the first live exclusive interview. We're about to run, stay on the phone, we'd like to talk to you too."

"I don't have anything to say. Could you give it back to my dad please?"

"Nina, it would give you an opportunity to put your side of the story across."

"It will be put across later this morning, could you hand the phone back to my dad please? . . . Dad, don't speak to them."

"Nina, I must go, the lady is calling me." He hung up.

I tried ringing again but the phone was off the hook and then a few minutes later I heard his voice on the television.

"Good morning Mr and Mrs Savani."

"Good morning," he shouted.

Both my parents were sitting on the Land of Leather sofa. My dad had changed into his red shirt and my mum was wearing her green sari. They had obviously been briefed on what had happened. As the reporter did her introduction the camera turned to photographs of me everywhere, photos that I was sure they had got rid of.

"So here we are talking to the parents of Nina Savani, the lawyer who managed to dupe the art world by getting a grocer to stand in for her as the artist." The reporter, realising she was getting vacuumed by the sofa, attempted to move to the edge of the seat. "An ingenious ploy and indeed some would say cunning. We're talking live to her parents this morning. So, Mr and Mrs Savani, did you believe your daughter was an agent?"

"Of course. It's the normal. She is one because I am one."

Oh God, I thought, he's misunderstood her: "Not 'Asian', Dad, 'agent'."

"You are?" Her voice sounded perplexed.

"Can't you see that?"

Someone must have told the reporter not to continue that line of questioning as she suddenly said, "Did you know about your daughter's scheme to fool the art world?"

I shook my head: "Please don't say anything, Dad."

"Definitely. I knew she was fooling them but not for one moment was I the fooled. I said fool them, do a good job and fool them."

"Is it because you agreed on her critique of the artist being bigger than the art itself?"

He looked confused. "What?"

She rephrased her question. "Did you encourage her because of the statement she was making?"

"No, I said this because when you do any job you make sure you do it properly. I have always told her this."

"Do you have any of her art here that you can show us?"

"We don't keep the pictures here, too expensive to leave in the house because of the burglars."

"Indeed. And what do you think about what she has done?"

"I am the proud," he bellowed.

I didn't know whether to laugh or cry and then the reporter turned to my mum.

"Mrs Savani?"

My mother nodded.

"Does she have any future plans?"

"Marriage, hopefully," she sighed.

"Mr and Mrs Savani, thank you. Now, back to the studio."

"Thank you, Sonia. I have Professor Landstein from Goldsmith University with me to talk about the nature of the duplicity." The presenter turned to the professor.

"Professor, what is your opinion on the statement Nina Savani was making?"

"The fact that she went to such lengths is an artistic statement in itself. She has opened up the debate even further; pushing forth the boundaries as to what one deems as art and it begs the question, can one call duplicity an art form?" He began going off "on the rambles" and she interrupted him by saying, "For viewers who have just joined us, one of the leading stories today is the lawyer who duped the art world by . . ."

Didn't they have more important news to discuss?

I couldn't listen to it and turned the television off, got ready and switched my phone on. The message box was full. I went through them quickly; most of them were from journalists and there was one from Jean and one from my dad. "Nina, did you see me on the TV? Did they get a picture of the sofa? They wanted us to sit in the dining room but we told them no, sitting room on sofa or no deal." And then I could hear my mum in the background asking if I was eating properly.

I got a phone call from Mangetti giving us instructions as to where he wanted to meet us before going to the Tate. The three of us met him in a grotty café where he briefed us.

He said to say that the judges had known all along that the paintings were not done by Foruki and the point they were making with the nominee Nina Savani, aka Foruki, was the extent to which celebrity had permeated today's society, so much so that people were fascinated not just by the subject matter but by the artist. "You are clear on this?" Mangetti asked. "You wanted to illustrate the nature of identity in today's society. You must insist that the judges were aware. Do you understand?"

I understood all of it but I wanted him to know why we did it — but he never let me explain. He wanted us to get into the Bentley with him so we could make our way to the Tate together.

369

"Not you," he said, staring at Gina as she was about to climb in.

"Rooney and I will walk then," I replied.

"You're not in a position to play with me, Nina."

"I'm not playing, I never was, it's the three of us or we walk." And I don't know where the courage to say that came from but I meant it literally because the side of Mangetti I was seeing was ugly and making him look good didn't seem as important as having my friend there.

"Get in," he mumbled, not even looking at her.

A few photographers pounced on us as we got out of the car and made our way into the Tate. We were taken to a room. It was packed. Photographer's bulbs were flashing away. Rooney and I were seated next to each other, alongside Mangetti, another judge and a spokesperson from the Tate. Questions were fired at me from all directions. I stuck to the story that Mangetti had told us to say: that we had gone to such lengths to make a statement about art and the best way to illustrate the point was to demonstrate the very nature of identity. The panel were asked at what stage Mangetti knew about it and he answered: he was adamant that it was from the beginning. They were then asked if I would still receive the £20,000 prize money, as technically I was not the one who had won. They responded by saying that the work was judged on its own merit and not by the artist and therefore the prize would still go to me. There were more questions but it was the one from a lady sitting two rows from the front that stopped me for a moment. It was a lady who

370

had wispy white hair, and she reminded me of the woman who had smiled at me on the tube a year ago. She asked me about the theme that ran through my first exhibition at Artusion and specifically about the painting of the hand, which I had named *Beyond Indigo*.

I wanted to tell her about my best friend Ki who had died in my arms two years ago — but how I wasn't lost any more. "*Beyond Indigo* is about believing and knowing that something exists even if you can't see it. It's about believing in all possibilities," I replied.

There were questions for Rooney — who he was, what he did. It was endless. After half an hour the press conference was brought to a close.

Mangetti had his arm around me for the press shots and was smiling, and then as soon as it was over he left without saying a word to me.

Gina and Rooney invited me back to celebrate at their house but I needed time on my own to take stock of what had happened and so I told them I would catch up with them later. After successfully dodging the press, I went to Green Park. It was cold, but not as cold and wet as it had been a year earlier. The trees were looking bare. Had the leaves jumped off the branches of their own accord or were they pushed along by the wind? A year ago I was here on my knees, stripped of everything, and a year later I had finally learned to see flowers; I had kept believing even when there was clearly nothing there. And in my moments of doubting, people were sent to show me otherwise. I had defied all odds and won the bloody Turner. How mad was that?

Was it because I had taken a leap of faith and done something out of the ordinary? Or was it because I was pushed and swept along? Whatever it was, on the journey I found parts of myself that I never knew existed.

The greatest irony in being someone else was that I learned to be me: to trust myself, to be myself. It was as simple as that. Maybe there were no concrete answers to anything, just experiences; to live each moment as it came.

There were press camped outside my doorstep so I went to the studio, packed up my paints, took down the buddha and wrapped him up. I then went to the rental company to hire the van again, loaded everything up and went to Gina's house.

Gina and Rooney were having lunch with Mrs Onoro when I walked in.

Mrs Onoro smiled. "Ohhhhhhhh, Nina, you done so good. I saw the TV and news; you and Rooney everywhere. They come looking for Rooney. I say I not know no man call Rooney. After, I go to Japanese Association and make them follow someone else, then I come here."

"It's all so crazy," Gina said. "You've been on every channel, Nina."

"I told you Rooney win prize. He always win everything when he was child. Lucky charm," she said, touching her necklace.

"It's mad, I still can't believe it," I replied. "They are camping outside the flat and the phone hasn't stopped ringing."

"What are you going to do, Nina?"

"I'm going to go away for a few months until it dies down."

"You can come stay with me," Mrs Onoro suggested.

"Thank you, Mrs Onoro, but I've decided to go to Ireland."

"Who's in Ireland?" Rooney asked.

"Man who you write 'go for it' to?" Mrs Onoro interrupted.

"No. Another experience, maybe?"

I stayed over with them all. Gina crept into my flat for me in the middle of the night to get a few things together, and in the morning I said my goodbyes.

"I'm going to make this quick as I'm not really very good with goodbyes and anyway I'm not going for long. I just don't know how to thank you all enough."

"You don't say nothing, you good girl, Nina," Mrs Onoro said.

"Yeah," Rooney added. "One of the nicest people I've met."

Gina was silent. I looked at her and tears streamed down my face. "Thank you for believing in me," I whispered as I held her. "This is for you and Rooney, open it when I go." I wanted them to have half the Turner Prize money because without them both, none of it would have been possible.

Tastudi Mangetti called to say that for everything I had put him through the least I could do was to sell him the buddha painting. He offered me £60,000.

"I'm terribly sorry, Mr Mangetti, but 'our sort' have some things that are not for sale."

"I will make sure you are unable to exhibit anywhere — I promise you."

"You go ahead and do that." I hung up on him. If the Mafia ever knocked on the semi it was my dad they had to fear.

Gina, Rooney and Mrs Onoro waved me off. I went to see Ki's mum.

"Auntie, open the door, it's me, Nina."

She came to the door.

"What happened, Nina? I saw you on the news."

I told her the story about Ki's name being mistaken and she began to laugh and then she cried.

"She's always here with us, Auntie."

"I know, beta."

"There's something I want you to have."

I went into the van and got out the picture of the buddha. She tore off the brown paper and studied it curiously, just the same way she looked at the pictures I handed her as a child.

"It's very nice," she lied.

She came up to Ki's room with me. We hung the picture of the buddha on the wall and her mum said maybe she needed to paint the walls and wash the curtains. Then she left me alone in the room.

"I still miss you, you know, but I can still hear you laughing. Are you laughing now? Only you could have orchestrated this, it's got your name written all over it. All I asked for was a sign not to win the bloody Turner." I blew her a kiss, "I love you, Ki," and then I went downstairs.

"Take care of yourself, beta." Ki's mum kissed me as I left.

"I will, Auntie, and you take care of yourself too."

The phone rang — it was Raj. I picked it up because that was the least I owed him.

"Congratulations, Nina, I saw it all on the news."

"Thank you. How are you? Are you all right?"

"I'm engaged," he said.

"That's fantastic news."

"To Pinkie, you remember her? She was brilliant after what happened with . . . with us, and then one thing led to another."

"I'm really happy for you, truly I am." Pinkie would make a far better wife than I possibly could have.

"Mummy's not happy about it but Pinkie and I have decided to go away and get married."

"Be happy, Raj. I really do wish you the very best."

"Stay in touch, Nina."

"I will."

I drove around the corner to my parents' house, checked that no one was waiting for me there and knocked on the door, unafraid if my dad would slam it in my face or not.

My dad answered it.

"Dad."

He smiled at me, welcomed me in and patted me on the back. "Nina, I am the celebrity in the depot."

"That's great, Dad, really great."

"All day yesterday we had the crews filming us. You see six o'clock news?"

My mum came out. I went to hug her and she was inert, like the biggest tidal wave had knocked her over and washed away everything she had left.

"You're still with the Jeannie?" my dad asked.

"It's not Jean, it's Michael, and no, I'm not with him."

"These things, they never last."

An enormous smile spread across my mum's face. "Raj," she gasped. "I prayed to Bhagavan and I knew it would work in the end."

"I'm not with him either. There's no one, and you know what? I'm happy."

"People will be queuing for you now that you are famous. Queuing I tells you. We might even be able to get the Kapadias' son."

The honchos considered the Kapadias to be the crème of the community. Their son, Hiten, was a barrister.

"You can move back today," my mum added.

"I'm not coming home."

"What?" my dad shouted.

"I'm going away for a few months to paint."

"We will let you do the painting in your room," my dad said.

"No, Dad."

My mum took her sari end out and sobbed.

"I only ever wanted you to be proud of me," I began to cry.

"Don't cry, Nina. You made us very proud. Who can say they have been on the news at six? Who can say they are going to meet the Cilla Black?"

376

"Cilla?"

"Yah, part of ITV deal for first exclusive interview. I tells them, nothing comes for free, I do this if you let me meet the Cilla."

He held out his arms to hug me. He never did that.

I held onto him and wept and then my mum did something I never thought she was capable of. She put her arms around both of us.

"Better go now, I'll call when I get there."

"I knew that there was no artist and it was you," my dad said on seeing the van. "I cannot be the fooled."

"You'll eat properly, no, beta?"

"Yes, Ma," I said, leaving.

My phone began ringing. I parked the van and answered it.

"Nina Savani?"

"Yes."

"Frances Evans, *Mail on Sunday*. We've spoken to a Mrs Malika Mehta with a story on how you duped her son Raj into marriage. She said that this is a pattern that seems to be recurrent with you. I just wanted to give you an opportunity to put across your side of the story."

I threw the phone out of the van and continued driving.

6th March 2001

I travelled to the west of Ireland and settled for a few months in Galway. The landscape and beauty that surrounded me was even more spectacular than

Michael had described and though the winter months made everything appear moodier that's not what I saw. I captured the energy of the roughness of the seas in vibrant reds. Beneath the grey clouds were piercing shafts of white light that made me look beyond them and see blue skies. Though the landscape was wet and damp with the rain, the raindrops glistened against luscious hues of green and when the snow came to settle I could still see the greens. Every day of these months, I painted. Solitude became part of my life and when I wasn't scared by it any more or trying to run away from it I knew it was time to go home — back to my flat and my studio.

Contrary to what Tastudi Mangetti said he would do, several gallery owners were interested in exhibiting my work. Contractually my first exhibition was supposed to be with Artusion and I wanted to exhibit there as Michael had risked so much for me.

Emanuel Hikatari had left Artusion to go back to New York and the gallery was run by a man named Stephen McCabe. We had arranged a date when he would come to my studio and go through the paintings with me. The same day I was supposed to be meeting him my mum called me to say that they had "a very, very big surprise" for me and I had to go round as soon as possible.

"Can't we do it later this evening," I said, thinking that I would be pushing it for my meeting with Stephen.

"No, now, beta, come now because it is a big, big surprise."

"Ma, I thought things had changed, please don't put me through this again," I pleaded, thinking she had arranged a meeting with Hiten Kapadia, the barrister. The excitement in my mother's voice could mean only this.

"Kavitha, get off the line before you tells her," my dad bellowed.

"Just come soon, beta. It's urgent," she said hanging up.

There was a black Fiesta parked right outside the door of the semi. It was an understated car for the Kapadias. It had to be them because although the space was permit free, my dad never allowed anyone else to park outside his front door.

"Get off," he would shout, holding a traffic cone he had taken from a crime scene and placing it in his space.

I knocked on the front door and instead of my mum or dad coming to answer it, a girl of about ten or eleven opened it.

"Hello Auntie," she beamed.

I thought it was one of the Kapadias' relatives. "Hello," I replied.

She grabbed me and began hugging me tightly. I was slightly taken aback by this child who was showing me so much affection — did she think I was going to marry her uncle or whoever Hiten Kapadia was to her? Affectionate child was sorely mistaken.

"Bring your auntie in here, Nina," my father shouted from the sitting room.

Nina? She had the same name as me.

My mother had the end of her sari out and was sobbing. My dad was sitting with his best red shirt on with a smile from ear to ear; the little girl went and sat beside him. There, engulfed by the sofa, was a woman with curly hair. It was no longer jet black as I recollected but had streaks of white. She was still beautiful; beautiful and elegant as I remembered her. It was my sister, Jana.

She got up. Tears streamed down her face. "Nina," she whispered.

I was unable to speak.

When we managed to disentangle ourselves she sat holding my hand. Jana told me she read all about me winning the Turner Prize and made contact with Ki's mum, who convinced her to call Mum and Dad.

She phoned Dad and instead of Dad claiming no relation to her, he asked to meet her again. They had met for the first time when I had been in Ireland and she had returned this morning from Germany where she was living, and was going to stay for the week.

"Why did you stop writing to me?"

"So many things happened, Nina, I will sit and explain it all."

Jana looked over at her daughter.

"Did you give your Auntie Nina a big kiss?"

"I hugged her," Nina said shyly.

"This girl," my dad said, pinching her cheeks.

380

I did not want to leave my sister but I realised that Stephen McCabe would be on his way to the studio.

"Go and see him," Jana said. "We're not going anywhere."

Reluctantly, I rushed off, saying that I would be back as soon as I could.

My thoughts were elsewhere when I got to the studio. I hadn't even arranged the pictures as I'd intended. The ones I wanted to exhibit were the ones on flowers that I'd done prior to the Turner Prize exhibition work. I was also debating whether to put in some of the paintings done in Ireland. I hadn't even taken off my coat when the door buzzer went.

"It's open," I called out, removing my coat, trying to get my head together.

"You shouldn't leave the door open, it could be anyone."

"Michael!" It couldn't be. I looked up and saw him standing by the door. I wanted to run towards him and throw my arms around him. He walked towards me without his hand outstretched.

"Nina," he said very calmly, "I know that you are doing an exhibition for us. I was in town and I've come to help select the paintings."

"Oh, right," I said, trying not to sound disappointed that he was there for purely professional motives. "I didn't expect you to come."

"Of course I would be here — I had to be, I mean look what happened the last time you had an exhibition."

"How are you? Are you well?" I asked. He looked incredibly well; his eyes still sparkled and his face was as warm as ever.

"Yes, very well, and you?"

"My sister's back," I blurted. "I've just seen her now for the first time in years, it's crazy. I have a niece; they're both waiting for me at home."

"Right . . . I mustn't keep you."

That wasn't what I'd meant. There was an awkward silence. "The ones I thought about exhibiting were the ones I've put out over here," I said, attempting to sound professional.

"Have you got over the shock of winning the Turner?"

"Yes. Thank you for helping me."

"No, we have to thank you. Since your win, business has rocketed and Emanuel is revelling in the publicity."

"Right. Well, that's good, then."

"Is it all working out for you? What have you been up to?" he asked, studying the various paintings.

"I've spent some time in Ireland."

"What were you doing there?"

"About what happened . . ." I began.

"It's in the past," he said. "You don't owe me anything."

Why had he come then? Was he married? Had he come to tell me that he had got married? I searched his fingers for a ring.

"So show me the work you did in Ireland, you must have done some."

"Over there."

He went over to the canvases. "It's Galway. You went to Galway."

"I've been there for the last three months sorting myself out."

"God, Nina," his face softened.

"I didn't marry Raj, I tried calling to explain but you never answered any of my calls, you never once let me explain. I know I made a real mess but I wanted to put it all right . . ."

"I called you a few days after you'd won the Turner and an old man picked up, saying he didn't know you."

"Was it my dad?"

"No, some old man who said he'd found the phone."

"What did you want to say to me?"

"That I'm really proud of what you did."

Was that it, was that all he wanted to say?

He looked away from me and began studying one of the paintings again. It was Cashla Bay. I had gone there late in the afternoon before the sun was about to disappear; the sea was green and although it was cold, and the sky was turning black, it was still lit with possibility. I captured this with indigo — colours that were there; colours that lay beyond.

"That's where I would go to make some of my biggest decisions. When I decided to go to America I sat there for hours, thinking. When Emanuel asked me to set up Artusion with him; when I was nine and mustering the courage to ask Lisa Flynn out." He smiled. "It's the only place I've found where you can really hear the silence of your own voice."

I knew what he meant. After I'd painted, I had sat there in the cold just listening.

"And so do you think that this is a sign?" Michael asked, taking his gaze off the canvas. He came towards me and held out his hand.

"Maybe, maybe not," I said, taking it.